MW00443979

Stellar Fusion
Infinite Spark Series, Book 1
—A Universal War Novel—
E. L. Strife

elstrife.com

Happy Reading!

~ Elysia Lumen Strife

Stellar Fusion
Infinite Spark Series (Book 1)
Version 3
Copyright © 2018 Elysia Lumen Strife
All Rights Reserved.
Editor: Jeni Chappelle
Some new material is unedited.
Cover Design: Amy Harwell

Thank you for purchasing an authorized version of this book and for complying with copyright laws by not scanning, reproducing, or distributing any part of it in any form without permission.
Stellar Fusion is a work of fiction. Names, characters, places, and incidents are the product of the author's imagination or are used fictitiously, and any resemblance to actual persons, living or dead, businesses, companies, events or locales is entirely coincidental.
ISBN: 9781520467252

For the farmers
And the soldiers
Thank you.

Hour Zero

NO ONE WAS BORN READY FOR IT—for the war on earth, the war of three hundred years. The stars beyond seemed so distant, unreachable, a dream delayed as earth fought over politics, cultural differences, and remnants of non-toxic land. After a long-overdue truce, the world united under common laws, electing a silent force of guardians to maintain peace and unity. Their system of justice: 'an eye for an eye,' as the saying goes. And it was effective. Until *they* arrived.

Man's deadliest disease used to be hatred.

They came in ships blacker than the deepest wormhole to a forgotten galaxy, ships that dripped with blood from starving mouths. Ships that didn't register on Earth's scanners until it was far too late.

They took Earthlings from their homes, from their broken families, their suffering planet, and enslaved them, slowly torturing each until they could endure no longer. And then they came back for more.

They leave galaxies swirling in fragments and chaos—the planets molten in rage—rendering countless species extinct.

They do it without remorse.

It has been like this since almost the beginning of time.

Because *they* were looking for me.

I won't be born for many long-cycles, but my kind, we surpass time. We live outside the boundaries of dimensions. We are the oldest spark, the strongest and brightest in the dark. And we thrive in the twilight, the shadows between all things.

They are an evil that spreads like blackened veins through the nebulae, siphoning life with a single touch. They feed off of us, drain our sparks without a moment's hesitation. There will be no warning. There will be no mercy.

I tell you this now. Find those you love and hold on tight for as long as you can. Life is a struggle—a chain of choices and fate. It is too short to let go.

May the stars of my ancestors guide you and protect you.

I know my mother and father will do their best.

But it is not enough. Not without me.

I am Luna.

This is my family.

And this is the Universal War.

—Sergeant Atana—

Chapter 1

BARELY COVERED IN SHREDS she'd stolen off the dead, Sergeant Atana stared at the ashen skin and sunken cheeks of the boy fighting at her side. Fighting ghosts—shadows that slung fire from fist. Pitchy clouds surrounded them, inducing claustrophobia like the endless walls of a maze.

The longer she stared, the more the image washed away.

Except the torches—the boy's blue eyes. She couldn't forget their crispness. Like beacons in the night, they burned bright, were always steady, and always locked on her. Even then, she couldn't quite recall his face. His name evaded her too. The memory was blurry as a watercolor painting in the rain. For the last thirteen years, it had haunted her. And the sense of betrayal that always seemed to tag along.

The images sharpened, following a familiar pattern. Flaming metal ripped by her. Then she was falling, tumbling through acrid clouds that seared in her lungs, her nose, and her throat. A spray of invisible shards battered her body with the throbbing sting of needles punching through her skin until she felt nothing but numb all over. Anger melted into confusion then into panic as her body hit the soft ground. Every time it ended with a consuming fear that something important had been lost. *Someone.*

A rumble, deep and spread, shook the sofa beneath her. Atana's heart bolted into a sprint, thumping up into her throat. Her eyes flew open, and through the window wall of her apartment, she scoured the smooth, amber mountains of sand surrounding the city. For a reason she couldn't place, she expected to see something more.

The screen strapped to her left forearm flashed, the speaker pelting her eardrums with rapid screeches.

Adrenaline Saturation 87% of Upper Tolerable Limit

Atana sat up, brushing the loose waves of hair from her face. Working night shift meant sleeping during the day. What she saw behind her eyelids made her never want to close them again. *Yes, I know. Shut up.* At her sigh, the alerts subsided, the screen flashing another minute longer, a reminder of her infraction.

Sliding open the security tab on her wristband, she tapped the Call Out button, hoping her security team could ease the concern clawing at the back of her mind. "Frank, Joe, do you copy?"

Resting her elbows on her knees, Atana rubbed a finger up the side of her head, the mark she hated the most, the one that stole every memory in a blink. Her body was a patchwork of scars, a result of lab tests run for years on end after her abduction. She'd uncovered enough pieces to understand that much. The rescue ship had crashed on Earth when she was fifteen, which is where her past began.

The shepherds had saved her life. She dedicated it back to their cause without objection. Repayment was simple, and Atana liked playing fair.

"Yes, ma'am?" a weathered voice replied. Frank was an old man in a job where men died young. He had been in charge of her residence patrol since her instructor passed, years back.

Atana picked a loose thread from a seam on her combat boots. Perfection was paramount in a shepherd's world. "What was that thundering a moment ago? It woke me."

"Likely one of our transports doing a fly-by. Couldn't see it from here."

"Understood." She planted her face in her hands. Something wasn't sitting right in her gut. She trusted few people and, least of all, the skies above.

Your subconscious cannot speak in words. Her instructor, Sensei, had told her the same line at the start of every meditation practice. *Clear your mind, and you will feel it in pressures, energy, urges. It will never lie because it does not know bias. Trust in it.*

Clouds of sand swept up and around her apartment, the granules whispering against the steel walls. The rumble she'd heard wasn't from an earthquake. The pattern wasn't right for an F-201 or a Med-Evac either. The amplitude was too great, the frequency too spread. She couldn't put her finger on it. It was just *wrong*.

Wisps of spicy-sweet steam from her Marusa tea drifted upward, folding in layers from the heated mug on the glass coffee table. It would calm the storm inside.

Lifting the ceramic burned her fingers, but the sensation faded quickly—like always. Marusa was her natural replacement for the serum, a medication mandated by her Command to regulate a variety of hormones in shepherds belonging to the Universal Protectors. Rio, the serum's designer, knew about her night terrors, the voices, the conjured physical pain. Yet he refused to dose her, and only her.

Command gave approval for two, critical reasons. When she was awake, she had complete control of *everything*. But the most important— Atana didn't *care* about anything but justice. She was completely apathetic. The ultimate soldier.

Atana had never *needed* serum.

She returned the mug to the table and walked to the glass wall facing the town's perimeter to scan again, the vibration that had woken her still winding through her thoughts.

Her wristband chirped, the speaker crackling. She lifted it to find the Security channel open.

"Intruder!" Frank rasped. "Knocked me over but appears unarmed."

Without hesitation, Atana leapt over the sofa toward the door. Grabbing one of her Standard Issue weapons from the storage slot beneath the intercom, her index finger slid over the trigger. The SI rendered a faint *peep*, the igniter whirring to life, primed for execution.

This was a regular occurrence for other Independent shepherds assigned a command post. Never her.

Soft thumps reverberated three times through the hollow steel. The intruder was slender at best. She took a breath.

Kicking up the lock handle, Atana slid the door open with her foot and directed the muzzle of the weapon on-point at the stranger's nose, every muscle tensed for a fight. A thin male, mid-twenties, met her gaze. His blue eyes opened wide, his hands rising in a startled, defensive rush.

Hi, an apprehensive voice spoke somewhere in the back of her mind. Her heart stuttered. His jawline and cheekbones, now lit in the teal light of her igniter, were unnervingly similar to her own. Dressed in a tattered, black sweatshirt and torn jeans, he looked out of place in the torrid environment.

"Sahara?" the young man asked. His body launched sideways and to the floor as Frank side-tackled him. Atana shifted out of the way.

The intruder's rough-cut, blond hair shook as he wriggled, trying to break free. "Stop! I'm Lavrion; she's my sister!" The hood on his sweatshirt slipped down over his face. "I just want to talk."

"Sorry, kid." Frank pressed a firm knee between Lavrion's shoulder blades, awaiting Joe's arrival. "Restricted area."

Atana dropped her weapon to her side, gazing upon the stray soul at her feet. She felt nothing, no pity, no anger, no sympathy. *But that voice—*

Frank's guard-in-training, Joe, a bulldozer of a man, thundered down the hall. "He's a fast one. Tripped me by the southern exit."

6

A deep inhale calmed his panting. Pulling a cataloger out of his pocket, Joe freed Lavrion's left arm from the tangled take-down. The scanner blinked red, detecting the chip in the young man's left wrist.

He read the encoded profile. "Lavrion, medic and spiritual healer, age twenty-four. Last log-in was eight years ago."

Lavrion's fair cheek, pressed to the warm floor, was already tinting purple. His focus jumped to the exposed wristband on Atana's left arm. He now knew what she was. He would have to be monitored.

Shepherds were forbidden from casual interactions with civilians. Separation was a component of their duty, the Code, which guided them in their protection of the people. Private residences were to be kept secret. Shepherds were to remain disguised unless on an immediate threat assignment.

Lavrion knowing what she was and where she lived was a major risk. If he was a member of the Kronos clan or was tortured for information, the Universal Protectors could have a problem on their hands. Kronos wanted control of the serum-compliant shepherds. They were power-hungry, post-war rebels and the Universal Protector's number one combatant.

Standing, the guards faced Lavrion down the hall.

"Sahara, wait. I just want to talk to you for a second," Lavrion protested.

Her eyes wandered over the struggling man. His look of confused rejection was unexpected. "My name is not Sahara. We are orphans, with no family remaining. What you say is impossible."

"Orders, Sergeant Atana?" Frank's iron grip evoked a wince from Lavrion.

"Detainment, H.Co.," she replied, flatly. "Get his information and put him on the Pending-Restraint list. Then send him on his way. If he tries to contact me again, move him to Active Restraint."

Lavrion stuttered. "What? Human Cataloging? No! You can't take me there!"

"Yes, ma'am." Frank dragged the fidgeting man down the hall with Joe's assistance.

Lavrion called out to her until the door shut on the level below. Atana stared at the floor, searching her broken memories.

Do I know him? His eyes weren't the right shade of blue. The boy from her dreams had sapphire eyes. Lavrion's were pale, almost white. *Definitely unfamiliar.*

A weighted sigh lifted and sank her shoulders. Without Sensei, finding more memories was hopeless.

The steel underfoot rumbled. She scanned through her apartment, out the windows to the sand. Inexplicable panic crept down her spine, prickling the back of her neck. The pulses through the floor grew until everything around her rattled.

She ran across the room to the window wall, scouring the dunes on the horizon. Several black specks tarnished the otherwise flawless sky. Before she had time to count them, they blasted down the street-side of her trembling complex and into the town, stirring golden granules up into the air.

The thundering hum that had woken her was woven through her darkest repressed fears.

A two-tone notification burst from her wristband.

Threat Level Delta: Invasion Underway
Initiate Safe House Procedures
Return to Base ASAP

She watched Frank, Joe, and Lavrion drop to the soft ground when the ships flurried by again. As soon as they were gone, Lavrion scrambled up and sprinted away, his heels flinging hot sand in rooster tails behind him.

The only warning was a single pulse, followed by a crackling buzz. In a flash of coiled, green lightning, Lavrion vanished. Her guards clambered back in shock.

"No!" She banged a fist on the glass in a surge of desperation, her first emotional snap in over a decade. Swallowing hard, she managed to shove her heart back down into her chest and call out to Frank and Joe, ignoring the infraction warnings on her screen. "Bunker, now!"

Atana slid the SI into one of her thigh holsters, watching the two sergeants scramble inside. Grabbing the gear bag she kept packed beside her door and her remaining SI from the storage slot, she flew down the stairs and out the front of her complex.

Sand jostled beneath her boots. She looked in the direction of the wave's origin. A cylindrical vessel protruded from the earth, fifty kilometers beyond the end of the city. It loomed above the world, extending up into the sky—a ghastly pillar of angry gods. Its surface absorbed light, punching a black hole in the radiant landscape.

These were new. She hadn't seen them in the records of the last abduction, or the first. Atana spun, slinging her bag over her shoulder. Through the alleys, she made her way to the end of the city.

Another sooty shape appeared in the hazy sky, the columnar structure plummeting toward the surface. Large panels peeled open, sending it spiraling like a drill bit into the land. Thousands of small propulsion engines sent out bursts, condensing the air into clouds and guiding the ship's descent. It impacted the earth, sending out another shock wave of leveling destruction, another pulse beneath her feet.

Hearing the ships return for another sweep, she ducked between two buildings on instinct. A mother and daughter ran along the street, fear stretching their faces, their long tunics lifted in white-knuckled hands. Atana opened her mouth to yell at them, but the woman disappeared, slung up into the sky by a green coil. The shadow made another pass, and the girl was gone.

Atana shuddered, pressing herself against a chipped, stone building. She knew that chill of the breath-sucking lurch wrapped in a green ribbon. It was a memory uncovered with alarming clarity.

A horn blared long and loud in the distance.

Atana peered around the corner at the first vessel to see the earth near its base sinking. Even at a snail's pace, she could track it.

The pillar was burrowing into her planet.

The shredded screams around her, some near, some far, were the tick of a clock, counting down the time remaining to fight back if it wasn't already too late. This was above the other shepherds' training. Her abduction and return was the only playing card her command would have. No one else from the rescue was left.

Atana squeezed her eyes shut and cursed.

Chapter 2

LAUNCHING out of the slide-chute into their secret bunker, Atana slung her arms through the straps of her pack, resituating it behind her. Frank and Joe were waiting.

"Why didn't you engage the alarm?" Atana demanded, hustling across the concrete floor to the protected panel in the hall.

Joe steadied his hands on his shotgun. "Guards don't leave their assigned post without order."

"Even then—" Frank trailed off as Atana reared an elbow back in front of the protective panel. She looked over at him. His peppered hair was mussed to one side, sand still clinging to the creases of his face.

"What's your excuse?" she asked.

Glass shattered with the first strike. Tugging on the lever, Atana engaged the alarm. Every siren within Nilsa Sand District Eight could be heard faintly resounding overhead, directing civilians underground.

"Not my job to make those decisions." Frank patted the R2 and Guard patches on his chest.

Sometimes the man had too much integrity. "An exception might've saved a few more from meeting Lavrion's fate." But there was no use in arguing. Code was absolute and the shepherds regulated. Everyone knew their place.

Out of the bunker, with Frank and Joe at her heels, she sprinted through kilometers of winding tunnel. Small lamps overhead lit their way, the air musty and damp from the river they approached. She called out over her wristband, "Sand Base Eight, Tango Sierra One One."

A female voice responded, "This is Dispatch. Go ahead."

"Initiate Protocol: Safe-House." She slammed to a halt at the edge of the Nilsa dam, a hydropower plant, and the desert city's main lifeline. The dwindling creek at the bottom of the reinforced ravine was barely visible. *It shouldn't be that empty.* Small bits of rock tumbled down the riverbank, from the vibrations overhead.

"Roger. Protocol in effect."

Atana lifted her wristband. "Dispatch, initiate Utility Conservation Protocol. Nilsa is dangerously low."

10

"Roger."

Grinding sounds of floodgates closing and turbines slowing echoed through the hollow expanse. They were now on emergency systems: batteries and generators. The lights of the passageway went out and flickered on again though dimmer than before.

They continued on another kilometer to a dead-end in the rocky cavern. Atana slid into one of the alcoves, touching the cool rock with the tip of her nose. The scent of wet slate filled her nostrils. Her left eye fixed on a familiar blue dot that spun a circle around her eye.

A *slam* of steel bars to her right opened the wall to the comfort of her command outpost: Sand Base Eight. Scanners in the doorway registered each passing member by their embedded H.Co. trackers and wristband codes, displaying their identities on the screens beside the two security guards on duty. The smaller desert base housed only twenty-eight shepherds.

Transparent computer stations hung from the ceiling before them, buzzing with a blur of people monitoring the invasion.

Atana walked over to Axel and Miranda at the central control desk. "What do we have?"

Axel's fingers danced on the clear, glossy surface, pulling up diagrams of the bunkers and scrolling through shelter summaries. Tapping and sliding open the active video feed logs, he sorted with a speed Atana respected.

"Twenty-one percent of the city's population is inside and climbing. At the current rate of accumulation, I estimate we will reach a total of sixty percent. The rest are—" He paused, his onyx irises darting up at her. "Being sucked up into the ships."

"Understood. Miranda, there are two visible pillars from the surface, about fifty kilometers out the east and west sides of the city. I think there's a connection between our new guests and Nilsa's low water levels. I want a team to check it out."

"On it." Miranda slid open a message board. Her black fatigues and blond bun were crisp and clean as ever. "Team?"

Atana tracked the movement of the ships from one frame on Axel's screen to another, the city's cameras catching mere inky blurs and green flashes. "Sidewinder Thirty-six." They were the most dependable.

"Roger." A window popped up, blinking on both of their screens. "Ma'am, we have a message coming in from Home Station." With a swipe of her finger, Miranda sent the feed to the main display. Only the peeps of the incoming data dared break the silence that fell upon the room.

A clean-cut face appeared amidst a gray background, his voice similarly smooth and colorless. "Every shepherd able to mobilize is requested on-site immediately for Assembly, 0900 hours. Ensure lockdown procedures are in order for the public and stand-ins are appointed as necessary. Set your transports to minimum visibility and low electrical priority. Keep your district links open, pending updates. Assembly will be broadcast live. Be swift in your travels. Home Station out."

"No details about our situation?" Joe asked.

Frank's sidelong glance at him displayed the typical sag from decades of clenched teeth. "They're not ready. At 0900, we'll know what they do."

Atana returned her attention to Axel and Miranda. "You're in charge. Spread the remaining field teams to the safe houses and keep Home Station posted." She spun around to address the rest of the base, directing their attention to the two at the front. "Any of you get any questions, they go through Axel and Miranda. Understood?"

"Yes, ma'am," the shepherds acknowledged in unison. Her stand-ins appointed, Atana headed to the rear of the building, where their small transport bay was hidden.

Frank caught the door before it closed. "Atana." She paused, glancing back at him. "Be careful."

With a sharp nod, she slipped away to weave between the parked personal transport pods. The hatch of hers unsealed and swung upward when it detected her wristband. A pale blue light illuminated above the seat.

Tossing her gear into the storage space behind the pilot's chair, she sprung up and slammed herself into the stiff cushions. Donning her headset, she flipped the transparent pupil location screen in front of her right eye.

A technical specialist in her earlier years, she had developed a device to turn electrical impulses of thoughts in the mind and degrees of pupil dilation into computer-generated actions. It had proven useful in a basic format for Home Station and on her own pod—a trial run.

Streamlined with six curvilinear airfoils, three directional electromagnetic propulsion thrusters, and a main hydrogen propulsion unit at the rear that was sectioned off in quadrants for extra control, the pod was one of the devices inspired by the first alien attacks.

Shifting in her seat, Atana pulled the five-point harness together and latched it, then commanded with her mind, *Pod One power-up, minimum visibility—engage, low electrical priority—engage.*

The manual controls lit the interior of the cabin sky blue, to the sides and above her. The propulsion systems hummed, the engines warming.

"Tango Sierra One One, Dispatch," Miranda called in on the pod's radio.

"Go ahead." Atana scanned the gauges, confirming acceptable levels for fuel, pressures for hydraulic systems, and cell response for cloaking abilities.

"I loaded a map of all reported locations of the unfamiliar vessels and included a course that should help you navigate between them."

"Copy." The pod lifted up off the supports, hovering over the concrete. "Dispatch, Tango Sierra One One requesting gates open: Pod One departing Sand Base Eight."

"Gates opening, airspace clear. Pod One, you are free to fly," Miranda responded. "Good luck."

"Roger, Pod One and Tango Sierra One One out."

The wall parted in the middle, and Atana blasted out of the bay, through the underground chasm, gradually lifting up to the elevation of the desert sands. In a cloud, the pod exploded out of the zip chute, zooming along the earth, sending small tufts of dust and sand swirling in helixes behind an invisible vessel.

The minimum-visibility setting, called 'chameleon skins' by the field sergeants, made the shepherds' aircraft move like the wind, leaving only their effects visible to the untrained eye. Atana swerved between the dunes, scanning the horizon for ships while monitoring her location relative to each pillar registered on the dash screen.

Through the glass behind her, she admired the graceful curves of the razorbacks painted with gold from the setting sun, the shadows expanding between. It was the closest to what she could have called a sense of peace, something she was, once again, leaving behind.

For her and many other shepherds, they would have to travel for several hours to reach Home Station. The ocean plains opened up before her. *Minimum visibility—disengage.* She'd use the extra power to reach Home Station faster.

The surface sparkled with the reflecting navigation lights of her vessel overhead. She gazed down, through the clear panels at her feet, to the dark fluid, in a way she knew the other shepherds couldn't. For a single moment, the stillness permeated her internal blockade, the one she used to keep the voices, and the human urges to feel, silent.

Her wristband flashed twice.

Restoration Necessary

Pulling up to auto-pilot level above the sea, she engaged the automatic flight control system. The hum of the pod's propulsion units softened, the engines cruising into a smoother rhythm. Slumping back in the seat, she stared up through the roof at the stars and sighed. She was never keen on the idea of rest, no matter her level of exhaustion.

The crashing waves of cerulean and white beneath reminded her of Lavrion's irises. Strong emotions flowed through his body. She was trained to see it in the shape of his face and his posture. But she could almost feel it radiating from his pink-white cheeks and hear the rapid thumping from inside his chest.

She wondered what happened to him, to the woman, and the girl.

They're not dead, are they?

The wind whispered through the airfoils of her pod. She could've sworn it said no.

She'd tried to run from the voice, block it out with noisy ratchets, anything to make it stop.

"Still don't know about you. Are you crazy?" Atana checked her gauges. *Or is that your subconscious? The voice of someone I have killed, maybe. What are you?* The nightmare of the boy's sapphire eyes loomed in the back of her mind. "Is that who you belong to?"

Within the silence that faithfully followed her string of questions, the ones she asked herself so often they'd lost their significance, she knew lay the answer to what she really wanted to know.

Who was I before the crash, and why am I the only one from the rescue left breathing?

She thought of the boy from her recurring nightmares, sprawled out on the chilled examination slab next to hers, his lungs gasping for air. The muted skin draped over his sack of bones had shone like morning dew beneath the spotlight. He'd fought harder than the others, jerking and writhing, his marrow the victim of the merciless surgeons' needles.

"Niema nigh, niema!" He'd screamed his voice into silence. *Please, stop, please!* Somehow she'd understood.

Their captors sauntered off, and the room lurched. The boy was knocked to the floor between their slabs. It was the tear rolling down his cheek that compelled her to break the rules. Grabbing two fistfuls of the cables plugged into her spine, with an exhausted huff, she tugged free the connectors to kneel at his side. Holding her fingers near his mouth, she felt a faint warmth roll over her skin. *Alive.*

"Niema, tuess evus!" *Please, get up!* She urged.

The boy tried to wipe the blood from a puncture on one of his emaciated arms, only causing it to smear. A groaning whimper rattled his chest. "Hu'te mocohas il amah yan veriia?" *What purpose is in this life?*

Taking the cleanest corner of her crusted shirt, she dried his tears. The stunning, brilliant blue that looked up at her made her body tremble, her fingers pause, and her heart beat a little faster. His cheeks flushed.

A barb jutted out below his collarbone, spurting blood across her front. Her body seized in terror. He was slung onto his table like a pig in the hands of a butcher. She cried out, straining to reach him. Pain exploded in her temple, and the room fell into darkness.

A loud beeping in Atana's ear snapped her awake. Before her, a pillar towered in the night, rigid despite the tepid, crashing waters. It was barely visible amongst the amassed vapors.

Minimum visibility—engage. The chameleon skins cloaked her pod in the dull navy and grays of the ocean mist. Grabbing the control levers at her sides, she slammed her pod into a high bank turn, around the column.

What had seemed like a smooth surface on the pillars from afar now appeared cragged in black, spear-like projections and pentagonal panels. There was no doubt in her mind. It was extraterrestrial. When she'd passed at a safe distance, she kicked up the power, sending her pod fleeing into the brume.

Chapter 3

A FLICKERING LIGHT, the homing beacon of a secret island in the South Pacific, stood poised, the pinnacle atop the world's aegis—the station concealed below the cresting liquid surface. The nine-level, seventy-square kilometer base housed the central command post for the descendant of the outgrown Shepherds United: the Universal Protectors.

"Home Station, Tango Sierra One One." Sergeant Atana's irises twitched, scanning for navigation lights and tracking the other pods popping up on her screen. Sharing the sky on low electrical priority could get dicey with the chameleon skins online, especially in the cover of night. But Home Station was always a reassuring sight.

"Go ahead," a modulated feminine voice replied.

Atana navigated the pod in a loop above the island. "Tango Sierra One One and Pod One requesting permission to dock."

"Permission granted. Proceed to dock station one-niner."

"Roger. Tango Sierra One One and Pod One proceeding to dock station one-niner."

The east side of the mountain opened. Pulling the manual controls toward her, Atana adeptly slowed the pod, gliding inside the narrow aperture. The propulsion stabilizers fired in small bursts, allowing fine-tuned positioning inside the terminal.

Cold, metal braces clamped around the pod, securing it. When the side hatch unlocked, the internal hydraulics lifting her door, she could hear the *tink* of cooling metal. The salty air was a welcome reprieve from the desert heat. An automated voice echoed from the deck, "Please vacate the pod. You have five minutes to reach the safe zone."

She unclipped her harness and tugged the headset off, slinging it over the back of the seat. Only managing a few glimpses of sleep, most of which were filled with fragmented memories, Atana swung her tired legs out of the pod, grabbed her bag and lumbered toward the narrow elevator beside the dock door.

The ocean shimmered moon-white across the tips of the waves that pounded into the cliffs. She missed the sound, the way they drowned out the voices inside. Placing a hand on the control panel to the left of the elevator, the wall retracted, pocketing itself to the right. She stepped inside and turned to watch her pod hatch seal up. The conveyor system engaged, taking her ride to the repository. The elevator door closed.

The voice spoke again. "Fifteen seconds to submersion."

Atana's stomach lifted into her lungs, jolting her awake. Lights blinked by increasing in speed. Repositioning her slipping bag higher on her shoulder, she sighed, heavy as the weight of a planet on her shoulders, silently wishing to be anyone else. At least, the brief silence was nice. *Staging is going to be packed.* The passing lights slowed, and the car came to a stop.

The door opened to the staging area fifty meters below. She scanned her surroundings out of habitual instinct. Home Station was a hive of people rushing out from other terminals, reading the screens lining the hallway, and teams regrouping in the main auditorium just beyond.

Her wristband let out a faint beep.

Personal Transport in Location: C5-J26

Heading down the main hallway to a vacant screen on the corner, Atana spoke to it. "Technical Specialist One One requesting access to UP Hub two three dash nine."

A digital voice responded, "Access granted. Welcome, Sergeant Nakio Atana."

The screen opened to a host of options: food services, maps, supplies, and lodging. Atana found her desired item. A pair of blue brackets appeared around the option on the screen. A double blink confirmed the selection: Independent Bunk Room 389.

Another beep from her wrist:

Assembly 2-CA, 0900 hrs

The time logged in the center of the top of her screen:

0814

Walking around the corner and down the stairs to Level Three, she assessed the people murmuring around her. Serum was about as effective on gossip as laws were to evil hearts. She'd heard so many circulating rumors over the last decade that she'd sunk further into her reclusive tendencies, hoping to avoid adding fuel to the fire. Atana used to try to communicate as her instructor recommended. She would give them no more reasons to talk about her now. Atana gave orders, with a glare. She needed to provide nothing else to get things done.

Tracking the hasty steps of a female, she acknowledged shepherd Yari's attentiveness to her position. The one shepherd not afraid of her. Yari just hadn't learned yet.

"Sergeant Atana! Have you seen Johna? I can't find him anywhere."

"I have not." Despite her straight face, Atana could see Yari's concern in the abnormally lengthy pause between her blinks, even for a girl who zoned out often. Yari was a new recruit, an R1: Assistant shepherd, not yet having acquired the rank of an R2: Sergeant status. The girl wasn't trained for this level of chaos. "Johna is experienced. He will be here when he can. Until then, check in with Ceilia."

"Yes, ma'am." Yari left in search of her instructor's field guard.

Shepherds, like all members of the Universal Protectors' community, were assigned partners. Sergeant Atana was one of the few exceptions. She knew she was too obstinate for other shepherds. No one would take the position, and those who had tried had given up or died. She'd been unmatched for most of her time in service. These days, it was her preference. Atana had yet to meet someone that could keep up with her.

Her wristband flashed teal against a navy background.

Meeting 1-CR, post Assembly, per Command

Few shepherds had the honor of speaking with Command. She received orders from them personally. So as one of them, Atana felt her fellow shepherds' eyes on her constantly.

She wasn't surprised Command wanted to talk to her. What she didn't know was what more they could ask. After the rescue, years back, they'd sat her alone in a windowless room and riddled her with questions via a speaker, most of which she didn't have answers to. Command eventually concluded their interrogation, determining her amnesia was the cause and not that she was afraid or wasn't willing to provide the information.

Her affinity for a variety of technical integrations, and the precision with which she designed and killed, had earned her other merits. Atana still wasn't sure she called herself 'lucky,' like so many of the other shepherds did—being rescued from whatever their hell was and turned into a machine created to impose order and justice on the world. Something darker and angrier crawled within her. She knew it from the cold weight around her heart and buried in the core of her bones. The blank faces passing her were mostly synthetic, induced by the serum. She was naturally void of emotion. Because something in her past had destroyed everything she was. Something before the rescue.

Reaching her room, Atana grasped the handle. Metal clacked in the doorframe, and she pushed inside. Each room was sixteen square meters, enough space for a bunk and a bathroom stall. She tossed her bag on the crisp, pale khaki bed with its tightly folded corners and set her Standard Issue weapons in the storage slot.

Sitting on the edge of the mattress, she buried her face in her hands. She'd only been five when it had happened, not old enough to understand but defiant enough to survive the collection, testing, and the Earth rescue.

Countless people had been taken. This third invasion rendered even more missing.

Being the only survivor of those to make it home, she knew she was Command's—and Earth's—last thread of hope.

And all she had were disorganized images, gut instincts, *pieces*.

"What in the bloodyhell can I do if I can't remember?" she mumbled to the floor.

Fight.

She wasn't surprised that the voice had returned. It always waited until she was alone. "It's not that simple. It never is." Atana raked her long bangs back with the rest of her hair, a heavy sigh puffing out her cheeks. The voice was hers and it wasn't.

They cannot win.

Rubbing her eyes, she nodded to herself, the urge to lash out boiling up inside her again. "But I don't decide that. I don't even know who *they* are or what exactly we're up against."

You do.

Frustration built on the inexplicable need for vengeance. She dug her fingers into her hair, feeling powerless. "But I *don't* remember!"

You will know what to do when you see them.

"Like always." Atana chewed a lip in disappointment. She wished could recall things, instead of being forced to wait and hope she recognized them. "It just doesn't make for a good *plan*."

Chapter 4

0900 HOURS.

Atana took her place on the floor with the other shepherds in 2-CA, the unfurnished central auditorium. Curiosity over what Command would say had her standing closer than usual to the open mezzanine outside Command's conference room.

The storm shields were up, concealing the murky ocean beyond the windows, the harsh LED light flooding the monochrome uniforms around her. Only a handful of earth tones dotted the black-clad mass—the Independents and Team Leaders.

From the frosted, glass room to the left, the Coordinator appeared. He presented Command's collective decisions, protecting their anonymity. Approaching the edge of the platform, he scanned the shepherds gathering in the open level below. His large hands molded confident and strong to the railing like they had thousands of times. When his gaze passed over Atana, it hung a breath longer than normal.

She knew then that there was more going on than Command had approved him to relay.

"We appreciate everyone getting here as quickly as possible. Updates will be posted under the Current Conflicts feed. This is now our primary focus." Stout and resonant, his words carried throughout the room and into the surrounding halls. Murmurs swept through the crowd. "Some of you might remember events from prior decades."

Atana's nose wrinkled a second in self-disgust before she could knock it down. *Remember.* Everyone else had memories. Even if they were bad ones, she was jealous. At least they knew who they were as people and where they came from. Hearing reminders like that only made her isolation more apparent. But she didn't dare flinch and draw attention to herself. She had enough of it already. If shepherds weren't looking at the Coordinator, they were looking at her.

"These collection vessels have been here before," he continued. "The columns have not. We have designated recon teams to research the new structures on Earth and what we believe to be the mothership above us.

We want to know what we are up against before we alert the invaders to our limited capabilities."

They already know, because they've been here before. They have to be watching us. Atana couldn't figure it any other way. How else would the invaders know where to hit and when to capture the people? The last two battles had been disastrously futile, from what she'd read.

Above, the Coordinator paused, his bright blue gaze falling on her. "There are approximately 130 vessels protruding from our planet. Thousands of our people have already been taken. The ones which appear to be targeted are those who are emotional. The current theory is these people are easier to lock on to, leading us to our reason for requesting minimum visibility and low electrical priority with transport use."

She always found an odd comfort in his stare—a faint piece belonging to a lost realm in the back of her mind. It wasn't him, just something about his eyes. *Like the boy.*

He looked away. "The main ship is currently on the sun-side of the planet and appears to be adjusting its orbit to remain in this location. This being the case, from 1030 to 1500 hours, we will remain on lockdown each day while we pass the threat in our sky. No transport traffic or surface walks. Wait for the command before engaging in combative maneuvers. Find and protect the people of Earth, and stay below the surface.

"Check the codes on your wristbands for your assignments. Send in reports immediately if you acquire any useful information. Make certain," he paused for emphasis, "your serum is properly functioning. We don't need to lose any more of our people. Good luck."

The Coordinator waited a few moments for the crowd to disperse before returning to the conference room, the door closing with a soft click behind him.

Atana watched the shepherds recede around her like a night tide, filtering out into the main hall. Most were checking their wristbands. A few had eyes on her. Lowering her head, she rocked forward on her feet and pushed herself toward the stairs leading to Command's conference room.

...

Every stony, insensate face turned toward Atana when she stepped inside. Ash kaftans hung stiff from their motionless figures. A twenty-member team, Command was responsible for reaching a universal, altruistic verdict on any operations involving the UP community and the planet under their protection. They worked together, a unified guiding body.

21

No one knew their names. Not even Atana.

The Coordinator stood from his seat at the far end of a long, interactive table. Ten members sat to each side: nine women, twelve men, in all.

"Thank you, Sergeant Atana, for contributing to this meeting." His stentorian voice carried across the room from his abnormally tall and brawny frame. "You will lead a team on this mission but work in conjunction with their leader. He should be here soon. This is the best recon and extraction team UP has to offer. They are in transit from the opposite side of the globe as you, Ocean Base Thirty-Three and Thirty-Four. The team was affected by the recent serum recall and have been off for some time. We have been assured their compliance with serum standards upon their arrival." He took his seat.

"Yes, Command." Atana stepped off to the side, straight-laced and rigid, tucking her hands behind her while she waited. She was accustomed to the unknown and unpredictable, making her the perfect option for many of the missions for which UP lacked significant background knowledge. Atana could work alone or lead and delegate as a commander. But a team? It was an intimate space she wasn't comfortable with. Working one-on-one with others meant they would have time to undoubtedly stare at the scars of a past she couldn't explain.

The door whooshed open behind her, and she executed a prompt about-face. An unfamiliar male sergeant stepped inside, hazel eyes frozen on her—dissecting, criticizing, lingering. His chestnut leather jacket over black tactical fatigues advertised his Team Leader status.

The Coordinator introduced them. "Independent Nakio Atana, Team Leader Jameson Bennett."

Bennett's callused hand politely extended, his reply deep and saccharine. "It's nice to officially meet you, ma'am."

Taking his offering, she felt the tiniest of zaps between their warm palms. The shock tightened her fingers around his on impulse, a tingling warmth spreading up her arm. "And you as well, sir."

His full lips parted with a breath, eyes widening just enough she noticed. Bennett's hand slid deeper into hers. He'd felt it too.

"We are depending on you," a male member of Command interrupted, one seated beside the Coordinator.

They abruptly released the handshake. Bennett cleared his throat, brushing the back of a hand across his mouth. His caramel skin darkened as the two of them turned to face Command. When his fingers hooked together behind him, Atana caught the tips of inked feathers peeking out from his collar.

She wasn't sure Command permitted such rebellious marks.

"We need critical information on how to take down this orbiting enemy so they stop coming back. Your goal is to infiltrate the mothership and give us something we can use against them. Destroy them if that's what it takes."

"Yes, Command," Bennett and Atana responded.

Atana couldn't help but wonder if this shepherd would be able to stick it out with her. Eyeing the filled-out shoulders of Bennett's jacket from the side, her doubts softened.

"Until we get a report from you or the invaders change up their game plan, we're going to lie low." The Coordinator rested his forearms on the table. "We're hoping they will just take what they need and leave. You both know we don't possess the volume of forces necessary to take out a fleet of this magnitude. We need to know what we are up against so our attack may be swift and effective."

Another member warned from a seat to the sergeants' left, "We do not expect you to return from this mission. However, we will hope and plan for it, adhering to the five-day limit, of course."

"Yes, Command."

But five days didn't feel like it would be nearly enough.

—Sergeant Bennett—

Chapter 5

SERGEANT BENNETT thought about it, quitting right then and there. The thought of never coming back wasn't ideal, and life-sucking space wasn't even crawl-out capable. He'd take the deepest hole in earth over the vacuum of black nothingness. But, living a caged life wasn't preferred either. Studying Atana's confident yet elegant poise, he was mysteriously compelled and nodded in agreement with her, accepting the mission.

They turned together, and he urgently reached out, pulling the door open for her. She gave him the oddest quirk of her brows, like no one had ever done such a thing before.

In the hall, she aimed for the open stairs of the central auditorium, scrolling through something on her illuminated wristband. "Message me when your team is five minutes out. I'll send you the room designation."

"Yes, ma'am." Bennett watched her hips sway as she hustled down the steps. She was nothing like he'd anticipated, like the whispers amongst others.

Atana was in constant pain. He read it clear as day in her eyes. The static in their touch exposed the rawness of her isolation, of the past that fit her uncountable scars. When Command had interrupted their greeting, Bennett saw that impassive shield lift again.

Her outfit was all leather, skin-tight, and the color of dried blood. *A justified camouflage for Command's lead assassin.*

Overhearing two wavering voices in the auditorium below, Bennett casually leaned over the railing of the mezzanine in the shadows.

"What did he mean, 'not lose any more shepherds?' How many have we lost?" one asked.

"I don't know. Not in all my service have I heard a warning like that."

Bennett's jaw tightened. A warning from Command was never a good sign.

In a haze, he headed for his quarters to inventory his ammo and medical supplies and mull over the mission his team had been assigned.

The walls and shepherds were a blur around him. Time seemed to rush forward, and he found himself staring absentmindedly at his closed door wondering how long he'd been there.

Atana had stood with confidence, yet her stern glare exposed a far darker truth: the enslaved forced to fight a war she cared nothing for.

"Something in common." Bennett rested an arm on his doorframe, unease twisting his insides.

A base commander, Atana wasn't likely to be swayed in her decisions. The mission was her purpose as was Bennett's. But dread she would overlook a small problem to fulfill a greater purpose could jeopardize the team's safety. That thought ate away at the confidence he could protect them. His shepherds were special, exceptionally gifted, and *his*.

At the mercy of the universe, like always.

"Sir?" A passing shepherd stopped in the main hall. He tilted, scrutinizing Bennett's posture.

Only then, did Bennett become aware of the dull ache hunching his shoulders. He straightened and waved a dismissive hand. "Nothing, just working through a new assignment." Catching the young man's boxy face with the crooked nose, Bennett gave him a nod and what he hoped was an encouraging smile. "Vellins."

"Your team's takedown of the terrorist cell last week has been playing on all the base TVs."

Damn cameras everywhere. "Yes, I'm aware." Bennett had watched it at every meal in chow hall. He wished UP permitted more channels.

"Thought you might be pushing through a bit of pain." Vellins paused to lean back and check the hall. "Heard from Danas you took a fifty-five-gallon drum to the back, then fought off twelve Kronos soldiers by yourself, saved Danas's life."

Bennett shrugged off the concern in the young man's voice. "Got separated from the teams. It happens. They have to learn to anticipate your command, just like you have to know what action they'll take. Mission was successful." Vellins had recently been promoted to Team Leader and his crew's first few missions hadn't gone *without* incident.

"Any update on the substation explosion?" Bennett asked to change the subject.

Vellins shifted between his feet, black fatigues rustling softly. "Used some of those tips you gave me on talking with civilians. Found out Kronos has been through the area a lot in the last few weeks and persuaded a teenager to set the bomb, making the usual false promises of gold and glory." A gust of air burst from his lips, his hands hooking over the back of his neck. He rolled his head and Bennett heard it crack. "I think I get close to sensing these feelings we're told civilians have, then my serum dose kicks in and it's all gone again. How does it come so easily to you?"

Shepherds said things like this to Bennett regularly. Bennett was good at hiding his truth, his battle with the serum. He'd practiced for years. Shoving his hands in his pockets, he studied the discomfort of the man before him. "I joined UP late, lived as a civilian a lot longer than any other shepherd."

"Somehow I think it's more than that. And whatever it is, is the reason you took a bullet for Sergeant Tanner, are always assisting us new Team Leaders even though you're not a listed reference, and don't hesitate to accept the assignments that intimidate most of the crews. I mean, the wildfire in Mountain Zone Eight was a death trap, and your crew put it out."

"Just doing—"

"Your job. Like every one of the rest of us." Vellins hung his hands from the front of his tactical vest and stood motionless as if every ounce of focus was on his next words. "Except you're different, more. We don't know what it is, us other TLs, but you're untouchable, with respect, sir."

Bennett, realizing they viewed him like he did Independents, shook his head. He didn't want to be on a pedestal built by intimidation. "Some of us just burn hotter inside." He tapped his chest. *And are always on the edge of serum burn out, the edge of retirement, of losing everything that matters.*

Vellins dropped his arms to his sides. He didn't look convinced but nodded. "Good luck with the next mission, sir. And thanks again for the advice."

"Any time." Bennett watched the man leave before pushing inside his room, his door clicking shut behind him. Resting back against it, he closed his eyes for a long moment. His shepherd status was always teetering because of his serum resistance. It's why he gave 110 percent every day. That, and his crew.

Bennett found himself envying Atana's independence from the system, breaking rules and not being discharged from service.

Crossing the small room, he dug through his issued duffle bag to busy his hands and refocus on the new mission. Everything was in perfect order as he knew it would be. Yet he felt profoundly ill-prepared.

Slumping to sit on his bed, Bennett raked his fingers through his short hair. For an entire week, he had been without his serum. Every vial at his base had been thrown out. Desperately gathering his pieces together, he caged the animal inside, the one that screamed his humanity.

The serum numbed the effects of hormones and neurotransmitters in the body, its effectiveness unmatched in the modern market. But someone had sabotaged the doses at the distribution center for Ocean Bases along the southern Pacific coast. The majority of the shepherds affected had to be put under quarantine until the withdrawal symptoms subsided.

Bennett was used to withdrawal. Hiding his emotions was second nature because the standard serum wasn't enough.

The smooth, ivory pillow on his bed reminded him of the blank faces he saw all too often, the personalities crushed by the serum. He longed to see something else, something to fill the hungry pit in his chest.

Leaning forward, a pair of dog tags swung from his neck, and his alone, black rubber around their edges to keep them silent. He had always wanted to be in the military, like his father. Just not like this.

His father had been a member of the Shepherds United. He'd had a family. But Bennett had been born into the era of the serum—the mission of protecting the world and keeping the peace more important than that of personal desire. His father had lost his life because of the job. His mother and younger brother had succumbed to a house fire when he was eight, leaving Bennett to wander the earth alone.

The liberated hormones in his system caused his mind to drift. He tried to imagine a woman sitting there beside him, calm and gentle, like his mother. But it would never be enough to make the loneliness depart. Rubbing his palms over his smooth cheeks, sticky with aftershave, he grumbled and raised himself from the bed.

Never going to happen, Jameson. Get on with it.

With the door closed behind him, he trudged toward the Serum Specialist Office, down his corridor at the end of an adjacent hall. His insides cramped up, knowing these were his last few minutes of being serum-free without getting in trouble for it. Squeezing his shoulder blades together, he straightened his back and prepared for the numbing hum that awaited him.

It was the burden of being a shepherd: sacrificing oneself—life, love, and happiness—for the betterment of Earth's population. But it was a debt paid—a life for a life. He'd been rescued from a violent death as a teen, a slave of the knock-pits in Tropic Zone Fifteen. He had earned himself the shock collar after stealing food for Meyriss, a homeless five-year-old girl he'd taken the charge of protecting.

There wasn't a day that passed that Bennett didn't wonder what happened to her. The raid had rendered him unconscious. When he had woken, he was in the Instructor's office, Master Yashina's dark eyes staring down at him. None of them recognized her name. He'd been the oldest recruit on record, signing on at seventeen.

Every shepherd had a similar story.

Turning the corner into S.S.O., he walked right into another shepherd. His hands rose instinctively in response to their bodies colliding. Grasping the sergeant's shoulders, he'd prevented himself from knocking them over.

The female jolted upright before sidestepping out of his way. Her glance was quick but long enough, the ice-blue of her eyes unmistakable.

Atana.

"I apologize." His fingers absorbed her warmth, the sweet hint of Marusa tea and spices tickling his nose. An elastic band held up the waterfall of merlot waves, a dress code rule only an Independent would have the guts to break. Women's hair was to be up in a bun.

A female Independent.

He couldn't believe he'd met Atana, and they were assigned to one another. Bennett admired the arch of her light mocha cheeks. Her soft strands brushed the backs of his hands. Beneath her leathers, he sensed the packed-in muscle. His stomach flipped, enthralled by every unfamiliar stimulation. He stood in fire and ice, burning with sudden and inexplicable lust and intrigue while frozen to the floor.

A woman in his grasp when he was off serum was a risky situation, thus why so many shepherds were in quarantine. To prevent an unplanned Awakening.

His opportunity was cut short when Rio noticed the commotion at the door. Bennett instantly released her, fumbling over his tongue. The older man in a white coat held the door to his private office open, Atana following at his request.

The attending nurse stopped in front of Bennett. "Sir, we can seat you on a table, end of row seven."

His gaze traveled behind Atana, even after she had disappeared, concealed by Rio's closed door.

"Sir, please have a seat."

"Huh?"

The nurse motioned to the back of the room. When he noticed the table's view through Rio's office window, he nodded and walked anxiously to it. He was now under observation.

Leaning his hips back against the metal table, he scanned the other shepherds to hide his desire to study Atana. A glint of light from an uncomfortably long and thin stripe on the side of Atana's head sent a pang through his chest.

Don't stare, Jameson.

But the way her plush lips delicately formed her words made his hands tighten around the rolled edge of the steel table behind him.

He needed serum yesterday.

Her eyes spoke louder than her muffled words. Rio shook his head. She sat, sliding her jacket off, exposing her left arm and several glossy striations in her skin, with an insistent nod. The man crossed his arms, the determination in his eyes unyielding.

Bennett had never seen Rio refuse an analysis.

Please, Atana's lips begged.

A hot pressure swelled in Bennett's chest, urging him to push his way into the office and make the demand for her.

Rio's shoulders dropped. He drew the Comprehensive Endocrine and Neurotransmitter Analyzer out of his pocket, placing it over her shoulder.

Bennett felt himself relax, and a realization hit him. He bolted upright, loosening his fingers. *What the hell is going on with me?*

The nurse broke up his view in her light gray lab coat. She lifted his left forearm and popped open the empty serum case on his wristband.

"Sergeant, you are from O.B. Thirty-Three, yes?" she asked, reading the chart on her illuminated tablet.

He leaned back discreetly to bring Atana's profile into view again.

"Ocean Base thirty-three," she reiterated.

Atana's leathers were shrink-wrapped to her curves. A hum started in his throat, and he coughed to cover it. "Correct."

Slipping, Jameson.

The nurse tapped her screen. "Seven-milliliter doses are your usual?"

Bennett took a deep breath to calm the hormones he knew were seething through his body. When he looked at Atana, he could feel them raising his heart rate, and inserting poorly rationalized ideas into his mind. "Yes, ma'am." He momentarily caught Atana's glance and couldn't resist a smile.

"Jacket."

Bennett promptly removed his leather coat, silently cursing himself for forgetting protocol.

The nurse pushed up his sleeve, resting the CENA analyzer over his shoulder. "O.B. Thirty-Three is one of the affected bases, yes?"

"Correct." The stirring flares through his core and the lightheadedness from his rapid heartbeat were deceptively encouraging. *I'm sure it's nothing. Serum will fix this.*

But he knew that was a lie.

"I'll get you refilled quick so those symptoms will cease."

Inside, Bennett cringed. He didn't like the way she said the word, like feeling an interest in another human being was a disease. They were the reason the human population still existed. Yet, he was a tad unnerved he might not be holding everything in as well as he'd thought.

"What symptoms?"

The device in her hands beeped. "You're feverish and trembling, sir."

—Fields of Gold—

Chapter 6

COLD STEEL punctured the surface of Atana's skin.

"What has you concerned this time?" Rio was the only other shepherd not required by Command to take serum. It covered his ability to catch those who were compromised. He was also the single one who could hold her gaze for more than a few seconds and not turn away.

A stiff inhale moved her only slightly.

"The thundering of the collectors—" She squeezed her hands into fists, trying to calm her racing pulse. "They woke me in a way most sounds don't. I regained control but—"

His slate-gray eyes scanned her face, a brow arching. "Nakio, I never tell Command unless your safety is at risk. Please, be honest about why you're in here."

Atana's lips curled inward for a moment. "A man broke through security yesterday. He said he was my brother. Looking at him caused a similar effect." Her voice dropped to a whisper. "Rio, sir, he *felt* familiar. I need serum."

"Felt?" Despite his hesitation, Rio's voice stayed modulated and calm. "Where all serum-regulated shepherds must use logic to complete assignments, Command has permitted your senses to override the mandate and for good reason. What you sense around you, our best technology doesn't always detect."

"Command expects use of my skills in relation to the missions, not personnel."

"It hasn't been an issue."

"Until now. Put me on serum, Rio."

The device shifted over her shoulder, the needle tugging at her muscle like a chilled, hard knot. He lowered himself to eye-level with her. She could see him silently probing for more.

Dismissing the uncomfortable sensation in her shoulder, a new one squirmed to the surface of her skin, all of it, with the urge to shiver and shy away. It was a mixture of vulnerability and failure. Rio studied her with a sympathetic depth far beyond her former instructor. Sensei had been unrelenting in his training, constantly pushing her combat skills, challenging her mental limits, and never letting her lose focus on the mission.

Thinking of him, the memory of the metal piercing through his chest crashed through her thoughts in a hot wave. But she held Rio's gaze, despite the agonizing image.

Atana had seen the frantic disbelief and regret in Sensei's eyes when he'd looked down at her, there in the abandoned office, his body sheltering her from the fragmenting bomb. She couldn't understand why he'd saved her, a young, R1 shepherd. Sensei's body had bloomed into a red-black cloud of mist, leaving her crouched in the darkness with nothing more than training weapons and the chunk of metal that had taken his life clattering to the floor in front of her. Three hours she'd fought her way through the Kronos rebels, back to the UP transport. Command had demanded an explanation for Sensei's disappearance when they docked. She couldn't answer, not verbally. The swelling hatred and confusion had tightened her throat, her jaw, every muscle, until she wanted to burst— as he had.

Rio had stared at her then like he was now, reading through her protective walls. He had told Command to let the matter go and then requested she be reassigned and put under his watch. Rio always listened and knew exactly what she needed when. She couldn't understand why he was resisting her need for serum now.

Atana preferred short communication and quick resolutions. This was taking too long. "I'm not leaving without it."

He frowned. Rio never frowned.

When the test completed, he removed the device from her arm to show her the results. "One spike in the last twenty-four hours, but it isn't even noteworthy for you. When you were first here, the numbers were off the charts, until we got your injury under control." He gestured toward her head. "It was like a switch."

"Why now? I haven't reinjured that area."

He ejected the spent needle into a red bin mounted to the wall and returned the device to the cupboard. "My guess—you haven't been sleeping enough and are running on adrenaline to keep yourself awake again. It's not healthy, nor is it allowed by Command. I know it plagues you, but you must sleep."

She hung her head with a bob, knowing he was right. "Yes, sir."

While Rio selected her doses from the chilled cabinet, she shifted focus through his office window to the crowd of shepherds and nurses in the other room. Someone looked in her direction from one of the exam tables: the one who had run into her. *Sergeant Bennett.*

He leaned against the edge, arms straightened, waiting patiently for the nurse to finish her assessment. Flecks of honey flashed in his golden eyes, sheltered beneath umber brows. The shallow divot in his upper lip stretched. His cheeks lifted.

The color on his face deepened with his smile. Bemused, she traced it again.

For a moment, the room slipped away. He was different from other shepherds, the few she'd interacted with personally. His high-and-tight haircut had grown out, still defying gravity. When his full lips parted, she felt the unnerving jolt of seeing the collectors and Lavrion's familiar face lance through her again.

"Nakio?"

She blinked and lifted her gaze to meet Rio's request.

Closing the faceplate, he pointed to the screen. "The program will notify you every twenty-four hours to inject your standard dose to maintain hormone balance and alert you if there's a need to inject before the scheduled dose."

"I'm aware, sir. I designed several components of the CENA-7 wristbands."

"Right. Well, I always monitor everyone's levels. So if there is an issue while you are at Home Station, I will find you."

"Yes, sir." Atana scrutinized Bennett in the other room one more time.

The ceiling fans stirred the air above. *Don't look away.*

From Bennett? She scanned his fit outline with more interest. *Why?*

Rio's voice summoned her back. "Are you ready?"

Atana swallowed. *Wasting precious time. Focus.*

She tapped in her sixteen-digit number as assigned from Human Cataloging. A swift click of mechanized parts, a tiny pinch, two seconds, another click, and the screen blinked.

Dose Complete

The cold serum flowed into her blood vessels, numbing her, the little voice suddenly dead quiet. She almost regretted it when she hopped up from the chair, the emptiness like witnessing the death of an innocent civilian. Zipping up her jacket, she shook Rio's hand.

"It was good to see you, Nakio." He smiled—an expression she'd never really understood.

...

The absence of progress on their situation was deafening. People were disappearing every moment she wasted. Atana stood in Private Conference

Room Five behind an interactive table, awaiting her new team. Her fingers drummed on the glass, whipping through all the Current Conflicts data received from the bases around the world.

The wall screen behind her flickered to life. "Sergeant Atana."

She spun to find herself staring at Command from behind the Coordinator's seat.

"We have accessed video clips of the vessel in space, acquired by Space Station Hope prior to their blackout. They should be loading in a few moments and will also be sent to your Electrical Integration Specialist, Sergeant Remmi Tanner."

"Understood." The screen went dark.

With a few moments to spare and the data available exhausted, she unclipped the straps holding in her SIs and drew them from her thigh holsters.

Her fingers swiftly disconnected the parts: wad and igniter magazines, radial vent chamber, and the accelerator. Slipping a small, opaque bottle from her pocket, she squeezed a drop of cleaning fluid on each component and inside the compression chamber and ignition barrel.

Scouring the individual curves and crevices, she diligently wiped away the charcoal film with the cloth from her pocket, returning each unit to the table top.

'Hurry up and wait' was never a good thing for an Independent. Atana had done and seen too much to be left alone without a task, something to keep her mind busy—and focused.

Bennett messaged her.

Five Minutes Out

Chapter 7

Sergeant Bennett rounded the corner of the staging area just in time to watch his team unload from an elevator. Each individual's band flashed with the message he'd sent.

They seemed unaware of his presence and, taking a step back, he leaned a shoulder against the wall to observe.

"Where the hell's that?" Sergeant Panton's voice boomed from above his massive spread of shoulders. "Better be near a lunchroom."

Sergeant Tanner pushed his floppy blond hair back from his eyes, searching the map on his wristband. "Nope, farthest thing from it."

"Damn it," Panton drawled, placing a hand over his grumbling stomach. "If I don't eat something, I'm going to wither away. Ten hours is too damn long without food. It's worse without serum."

Sergeant Cutter adjusted the faded ball cap hiding his smooth, coal-black hair and lugged his duffle bag over his shoulder. Catching up to Tanner, he dipped his head beside the young man's ear. "He couldn't wither in a million years."

They shared a chuckle before passing Panton.

Bennett arched a brow. Cutter never joked. *Must not have picked up his doses yet either.* Serum never knocked the emotions completely dead for Bennett, but Cutter became as steely as the color of his eyes. He'd been worried about his munitions expert for years, with the utter lifelessness of his face. It was reassuring to know that beneath he still held elements of humanity. It was also, unfortunately, wrong.

Panton squinted at the two snickering sergeants. "Y'all don't understand. I'm so hungry I could— Wait, are y'all saying I'm fat?" He glanced back at the last member of the team to unload. "Josie, do you think I'm getting fat?"

"We'll eat after the meeting." Josie's drawl was softer than Panton's yet strong in volume despite her petite frame. Her strawberry-blond bun bounced as she hopped out. Adjusting her black tactical vest, Josie slung her e-rifle over a shoulder. "And no, Panton, you're the size you need to be for your job. You know that. Relax."

Sergeant Tanner caught Bennett's position, relief lifting the man's features. "B!"

"About damn time. I was starting to wonder if I was going to get switched to another team," Bennett teased through a grin.

"I was getting mighty tired of bossin' these three around." Josie jerked her freckled nose at the team. "Please, take them back."

Panton scoffed incredulously. "Aw, c'mon, we're not that bad!"

Cutter pursed his lips, his silver eyes glinting with amusement.

"So who's our new Team Leader?" Tanner asked. "I mean you are always our leader, B. There's just—the female Independent assigned to lead us?"

Bennett's smile faded. He led the group down the hall to the stairwell, his feet sinking heavily against the steps. "Yes, she will be calling the shots. She's quiet and hard to read."

"You already met her?" Panton asked.

"Yes." Bennett was still tripping over himself trying to figure Atana out. Flashing Cutter a glance, he hoped their psychologist might offer some insight. All Bennett got in return was a doubtful twist of the man's mouth.

Tanner followed at his heels. "Don't worry, B. We'll take her orders, but we'll always operate by your rules, right, guys?"

The team concurred behind him, settling some of the nervous energy in Bennett's muscles. Independents weren't used to accounting for the safety of others. Effective or not, Atana was a lone soldier for a reason.

"Make sure you call her ma'am," he warned, lifting an open palm to the room.

The team filed in ahead of him. Bennett stopped in the entrance, studying Atana as she straightened from the interactive table. Those bright eyes were why so many shepherds couldn't look at her, that and the proudest scar on the side of her forehead.

He'd heard a shepherd say once, "I feel like she's looking into my soul."

Atana was intimidating, yes. But more so, her mysterious past intrigued Bennett. Her eyes held a depth he wanted to sink into, something rare in their emotionally sterile environment.

Settling in against the doorframe, he let his team introduce themselves. He was proud of his crew. They had grown together over the years. He had coached them, protected them, taught Panton and Cutter the tricks and secrets he knew from being a guard. He had learned from the younger, innovative Sergeant Tanner, and he now knew when to step back from Josie's fire.

Cutter pulled his hat off, to Bennett's surprise, and met Atana's gaze. He was studying her without serum? "Ma'am, I'm Sergeant Cutter. This is Josandizer. She stands in for Sergeant Bennett when he is away on assignment."

Atana scanned the nametape over the shorter female's left pocket when Cutter directed to her with a hand.

"The guys call me Josie," the redhead offered.

Atana's brows pinched. "You think it's acceptable to disrespect the name Command coded you?"

"No, ma'am. My full name is just lengthy and ridiculous. Josie is easier and quicker to say." Josie threw Bennett an anxious glance. "More efficient."

After an awkward moment of silence, Sergeant Cutter gestured to his other side. "This is Tanner, and the tank in the back is Panton."

Panton lightly punched Cutter's shoulder and mouthed *hey* when the man turned around. Cutter responded with a wink.

Shoving his hands in his pockets, Bennett had no doubts now. His crew needed serum.

"Josie and Tanner are the specialty sergeants, sniper and electronics emphases, respectively." Cutter hooked a thumb over his shoulder. "Panton is Josie's guard, our blunt force as needed, and I am Tanner's, team psych and trained in freeform munitions. I hear you've already met our Team Leader, Sergeant Bennett."

Atana's gaze fell on Bennett once again, cementing his feet to the floor. Behind that familiar shepherds' disconnect hid a shimmer of pain and a glint of something sinister. Bennett couldn't place it. All Independents displayed a similar façade, but not to Atana's intensity. She was something more.

The muscles in Atana's jaw visibly twitched when she looked down to scroll through the screen in front of her. "Upon reviewing the information available on our upcoming task, it's possible we may not be returning home. With this in mind, if anyone wants out, now is the time to do it."

"I just want out so I can get a sandwich," Panton mumbled.

Josie glanced over at him, brows raised. "Sorry. Our unit had a batch of serum get contaminated. We've been off for some time." She jabbed a pointy elbow into his side. "A little mouthy is all."

"Chillax, feisty. I'm just hungry." Panton chuckled.

She rolled her eyes. "When are you not?"

"You may elect yourselves out if you prefer. I can arrange for another, more stable team." Atana surveyed every member of the group.

Her words cut into Bennett like a hot knife. His fists clenched in his pockets, but he managed to smooth his voice. "Command wouldn't have picked us if they hadn't thought we were the most qualified, serum issues or not."

"We just need food and serum, and we'll be good-to-go, ma'am." Josie gave her a reassuring nod.

Atana pulled up the schedule, displaying the daily blackout and shuttle availability. "Same room, 1630 hours. Shuttle departs 1700."

"Thank you, ma'am!" Panton leapt out of the conference room, gear bag in tow, the others racing to catch up.

Bennett leaned through the door, calling after them. "Serum. I'm checking in one hour." He tapped his wristband.

The team shouted their compliance over their shoulders. Bennett opened the tab on his screen, displaying their stats. Atana's face now appeared with theirs. Panton was the worst offender, the bars of his hormone graph already bouncing like a serum-free civilian. Cutter was second, followed by Josie. Tanner never seemed bothered by serum withdrawal. His levels only rose enough to hit the bottom of the warning threshold.

Bennett sent Josie a message to watch Panton carefully. She acknowledged. Panton's testosterone level spiked then slowly dropped back with the others. Bennett rubbed a callused hand over his mouth. Kronos had really screwed them with this serum disruption right before an invasion.

But Atana, she was flat across every recordable unit. If he didn't know better, Bennett would've thought she was dead.

He stepped into the room where Atana was back to work on the table. "The serum issue isn't their fault. Why are you being so hard on them?"

She scrolled through the images popping up on the screen. "All I need to know is if I can rely on them to act accordingly. Rule Two, serum for stability."

"I know what it is."

She leaned over the large display. Zooming in on a photo of the ship orbiting their planet, a section of a pillar-like structure sharpened. "What do you think this is?"

Bennett walked around the table to view what she had been studying. "Not sure, maybe a dock door?"

His subconscious had thankfully responded. He was, once again, lost in the marred curves of her face. It wasn't permitted, shepherds conversing in length about who they were or where they were from, per Rule Six of the Shepherd's Code. There were only stories circulating about her, bits and pieces he had heard from other sergeants.

Carries a blade into village territory battles, nothing more. Tears her band off when she works alone. So risky. How can Command trust her if she doesn't follow the rules?

Cleaned out an illegal fortress, Mountain Zone Nine, the cannibals picking off travelers. Thirty-some rebels. An entire team of shepherds down. Blew up the cave. When she brought the Sheps' bands in for the download, there wasn't any data. Maybe she killed them too? Wiped the hard drives?

Heard she ripped the throat out of a Kronos with her teeth. Got herself caught just so she could get in and take out his posse. Gotta say, the guy had it coming after beheading the last team we sent in.

Bennett cringed. *That last one, no way.*

"I've heard a lot about you." He paused. "Rumors are, uh, usually inaccurate though."

"Usually." Atana's focus jumped to another image of the mothership, one farther out. "What rumors?"

He wasn't the first to pry and stumble, judging by her impassiveness. "I apologize. It's—nothing."

She squinted up at him. "I should have requested a different Team Leader."

His eyes locked on hers. Challenging an Independent was a bad idea. *Lifting Pandora's lid, Jameson. Stop it.* He looked away. "I only want to know what artillery I'm playing with."

"This is not a game, Sergeant Bennett." Atana sighed through her nose, bracing her hands on the desk. "Stiff shoulders, particularly when you sleep, repeated wrist fractures from punching bags and bodies, and regular serum noncompliance. To name a few."

His eyes closed, his lungs releasing with force. How could she know? He cursed himself inside.

"Why were you—*are* you studying me?" He arched his spine and interlaced his arms. The position was comfortable, safe.

"I have to calibrate myself for your system, to know what you're capable of and where I have to compensate. We could be overrun when we get up there." Her voice dropped to a whisper. "If we even make it in one piece."

The air in his lungs heated. He wasn't sure if he was angered by her accusation of his instability or riled up by the idea of her 'calibrating herself for his system.' "We could spar for an hour."

"I need to work on our plan." She returned to the images, unfazed.

She said I, not we. He paced around to the opposite side of the table. His team was involved, making him responsible for their safety. There was no guarantee Atana would consider it a priority.

"Thoughts, then, on the plan?" He opened the diagrams of Hope's operating spacecraft on his side of the interactive table.

"The 501, and Goss is piloting. It's once we get up there. That's what I need the plan for."

Bennett stopped scrolling. "Seems like you really know what you're doing. Why?"

She offered no response.

Growing irritated, he rounded the table and planted a hand in the middle of her screen. *Look at me.* "We are a team now whether you like it or not. You need to include me so I can prepare my sergeants for whatever you need. My job is to protect all of you. Give me something to work with."

Atana uncurled herself from the table to glare up into his eyes, her nose merely centimeters from his. A few strands of her wavy hair had slipped out of the elastic band holding up her ponytail hiding the tail ends of several scars.

Her spicy-sweet scent cut down the molecules of serum in his blood with ruthless prowess. His heart broke into a sprint. He desperately wanted to take one finger and draw the tendrils from her cheek, concerned over the extent of her painful past. How far back did the scars on her face reach?

Sensing the motions of her fingers near his hips, his wristband signaled its alerts, evoking a single slow blink. He couldn't think. All he could see was her and feel his blood rushing through him with a fury he'd only heard of from the pre-serum era. Reckless. Wild. Free. It was an addicting and powerful sensation, tingling in every muscle, filling him with energy. He didn't want to stop it.

In one swift move, her hands unsnapped his holsters and grabbed the two SI units, yanking them from their cases so hard they spun in her palms.

"Here's something to work with." Atana shoved the handles into his gut, knocking him back a step from the force. Bennett accepted the SIs she held against his tensed sides with a heavy heart.

"Keep your head in the game, Sergeant," she asserted with a petulant shake of her head. "And let me do *my* job."

Their wristbands beeped, flashing notifications on their screens.

Body Status Reaching Peak Performance Limit
Restoration Necessary

She broke his gaze to gesture at the door. "Get a serum check with your team before we depart. I need to know I can trust you."

Bennett holstered his SIs in one thrust. Atana ignored the alert on her screen. Biting the inside of a cheek, he kept himself from pointing it out and made one final plea. "I need to help. You just have to tell me how I can."

Her body locked in determination. "I have to do this alone. I can't focus with you hovering. When I have a plan, I'll send it to you."

Something about the way she said 'alone' made a cold emptiness spread through his core like a person who'd been starving for days on end. It crushed his high in a blink.

"Meeting at 1630." Her eyes darted to the exit and back to him.

He turned to leave but caught the doorframe in a hand and stopped. "If you change your mind, message me." Atana's leathers gleamed under the hard light when he looked back. She didn't move.

Patting the jamb in defeat, he left to track down his team.

Chapter 8

THUD, THUMP, THUD.

Bennett's fists pummeled the punching bag, frustrated he was helpless, at the mercy of an Independent for the safety of his sergeants. Home Station was locked down in blackout status, and he couldn't sleep.

Atana clearly didn't want his help or need it. It was like he was back in training again. He wasn't used to being bossed around. And on top of it all, Bennett felt things for her he knew the serum was supposed to keep quiet.

Even the higher concentration Rio had synthesized, specifically for him, wasn't enough. Not today.

It was more than a typical interest in a woman when the numbing hum faded. He wanted to stay by her side, watch her, watch *over* her. There was no rationale for the urge, just a deep, consuming need. But Atana didn't want him there.

Releasing a growl, he swung for a roundhouse kick, connecting hard against the tough, fabric surface. Granules sprayed out, pouring from the tear in the deforming bag and into a pile on the floor. Bennett slapped a hand over his face when he saw the mess beneath.

"It's nothing to be upset over." Rio's soothing, fluid voice carried in from the doorway. "Sergeant Porter will clean it up before the shift change. What's your trouble, Jameson? I'm here if you want to talk."

Bennett spun to see Rio in dark cargo pants and a long sleeve shirt, his white coat gone. "Poor kid just lost half his leg. I'll clean it up myself."

"Command put him in here to get his strength up, to learn to use his prosthetic," Rio stated softly. "If they didn't think he was capable of continuing, they would've retired him."

Bennett plopped down on the mat listening to the whispers of falling sand. "Yes, sir."

He hung his head and opened up. "Sir, the serum—it's not working. It's worse than normal, and I have a crucial mission in a few hours. I'm not confident I can perform to the expected standards if this continues."

"Sergeant Atana is giving you trouble." Rio lifted one corner of his mouth.

Bennett stilled. He should've known Rio would figure it out.

45

"You two are polar opposites. She has never needed serum, and you have always needed more than anyone else in the system. I have shadowed both of you closely for many years because of this."

Bennett twisted his neck, evoking several pops. "I don't know what to do, how to handle her self-righteous attitude. I can't seem to get a word in without getting glared at. She doesn't want to tell me what she's thinking or even ask for my opinion. It's not equal."

Rio scanned the otherwise vacant gym. "Do you want to die here on Earth, doing nothing? Or do you want to bear the burden to protect the people?"

"Protect the people, of course."

"I have looked the other way for many serum users because, in their situations, it was better to be emotional than not, though I never disclose this information to Command."

"Better?"

Rio gestured toward the fabric swinging from the chain. "When was the last time you split open a punching bag like that?"

Bennett peeled the tape from around his knuckles. "Never."

"I know she can be intimidating and occasionally frustrating." Rio interlaced his arms and sighed as if he'd given the speech many times already. "An R3 status isn't a lower grade than an R4. You two possess the same leadership qualifications, field skills, and experience, and your words hold similar clout. You just play better with others, which is why you have an assigned team and she does not. Be a reflection of her stubbornness, and she'll see she has to adapt to get you to do what she wants."

Rio turned to the door. "One more thing. When her instructor, Sensei, passed, she was assigned to me. Though no one else is privy to this information, Atana is the closest I have to a daughter. If anything happens to her, it will be on you."

Bennett knew Rio started with the Shepherds United when families had been permitted in the beginning. After Command discovered the underlying weakness of selfish motivations to protect oneself and one's family, lessening the vigor with which certain shepherds performed their duties, Rio had been tasked with creating the serum.

Families were a concept Bennett didn't fully comprehend because he had come from a torn one, like every shepherd. But he respected the significance of it, nonetheless. It's ultimately what they guarded with their lives.

"Command wants to see you when you have a moment." Rio glanced back, his quiet voice diamond hard. "Until every last drop is spent, Sergeant."

Bennett popped to his feet. "Yes, sir."

...

A deep breath helped calm Bennett's nerves. His hands opened and closed, trying to relieve the swelling. He had mulled over every possible reason Command could want to speak privately with him and concluded it must have to do with his team's serum noncompliance over the last week.

"Have a seat." The Coordinator waved him inside the conference room.

Bennett hesitated. "Yes, Command."

They'd brought in an extra chair just for him. He sank uneasily into the stiff mesh at the end of the table, staring across its length at the Coordinator's blue eyes. Even seated, the man towered above the others.

"Sergeant Nakio Atana, your assignment leader, is one of the few to survive the initial attack from over twenty years ago. The main ship re-entered our orbit, thirteen years back, taking more of our people."

Bennett nodded, relieved his team was off the hook. He had heard these things before and was now left wondering what the purpose was of such a private meeting.

The Coordinator folded his hands, resting them on the desk. "We sent a rescue team in to try to recover some of our people via our H.Co. tracking system and learn a bit from the ship. However, our Hope Transport Six was destroyed shortly after arrival. A shepherd made an impromptu decision, flying one of the invaders' ships to the ground, which regrettably crashed. It was not ground-worthy. We lost many people during that encounter." Every cold, blank face became uncannily astute to Bennett's position. "You must swear not to release the following information to anyone, ever."

"I swear."

"Not even your team," another muttered, a woman, the only one whose head was down, the scratch of her pencil pausing at the silence.

His jaw tensed, teeth grinding as they repressed his growing fear. *How could they know about my team rule? Those guys wouldn't say anything.* "Yes, Command."

"When the transport crashed," the Coordinator continued, followed by the woman's pencil, "some of the cabin remained intact. We believed it was luck or fate at the time, possibly the softer dunes. The shepherd who rescued Atana reported seeing her stumble out of an area of the cabin entirely engulfed in flames.

Bennett ached to shift in his seat. Atana had survived a transport crash? *She's been on the ship?* He honestly hadn't heard much about her beginnings, only that she wasn't "to be fucked with," in the words of more than one shepherd that had served under her. *God knows what she's seen. That explains why she didn't want my help.*

The Coordinator tilted his head just enough for Bennett to notice. "Oddly enough, the fire did not burn her skin. Unfortunately, for her—and us—she lost most of her memory during their return to Earth when a piece of metal debris struck her in the head."

That's where the scar is from. Bennett cringed inside. "So she's what—fireproof?"

Another member spoke up, a man seated beside the Coordinator, one Bennett noticed had a permanent furrow between his brows. "She can take a lot of heat in more ways than one, yes, Sergeant Bennett. Atana has always been unique because of her technical skill. She also has the highest kill record of any we have ever had on the force."

Bennett ran a couple fingers over his lips in contemplation, dropping his eyes to stare at the speckled gray linoleum floor. *Atana doesn't remember. Sounds like she's always in go-mode. Must be why she couldn't plan with me in there.* "You need my team to work with her, at her pace, and be prepared to change plans without explanation."

The woman's pencil stopped. Her head didn't lift. "One of the reasons we selected you—your ability to adapt."

Several members concurred with murmurs.

"Something about Atana is different from the others we rescued, something we've never been able to tack down." The Coordinator leaned forward. "Sergeant Bennett, you have always been our most capable and reliable guard. You have led your team successfully for several years. We are entrusting you with her safety, the team with her mission. You will need to do whatever you have to up there to survive and return Sergeant Atana to us. She is our most valued asset."

Bennett's heart jumped erratically, threatening to crack his voice. They had given him the charge of protecting the silent zenith of the Universal Protectors.

"Yes, Command."

Chapter 9

IT WASN'T WORTH IT most nights. Sergeant Atana lay on her bunk, eyes wide open. She'd completed the plan and sent it to Bennett. Now, she was stuck waiting for the blackout phase to end, for 1630, for her chance at answers.

Restoration Necessary

Her exhale was voluminous and forced. She hated those two words.

Black, drift-less sleep, peace, quiet, warm, soft dunes—she pleaded, focusing on the words, hoping they would send her into such a realm. But she knew better. The mission would open another window into her past, giving her a fragment of something bigger. Stress induced it. New experiences built tiny bridges. She just couldn't search unprompted on her own. Not without Sensei.

Allowing her eyelids to hang low, she steadied herself for whatever would play, and let herself slip away into another memory.

Her body was rejecting the implants along her spine and in her brain, her skin irritated around the metal nodes. The chill of the unforgiving steel beneath her, the bright procedure light overhead, and the faint sounds of a life teetering on the edge of death echoing from another room told her right where she was: testing.

An electrical probe contacted parts of her spine and brain, causing hot, snapping arcs and involuntary movements. She could smell the sizzling tissue—her skin, her muscle, her bones. She was pretty sure she didn't know what to define as pain anymore.

Two large creatures dragged a limp body in, tossing him onto the slab next to hers. His malnourished frame hit the surface with a light thud, a sticklike arm dangling off the side.

Everything became hazy. She choked, suffocating without the use of her lungs, hope fading with her consciousness. At a groaning creak of metal, she dropped to the sludgy floor like a forgotten marionette. A meaty hand tossed her onto her slab, the nodes along her spine scraping the surface. The friction took hold, digging in, vibrating, and manipulating every vertebra with a screeching racket.

49

Her body convulsed, the agony inundating her system. They tied her down, jabbing a needle into her neck. She writhed in their grasp until the muted lights faded out completely, and she was left again, in darkness.

Atana's lashes lifted, and she peered up at the ceiling in her bunk room, cursing the stars she knew were beyond its metal shield. She covered her face with a hand, breathing deep to control the reverberating images as they evanesced into memories. But pushing away the sensations—the trembling radiating out from her spine, the desperation for air, and the ache of staring at the boy's emaciated and neglected body— was nearly impossible. Those things had to fade with time.

Some nights, she feared they never would.

Chapter 10

1630 HOURS.

The team reassembled.

Bennett remained in the doorway, leaning against the frame, like he had done the previous day, studying Atana. He hadn't slept much with the additional responsibility now on his shoulders. The trouble was going to be protecting someone who didn't appear to want him around.

"Is everyone stable?" Atana calmly scanned each sergeant.

They nodded, every face now apathetic and patiently awaiting orders.

Atana didn't even glance at Bennett.

"After reviewing our options with Command, we have decided to take Space Station Hope's 501 and drift, to this port here." She pulled up the images of the enemy invaders' main ship, pointing to the door where they planned to connect.

"It will take us about fifteen minutes from Hope on the moon to reach this large fortress. We will do it in silence, propulsion off, like we are some of the space junk already up there. Sergeant Goss will be our guide pilot. He works primarily with our Space Department. He's prepping the 501 now.

"When we have docked to the invader's ship, Sergeant Tanner and I will go inside to find a control panel we can hack and get some more information on what we are up against. The rest of you will be cover and protection. When we have a concept of layout, we'll split up to assess capabilities, regroup, and get the hell Home. Nod if you reviewed the plan I sent out." Every member complied.

Bennett noted the paleness of Atana's face as they headed up to the main hangar. The shadows under her eyes, the fine lines between her brows, and her constant deep breaths and sighs, indicated adrenal fatigue. It was a common problem in overtaxed field sergeants, especially those whose sleep was cut short on a regular basis.

When they boarded the shuttle, he chose to sit across from her, steadfast in his watchful position, wondering what she would be like on the inside after all she had been through. The combined experiences she'd had should've equated to PTSD. Somehow she remained vigilant and strong. Too strong.

It's locked and buried—something he could relate to.

His team clung to the unusual straps across their chests. It'd been years since they'd all completed Astrotech training on Hope. Bennett followed Atana's scarred hands as they latched her in, brushed the loose strands from her closing eyes, and then rested comfortably in her lap. *She's used to this.*

Tanner whispered in his ear. "You good?"

Bennett blinked lethargically at the distraction of answering Tanner's question. "Yeah, I got my serum adjusted. Again."

"Rio had to increase a couple of our doses faster than normal too since we went without for so long," Tanner offered.

Panton nudged Josie. "You hear they retired Wilkes last week?" The ship rumbled like his words, and they sank heavily into the seats.

"He was one of the rescue survivors, wasn't he?" she asked.

Cutter's voice was dull and lifeless. "He was having emotional instability issues after one of his missions. The serum wasn't working for him anymore."

Panton eyed their new leader, whispering, "They seem to go one way or the other, don't they? Some crack after a month, and others— It's like they're dead to the world—no emotions, no desires, no serum, ever."

Holding in a sigh, Bennett glanced up at the nearing pockmarked, lunar surface through the windows. The rush of wind and drone of burning fuel always meant something was about to drastically change in his life.

Command was sending a recently serum-compromised team with a worn-out leader on a suicide mission with the hope they would save them all. Bennett cursed in the privacy of his mind. This was bound to be a shit show.

Stars help us.

Chapter 11

STATION HOPE'S Commander greeted Atana when they unloaded from the transport. He waved for the team to follow. The silver cording and UP pin on his black uniform jacket glinted every time he passed beneath a light. His war-wrinkled face looked particularly weary tonight. "You're docked in 1B. Goss is ready to begin the launch sequence, pending your arrival."

"Thank you, sir." She had no doubts with Goss as their pilot. He'd been flying space missions longer than she'd been alive and had survived the two previous encounters. Both had been fiery, futile battles against the mothership and her swarm of collectors. He'd told Atana the stories when they'd take a space pod out between training sessions. An Independent shepherd like her, they'd connected quickly when she'd been temporarily reassigned to assist with remodeling Astrotech and Space Station Hope.

Atana led the pack, Bennett tracking unusually close to her side. The team lagged behind enough that she realized they weren't familiar with the layout. To her, it was like a second home.

Bennett's team worked field-missions on earth, not in space. She gritted her teeth. The potential success of their mission just took another hit. But Hope's teams weren't as good with infiltration tactics. They were specialty sergeants in technical integrations and space flight operations. As she'd heard several shepherds say, they were *screwed,* one way or another.

"Since we don't know if it will be a survivable environment, we have provided suits for all of you." The Commander had shepherds with him carrying the body gear, one sized to fit each team member.

"Thank you." But Atana had a feeling they weren't necessary. She stepped into the bay where the 501 navigation lights blinked in warning of its hot propulsion status. Pale blue orbs lit the three rear thrusters below the main deck, a welcome sight. Something familiar.

"If any of you get stuck outside, you listen to Sergeant Atana. I know she's not your usual leader. Command briefed us." The Commander acknowledged her with a terse nod. "But we've never lost a shepherd up here because of her, only ones who wouldn't listen. And Sergeant Goss is a damn good pilot. Keep him safe."

Atana hiked up the starboard ramp, jumping into her dark-graphite space suit. The Commander's crew helped the loading team don theirs.

Panton's was a bit of a tight squeeze. Josie reached over and zipped him up. Her eyes crinkled on the edges, grinning, though her lips didn't move. Sniper guards were the largest members of UP and the least likely to be assigned space flight missions.

"What'd I do without you?" He drawled.

"You'd be unemployed." Looking up at his playfully offended face, Josie snorted. The smallest suit available was bulky on her petite frame.

Atana finished with her own airtight seals and clipped her gear belt around her waist and thighs. "Sir, do we have any updated images of the ship? I want to check the status of our dock point, in case something has changed."

The Commander signaled to one of the crew who brought over a tablet. "We have a few from the David satellite. The base went into blackout status shortly after we saw them enter orbit."

Atana took the tablet from the crew member with a nod and called Tanner over, who fiddled clumsily with one of the body seals on the left arm of his suit. Handing him the tablet, she directed him to copy the images so they could study them later on his laptop if necessary.

Tanner disregarded his seal to flip open the case loosely strapped outside his suit. The screen illuminated his face as he linked the two, transferring the files.

Atana reached over and adeptly secured the body seal he'd left open. Growing concerned the team was unprepared, she spun, prepared to direct the others on the process.

Across the narrow cabin, Bennett helped Josie latch Panton's upper and lower body sections around his waist before inspecting Cutter's suit. "Dusted off my old Astrotech books last night."

"While we slept?" Josie's mouth hung partially open, her brows knitting upward.

"Does that really surprise you?" Cutter asked, watching Bennett fix his right boot attachment.

"Well no." Josie shifted the gear belt around her waist. "I just wish he would stop doing that shit, task one of us with sacrificing sleep."

Bennett sighed and stood, pointing at himself. "Team Leader." He pointed at her. "Kick ass when I tell you to."

A corner of her mouth quirked downward. "Yes, sir."

Beside Atana, Tanner spun his laptop around. His attention drifted to his team getting instructions on donning their helmets, then leapt back to her.

Atana cinched his tech harness tight against his chest. "Tuck the thermal, isolation barrier inside. Twist the lock rings together until the external iris snaps twice."

"Yes, ma'am." Tanner glanced uneasily up at her.

"Helmet is the same pattern."

"Thank you."

"Please refresh your memory of Astrotech at your next opportunity." Atana gave him a warning glare. "You can't work if you're dead." He bobbed his head but stumbled over his tongue. Returning the tablet to a crew member outside the 501, she looked down to study the shadowy pictures on his screen.

A network of support structures connected several hundred cylindrical containers in multiple levels, encompassing an immense central core. At one end, the framework sat empty, *where the pillars on Earth would be docked normally*, she supposed. At the other end, a fuming, blood-orange power source could be seen, its light broken up by arced spires, thicker at their base, where they attached to an outer ring, jutting up far past the nucleus.

Atana took a few steps away from Tanner. The last two invasions, Earth had fought back. This time they weren't, not the same way. Whoever or whatever was orchestrating the takeover had to be watching for an attack.

She repressed the panic and fear, knowing this plan still had a high success rate of evading radar. UP was risking a lot based on her theories. But she was sickeningly never wrong and knew she could access the mothership's system. She hadn't perfected the how. When she saw it, she would know. The recall portion of her mind was always hazy, but her recognition was infallible.

Staring at the rough surface of the ship before her drew another broken memory of testing forward in her mind. *Hoses swinging over her head, the light dancing, the steel beneath her bare back vibrating, her hand stretched to the boy's on the slab beside her.* The walls of the exam rooms were painted so thick with dried blood they were black as space itself, the sickening chill of staring at them much akin to the sensation the mothership sent coursing through her.

Atana turned to the Commander who stood outside the ramp to the 501, two sergeants at his sides, staring hopefully and fearfully with him. Summoning a steady breath, she forced out the confidence she knew everyone needed to see, even if she felt less of it herself, with every passing moment. "We're ready."

"It's commendable, what you're risking. We wish you the best." The Commander's gaze hung over her as if to map her face one last time, despite the fact they'd worked together for years. She didn't like the fate his attention suggested.

"Doing our job, sir," Atana and Bennett replied in sync. Their heads swiveled to scrutinize the other.

Strangely uncomfortable, Atana yelled up at Goss to get them on their way and buckled in on the end of the bench, behind his seat. Resting her chin on clasped hands, she stared unfocused at the floor, breathing slowly to calm her rapid pulse. *Stars, I hope this is right.*

"Roger. Initiating launch." Goss tapped a slowly pulsing light on the dash and the side ramp closed.

After reviewing the pairing order for infiltration with his team, Bennett knelt in front of her. "You get enough sleep last night?"

Rest was the last thing on her mind. "I'm fine."

Goss lifted the 501 from its support locks and directed them on course, out the security doors, and into the darkness. Bennett tugged up one of the tie-down handles from the floor, holding him in place.

At the clank of metal on metal, Goss glanced back, salt and pepper eyebrows crushing together. "Sergeant Bennett, why didn't you strap in when Atana gave the command?"

In front of her, Bennett's head swayed. Atana recognized the movement—a sign of emotion. *He's frustrated. Over what?* Ultimately, it didn't matter. There wasn't enough serum in his veins, another potential risk to mission success.

"Why didn't you wait?" Bennett asked, a twinge of acerbity in his voice.

Atana looked to Goss, curious how the older shepherd would respond. He had lived and worked serum-free when he was younger. Would he pick up on the emotional inflection? Turn the ship around? Execute his right as a shepherd to report Bennett and make the arrest?

Cutting the thrusters, Goss rested his hands to the sides of the controls. The 501 floated through space, slowly gyrating, the moon rolling across the windows, shrinking with each rotation. "Because Atana is lead on this assignment," He said coldly, over his shoulder. "I follow her orders. As should you."

Ignoring the emotional infraction was not what Atana expected.

"Yeah, yeah, I know," Bennett muttered, peering up at her.

She studied the moonlight reflecting in his narrowed eyes, impassive to the concern they displayed, but curious about him. He was acting like Rio.

"Holy hell in the sky," Panton muttered.

Glints of sun and carmine lights from within were all that distinguished the nearing structure spread before them from the void. Closing in on the invaders' ship, Atana heard the voice that had been silent since the serum that morning. It was nothing more than the essence of a notion, a distant cry in the ether.

Rio didn't give me enough? Her breath hitched. *Of course, he did. He designed it.*

The weaving, pulsing thread brightening in the sky before her made her wish he had given her more.

"Do you see that?" she asked. The blue-white jet stream in the darkness called to her like desperate fingers sinking into the sea.

"See what?" Bennett hesitated then followed her gaze.

"The enormous, alien porcupine ship? Yeah, I think we see that," Panton smarted.

Josie fidgeted, trying to reach over and smack him. "Obviously she's seeing something else."

"Yeah, but what?" Tanner whispered.

Ignoring their chatter, Atana unclipped her harness and tossed it to the sides. She grabbed the internal structure of the gravity-free 501 and pulled herself to the pilot's window.

"Can we change the dock location to a pillar structure over there, three to the right and two levels down?" She pointed to a black column with a similar dock point. She was following the trail that seemed to sparkle at its base.

Goss responded, "Yes, ma'am. May I ask why the change in the plan?"

Impulsive. But the voice was strained as it cried out to her, more distinguishable every passing moment.

"We want to ensure we have the element of surprise on our side, in case they've somehow been paying attention to our trajectory." It came out more purposeful than she'd expected. "Even if they think we are floating junk like the plan, they may still try to destroy us so we don't damage their ship. We want to mislead them and avoid potentially being shot down."

"You always did keep me on my toes." Goss let out a short laugh. "I see nothing has changed. I'll have to run the generators for that much deviation." He gave her a patient, sidelong glance.

She waited until they were two rotations closer. "Now."

He powered up the thrusters and directed the vessel off their original course.

Bennett let go of the handle on the floor and pushed himself up to the pilot's box, beside Atana. "You sure about this?"

"Yes." Atana didn't want to try to explain. She saw things other shepherds called her crazy for. Silence had become her shield.

Goss maneuvered them carefully up to the port while the team donned their helmets.

"Anyone else feeling a little—gravity?" Cutter asked.

Goss nodded beside Atana as her feet and Bennett's drifted back down to the floor. "Struggling a little to keep her steady. I didn't expect it." He unlocked the magnetic dock feet. "I hope whatever material that is, it's ferrous."

Atana watched through the rear window, unsure where her confidence came from. "It is."

A jolt shook the 501 and the shepherds in their seats.

"Locked and holding." Goss tapped a screen, darkening the dash controls.

She set a hand on his shoulder, feeling the curled edges of his Shepherds United patch beneath her glove. A good luck charm. "Sky watch?"

"Watching sky." Goss winked up at her under the light of the stars.

Panton and Cutter opened the 501 door and stood to either side of the opening: her protection in case the dock feet failed and they floated out into space. Atana scanned the port and frame before them with Tanner's electrical locator. Using the knife from her belt, she wedged the blade into a panel seam and slowly peeled it open. Its outer layer crackled with white sparks.

Panton gasped in shock behind her.

Ignoring him, she reached in and drew out a bundle of wires with illuminated mesh casings. Tanner hooked up and, with her help in reading the codes, typed in a command and the door unlocked, rolling down inside the hull.

Bennett held up both of his SIs, their blue-green igniters glowing, hot and ready, as the team became exposed to the interior. One by one, the crew followed him into the main ship. Atana hung back, waiting for Goss and Tanner.

On his wristband, Goss prompted the 501 door shut. Selecting Secure, the small vessel darkened completely. When Atana and Goss were inside,

Tanner sent another command to the airlock door. Unclipping from the wires, Cutter tugged him inside, the metal panel separating them, once again, from space. The room pressurized with a whoosh.

An internal door parted in the middle, and they stepped out into a metal passageway, cloaked in the lightless chill of continuous night. The room was dank and smelled of mold and wet iron.

Unanticipated fear sliced through Atana, making her shiver. She wanted out of this place with an urgency she hadn't felt in decades. Her shoulders hunkered forward in instant defense, the scars on her body throbbing like they were fresh wounds all over again.

Goss held up an environmental diagnostics device, taking a few more daring steps inside.

"This section is suitable. Tanner?" His discordant voice transmitted over the headset in the airtight shell surrounding his head. "Any idea if this is the system for the entire ship?"

"Hard to say. Didn't get any useful information from there. Atana and I need a hub station connected to the grid, not an independent post."

A hand atop Atana's shoulder made her jump. Looking back, in the faint light of their equipment, she saw Goss's eyes filled with sympathy. His fingers gave her a reassuring squeeze, followed by a nod.

"What the hell y'all suppose this place is?" Panton gawked at the maze of tanks and the hoses hanging down from the ceiling of the long, narrow room they found themselves in. Josie shrugged beneath the bulky suit.

Pushing on through the space, Atana searched for an electrical junction, something they could connect Tanner's laptop to. There were far too many lives counting on her for her to back down now.

"What about that?" Cutter pointed through the room at a rectangular cutout in the wall at the other end.

After inspecting the system, Atana dismissed the box. "It's for the plumbing system down here."

"There's a stairwell," Bennett stated quietly from around the corner. At her signal, the team followed him up the unusually tall steps to the next level. He leaned briefly around the corner into the hallway. Raising his SIs, he walked out, checking both directions as the six others followed.

Tanner waved Atana over, showing her his screen. There was a potential wiring junction at the far end of the hall. As they stepped out, two warm spots appeared behind them on his screen. "Shit. Everyone cover!"

Chapter 12

THUNDERING FOOTSTEPS rounded the far corner of the metal passageway. Bennett squinted at the pair of monstrous creatures. Harnesses over their chests held rows of glowing canisters, their belts a myriad of batons and tools. Their patchy, multicolored skin jiggled with every step, a mere strip of fabric dancing between their meaty legs.

They outstretched ellipses-shaped weapons, glinting like hematite, a pulsing, orange radiance circulating through their interiors.

Before Bennett could free his palmed SIs and take a shot, Atana grabbed him by the jacket, shoving him against the shadowed wall, across from his team.

Several flaming streaks whizzed by the team as they retreated to shelter.

Lifting his SIs to his shoulders, Bennett felt the hot rush of adrenaline pump through him. Atana's hands patting him down weren't helping him focus. *What is she doing worrying about me? Now is not the time.* "I'm fine."

Atana bolted upright, her bewilderment contorting into anger. Releasing an SI from one of the thigh holsters, she fearlessly leaned out and, with vengeful alacrity, fired two shots at their attackers.

Bennett peered around the corner, shame clawing at the back of his brain for having been saved by her when it was supposed to be the other way around. The beasts collapsed, wounded, their dark blood seeping from the smoldering holes she'd created.

Drawing her other SI, Atana spun the intensity dials of both to maximum wad and ignition release. Walking toward the writhing bodies at the end of the hall, she stepped one boot onto each of their bulbous chests. Her head cocked in the way a vulture curiously swoons over fresh road kill.

Their thick, stubby-fingered hands wrapped around her feet but made no progress in defending themselves against her onslaught. Gnarled knots of blue and green flames left the barrels she held, impacting both in the face simultaneously. The floor beneath them painted plum, the walls with a cold flash of light.

Atana spun around. "Dial up your weapons for these ones. They take an extra punch." She paused in her tracks and dropped her SIs in their holsters. "Goss?"

Bennett turned to look as she ran to where the shepherd lay on the ground. Atana knelt next to Goss, slipping her fingers in his.

His stomach was covered in blood, his spacesuit charred. He wasn't moving, and his wristband wasn't detecting a pulse. It signaled significant blood loss with rapid flashes then darkened with one final message, recognizing an irreversible state of damage.

Final Mission Completed

Please Return to Home Station

Atana's silenced wristband blinked furiously, catching Bennett's eye. She glared at it. The light softened and stopped.

Letting Goss's arm rest gently on his chest, she unclipped his wristband and shut down the computer, handing it to Cutter.

"I can take him back to the 501," Panton offered solemnly.

Pointing at Cutter and Josie, Bennett gave them an order with a swift tilt of his head. Panton slung the older shepherd over a shoulder. The three acknowledged and headed down the stairs.

Bennett corralled Atana away, a hand to the small of her back. Her blue eyes looked to him for only a second, but her gaze was so unexpectedly flat and somber he felt a twinge of her loss through the serum.

Proceeding up to the terminal pointed out by Tanner, Bennett kicked in the large panel, flaring the edges. Together, the three sergeants pried it off. Tanner sorted through the grids of illuminated cables. Atana hovered over him, helping him navigate. Bennett stood with his back to them, SIs raised, on guard. They hadn't been on the ship for ten minutes, and one of the team was already gone.

When the others reappeared, Bennett directed Josie and Panton to set up a post at the intersection they had come from. He called Cutter to stand guard with him at the opposite end.

They took a few paces farther away from Atana and Tanner so they could talk.

"Is she a tech too?" Cutter whispered. "Not even a profile in the database for psych evals; otherwise I'd know."

Bennett shrugged, checking the far post. Josie had her e-rifle crammed on her shoulder, the muzzle just low enough that she could scan over the top of the scope. Panton's SIs glowed beside her.

"Screw. It's probably in Rio's office," Cutter muttered behind him.

Bennett examined Atana's frame at length before returning his focus to the task at hand. Rio had called her his daughter. It seemed likely he would protect such sensitive information.

"You need to talk about something?" Cutter whispered in his ear.

Atana broke up their conversation. "Oxygen is sufficient. We can unsuit."

The team pulled their masks off.

"Company!" Panton yelled.

Two more large guards found the first set down. One clumsily unclipped a device from its belt and yelled gargled sounds into it. Josie took out her targets with precision. Atana frantically helped Tanner grab cables and cram them inside the pouch beneath the laptop.

Two sets of thundering feet approached on Cutter and Bennett's end. The second the creatures became visible, they promptly backtracked, vanishing into the shadows.

Dropping her helmet to the floor and drawing her SIs, Atana took off down an adjacent hall without a word. Bennett signaled the rest of the team to follow the last pair before racing to catch up with their leader.

Where's she going? We shouldn't be splitting up like this.

Taking a deep breath, he tried not to worry about his team. They were trained for this, *hypothetically*. Astrotech video simulation was a far cry from this reality. He hoped their field skills were good enough to compensate for the unknowns of real alien combatants.

Sprinting down a long hall, Atana came to an abrupt stop in the center of a blackened opening. Lifting one SI, her arm outstretched and directed into the shadows, she fired two shots. Two thuds and she disappeared into the passageway.

Bennett clicked on his pocket flashlight, the bright beam flooding two decommissioned beasts on the floor, shot through the head, with Atana standing over them. When she looked back at him, Bennett caught a glint of nocturnal silver in her eyes.

He flinched, clumsily holstering his SI. "How did you—"

At the sound of footsteps too heavy to be one of his team, he spun and met another pair of the creatures.

With no time to think or draw his weapon, he elbowed one in the side and kicked the other in the stomach, throwing it against the wall. The flashlight tumbled from his grasp, hitting the hard floor, the light winking out.

The first one grabbed him from behind. Bennett dropped out of the hold and rolled, standing into a roundhouse kick to the guard's knee.

It went down. The second picked Bennett up by the throat, slamming him into the wall. Strings of saliva dripped from its gaping mouth, exposing several rows of long, black, spiny teeth. Its breath like raw steak, Bennett choked on a gag and grabbed its wrist.

Bracing himself, he threw a punch straight into its throat and felt its windpipe crunch beneath his knuckles. It dropped him, slumping to the ground.

The first one managed to stand, wobbling and angrily reaching for Bennett. He spun out of the way, and lunged off the wall, catching the creature's head between his knees. Swinging into a somersault, he used his bodyweight to throw the larger life form to the ground. Jumping up, Bennett took it by the head, and with a swift jerk, broke the creature's neck. *Just to be sure.*

Bennett turned his head to the side with a snort, trying to get the beast's stench out of his nose. He looked up to check on Atana and soaked in the surprise on her face. "We need to find a secure location to discuss our next steps."

The team rushed into the far intersection, weapons up, and flinched at the sight of their leaders.

Josie yelled from down the hall, "Hey, uh, guys?"

Bennett quickly had his SIs squeezed tight in his palms. Josie never hesitated. "Report."

"I—I don't know, sir." She urgently waved them over.

A warm, grassy-sweet breeze escaped through a crack. Panton slid open the heavy door, and a sharp angle of light burst out into the hallway. The blood-covered steel beneath their boots was a violent contrast to the hopeful shimmer of gold.

Bennett cautiously followed Atana inside, the team at their heels. Panton quietly closed the door behind them.

Tall, flaxen grains, with long awn strands like wild emmer, waved in the generated winds. In the distance, a small, rocky peak pierced through a grouping of bushy indigo trees. A narrow, dirt path lay before them, leading out into the large facility. Looking up 150 meters, the light radiating over the land danced like millions of fireflies in a mirage of atmosphere. Dazed by the similarities to their home planet, the team meandered, awestruck, through the field.

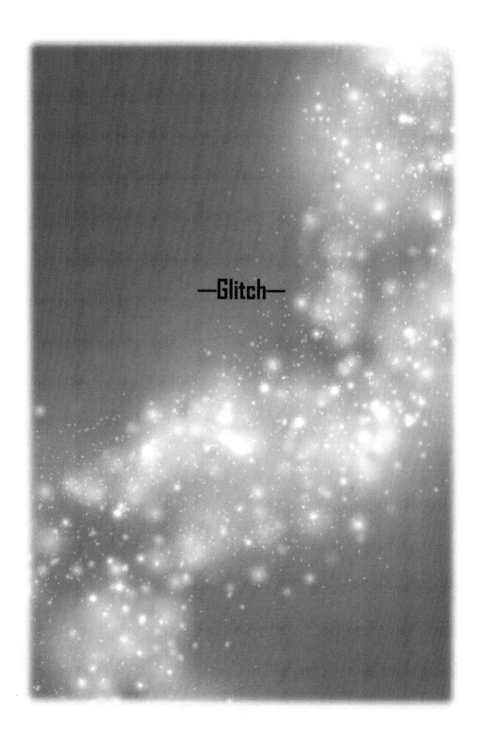

—Glitch—

Chapter 13

THE WAVING FIELDS weren't the only thing whispering around the team. Gripping their weapons tight, they crept soundlessly along the path, venturing deeper into the vault. Dirty heads bobbed like timid gophers among the crops.

Excruciating twinges ricocheted through Atana's brain. The golden sea spun around her. Unable to focus enough to stand, she dropped to her knees. Her fingers dug into the olive-brown clay of the path, eyes squeezing shut as a thousand voices swirled in her mind.

It was an agony she'd only felt once before, one that had put her out of commission for two days. The memory-nightmare she'd had that day was of her and the boy, harnessed to a machine shooting sparks. It sent venomous needles coursing through their brains. That day had changed her. She knew it, even if she couldn't quite remember how.

Not now, please.

Bennett knelt beside her, a gentle hand to her shoulder.

Inhaling painfully slow and deep, she cleared her head enough to see through the haze and nod at Bennett.

His touch slid over her back. He lowered himself until his eyes were level with hers. Bennett didn't look convinced.

A rustling in the fields surrounding them pulled the team to the ground with them. Crouching with weapons up, they scanned through the tops of the grasses, watching, waiting.

Through a gap in the swaying stalks, a small hut appeared, making Atana pause. Crooked, wood poles held up a twig-and-straw roof. Strips of tattered fabric hung from the top side of the windows and door frames, dancing and twirling in the subtle winds. Ochre branches had been woven together, creating a barrier between rooms, barely protecting its inhabitants from the oddly Earth-like landscape.

Standing in the doorway was a tall woman in dark brown robes, long, black, twisted hair draping down her back. She squinted, scanning the fields. A stole of bold hues hung from her shoulders.

The woman's voice came out strong, flowing like a deep ocean current, carrying out across the grasses. "Welcome newcomers. Our intent is not to harm. We are not the ones on the surface of your planet. We are their slaves."

"English?" Panton whispered.

Josie lurched at him with a fiery green glare hissing, "Shut up."

The team remained in their tactical defense formation, awaiting a command. Atana tried to stand until a fist grabbed her jacket, yanking her down.

"What are you doing?" Bennett mouthed.

Drawing a loop in the air with a finger, she mouthed back, "We're surrounded." Flattening out her hand, palm to the ceiling, she scoured his face. *What else are we supposed to do?*

"You have no idea who she is," he whispered hoarsely with a shake of his head.

"Keep them low." She spun to face the hut. *We should not have come in here.* Goss's last wink up at her flashed its painful reality in her memory. *If anyone is taking this risk, it's me.* SIs prepped in hand, Atana was ready to fire from the holster at the slightest aggressive twitch. "I'm coming out."

When she slowly crested the fields, the stranger stumbled closer. Other life forms peeked up above the grasses throughout the landscape. "Please come, and your companions. Come into our home!" She bowed.

Bennett stood, exposing his head and chest above the fields. "Atana—"

She looked back to see Tanner flinch at Bennett's side, his SI up and ready. Raising their weapons, the team spun out, covering their leaders 360 degrees.

"The workers will not harm you. Please, come!" the woman called out.

"I don't think this is a good idea," Bennett contended.

Atana always made a plan and ended up changing it depending on what felt right. And this seemed a much better option than the hallways outside. "Got a better one?"

A twitch of a frown crept over his face, but he signaled for the team to follow.

Multiple sets of eyes tracked the team when they stepped into the clearing in front of the humble structure. Atana's nerves were primed for combat after their encounter in the halls. Unnerved by this contradiction, she eased through the wooden arch at the woman's insistence and nodded Bennett toward another room. Together, they checked the small spaces, finding only bone-thin workers and splotches of sick and blood in the dirt.

With the hut clear, the fields outside given one more scan, the team gathered in the front room where the woman waited.

On a baled-straw stool, the stranger patiently took her seat. "I am Saema Chamarel. The workers of the Hatoga fields call me Saema, or Ma for short. Please, sit."

Not knowing what else to do, Atana stepped inside the ring and rested on one of the natural chairs. Before her, in the center of the circle, rested a single wider bale supporting a host of misshapen clay containers. The team joined her, all except Bennett. Chamarel tracked him, pacing the doorway. "The Suanoa are the ones responsible for the invasion, not us, Sergeant Bennett. Please, sit, so you do not concern my workers. They have much labor left to render the harvest to the Suanoa's demands."

Bennett stopped in his tracks. "How do you know my name?"

Atana observed the many shades of human skin tones on Chamarel's face when she inclined it his direction. Beneath the metallic sheen, her cheeks blended and caramelized to match his darker complexion. Chamarel motioned casually at his chest.

The nametape. She can read English too.

"I am the Sacred Mother here," Chamarel continued. "The life forms outside are from many different planets and galaxies, taken from their homes. They come to me for food and healing."

Panton circled a finger in the air. "So the flash we see is transporting our people to one of these containers?"

"Yes, by Linoan collectors. Sorting occurs in what we call 'the sway,' an area in between the gravitational control systems for each unit of fields. There is a sway level above us and one below us. Initial retrieval always designates the first groups go to testing. If the life forms are considered usable, the Suanoa return to the planet, take more, and pick through the healthy ones for their abilities. Some go to Maintenance; some come to Production, which is one of the many locations, like this one, where we are. The weak ones are eliminated." Chamarel turned to check the fields outside. "Dumped out the airlock, alive."

The concept didn't startle Atana like she knew it should have. But it built on the fever welling up in her core after Goss met his fate.

A thin teenager with scraggly clothes and light-gray skin peeked in from behind a curtain. One of the tufted ears near the back of his head was missing a small chunk.

"Ma, you want me bring tea?" His abnormally large, sunshine-yellow eyes focused directly on the woman in the long robes.

Chamarel directed toward the youngster. "This is Teek. He is my most recent helper."

"Giyam!" Teek lifted his long, curved fingers with a smile.

"Let's hold off for a few moments. It's almost meal time."

"Tsu, Ma." He bowed and disappeared through the doorway.

Soft chuckles slipped Panton's lips. "More like geek than Teek, huh?"

Josie elbowed him in the gut with a condescending glare.

He barely flinched. "You're right, bad timing."

After a careful inspection of Panton, Bennett rested his palms over the handles of his SIs and dragged his attention to Chamarel. "Why our world?"

The woman scoured his face as if seeing something more and then watching it fade. "You have what they need to survive."

"So this land we're on is from another planet?" Tanner glanced down.

"Yes, Lizra. My home." Her robes shifted near the floor. "The Suanoa force those they select to do the labor, with the threat of death to us, our families, and our sectors, if we do not obey. For now, you are safe. And you will be here a while."

Pangs of unsettling noise erupted in Atana's mind. She flinched, straining her neck, her brows pressing together. Releasing a slow, deep breath from her nose, she attempted to calm the re-emerging ache in her brain. After a moment of meditation, she sorted the sounds.

If not forever.

Bennett shifted behind her, his voice muffled through her pain. "We must get back to our Command, let them know what is happening to our people."

When the throbs softened, Atana realized his hand was resting on her shoulder. Despite its unwanted and unexpected presence, she found herself absorbing into its warmth.

Chamarel shook her head. "Individuals attempting to make contact, whether physical or by radio, are dumped. Those of us associated with them are as well. The vessel you arrived in has already been discarded by the Linoan survey crews."

"Discarded?" Tanner scrubbed a hand through his hair.

"Incinerated."

Atana squeezed her eyes shut, grinding her teeth. *Goss's body.*

Straightening in her seat, Chamarel appeared to steel herself for what she was going to say next. "It is not safe for you to leave. I know you have a mission. All infiltrators do. But the Suanoa are too smart. After thousands of years running these vessels, they have seen it all. Why do you think we do not have any ground-worthy vessels?" She arched a brow. "Even Linoan collectors shut down at a certain distance from Agutra. *They* cannot leave unless they wish to die a slow, chilling death."

Inside her mind, Atana shook her head. She felt like she should know this, remember it. *Why can't I remember?*

"What the hell—" Panton grumbled. "Who do these people—things— think they are?"

Chamarel's tone hardened. "They are the farthest thing from any life form containing what your kind call humanity. They learned of the eventual supernova of their sun and, to save their species, developed these container ships and space travel technology. Leaving their galaxy meant they needed to find new sources of materials to sustain their existence. It is their desperate, self-preserving nature which causes them to act so brutally toward all new forms of life."

"So much information couldn't come so easily to an unwilling participant," Bennett remarked, gesturing his free hand at Chamarel. "You must understand our doubt to believe you after the greeting we received out there."

"You feel it."

Atana twisted to look up at him. Bennett furrowed his brows, not breaking eye contact with Chamarel.

"It bothers you I said that." Chamarel visually addressed the team.

"We're on serum, shuts down emotions," Tanner offered, his laptop screen lighting his face with streams of data.

Bennett's voice burst out with invigorated depth over Atana's head. "You didn't answer my question."

Chamarel waved a loose hand in hopeless abandon, dropping it into her lap with a flop. "It doesn't take long to catch the pattern. I've been a slave more long-cycles than any of you have existed for. Us Saemas and Healers train under one another. We exchange knowledge."

Eager to get what they needed and find a way back to earth, Atana slid forward on her stool. She didn't want to stay any longer than they had to. Everything around her prickled her memories with notes of horrid familiarity. For once, she didn't want to know more about that part of her life. The fact she couldn't recall them with any clarity, and kept trying to, had her distracted from the mission. "What are their weaknesses, the Suanoa?"

Chamarel was silent for an uncomfortably long moment. "They move slower because of the tough exterior of their physical forms. They can be easy physical targets in battle, which is why they employ guards to protect them and their assets. But do not think this makes them easy to kill. They have telepathic abilities so strong that they are capable of knowing what action you will take before you make it."

"With such constant threat of death, how do the workers remain focused enough to survive?" Cutter asked.

Chamarel rolled her head. "Most do not. But generally, the Suanoa leave us alone because we make the food and supplies they need. Maintenance workers in the core of the ship do not get such independence. Linoans monitor them, keep them in line with Arc Bows. Here, those weapons are a risk to crops. If too many field workers are harmed, food production falls, an undesirable result. Inefficiency is something Suanoa despise. Many died before we gained such freedom from their watch. Workers have designated routes. But even then, Linoans aren't known for self-restraint."

"Won't they search for us?" Atana asked.

Chamarel adjusted the robes over her knees. "Typically, only new slaves get inspected by the guards. With the greeting you received, I believe the Suanoa will consider you 'threatened into assimilation.' But I cannot guarantee anything. However, us Saemas and Healers also have our own guards on the perimeter, to warn us if they do.

"And no, Sergeant Bennett." Chamarel looked over Atana's shoulder to him. "The Warruks you killed on your way in are not our guards. The Warruks have already been removed."

Bennett fidgeted, shifting between his feet. He threw Atana a wild-eyed glance that confirmed the woman had read his mind. "Will it be a problem later?"

"They are no more than bullying beasts. They will assume horseplay, like your kind say, and send more this direction at the next rotation."

"How does it not set off alarms with the Suanoa if they are so controlling?" Cutter asked.

"Warruks are like any other form to the Suanoa: expendable."

Atana, feeling a bit overwhelmed with the onslaught of information scanned the fields to remove herself for a moment and think. "We haven't deployed any offensive measures on Earth yet."

"Good. It will buy your planet more time," Chamarel replied. But the way her voice fell suggested it was more a hope than a truth. "This is our third visit to Earth. It will be our last."

"That's a good thing, right?" Tanner asked.

Chamarel's hands knotted together. "Good things in this life are rare."

The fluffy tip of a long tail drew the curtain open at the back. Teek stood again in the doorway holding a wide, shallow basket filled with rolls.

"Ma, we ready."

His outer coat appeared soft, a texture of short, velour fur. It struck familiarity in the corners of Atana's memory. His gray cheeks flushed violet, his tail swaying, stirring up the loose, dry surface of the dirt floor beside her.

Chamarel stood and invited the team outside with a wave of her hand, seeming eager to end the conversation there. "That will be enough information for tonight. Please join us for the end-of-cycle meal. We shall discuss more in the morning. It is not safe for you to wander the halls this night."

She walked between the fabric strands, following Teek, and tied the curtains open, displaying the bunk room.

"You may sleep in our new recruit housing. I will situate any other arrivals elsewhere, though I doubt there will be any. We are at full capacity." She gestured for the crew to follow Teek.

Letting the team select bunks, Atana passed through and stepped outside.

"You wish to know if I was the one who called to you." Chamarel gave her a minimal sidelong glance from beside the hut before returning to her patrol of the fields. "I was not."

Atana regarded her unprecedented comment with caution. She had wanted to ask but didn't for fear of the team's reaction. *A glittering thread in the sky and a voice where sound waves don't exist*— Chamarel had made her point. Atana wasn't crazy.

"I must tend to the workers. Pelaeso sur ahna: blessings on you." Chamarel bowed and proceeded through the growing crowd, leaving Atana standing alone in the doorway at the edge of the backyard.

This place was nothing like what they'd anticipated. She was stumbling over her tongue, her thoughts, and what to do next. The indecision alone unnerved her.

Chapter 14

SHELLSHOCKED, Bennett fixated on Chamarel, who reached out and touched a worker awaiting the evening meal: a creature with white, segmented extensions protruding from its scaled body. Their choppy movement relaxed to her touch, flattening against the individual's core as several thicker, arm-like units shifted underneath.

Chamarel's form folded in on itself, molding to match the appearance of the worker beside her. Leaning around to greet the worker, she smiled, verbalizing sounds Bennett couldn't decipher. When she had received an acknowledgement, she patted one of the worker's shoulders and moved fluidly across the uneven soil to the next, her figure sprouting broad bands of dull, brown cartilage, layered up like armor.

Faint music mixed with the chatter. Over a hundred life forms of different shapes, sizes, colors, and languages mingled amongst the stools gathered around the fire pits.

Teek scurried over to a smaller collection of fibrous seats with food on a central bale, encouraging the team to sit. "I think you want separate from others. I imagine it much strange to you."

Seeing children collected around a gray and yellow life form, seated on one of the stools, Bennett stopped to watch. The ruffled ribbon-like skin draping down the back of its head shook when the creature resisted the children's requests. "What are they asking for?"

"He a Gunre Tokta. They want see him eat." Teek pointed a bone-thin finger at his chest, drawing a vertical line to his belly button.

In the distance, the Gunre Tokta's barrel-shaped rib cage peeled open from the middle. His single, beige eye warily scanned the gathered youth. Bennett watched the flaps of skin curl into extensions resembling arms. The misty, blue core of its being showed a suspended orange and purple Brocanip fruit, atomizing from its exterior layer inward. The children released sounds of amusement, pointing at the particles of food absorbing into the Gunre Tokta's hazy organs.

Teek rubbed an arm, leaving tracks in his short fur. "They not many left. Must keep cover when eating, so cannot work. Suanoa get impatient. Gunre work hard."

"How do you feel, being stuck in here?" Cutter asked.

The teen glanced around at the group as if it were obvious. "Chamarel take pain and give purpose. I help now. They too much for one Chamarel."

Josie directed to other beings similar to Teek playing in the trees off to the side, their chatter incomprehensible. "You speak English very well."

"Thank you. Chamarel is good mother." Noticing Atana heading for them, he bowed. "I leave you now."

Bennett tracked Teek as he hurried away to attend to other workers. He'd given Atana space at her nonverbal request. As she passed Teek and joined the group, Bennett gave her a lengthy visual inspection. The corners of her eyes were wrinkled as if in deep contemplation. When she rested on a stool, Bennett took a seat across from her, the team joining them.

"So what now?" Panton asked.

"Assess capabilities of combatants and perceived local civilians from a safe location," Bennett directed.

"Which up here means—what exactly?" Josie asked.

Atana rested her elbows on her knees, a hand over her lips, looking deep in thought. "Do you all remember what this ship looked like on the outside?"

The team concurred with murmurs.

"The core is like the spine. All the critical components are logically situated there. The field containers attach to it like rings of ribs. This is where most of the workers are." Atana leaned over and read the hacked schematics Tanner pulled up on his screen.

He glanced at her, apprehension in his multicolored eyes. "Sorry, ma'am. It's all on you. I haven't got a clue what this language is yet."

"Pull up your coding platform, and I'll give you what I can understand." Lifting a hand she listed locations in order from top to bottom. "Abaddon deck which is the summit observation room. Imperial ring—where their command center is located. And from which, the Suanoan residential spires jut up. Below is Plasma Engineering. Then the Linoan and Warruk dens." Atana set a finger on Tanner's screen and slid a schematic up, exposing the lower half. "These containers start after and run almost the length of the core. At its innermost space, are the propulsion systems. The exterior rooms of the core are dedicated to consumables and medical storage. There are separate ones for Suanoa and slaves."

Bennett was starting to pick up on why Command valued Atana so much. It wasn't just her skill. She knew things the others had no basis for beginning to understand.

"So the top half is where the rulers exist, extremities are where the slaves are?" Josie asked.

"Generally." Atana directed Tanner through a few quick translations.

Bennett surveyed the diagrams. "Probably some Suanoa in the core if they have storage there and key parts of the ship—power systems and what looks like plasma *weapons.*" Double tapping the screen, the schematic zoomed out, exposing the full image. The field containers and their structures were lit in a duller green than the rest of the ship. "I think they can separate—top half and core from the containers, like a sword from a sheath."

"That is an interesting observation." Atana met his eyes with distinct approval, giving his confidence a congratulatory nudge. "We will need to break up the team to cover this much ground. Three pairs." She nodded at Tanner and Cutter. "Best suited for plasma and propulsion sections. Josie and Panton get civilian duty. It shouldn't be difficult with half the rows empty. Bennett and I will take a look at their command. We'll regroup and make our escape."

"Sounds typical." Panton shrugged.

Atana glowered at him. "Do not become complacent, Sergeant."

"She's right." Bennett could sense his team was on edge with all the extraterrestrials walking around and the news they'd just received. "Everyone needs to be game on, no exceptions no matter how unusual the sights, and no rest until we're at Home again. Tanner, you're going to have to be the backup pilot. Find us a way home."

"Already working on it, B," he replied.

Atana swiped a strand of loose hair out of her eyes. "If we are stuck here. It is possible we will have to relay encoded information through our David satellite to Station Hope. But even then, like Chamarel said, that may still bring unnecessary pain to these workers. And harming innocents puts that option lowest on the list." She looked up at Bennett. "What do you think?"

He couldn't believe she was asking. An Independent asking a Team Leader for his thoughts was about as common as a shepherd being permitted non-serum status by Command. To date, he only knew of two instances. "Agreed. I say we see what other information we can acquire from this Chamarel, first." Then he tested the part he was most bothered by. "I get the notion you think we are stuck."

"I do." Atana surveyed his face in length. "But that does not mean I accept it as our fate."

"The translation program is almost complete." Tanner showed Atana the screen, and she helped him through a few more adjustments.

Bennett broke his gaze from her to scan the yard for threats. Many of the other life forms on stools across the open area from them were also locked on to her. The whispered languages weren't familiar. But the tone and the way they leaned into one another made him itchy for a weapon.

"So, Sergeant Atana, why did that metallic-skinned woman take to you so easily?" Josie asked. "If she's even a woman."

Atana stilled. Bennett followed her gaze to a man standing stone-still along the distant tree line. His eyes cut into her like luminous, blue daggers. Gray, virile arms folded over his chest in apparent contempt.

His space suit stretching and crinkling with his movement, Panton tilted toward Josie, lowering his voice. "Rumor is she was picked up by an alien ship as a kid an' came back with the rescue. Maybe this Saema Chamarel actually knows her. Maybe it was this ship. Maybe—"

Atana threw Panton a glare, then leapt up and stalked into the depths of the forest bordering the encampment. The stiff branches of short indigo needles sprung back into place behind her, concealing her position.

Her change was so sudden that it snapped Bennett to his feet. *Where is she going?* He hustled several steps after her, confusion twisting into frustration.

Bennett stopped. "Seriously Panton, what the hell's wrong with you today? Didn't you get your serum checked?"

Panton hung his head. "Sorry, boss, I don't know. Rio upped my dose. Guess it wasn't enough. I've sorta lost the filter between my brain an' my mouth."

"That was not covert." A deep sigh released from Bennett's lungs. "What mils are you on?"

Panton inventoried his wristband. "Five, now."

Bennett clicked open the faceplate on his arm and pulled out a tiny, glass vial with a number seven etched in its curved surface, extending it toward him. "Here, this is stronger."

"Thanks, man." Panton stuttered. "I mean, sir."

In an attempt to lighten the mood, Bennett chuckled. "We can't have you compromised on this assignment. You're too damned big and hard to tolerate during that time of the month."

"Oh, haha, you're so hilarious," Panton responded sarcastically.

Bennett dropped the vial into his open palm. "Sorry, Josie, no offense meant."

She glanced up at him with a crinkle in her nose, then winked and whispered, "An excuse to be *Super*bitch."

Licking his lips to hide his smile, Bennett acknowledged Panton's position with a terse head tilt, suggesting she help. Josie silently obliged. Clipping his case shut, Bennett excused himself from the group to follow Atana, concern burning in his chest. Serum-regulated shepherds didn't storm off.

...

Panton, frustrated, set the vial on the stool between him and Josie. Pulling his hand away, he squeezed it into a tight, angry fist. Josie hopped up and nimbly collected the dose. Sitting next to him, she braced his left arm and opened his wristband.

Slipping the vial into position, she looked up. "You ready?"

Panton gawked at her for several moments. She looked different today, her hair the bolder shade of a blushing rose, her features softer under this artificial sunlight. The freckles he'd stared at for years over her nose looked like crushed cinnamon on pure divinity. Panton couldn't stop himself from wanting a touch of such a curious texture. He inched a callused fingertip toward her cheek.

Her presence was so—relaxing.

She let out a short breath. "Josh?"

"I was born ready, miss," he murmured, leaning in.

Tanner rolled his eyes with a groan, Cutter intently observing beside him.

Panton didn't care. He knew Tanner thought his jokes were terrible, and Cutter always stared. Right now, all he wanted was to know the feeling of his little, fiery sniper against his hand, the *real* feeling. He was so close.

Jerking his wrist down, Josie clamped the cover shut and tapped Inject.

"Ow, Josie!" Panton inhaled through his teeth at the twinge radiating up his left forearm. As the serum stilled the desires, Panton flushed with embarrassment. "Thanks, don't know what came over me."

"Hormones." Josie's reply was prompt, but her gaze hung a moment over him. She turned to look at what had Cutter's attention.

Chamarel was following Atana and Bennett's path.

Panton withdrew in a moment of self-reflection. Josie was starting to have her doubts about his serum tolerance. He had to get control of himself or risk being taken away from her and the team.

He needed a serum upgrade. Whatever formula his boss was on was heavy shit, numbing him to almost the point of a cold lethargy. Panton liked the effectiveness. It was just a bit too much. He would have to mentally keep himself in check better at the next dose cycle. For now, he was 'in the clear.'

"She was too calm like she knew we were coming." Cutter rested his chin in a hand. "Humans I can read. Her— I don't know."

"Well, maybe we can get more information in the morning," Panton suggested.

Josie pulled her e-rifle from her shoulder, resting it across her thighs with steady hands. "Let's take shifts on guard tonight, just in case."

Chapter 15

BENNETT KICKED INTO A SPRINT when he broke out of the tree line. Atana was surrounded. A growing crowd of grungy, emaciated life forms reached for her, their fingers aching for a touch.

"We have prayed for you, blessed one!" one shouted. Then another, "You will help us, won't you?"

A girl responded to someone's question in the back, "Of course it's her! It's in the prophecy! 'From a blue planet, hair like fire, eyes like ice.' Ask Ma. She heard it in Ether!"

Several more joined in until the ruckus was indecipherable.

Atana's hands flared open to the sides, theirs gracing her like she was a golden chalice.

Bennett knew he had to get to her, shield her from the masses. It was something no Independents could handle. The workers didn't look like a threat, but there were too many to know there wasn't trouble among them. The panic on her face compelled him to push inside. "Please, let me through."

Her ribs swelled and released rapidly. Several bodies stood between Atana and Bennett. He called to her. She spun left, then right, back-stepping as the crowd moved closer.

Reaching between the others, he managed to place his fingertips between her shoulder blades. She whirled around. The chatter lightened, the workers suddenly moving out of his way without a struggle.

"Bennett." With a slow blink, her body wavered. Adrenal shock was setting in.

Bennett hooked an arm around her waist.

She sank in against him, holding her head. "Too many voices."

"You need rest." Bennett clutched her to his side, helping her toward Chamarel's hut. The readiness of her compliance was alarming. "Serum doesn't work if you don't sleep like you're supposed to."

Someone shouted, "Who cares about the prophecy? A new crew means another chance at freedom!"

"You will free us, won't you?" another asked, joined by a multitude of concurring sounds.

Bennett extended his free arm as a bumper in front of Atana, blazing a path through the cluster. He raised his voice to the crowd. "There's nothing we can do until we have more information."

A strawberry-red hand waved a scrap of stiff pulp-paper toward them. The matching, red quills on the teenage boy's head swayed every time he jumped to see over the shoulders in front of him.

Atana stopped. Bennett paused with her. She hesitantly took the item, turning it over. Charcoal hash marks and dots lined the paper in no decipherable order.

An older female with copper hair, skin like frosted feathers, and vibrant green and black eyes pulled the youngster forward.

She rubbed his back. "Ekiipa's voice doesn't work anymore, shredded it when they sent his mother out the airlock for working too slow." With an owlish twist of her neck, she read the note. "We give our blood to nourish the soil that feeds them, and then we are nothing, discarded, sent to the stars and—forgotten."

The woman turned to him, resting her head to his and muttering softly.

Ekiipa touched the older woman's arm then gestured at them, spikes flaring from his red skin with every movement.

"His father is a perimeter guard for the sector below us. He will fight with you—" The woman trailed off when the boy firmly pounded his chest with a fist.

Bennett gathered Atana closer, eyeing the young man. "What does he want?"

"To fight when you do." She scowled at the boy. "Ekiipa, you are too young. Go on."

Atana's voice was faint at best, her fingers back to rubbing her temples. "We're not here to fight."

"I know. The young ones are hopeful, always are." The woman said several words in other languages and pointed to the fire pits in the meal yard. The group grumbled, murmured, and wandered off. She lifted her hands toward Atana's.

Bennett drew Atana a step away, with a glower. "I think she's had enough for one night."

"I will not hurt her spark, seer." Before Bennett could stop her, she took Atana's hands in her short, thick fingers with haggard dirt-embedded nails, giving them a feeble squeeze.

"You can help us. You have skills beyond your knowledge and our capabilities, prophesied or not." Her eyes locked on Bennett's. "A life knows when it has seen the suns in the sky and felt the warmth that radiates from them." Releasing her hands, the woman sauntered off to join the crowds, leaving Atana to sag in Bennett's arms, the note clutched between her trembling fingers.

Chapter 16

BLOOD-ORANGE colors washed the wall at the far end of their agricultural prison. Atana's limbs felt cold and her body too hot. At her nod, Bennett released her.

She had never been recognized or focused on by so many strangers and was glad he stepped in when he did. She was getting antsy for a weapon just to get them all to back off.

Why did they act like they knew who she was? She was supposed to save them? And why did that woman call Bennett a 'seer'?

With Bennett at her side, the two of them silently mulled over their situation.

Four tall, slender legs ambled toward them, the creature's barbed coat leaving a trail of silver mist in its wake. Calmly, Bennett rested his palms over the handles of his SIs.

The vivid lime and violet striations of her irises relaxed from vertical ellipses to humanoid circles. She straightened upward, from four legs to two, her spikes morphing into shallow scales and then into small feathers before folding in against her, a skin-like texture forming.

You cannot fight what you are, sentinel. Chamarel's words echoed like bad reverberation, pounding in Atana's skull.

A congregation of voices followed, shrieking and wailing, shaking her to the core, their cries pummeling the insides of her bones. Atana crumpled to her knees with a groan. *What is this? What's happening to me?*

Bennett leaned down to her side. "Atana?"

"Can you give us a moment?" Chamarel asked overhead.

In a breath of silence, Atana grasped Bennett's wrist, unable to look at him through the clouds of pain. She couldn't explain why Chamarel had her trust so quickly. It was just a *feeling*. "It's okay."

He sighed heavily in disagreement. "Twenty paces to your six."

"Understood." Atana listened to the barely audible compression of pine needles as Bennett walked off. He stopped at nineteen.

A warm hand tenderly rested between Atana's shoulder blades, calming the ache. "Do not fear what you do not understand. This is normal."

Atana let out a forced breath. "I hear so many voices, like in my sleep but exponential in volume. Why can't I suppress this? My serum, I need—"

"Control."

"It's my job." Atana rubbed her fingers over her forehead. "Was that you? 'I cannot fight what I am'?"

Chamarel hummed. "My species is telepathic. We can communicate to open minds, like yours. Some have the ability to block and control what others hear, like the Ari species."

"Is that why you know so much about the Suanoa?" Atana pushed herself up, spreading her feet from the head rush. She heard Bennett shift in the trees behind her.

"No. We have to be close to one another for the connection to be strong enough. It is information passed down."

"And myself? Are you that voice I've been hearing?"

"Yes and no. Your escape is well known among our sectors. We can discuss details later." Chamarel glanced back at Bennett.

"I want to finish this first thing tomorrow," Atana insisted.

"You have questions that need answers. I know." Chamarel gave her a sedate smile and headed for the yard, leaving the sergeant with a few last words for the night. *Your mind is open. Is your heart? It holds the key to what you truly seek.*

Her thoughts rattled between Atana's temples.

Pondering Chamarel's comments, Atana returned her focus to the fading light, massaging the sides of her head. *I cannot fight what I am? She's implying I'm hiding something.* The breeze whispered through the trees. *From something.*

...

Bennett approached with caution, eyeing Chamarel's silhouette fading between the branches. "Are you all right?" *I know you're not.*

In the silence, he studied the profile of her glossy eyes. As steady as her eyes seemed, she hid behind them. Command's most effective assassin had been taken down by a force he couldn't see to fight.

"I apologize for Panton. It won't happen again." The 'daylight' disappeared. Small lights began to shine overhead. Knowing what was at stake, Bennett did the best he could to hold his personal concerns inside. "Their synthetic sky is intriguing. I'm curious how they make the stars look so real. Some are even twinkling."

"It's the atmosphere. Refraction of light." She glanced at him. "What do you want from me?"

"I don't want anything from you. I just want to be—" He paused, carefully considering his words. When dealing with the single remaining rescue survivor up close, the rumors from others fell away. "I want you to know I'm here if you need anything. I would like to know what happened to you since we are on the same team."

She was not the brash, reckless, lawless sergeant like everyone had gossiped. Atana had a heart, buried deep. He could see her doubt when the first airlock opened, regret over Goss's death, and confusion and panic as she stood surrounded moments ago. She'd leaned into him and Bennett had felt her instantly calm.

"I need to know why you had to be put on this assignment, why you're special—from you. Otherwise, I'm running through a maze without a map."

"Right—special," she grumbled.

A few moments passed. Her lips parted then pursed.

"No pressure, if you don't want to tell me. I'll try to understand and promise I won't ask again."

Her eyes flicked up at him with the seriousness of her words. "You can never talk of what I am about to tell you, to anyone else, including Rio."

"Understood."

She rested her hands on the grips of the SIs in her thigh holsters. "The stars are a symbol of hope for most. To me, they are a symbol of suffering." She cleared her throat. "I have only bits of memories from my time before the crash. They come to me in disorganized nightmares. My instructor taught me meditation to help me consolidate the few I acquired, over the years. When he passed, I couldn't focus enough, haven't been able to since." She shook her head. "Now they come and go in no order and never progress in detail or context."

Bennett thought of his own nightmare, the memory of his mother and brother, the house in flames. He could understand that, but not the concept of never knowing where it fit into the past timeline.

"What I do remember, the pieces, are all I have left of who and what I was before UP. My earliest memories are from a mountain with a cabin and a creek. Then a green light wrapped around me, and I awoke in a room packed with bodies, some humans, most were not. Some alive, most not. Large creatures, like those Warruks, dragged me to a cell. I could kneel, couldn't stand up. I think I was around five.

"My skin was constantly covered in this red, gritty sludge, occasionally other colors. Eventually, I got used to the cold and stopped shivering. But, the stench was unbearable. I didn't get much light through the bars of my cage." She stared, unfocused at the distant end of the fields. "Took me a few years to adjust to the sun, back on Earth. Still prefer the shadows, night."

Her eyes glinting in his flashlight came to mind. *Adapted to the darkness. Such a shame when she's so beautiful in the light.* His throat tensed. *Knock it off, Jameson. Pay attention. She's finally opening to someone.*

She paused, making a quick scan behind them. With a quirk of her mouth, she continued. "These thinner beings, with a sort of white, marble skin, went through cycles of testing on me, on us. They implanted devices along my spine, my joints, and in my brain, that, when connected to the harness, caused involuntary movements of my body. They took control of my arms, my legs, my lungs, never got to my eyes."

Bennett cringed. *Someone's puppet?*

Her fists curled up then relaxed. "I was in the muscular and neural test group. The people with their internal organs and other tissues studied didn't survive the first day."

His nerves prickled, wondering what she'd actually seen.

"One session, they adjusted a node they had rammed in my brain. It created such a racket I couldn't think straight. I covered my ears instinctively, though I was born without the ability to hear." Her voice quieted. She gave her wristband a slight twist as if its positioning was off. "The testing kept us in this cycle of unconsciousness and consciousness. It messes with your sense of reality. Was a little more than a decade ago, now."

His hands slid into his pockets, scanning the needles beneath his boots, oddly hued despite the darkness. He didn't quite know what to say. But he knew what he saw: a familiar internalized ache from howling loneliness compounded by guilt, rejection, and torture.

"The workers abused and mutilated the life forms, alive and dead, to see how they would hold up. They got a kick out of it, thought it was fun to poke and prod us to see who would crack, who would fight, and who would die." She grabbed her arms like she was suddenly cold. "I saw bodies chopped in pieces. There were hides, people and other forms skinned and stretched out on the walls like they were art: prizes of a hunt. I watched Warruks fight over one that hadn't moved on its own in days. It was gray and thin, somewhat like Teek—"

Her body visibly tensed.

"They tore limbs off and fought one another for who got to eat which part." Choking down a gag, she waved a loose-fingered hand over her face. "Why their breath smells like iron."

Bennett's stomach turned, thinking back to the fight in the hallway, the rot-black teeth. His upper lip curled.

"A worker kicked the table over, yelling in a language I didn't understand. The body rolled onto the floor, and the worker—" Atana stopped.

Bennett looked over to see her zoned out, jaw hung open. "You don't have to tell me."

She gritted her teeth. "It just left them there. They left the body lying there on the floor for five more of my sessions before they dumped her with the other failures." Atana's lips quivered. "They never sedated anyone in that room."

He placed a hand timidly on her shoulder, giving it a gentle squeeze.

Atana hid her mouth behind a hand. "I tried to help someone once. Another life form fell off his slab, too weak to stand on his own. I climbed down to help him up, but a hook went through beneath his collarbone. They slung him over his table, and he just slumped in a pool of blood. They hit me in the head, and the memory fades."

Bennett didn't know what he could say to comfort her. He couldn't understand, but he wanted to. He slid a half step closer just to give her the reassurance she wasn't on her own, anymore.

"They fed us this white, mushy composite, Izanot, and dirty water. I think whatever the mixture was is the reason I healed. No one should have been able to survive any of that." She looked away. "Kept us alive to continue the torture."

The chilled edge to her voice burned him inside. "Oh God, Nakio, I'm so—"

"God had nothing to do with this!" A tear teetered on the brim of her lashes. "Such beings of hope are lies, lies to cover the truth that people can't handle!"

"Okay, I'm sorry." He backed up, palms in the air. "I didn't mean anything by it. Just an expression."

She sighed, swiping a cluster of bangs from her eyes. "I apologize for my outburst. That was uncalled for."

"Not after what you've been through. I think you're handling it better than most."

"By default." Her brows knitted downward. A tear fell to the dirt underfoot. "I'm the only one left, Bennett."

"What does that mean?"

She flung her arms straight at her sides, anger darkening her face. "They're dead. All of the others that survived the rescue crash. Dead. Wilkes was the last. He shot himself. He couldn't handle the voices anymore. He retired *himself*."

"Oh." Bennett fumbled over his tongue. "I'm sorry."

"Sorry doesn't bring good people back." She huffed and spun a circle. "They lost it." Atana waved a hand at her head. "For some reason, I haven't." Her wristband sent out its warning peeps, flashing in the evening light. Rolling her eyes, she cursed.

Command Threshold Met. Reporting Protocol Initiated
Insert Relief Vial or Tap: Inject Standard Dose Ahead of Schedule

Atana wiped the weakness from her eyes with shaking fingers and clumsily unsnapped her wristband cover. "I don't know how I got out of there. It doesn't make sense."

Bennett took her hand, preventing her from removing the vial.

"Let me help." He steadily took the glass tube out of the storage slot. "No one wants to drop the only extra-high dose they've got."

Atana lifted her fingers to her mouth, shielding the tremors a moment too late.

"You don't have to hide it from me." He dipped his head, reconnecting with her eyes. "It was a traumatic time in your life. You have a reason for your emotions. Believe me; I know what it's like to have to fight them."

Her gaze showed apprehension—an abused animal cornered by a stranger unknowing of her injuries.

"Hey, it's okay." Grasping her shoulders, he drew her into a hug. "You made it out. That's what matters."

Holding her was strangely soothing; it felt right. But, by UP's Code of Appropriate Actions, it was not permitted.

She pushed away, sniffling. "What are you doing?"

"I thought that's what people do when someone is—" Bennett stuttered nervously, searching for a distraction. She had fallen into him minutes ago and now guarded herself from him.

He slipped the vial into the Emergency Injection slot with a click. "So you began to hear while you were in this place?"

It seemed so wrong to be dosing her when he knew that if he let her go, there was a chance she might feel the same as him. He had seen her eyes connect with his in S.S.O. She had studied him when they were in the private conference room. There was something there, between them. He just couldn't place it. With a sigh, he snapped the cover shut and injected the dose.

Her eyelids closed, her shoulders slumping with relief. "I was born deaf. At some point after the second or third time I was on the table, I started to hear things."

Her first sounds were of people being tortured? Maybe that's why she's so callous.

She returned to a collected, unemotional state. "Well, now you know my story. So you got what you wanted, yes?"

"Atana, I didn't mean it that way." He shoved his hands in his pockets, ashamed of his impulsive action.

"Everyone wants to know," she stated flatly, scanning the trees. "Rio had to give me serum before we left. Never needed it before."

Bennett stuttered, trying to come up with something to say to ease her discomfort. "He increased the doses for my team too. We're all a little on edge. Hopefully, it proves useful for us."

She ignored his optimism with a stern glare. "Do you trust me now?"

"Yes, Nakio. My team has no secrets, no matter what they are. It's a rule of mine, and because of this, we are strong, together." His weak attempt to smile faltered, his attention yanked from her to the trees behind them, thinking he had heard footsteps.

When he turned back around, he found her nose almost touching his. *How did she— I didn't hear anything.*

Being a shepherd was a confusing mix of preventing anger, lust, depression, and personal agendas from taking control—yet they were to be kind, polite, and understanding when working with one another and the public. It was too much for him to sort, so he played nice with everyone to keep it simple.

This situation was different. His last encounter with her, in such a position, had bruised his sides. He lifted his palms in innocence.

Her fingers timidly contacted the warm leather covering his chest. "Why does your heart always beat so fast around me? Do I intimidate you?"

Bennett let out a short, flustered laugh catching the blinking heart icon on his wristband. "In a way, I guess one could say that."

"I do not prefer to be this way. Intimidating others is not an effective way to lead. Did I say too much?"

"No." *That's all you've got? No? Say something, you idiot.*

His lips parted, his breathing rapid and hot. Bennett visually traced down her soft, mahogany hair to her curvy legs and back up to her bright eyes. *I can't console her, but I should, shouldn't I?*

Thinking over what he could say, he brushed the single wet streak from her cheek with the tips of his fingers trying, again, to be comforting. The heat of her skin beneath his was so distracting, every thought he had tumbled to the ground. Her long lashes sparkled with human vulnerability, her plump lips like rosy pillows looking for a fight. He craved the feeling of them against his. His spine tingled with an urge bordering on a level of insanity.

Sliding his hand under the elastic band holding up her auburn waves and one arm around her waist, he delicately ensnared her, all reason melting away like his burning serum. Hesitantly, he pressed his lips to the ones so delightedly taunting and tasted the sweet nectar of her skin.

Chapter 17

EMBERS SPARKLED across the backs of Atana's eyelids. She responded to Bennett on instinct, her mouth captured by his.

His larger body curled around hers, pushing back her injurious memories—a shield. Bennett's lips, full and soft, surprised her with their strength. The tips of his fingers dug tenderly into the skin of her neck. Her heart skittered.

She was processing her serum too fast, the numbing hum already fading. The heat edging into her stomach made her want to never let the feeling of him slip away. She had suffered too long and too much.

He ignored the alerts flashing incessantly on his wristband and caressed her lips again, deeper. Lingering. Exploring her mouth with an intensity that left her knees trembling.

Her body fell against his without objection.

When his fingers pressed into her low back, creating the faintest pressure between their hips, shouting out the need he had for her, her eyes flew open. Currents of energy flared through her body, waking the ghost beneath her ribs. She gasped and blinked to survey the dark whirls of smoke for lashes on his soft-featured face.

It wasn't the serum mix-up. It was him.

He was doing this to her.

Her hands lifted, weakly bracing against his muscled sides, torn between pulling in and pushing back. Could Chamarel have sensed they were burning out and intentionally gave her a false sense of security to try to destroy the team from the inside? Or could it be a good thing? Either way, Atana now knew exactly what those little, red flags in the back of her mind meant, the ones waving furiously just before his kiss coaxed her under his spell.

She was losing sight of the mission, breaking code, toiling on the middle ground between duty and desire. *People are counting on me.*

Her arms ached in protest when she pushed back.

...

Bennett tried to follow, not wanting to let go. Her warmth had penetrated the uniform he wore, seeping in to rest against his skin, stirring up desire in every cell of his body.

90

Nuzzling her cheek, his words fell down her neck like a summer breeze. "Nakio, I—"

Seeing her reddening face, he released her in an instant. "Oh, Nakio," he stammered. "I didn't mean—" His hands lifted, his feet sliding back a step. "I mean, I didn't think. I just— You're so—"

Breathless and wide-eyed, she spun, vanishing amongst the trees.

He ran an anxious hand over his tingling lips, embarrassed at his actions, befuddled by her response, and silently pleading for her to keep their moment a secret.

The trees rustled, nearly inaudible, behind him. He twisted to find the tall man slinking out from the indigo forest with wild, blue eyes like torches. Muscle rippled beneath his navy-striped gray skin, his square jaw level with the top of Bennett's head.

Bennett palmed an SI. They scrutinized each other for a long breath before the man crossed Bennett's intended path, heading into the camp. "Who are you?"

He glared back at Bennett with an irascible grunt before joining the others in the yard.

At a loss for words, Bennett trudged back to the team. They'd moved into the hut where Panton stood guard in the doorway.

"Are they all asleep?" Bennett asked low.

"Yes, sir."

Seeing Panton so hollow-eyed, his voice now monotone, Bennett swore he'd never give the man one of his doses again. Slumped against a post of the doorway, Panton stared out across the fields. He looked too dead inside, too much like Cutter.

Bennett quietly clapped a hand to Panton's shoulder and stepped inside. Resting an elbow on his top bunk, he gazed down at Atana as she slept on the bed beneath his. In the low light of the night sky from the doorway, he admired the skin he'd caressed moments before. Her copious scars reflected the pale blues a hair brighter than the unmarred areas, making her almost sparkle.

He didn't know what to think or feel. She was more than a shepherd, though she acted like it was nothing. *Maybe she thinks it is nothing.*

Bennett grumbled inside, trying to formulate a plan. Command needed information. These workers needed her, or so they thought. He was supposed to protect her. Torn between duties, he stood watching her sleep quietly—rolled away from him, the boy's note tucked in a pocket of her jacket—enjoying the peaceful moment.

Earth was under attack, but she was safe. He knew it wouldn't last and dreaded the second it would change. It was coming. Unpredictable and unknown danger ate away at his confidence.

Things weren't going to be okay. More people were going to die. He could feel it.

And now it bothered him because he was emotionally broken down, burned out, and invested in her.

It didn't upset Bennett that he was violating the shepherd's primary rule. The anxiety is what concerned him. It was different from the other missions—a more intense, attentive, worried focus.

Worried about her or the team? For once, just think about your job. They can take care of the rest.

But he wanted to understand. He wanted to help her. She didn't deserve the burden she carried. No one did.

...

Restless, Atana jolted in her sleep, her dreams more detailed and vivid than they had ever been before.

The chilled surface of the table fogged beneath her lips. Metal clinked above, the screeching whir of a small drill bored into her bone. Hot liquid that tasted of iron filled her mouth.

Her eyes popped wide open in the dark, her heart trying to beat its way out of her chest. The seizures evoked by that node left her quivering upon waking. Atana covered her mouth with her hands, repressing an outcry. She barely noticed her wristband beeping.

After several deep breaths, she forced her heavy limbs to put her upright on the bunk. She was accustomed to this kind of event. But her recovery time was slowing.

Setting her boots on the floor, she rested her elbows on her knees, brushing the hair from her face. Her head fell into her hands.

The striations on her neck, below her hairline, were smoother and lighter than the undamaged skin, what was left of it. The glossy zigzags formed a pattern, framing the rounded process of each vertebra in her spine. The scars stretched, her fingers hopelessly massaging the knotted muscle at the nape of her neck.

She stood and glanced at Bennett, sleeping soundly, the contours of his face easily visible to her in the shadows. His left arm, with his wristband, lay over his ribs. Atana checked their posted guard. Cutter had his back to her.

Gently, she slid a hand into Bennett's, lifting his arm up to where she could read the screen. Rousing the computer from sleep mode, she put her finger on Serum Status. The screen lit up.

Next Dose, 22 hours
Two Vials Remaining

She looked up, calculating. *He should have four.*

Bennett stirred, squeezing her hand in his. Atana's reflexes kicked in. Her hand twitched, wanting to retract. For the first time, she noticed how much larger his hands were than hers. But like hers, they were marked with scars and padded with calluses. Part of her clung to things like that in others, longing to be something she knew she wasn't. She cautiously slipped her hand out of his and crept out to Cutter's position.

"Sergeant, I can take over," she offered.

His silver eyes glinted in the starlight when they fell on her. "Ma'am?"

"I can't sleep."

He stood stark still, inspecting her with a sidelong glance. "Bad dreams?"

"Something like that." She jerked her nose toward his bunk in the back by the stack of folded space suits and helmets.

"If you change your mind, come get me." Hanging his shotgun at his side, he slipped through the doorway.

Atana leaned against the side of the hut. Staring up at the stars with a weighted sigh, she wondered how the real thing could burn amidst such frigid abyss, such desolation, without winking out.

Chapter 18

RATTED FABRIC strands swung gently in the windows, the morning light humbled by their presence. Chamarel flowed into the bunk room, her movement smooth, without step. The hem of her robes draped to the floor, dragging in the dirt, concealing what hid beneath. She stopped beside Atana. *We need to talk. Come with me.*

Taking one last wary glance across the fields, Atana signaled Josie to take her place then left her guard post to follow. She was anxious for explanations. If only she could solidify into words the ambiguous feelings rushing at her since their arrival, maybe she could make some sense of herself.

"It will rain today, so the workers will be inside their own quarters. It will let us get much accomplished." Chamarel addressed the team. "For now, Teek will take the rest of you to the first meal." His gray face peeked in, a smile spreading his sunken cheeks, tail swinging behind him.

Panton stood authoritatively. "Sergeant Atana needs food too."

Josie jumped down from her top bunk and stood next to him, equally attentive to her response.

The team's concern was unexpected. Most shepherds took her orders without as much as a glance at her boots. Her growling stomach appreciated their response, begging to join. But her integrity overruled. "I'm fine. You go." Atana gave a terse tilt of her head toward Teek. "We'll talk after."

Upon entering the front room, Atana noticed Bennett following them and spun around. He slid back a step.

Without his jacket on, the slender, inked feathers hugging the base of his neck were more apparent. She studied them long enough to see a wisp of fire colored between.

On serum or not, Bennett had broken a physical contact boundary, and she needed to put it back into place. "What do you need?"

"Can I bring you something to eat?" His honeyed eyes danced over her face, the hunger in them repressed to a glimmer.

"Oh." Only Rio had ever made such an offer. "I'm fine."

She watched him join the others, finding it unnatural he was so interested in her. Disconcerted her wall was still in pieces at their feet, she

94

slumped on the straw stool across from Chamarel. "So what did you want to talk to me about?"

He seems to care for you.

Atana winced at Chamarel's voice between her ears. "He's not supposed to care about anyone, just do what he is told to do: protect."

I don't see how he has been harmful.

He's violating codes. Atana's mind was warming up. It was the first time she found talking easier than listening.

And you don't? Chamarel tore a scrap of fabric from her robes, gathered her strands of twisted black hair, and tied it in a bundle over a shoulder.

I do, when it benefits Command's mission.

Is that the only mission that matters?

Atana didn't know what to say. Protecting others and preventing them from knowing pain and prejudice by stopping the offenders was the only goal she'd ever known. Or, at least, the only one she remembered so clearly. Despite not having the memories, she knew she had felt its necessity since she was very young. Always fighting for life. What else could be as important? "I'm here because of the mission. There is little time to waste. Can we please move forward with what we *can* do something about?"

"I told you last short-cycle, yesterday, that you cannot leave. It isn't safe yet." Chamarel said it like a broken record. "My guards will let me know when the Linoans and Warruks are back to their typical routes, then, maybe, we can discuss your options. This *is* what we can do, for now. Work on you."

Chamarel brushed something off her knee, sending a small cloud of dust settling to the floor. *How does Sergeant Bennett make you feel?*

I'm not answering that. Atana didn't want to think about her momentary loss of control. Or the warmth of his skin, the perfect tenderness of his fingertips. The strength in his kiss made her heart pound and her world of hurt melt into clouds of harmless colors.

It was addicting. And wrong.

Gah, stop! Atana slapped the sides of her head.

Chamarel smiled. *So secretly, he's intrigued your heart.*

It's this place. The ship is screwing with me.

That's only part of it. Stop lying to yourself.

I'm not. Seeing Chamarel's brows lift, Atana silenced.

It was the truth, just not the right one.

You need to stop fighting your emotions. We are designed with them for a reason. Train unrelenting control into someone and give them a weapon that intensifies their skills, like motivation, and they will gain the upper hand.

Atana's mouth twisted to one side. *I guess. But the first few days off the serum are the most uncontrollable and unpredictable.*

I don't sense any troubles from your team, including Bennett.

He's acting on impulse.

Chamarel sighed. *You are the one having trouble—finding the boundaries.*

I'm fine.

Yet your control slips.

Atana fidgeted with the straps of her wristband that rubbed against her continually rolled up jacket sleeve, anger thumping to life in her chest. It was a reality she didn't want to face. The mission had to succeed. People were counting on her. Billions of them.

Because of your control, you have the most amazing gift of all: the ability to utilize your emotions when the moment calls for it. You should not hide from this. Bennett is more human in that he feels something all the time. This is why you think him so uncontrolled.

Atana's thoughts blurred. Everything Chamarel was saying broke Command's Code. *Wait, what do you mean?*

Teek entered, a small woven tray in his hands. "I bring tea."

Atana sat back, not paying much mind to the teen as he poured a cup for Chamarel.

Being here was changing her. The serum was losing effectiveness. And Bennett was 'more human' than her?

The sweet notes in the spicy steam roused Atana from her confusion to soak in its odd familiarity.

"What is it made from?" she asked, looking up at the friendly, youthful face now standing beside her. "It smells like something we grow on Earth."

His hands quivered. "It is Jesiar, from dark red flower."

"Here, let me help," Atana offered, taking the fired-clay cup. He held the pot handle with both hands, attempting to pour the tea into the cup she held. But the steaming liquid splashed over the rim and onto her hand. The bold sting was nothing new or shocking. A nuisance at the most. She held the cup stable, not bothering to wipe the droplets from her skin.

"Oh, my sorry!" He squirmed.

"It's okay. Let me take the teapot." Trading hands with the cup, Atana reached up to the kettle with the affected hand and finished pouring.

The stinging would pass quickly.

She would heal.

Eyeing Teek's fur coat, hanging from a gangly frame, any annoyance she might've felt crumbled. She couldn't understand why he was serving her and not himself.

The surface of Atana's thumb and forefinger paled and crackled with iced sparks like usual. It returned to its normal light-mocha color within seconds, undamaged. She shook away the prickling feeling.

He drew in a sharp breath. "It is her, Chamarel!"

Chamarel nodded at her helper. "You must not say anything, to anyone. Do you understand?" He bowed. "Go tend to the rest of the crew so I may continue."

Teek spun and left with a bounce in his step.

Atana sipped on her tea, trying to appear innocent of whatever Teek was suggesting. The taste was a hint spicier than Marusa, but its calming effect was no different. For a moment, she closed her eyes to linger in the stillness.

How long have you been able to pull off that trick? Chamarel motioned with two glittering fingers, in approximately the location the blisters should have occurred.

Atana glanced down, wishing they could move on to a more pressing matter: the mission. Tiptoeing around conversations to earn trust and acquire critical information from civilians was not her strongpoint. It was boring, irrelevant, and often filled with inaccuracies and exaggerations.

Team Leaders were better at it.

Nothing about this mission made sense. She couldn't even figure out what was going on within her. What in the bloodyhell else was she going to do?

I've always been like this. I think I used to play with candles when I was a child. So please explain how you have reached this conclusion about Bennett again?

It is not so much Bennett as it is you.

Atana sighed, a silent curse slipping through her lips. There it was again. All she wanted was some sort of normalcy in her life: to live peacefully in the shadows. She leaned forward, elbows on her knees, the teacup in her hands, and hung her head.

Chamarel's voice sung in her mind. *Bennett is human. Human nature is to be emotional.*

Atana took another sip. *How do you know that, and why are you saying it like I am not human?*

If you remember, I have already been introduced to Earth's inhabitants via the Suanoa's last two invasions and have acquired many as workers in my fields. And you are not.

Choking, Atana set the cup on the straw table. She covered her mouth, sputtering. *Excuse me?*

Chamarel's words were strong, definitive. *You appear human, but the majority of your ancestry is not of Earth.*

Atana nervously rubbed her leather-clad thighs. *I am from earth, was born on earth.* But the uncountable anomalies setting her apart from the other shepherds—

Are you certain? One of Chamarel's brows arched.

Atana bit her tongue. Her insides hollowed, blood chilling in her veins. What was she implying?

Teek burst back into the hut. The fear widening his yellow eyes made both women leap to their feet. He rattled off a string of words to Chamarel in a language Atana didn't understand.

"What's going on?" Atana asked.

Chamarel bolted through the bunk room, the ends of her colorful stole flapping behind her like a ribbon in the wind. Teek trembled as he followed, clutching the strap of his satchel.

Tracking behind them, apprehension building within, Atana pinpointed the team at the edge of the clearing. Chamarel hadn't answered her. With the rapid pace of the woman's movement, Atana couldn't figure this was expected. Drawing her SIs, Atana zigzagged through the mass of workers toward the other shepherds.

Chamarel shouted across the meal yard in multiple languages. Her face was blank, but her words, however indecipherable, were clipped with urgency. The workers were instantly up like ants on a mission, hiding food and supplies.

Bennett broke away from the team and jogged up to Atana, meeting her halfway. His lips parted as he scanned the hive of workers.

Atana lifted a finger to silence the question she knew Bennett would ask, the same one Chamarel hadn't answered for her. Chamarel made eye contact with an incoming worker who stood a little straighter than the others, more muscle on his frame. The metal handles on his belt were caked with something too dark to be dirt.

Opening her mind, Atana overheard the silent words he and Chamarel exchanged. She canted toward Bennett as she relayed what she understood. "Linoans escorting twenty injured from Plasma Engineering."

Chamarel swayed in disappointment. She turned, in the distance, toward the team. "You must hide in the trees. We will be inspected." Meeting Atana's gaze as the team picked up their weapons and promptly disappeared into the forest, she sent her a private warning. *Linoans may not be telepathic, but you do not want to give them any urge to search. If they find infiltrators, they will shred every last one of us.*

The notion spiked a nauseating twinge in Atana's empty stomach. She managed a nod and encouraged Bennett after the team. The two of them wove back into the depths of the poles with silent steps until they found the group.

Wanting to watch, Atana touched Bennett's shoulder and signaled she was breaking off. He turned, forming an objection, but motioned he would join instead. At his command, the team backed up to one another in a circle, weapons ready.

Atana paused by Panton, a growing worry his big mouth might alert the Linoans. Leaning close to him, she lowered her voice so only he could hear. "Don't make me want to cut your tongue out."

His face paled, and he mouthed, "yes, ma'am."

"If we don't come back, you continue with the mission." Atana scanned the team until she'd received a nod from each.

Bennett pointed to Josie. "Lead." Then he looked to Tanner. "Find them a way home."

With one last inspection of Panton, Atana crept through the branches back toward the yard, Bennett at her heels.

Atana slid her SIs into their holsters, darkening the igniters. Crouching, she and Bennett took up a position several trees deep from the clearing. Between the indigo needles, they watched a group of workers stumble in from their shift, several bearing paired burn marks on their skin and clothing. From their arms hung twenty-one bloodied bodies. At their backs were four Linoans, pushing them along. In the Linoans' hands were bows strung with dual bands of flaming string. Their fists and heels bore crisp metal that flashed in the artificial light.

Chamarel stood alone between the forming row of males and the row of females, waiting. One Linoan yelled words Atana couldn't understand.

The creature spoke as if its vertical mouth was full of honey and its throat abraded by acid. It pointed the end of its bow at Chamarel as the bodies were deposited in the yard, and she was on them with lightning speed, assessing their injuries. Lifting the bow to the crowd of workers, it barked another order.

The slaves from Plasma Engineering quickly joined the others in two lines on opposite sides of the main path. The men made up more than three times the population of women.

As the congestion cleared, a man broke out of the lineup, running to a body on the ground. He collapsed into the dirt, clutching the woman in his arms, crying out. His song of torment was so harsh and raw it made Atana's heart stall for a beat.

Teek, she noticed, stood in line with the others, head down, his satchel missing from his chest. Chamarel frantically passed over each of the injured while the leader watched. The other three Linoans scoured the crews, ramming the end of their bows into stomachs, grabbing faces and shoving the workers back with a sharp word, the men taking the abuse before getting back in formation. When the Linoans inspected the females, the male row fidgeted.

Females received the same rough handling. The younger girls cried. The older women stood firm, jaws locked in defiance. At the inspection of a pregnant, humanoid female with diamond white hair, a male tried to break out of his line, shouting desperately as the young woman took a Linoan hit from a bow point to her stomach. Other men in line grabbed him, keeping him in place. The Linoan made a noise of disgust and moved on.

Beside Atana, Bennett looked down with a subtle sway of his head.

The lead Linoan barked another chain of grating sounds. This time, Atana heard someone in the distance speak through Ether, though she couldn't understand. Not until the fourth voice joined. *You fail again, you will be purged.*

Chamarel stood from a worker, hands curling into fists. She leaned forward and, with eyes contorted in anger, raised her voice to a challenging bellow.

Again, the fourth voice spoke. *You are killing too many! We cannot keep up with Suanoan demands this way!*

The Linoan spun its bow, the strings brightening with its swing. Fear ripped through Atana, and she grabbed Bennett's wrist, holding her breath. Beside her, Bennett did the same.

Two stripes of red-orange light painted Chamarel's glare but stopped. A reminder of her vulnerability. The fiery bands hummed and crackled beside Chamarel's cheek. A wisp of smoke curled up from a twisted strand of her hair. She held her ground, glaring right into the Linoan's eyes.

The Linoan cocked its head, talking slowly.

Pregnant females work too slow, make mistakes, the fourth voice translated.

Chamarel's hands squeezed tighter until dark droplets fell from them.

They make more workers at no expenditure of your own.

The Linoan studied Chamarel a moment, retracted its bow, and then signaled the others for the exit. Shutting its bow off, the Linoan folded it up and slapped it to its back. After one final scan of the fields and the trees, the creature dropped to all fours, bounding out across the fields toward the bay door with the others.

Teek and the others broke formation to help attend to the injured.

Atana sighed with relief. Only then did she realize how much her body had tensed during the encounter.

"Come on," Bennett tapped her, leaping out of the trees. She watched as he sent his team a message, then pulled his medical kit out and collected the burn patches. "I was informed you don't need these." He handed a dressing to her.

"By who?" she asked, stopping beside one of the injured workers. Inspecting the pair of charred and blistering stripes on the man's thigh, she applied the bandage. The worker remarked something Atana couldn't decipher, but his face showed appreciation and likely a little relief from the analgesic.

"Command."

She didn't have much to offer in response. Command was contradicting their own rules, telling Bennett such private details about her. Atana knew it made sense to explain things to a Team Leader on a mission this critical. But what else had they said?

Atana watched Chamarel hover her hands over the workers squirming in pain. Peach light danced like a thick sheet of static between her palms and the wounds, slowly healing them. For the more devastated workers, Chamarel leaned over and touched her forehead to theirs, appearing to heal from the inside out. But nearly half, she just shook her head and waved over a group of workers to carry off the body. The man crying over the limp woman had to be peeled away. He struggled to hold on, throwing punches at his fellow workers. Chamarel braced his shoulders as he broke and fell to his knees. She whispered in his ear, drawing their heads together.

His sobs calmed. "Paramor will release her?"

Chamarel nodded. "Yes, my son."

Atana couldn't sort what was meant by such a statement. The woman was gone, dead. What more could they do?

Approaching the team, Teek wiped his bloodied fingers on his clothes. "They push maintenance workers hard when we near a planet. Want plasma ready for terraform. Want power ready for escape."

A perimeter guard, helping to lift the last body added, "The Suanoa could do the tasks easily, telekinetically. But they get a sick joy out of seeing us suffer through it instead."

"Terraform?" Atana asked, grabbing Teek's arm.

"They cleanse the planet after the siphoning has completed." Chamarel stood and made her way to the team. "This is why you mustn't act until we are sure it is safe. Your mission must wait if it is to succeed. Had you arrived earlier, you would've had more time."

Atana and Bennett exchanged worried glances.

"I didn't want to say anything," Chamarel added. "I know you will push to leave, to continue your search. But you will only become another body sent into the void if you do not wait for the right moment."

Bennett placed his last burn patch on a young girl's shoulder then looked to Chamarel. With a shake of his head, he appeared to reconsider what he was going to say. "Do you need us to clear out the bunk room?"

"No, those who are alive have been healed enough to return to their own huts. The others will be sent to the stars after Healer Paramor frees their life-spark. Not every Agutra is lucky to have an Orionate onboard. Only someone like him can send their spirit home from such a black hole as this." Chamarel's mouth twisted in disappointment. "Even a soul cannot escape the gravity of a Suanoan ship, not without the help of an Origin Elite life form." She lifted a hand toward the baskets of food reappearing in the yard. "Please rejoin the others. Atana and I must continue."

The team followed Bennett back to the yard, their eyes trained on their surroundings. He described what he and Atana had seen as she and Chamarel headed for the hut.

In the front room, Atana sat on a stool, reeling from the events. She couldn't seem to focus on anything but watching Chamarel. The dark stains on her brown sleeves had an obvious cause now.

Your skill, Chamarel directed toward Atana's hand, *is a rare Xahu'ré characteristic, from a very specific lineage. It is the reason you are different and that your team has a chance to succeed. The workers sense it. A few are Xahu'ré. They are also telepathic, like me.*

It was clear by the way Chamarel moved on that this was normal—the violence of inspection, the severely burned workers, carrying off the dead. On Earth, Atana would've gladly killed all four Linoans without hesitation. But this time, she knew that would only bring more trouble. She and the team had to make the right move at the perfect time, no sooner or later, to not draw attention.

Chamarel's insistence was well-placed.

So, are you Zuh-who-ray? Atana asked, sounding it out internally. *Is that why we can communicate this way?*

No, I am Mirramor. Our species are distant cousins.

Atana palpated her hand with her opposite thumb, sorting through her life experiences, trying to rationalize the information she was being given. She wondered why she seemed so connected to Chamarel. *Could it be the mere telepathic link? Or was I here before? Maybe it is her. Cousin species? I'm not human? Maybe this is a dream? Or—* She thought about the man with the blue eyes from her night visions.

Chamarel's face pinched like she was in pain. *Remember, I can hear everything. You are a mixed breed: Xahu'ré, human, and partly like me: Mirramor. Xahu'ré look like humans, though their structures are built significantly sturdier.*

Three different species? Atana's mind went completely blank.

Xahu'ré skin is usually a medium gray, with dark-navy, symmetrical thermo-stripes. The human children call them zigzags. And all true Xahu'ré have blue eyes. Mirramor can change shapes, so unless you can learn which individuals are my species, you won't be able to tell.

After a long breath and a crack of her knuckles, Atana managed to wake her brain from its shocked slumber. *Does your, or rather our, species have a natural form?*

Yes, for full-bloods. Partials, like you, get some of the traits and skills. Which ones, we never truly know until they appear. Mirramor Saemas and Healers are under sworn oath to never show ourselves. It frightens too many species.

Chamarel leaned back on her seat, watching Teek help a bandaged worker up from his cot in the spare room. *We have all been long-awaiting your arrival. It has been prophesied by many before me that a life form would come from a blue planet to return us to our homes.*

Aren't your homes many light-years from here? Atana asked, ignoring her implication.

Home is not a location. It is inside us all, a peace of mind we get when surrounded by loved ones, familiar things, and a safe, stable environment.

Atana inspected the woman across from her. She was saying a lot of unbelievable things. *What does this prophecy say exactly about this individual everyone seems to assume is me? I heard someone in the yard, but a physical description is hardly determinate.*

Chamarel's smile was grim at best. *Her heart tormented by vengeful desire, with a soul of light, a mutiny will transpire. Empathetically pained, with fearless might, she will kill three. Embodied in flames, the afflicted shall fight and set the innocent free.*

Atana mused vacantly over her scarred hands. *I am effective. But vengeful? No.* She lived by Command's Code. *Empathetic?* UP assigned serum for such weakness. *Embodied in flames? Definitely not.*

It was her responsibility to protect and save her people. It was clear, these beings needed help too. Ultimately, the end goals were the same. But what were the long-term effects? This land was from another star system. *After us, they will move on and tear apart other galaxies, won't they?*

The way Chamarel's eyes darkened and fell said enough.

"How?" Atana asked, realizing the additional obligation now hanging over her head. "How do we end this? All of it."

"Only you and one other have ever killed Suanoa. You don't remember how you killed the last three?"

Atana couldn't even recall what one looked like. "No. Is there any way to find out how to kill them? Is the other individual here?"

Chamarel's words were slow in the way a doctor announced a fatal diagnosis. "I'm afraid not."

The silence that followed seemed to stretch forever. She offered nothing more, no explanation.

Chamarel was hiding something. Something horrible. Something about the other person.

Picking up on this, and feeling they'd wasted enough precious time, Atana nodded and moved forward. "Are there any known methods?"

Telekinecrosis, otherwise known as the Grey, but it too often results in the death of the infiltrator. Chamarel's lips pursed.

Command's words about this potentially being a suicide mission resurfaced. Atana knew her place, to serve and protect the innocent. A life as mechanical as hers was incapable of understanding the higher value of an innocent. Death was always dripping from her fingertips. It seemed only fair, for once, it might be hers.

The risk was accepted, permitting Command got the information they needed to defend Earth.

How does it work?

Chamarel hesitated, the slight sway of her body like a rat in a maze trying to find an escape. *It is a more permanent state of being in the ether, the telepaths' network. If one meditates deeply enough, the brain impulses will be so minute the Suanoa can't detect the intruder. It is, however, not safe for anyone and requires years of experience in meditation. It has always, and only ever, been a last resort.*

Will you teach me?

"No. It is too dangerous. We must find another way."

Denial did not fit Chamarel's recent pattern of behavior, throwing the plan Atana was constructing into the dirt. "I was sent here for a reason. I'm not like the others, like *anyone*. You said it yourself."

"You are different. But the risk is not worth it." Chamarel dug her toes into the dirt beneath her robes. "We cannot lose you."

"*You* cannot lose me? What about the people of Earth?" Atana let out a breath, realized how arrogant it had sounded, and dialed down her tone. "At least train me so we have a chance. I won't use it if we find another option."

Chamarel's skin shimmered, her colors changing in rapid gradients. "I will not."

Footsteps approaching Atana's back made her leap up from her seat. A hand rushed to her SI as she spun to step away in defense, heart pounding.

Bennett, looking stunned, stood holding a small woven plate and a gourd with water. "What's going on?"

Kernels of water tapped the straw overhead. Within seconds, they were sheltered from a total downpour, the soil pooling outside the hut, the air gray with mist.

"We will talk more later. Think about what I said." Chamarel rose and walked out the front opening right into the rain, shoulders sagging.

Bennett's mouth slacked, his gaze following Chamarel closely. "What did she want?"

Me. And Atana didn't like that thought. "Nothing relative to the mission."

Chapter 19

THEY STARED quietly at the rain, pelting down from the roof of the container. After several minutes, Bennett inspected the bundles of straw above them. "Amazing how well they have it tied for how little they have."

Atana plopped onto her seat. He took the bale next to hers, placing the plate and gourd on the large, central stool.

"I know you're hungry." He pushed it toward Atana, concerned by the redness of her face. Chamarel had lost points with him. Whatever they'd talked about wasn't worth this level of stress in Atana, or the concern forming within him. At least the workers had pitched in extra food for her. "Please, eat something."

She took a golden roll. "Thanks. You didn't have to."

Tearing off a small piece, she placed it in her mouth. Atana pursed her lips, looking like she was chewing more on her thoughts than the food.

Fluffy and light on the inside, it reminded Bennett of Earth's coarse-ground wheat bread. It had a surprisingly sweet taste beneath its lumpy exterior.

The spice of her lips lingered in his memory. He still couldn't tack down what had happened to him in that moment, why he'd caved. "I wanted to." So did the workers. And he was now at her mercy to keep his job. "My team takes care of each other. Another reason why we—"

"Work so well together." She swallowed, straining her neck. "I know."

He genuinely hoped she would see his priority was her, not himself. "I'm sorry about last night."

Atana chewed another bite, staring vacantly out the doorway. "It's not you."

Soft words from an Independent were never a good sign. Brash, sharp-tongued, and impatient might describe them. Bennett had worked for others enough to know this behavior indicated fading health, or their mission had already failed.

Ignoring his physical contact infraction, one worthy of dishonorable discharge, meant whatever was on her mind was far worse. Bennett cautiously pried. "Trouble sleeping?"

"It's nothing," she huffed.

It burned Bennett inside how overworked she was, and how thin a sliver of self-care she appeared to allow herself.

"Bull." He said it then cracked a light smile. Atana's eyes darted to his mouth, hung in place for a breath, then jumped to meet his. She looked confused.

The urge to lean in close, touch her, feel her heartbeat against his had him scooting to the edge of his stool. The sound of dry grass scratching against fabric made him stop. Gripping his knees he swallowed the impulse into submission. She was a rush, one that had turned him into an instant hot mess without rationale.

Most wouldn't have called a scarred patchwork like her beautiful. But to Bennett, she was. He surveyed the marks again, an anguished respect for her building within. He knew the high level of pain one endured for a scar to be left in its place. He didn't think he could count all of hers in a single day.

"Is there anything I can do to help?" *Please let me help.*

"I'm not one of you." Her exhaustion was apparent, her words quivering. "There's nothing anyone can do."

He hadn't heard it stated in so many words. But the isolation always shone in the gaze of Independents. Few shepherds took the time to look. Bennett watched everyone.

"Whatever Chamarel said doesn't make any difference to me. We are a team, whether you're an Independent or not."

"Bennett, you don't understand."

Resting a timid hand to her shoulder calmed little of his growing worry. "Well then help me. Please, Nakio. I want to."

"I can't. I don't know how." She set what was left of the roll back on the plate. Her fingers rubbed her temples so hard her skin paled. "It's too complicated."

She was right. He didn't understand. But why wouldn't she open to him? It was Rule Seven of the Code. Honesty Prevents Failure. He had to admit, there was a gray area between Rules Seven and Six: not identifying personal information.

"This is not the time to be keeping secrets, Nakio. If something is wrong with you, I want to know. I need to know, for the success of this mission and the safety of our team." Seeing her jaw muscles twitch, Bennett instantly knew he had hit a nerve.

"Nothing is wrong with me." Atana's words came out forceful and paired with clenching fists. She rose from her seat and stalked out the door.

Bennett scrubbed his fingers through his hair. *If something is wrong with you— What an ass, Jameson.* He groaned. It was a legitimate question. But his desperation to resolve the issue had tightened his tone and exacerbated the situation instead.

Tanner slipped into the room, shifting out of Atana's way. "What's wrong, B?"

Bennett tilted back, confirming her disappearance. "I need to invoke Bravo Sierra, for myself."

He took the seat Atana had left empty. "Sure, B, what's up?"

Trust and respect were hard-earned bonds, easily destroyed, in the civilian world. Bennett felt honored and lucky to have such willing relationships with his team when UP created it innately with the Oath, Code, and training. He had never opened up about something so personal to anyone, except Rio. Rio wasn't here. Bennett, perplexed by Atana's withdrawn behavior, wanted some peer validation for his concern. "Have you ever wanted something that, by the Code, you weren't supposed to want, but you couldn't stop it or shut it out of your thoughts?"

Tanner nodded.

Relief flooded him and he found himself slumping forward. Someone else knew a similar struggle. "Can I ask what you've wanted?"

"Under Bravo Sierra, you won't report me?" Tanner studied the hem of his cargo pants and dusty protective casing over the laptop against his chest.

"Of course not. That's what it's in place for. Because you guys, and Josie, are the closest thing I have to—" Bennett stopped himself, throwing his gaze out the door, afraid he might give away the entire intent. And his weakness.

"A family, yeah, I know." Tanner ran a hand over the blond scruff on his jaw then looked over at him with a half-cocked frown.

Bennett glanced around the hut for Sergeant Cutter. With no sign, he leaned toward Tanner and whispered, "Have you ever wanted one or at least wondered what it would be like to have one? A normal one? Parents, a spouse, kids?"

"I think we all have." Tanner chewed a lip and promptly added, "Because none of us know what it really is."

Cutter lurched into the room, his boots sliding and scraping to a stop in the dirt. His face was expressionless, but his speed suggested there was a problem.

Bennett's heart thumped in panic. Had Cutter heard their conversation? He and Tanner stood from their seats.

In Cutter's eyes was a raw emotion, a tiredness within a pain. A door long-shut in his mind had been reopened. And it wasn't pretty inside.

Bennett knew better than to ask, putting one soldier on the spot in front of another.

"There's a scuffle outside. You both need to see it." Cutter whipped around and stepped back outside.

Exchanging nervous glances, Bennett and Tanner followed him through the doorway.

...

A gaunt boy, of Xahu'ré decent, stood yelling at another child, who lay sprawled out on the soaked clay. "Dak ras!"

"Niema, nigh!" The smaller of the two cried out, his words choppy through his sobs, clutching his soggy roll.

Atana had been heading for the trees to clear her head, the forest a shield from the eyes of others in this cage. When she heard the commotion and for some reason understood their language, she slowed and listened.

The larger boy demanded, "Give it!"

A higher pitched voice cried, "Please, stop!"

It sent a stabbing pain through her heart. *Please stop.* Those two words hung in her thoughts like they did in her dreams, a jarring pair of verbal bullets. Her feet stopped moving. The plea replayed. She looked back.

A foot slammed into the smaller boy's stomach. It splashed a sheet of dirty rainwater in his face, causing him to cough and sputter. With a whimper, he curled up into a ball. The boy towering above reached a clawed hand at the disintegrating food.

Watching children fighting over scraps had a sickening familiarity to it. She found herself backtracking toward them, faster with every step, until she was in an all-out sprint, desperation and anger boiling up in her voice. "Hey; asii!" A sympathetic ache crawled through her belly as the larger boy drew back for another kick, the younger one still struggling to hang onto his roll. "Asii!"

Upon Atana's approach, the bully took a swing at her, freeing pieces of the boy's soggy roll in his other hand. She caught his arm and spun him around, down to his knees. Drawing her hooked blade from the small of her back, Atana pressed its point lightly to the side of his Adam's apple.

"Everyone is hungry. Not just you," she growled to his ear. "Don't ever do that again."

Shoving him into the mud, she stood and slapped her blade into its sheath with a glower.

Kneeling to the smaller of the two, who now lay motionless, Atana slipped her arms gingerly beneath his beaten body, scooping up his frame. The boy groaned, water pouring from his shredded shirt and pants, draining to the soppy dirt beneath.

Mud squished beneath her boots as she pushed past the team filling the doorway of the hut. Her head and shoulders soaked from the pouring rain, she called to Bennett. "Is there food left from what you brought back?"

He picked up the woven plate and followed her into the smaller of the rooms, adjacent to the front, with a single bed. Setting the boy down carefully on the faded blankets, she summoned Chamarel, who was out front speaking with a worker.

"His ribs are fractured," Atana said.

The boy groaned and held his stomach, dragging his knees toward his nose.

Chamarel looked down upon the pale face. "How do you know this?"

"I'm guessing, based on the bruising." Atana lifted the side of his outgrown shirt to show the black, indigo, and violet colors surfacing below his gray skin. "Can you do anything for him?"

Chamarel acknowledged the discoloration. "There are several stages of bruises here. This is not the first time he has been hurt."

"Where are his parents?" Atana took the plate from Bennett's outstretched hand, setting it on the table next to the bed where the boy lay.

"Killed by Linoans. That's the rumor. Kios has been alone for a few months." Chamarel inspected the bruises with her fingers.

"Who's supposed to be raising him?" Atana asked.

"There many like him, and we not enough," Teek interjected upon hurrying inside. Worry pinched his brows when he saw the boy. "Try to be."

Gazing down upon the shallow, rapid breaths of the innocent child on the bed, Atana's heart twisted in knots. His tousled, dark charcoal hair reminded her of the boy in her dreams. It made her wish to brush the thin, muddied strands from his forehead if nothing more than to reassure him someone still cared—to not lose hope.

She became immersed in his presence, studying every inch of his shivering form. This child's Xahu'ré markings were of uneven thickness and not symmetrical in the least. He was unique and alone, like her.

"You are safe now, Kios," Chamarel whispered, drawing a shabby blanket up and over his waist.

Thinking her compassion might be in violation of Code, Atana quickly switched focus to removing herself from the packed room. Something cold and clammy caught her fingers, stopping her. Looking down to what held her, she found the boy straining to hold on, his eyes barely peeking out from under his drenched, swollen eyelids—a deep, slate blue. *Like the night sky from Earth.*

"Eih ahna, miia zi du viia," he squeaked out before his weakened fingers lost their grip.

Chamarel sat on the bed by his feet. "If you see any others like this, please let me know." Hovering over the boy, she gently wrapped her palms over his ribs. "I'm sorry, Kios, this is going to hurt. I have to fix your broken parts. Can you be strong for me?"

He managed to wheeze, "Yes."

She quietly chanted her healing prayers. Bright peach light danced beneath her hands. His young vocal strings screeched. Sparkling drops escaped the corners of his squeezed-shut eyelids, his hands pushing on Chamarel's shoulders, his legs kicking beneath.

Atana stared at his writhing frame unable to move, to breathe. His cries rang in her ears causing her fists to curl, thinking of those who would cause such misery, such desperation over food. The bully wasn't the problem. The children were equally hungry and scared. The ones who had created such a cage—they should pay. *They will pay.*

Chamarel leaned down to meet his forehead with a kiss. Then, gently touching her forehead to his, Kios's legs relaxed, his arms dropping to the sheets as his eyes closed.

Panton whispered from the back of the group the way distant thunder rumbles. "Is he going to be okay?"

"Yes, but Kios needs rest. It would be best if everyone would give us space. I will meet you in the other room soon so we can further discuss what you need to know for your mission."

The team slowly filtered out.

Atana knew Kios was too young to defend himself in such a manner and, least of all, over food. He couldn't have been more than four years old. Many shepherds had been in similar positions at his age but had been rescued by members of the Universal Protectors. Up here, there was no salvation.

She glanced outside to see what had become of the situation with the bully. A group of Xahu'ré males had surrounded the boy, all wearing the same stoic expression and threadbare clothes with belts. *Must be perimeter guards.*

One man stood close but separate from the others. When she looked, she found his blaze-blue eyes on her. It was the tall man from the night before. His arms were uncrossed this time, and he looked prepped as if to run. *Shit.*

Spinning around the corner of the hut, Atana hid from his line of sight, pressing her back up against the twig wall. She prayed he wouldn't follow as Kios's words echoed between her ears. *Thank you, female of the light.*

Chapter 20

BENNETT WAITED FOR HER, his body blocking the doorway. When Atana shared the entrance with him, he reached out and softly touched her arms. "Are you okay?"

Atana nodded, slipped his grip, and went to stand in the corner opposite him. Gesturing toward a stool, she encouraged him to sit this time, to which he shook his head.

A guard was to be twice as strong, fast, and vigilant as his assigned co-shepherd. He didn't like the idea she'd patrolled last night without telling him, letting him sleep while he should've been posted beside her, instead of her.

Chamarel took her seat. "Please keep your voices low so we do not wake Kios." The group acknowledged with murmurs. "I will give you the answers to the typical questions first. Then you may ask yours after.

"All Agutra ships, like Semilath, this one, hold 270 agricultural containers. Each container, plus their attached facilities, is what we call a 'sector.' The central axis of the ship holds the stored food, consumable water, medicine, and other supplies. There are fifteen levels of sectors attached to this axis. Each level has an inner and outer ring housing six and twelve lateral sectors, respectively. Propulsion systems, power generation, Linoan collector docks, and sway and testing areas are located along the core, between the levels of sectors. The Suanoa live in the top, beyond Plasma Engineering, in the spires." Her voice darkened in warning. "There is also a smaller set of mechanical iris spires in the stern that open when the plasma weapon arms. This is also what they utilize to terraform planets."

The entire team looked up at Chamarel in a moment of heavy stillness.

"How many individuals are there per sector?" Josie asked.

Chamarel paused to scan the team. "It is hard to know for sure. We have to move everyone around when the Suanoa do a resource reload. Then there are the new recruits from your planet which have not been completely accounted for yet. At the fewest, we have had twelve to work a container, sometimes upwards of three hundred. The population tends to dwindle the closer the sector gets to the end of the cultivation shelf life."

114

Bennett studied Atana, working away on her wristband, sliding tabs open and typing information in. Tanner's fingers rumbled across his computer keys. The others leaned over his shoulders.

After a few moments, the team looked up at Chamarel and she continued. "I am going to see about getting the maps with the hidden routes we have drawn out from one of our neighboring Healers, Paramor. They are what our perimeter guards use on a cyclical basis."

"We're going to work on a plan when we have the maps in hand." Atana stopped to rub a temple as if a headache had abruptly switched on. "We will proceed with the mission tomorrow."

Chamarel twisted her hands together, her robes shifting near the dirt. Her colors faded from light mocha to her usual diverse palate. "Many individuals and teams have tried what you are about to attempt and have failed. Please understand the importance of your success. If you fail, it also causes suffering for the rest of us up here."

"Then why encourage us to go through with this?" Bennett asked.

"We hope someday our kind will be free, not necessarily that we, ourselves, may be." Chamarel produced a faint smile. "The Suanoa have been known to dump these agricultural containers and kill everyone on board to prove the point that they are in charge; they control our lives. There is no guarantee of a tomorrow for us. And unfortunately, we are one of many Agutra."

Bennett hung his head, shaking it in disgust. "They have to have a weakness. Every living thing has a weakness or a breaking point."

Chamarel swayed in her seat, looking uncomfortable. "Since they are the first species to call space their home, they believe they are the most intelligent and don't think anyone is smart enough to take them out. They do not see the imperfections in their systems because they don't believe anyone will defeat them. But knowledge is power. They have studied countless species, though mostly ones with narrower footprints, for efficient use of the limited space." She hesitated. "I believe there is one type you didn't encounter on your way in, mostly because you're still alive."

"There's something worse than Warruks?" Tanner stilled over his keys.

Chamarel's fingers tensed around one another, enough that Bennett noticed. "They do not usually show in containers unless the Suanoa specifically request it." Her eyes darted to Atana and Bennett. "Their typical workstations are keeping the crews in propulsion, power, and plasma areas in line. They also operate as the Suanoa's assassins and are the ones piloting the collectors on your planet."

"Linoans," Atana said quietly.

"Yes. Their skin has a muted, dark-red tint to it, with small, black markings near their joints. They operate mostly on passive tendon-tension, so their movements do not require much energy, making them swift killers. You have to hit them hard and fast if you hope to survive an attack." Chamarel's irises flattened and dulled when her gaze fell to the floor. "We have lost many guards to the Linoans and innocents undeserving of the end they received.

"They don't carry propulsive weapons. However, they do wear pairs of arced blades over their knuckles and the backs of their heels, wield Arc Bows in maintenance sectors, and always work in teams of four. It is easier to kill them if you break them up and take them out individually." Her voice hardened with an uncharacteristically venomous edge. "You must kill all of them."

"And these Suanoa?" Bennett interjected, hoping to distract her from whatever was boiling her inside.

She wiped her palms on her skirt. "The first time you meet one, you will hesitate. Even non-telepaths can sense the weight of their aura." She shuddered. "They wear armor made from the hides and bones of the Noriamé, a creature from their home planet, long since extinct. There are two black stripes which run crown to jaw, to either side of a central, knobby ridge."

A trail of cold stabbing signals prickled down Bennett's spine.

Chamarel's face radiated Atana's light-mocha color for a moment before returning to its multi-shade, calico state. Atana squirmed as if fighting a battle inside.

Secrets. The reason Bennett had created the team rule. Not being privy to all the available situational information could end in disaster—and had. All of his tattoos were reminders.

"Their skin is a dull white and contains a plasma-permeated layer. Blunt force will do you no good. It's like hitting metal or stone. You can puncture them with a sharp object. If you are quick enough to get something hot against them, you can change the state of the plasma and cause serious harm to their exterior layer. They do send out their own telekinetic fire blasts from plasma devices they embed in their palms and fingers. You have to be careful if you get within visual range."

"For right now," Bennett interjected, "let's concentrate on getting the information Home Station requires about what is up here and try to return in one piece."

"Agreed." Atana stepped forward. "Bennett and I need to talk with Chamarel more about the best routes to the locations we tagged in Tanner's maps first."

Chamarel's eyes twitched toward the back of the hut. "I will bring in a few of our perimeter guards to help."

"This is a recon mission first and foremost," Bennett reminded his team. "Do not engage unless innocents are at risk."

"Dismissed," Atana said quietly.

With the team in the bunk room, leaving Bennett, Atana, and Chamarel, Bennett broke the silence. "So what is going on? You keep leaving me out."

Atana threw him a pained glance.

Right. His only job was just to *protect her.*

A Xahu'ré male peeked in the front opening. "Ma, I couldn't get him. He's in Sector Seventy-nine," he paused, catching Atana's gaze on him. "Scrubbing."

Teek had explained different species to the team at first meal. Bennett still couldn't get over the shock of seeing the glowing eyes of Xahu'ré.

Chamarel waved at a seat. The thick-striped male sat as requested. "This is Kylo, one of our most experienced guards."

He surveyed the Earthlings in length. From his belt hung four crude blades. "Bennett and Sa—" Chamarel cleared her throat. Kylo paused, snorting at her. His bare toes clawed into the dirt. "Sergeant Atana. I hear you want help navigating our network. I can send each of you out with a guide at sleep-cycle."

"Thank you." Atana graciously dipped her head.

"Our team works in pairs," Bennett stated, trying to keep some level of control over their safety. "I want to see them stay that way."

Kylo glowered at him. "I will discuss this with our lead guard." His eyes settled on Atana. "We will find you after the last meal."

He stood promptly and left.

"I apologize." Chamarel sighed. "Kylo is effective but a member of the Verros, a group that believes we were saved from extinction by being enslaved, a sort of salvation on the backs of the Suanoa."

"That makes no sense," Bennett said. "With all the horrible things that happen here—"

"Some do not know any other life." Chamarel nodded to herself. "For some, it is how they cope so they may continue. After Kylo's mate was killed, he joined their cause. He protects because, to him, this is his home."

Chapter 21

THE TEAM twitched at every sound while they waited inside the hut for Kylo and his guards.

"I don't like this." Bennett sat beside Atana on her bunk, leaning onto his elbows. "We walked in here too easily, have been given a lot."

Atana inspected the edge of her hooked blade for nicks to keep her hands busy. The heat of Bennett's body, inches from hers, was more noticeable today. "By those who have so little, I know. I don't like it either. But if there's a chance they can teach us how to find our way around without getting caught—"

"Again, too convenient." Bennett's words made Josie shift on Panton's bunk across the room.

"Guys," Tanner called from the doorway. Atana slapped her blade back in its sheath and freed her Sis.

The four of them sprung to their feet. Atana burst out first, between Tanner and Cutter. A ring of shadowed figures congregated around the opening to the hut.

The posture of the circle was that of a pack of hunkered, starving wolves, but she could see them clearly enough. Four guards had shown, without Kylo, the guard they had spoken to earlier. He'd seemed less than pleased with their request. She could easily disregard his hostility as a result of impatience, pains from starvation, or reluctance to take a chance on another crew. But Atana considered it more likely distrust, leading her to expect one of two things. He was intending to test them and their intent within his territory or trap them with the goal of removing a threat to his people.

"I am Tohsa. Come with us," one of the guards said as they walked away. Bennett promptly moved up to Atana's side, the team following in pairs behind them.

"Below us are the gravitational maintenance rooms and the drainage systems for the fields." Tohsa guided them out of the agricultural fields, into the hallway, and down the stairs, directing with a hand as they meandered through to the other end.

"To either side, you will find hydro-facilities that pump the filtered water overhead for the rain." When they'd climbed the stairs again, he pointed to the pipes. "There are a lot of open spaces around the plumbing systems with no structured access, but every sector has them marked. Above are the light and ventilation systems. There are maintenance closets and chambers you can use to hide in when transitioning between levels. Like this one." He pointed to a set of etched triangles on a wall panel. "To make moving between levels fast, if you are being chased."

"You want wander ship free, get information, put our innocents in harm," one of the guards growled. "You must earn right."

Atana knew by his forced tone, this was a test. Since they were still getting useful information, she considered it a worthwhile risk.

"Jeniah, not now," Tohsa scolded. "He is not as good with English. We go through many long-cycles of training to be guards and to learn the different languages."

"What do they teach you on blue planet?" Jeniah interrupted. "How to be spoiled?"

"We are like you, Jeniah." Atana stopped to look at him. *I know what your game is.* "Our purpose is to ensure the safety of all Earthlings."

Tohsa let out a grunt, and the guards disappeared, leaving the team completely exposed to the hallway.

Atana straightened with an irritated sigh, keeping her senses open to the shadows.

"Now what?" Panton whispered, guiding Josie closer to him as he checked their perimeter.

"Perimeter Guards are testing us." Atana steadied her SIs.

"Testing?" Josie stammered.

Cutter stepped in front of Tanner, wrapping a firm hand around the shotgun strapped across his chest. "Panton, six o'clock!"

Swinging an elbow back with his SI in hand, Panton landed the hit to a guard's face, sending Jeniah stumbling backward. Several more unfamiliar guards appeared around them, countless hands clawing at his body before dragging Panton off into the darkness. Frantically calling out his name, Josie hustled after him, releasing a shot to her right.

Seeing Panton disappear sent Atana's heart pulsing up into her throat. For a moment, she second-guessed her judgment. Maybe it wasn't a test.

Two guards dropped in front of Cutter and Tanner, leaning out to kick their chests. Both sergeants deflected their attack and engaged with skill. Thuds of scuffling footsteps mixed with grunts and swishing fabric faded, leaving Atana and Bennett alone in the hallway.

They spun back-to-back, four guards closing in on their position. SIs outstretched, igniters glowing, the shepherds' radial vent chambers illuminated the stunned faces upon discharge. None were in Tohsa's original group.

Dread sank like a cold lead weight in Atana's middle.

Ducking to avoid the flames barreling overhead, the guards were swiftly on them throwing punch after punch, searching for a weakness, Atana swung a fist into the ribs of a guard, sending him crashing into the wall. She needed the team to be safe or the mission would fail.

Bennett lurched around her side, knocking her second attacker down by merely being the barrier the guard collided with. The gust of wind in his wake combed through her loose hairs with warm fingers. Atana whipped around to find his two were also writhing on the floor. An urge to thank him stilled in her throat. This was just work, their job, nothing more.

"Doesn't take much to stop them." His voice was low and soft but edged with ice. "Don't see the point in unnecessary force, even if they did attack first."

She didn't think Bennett could see the same degree of detail she could, with the way he blinked and squinted. The guards scrambled up. They were emaciated next to the average human but strong compared to the workers of the fields. Atana spread her feet, anticipating another attack.

Instead, she heard quiet vibrations come from every guard, originating from the faint blue light now pulsing in their pockets.

"Hide," the guards whispered. "Linoans spotted."

The hallways emptied, except for Atana and Bennett.

They're warning us? Atana knew then that it *was* a test and bolted back the direction their team had vanished.

Bennett caught up, urging her toward a marked space.

Sliding open the panel, she shoved him inside and placed a finger over her lips. He resisted, trying to push his way out. "I need to make sure my team is safe."

Grabbing his jacket she forced them back in the space and gritted her teeth. Why couldn't he just take an order? "I will find them. I see better in the dark than you do."

His lips parted in shock, a breath warming her face. "If you're not here in five minutes, I'm coming to look for you."

Stepping back, she studied his hazel eyes as they burned into hers through the shadows then slowly closed the door between them. Atana continued her search, unable to push Bennett's protective actions toward her and the team out of her thoughts. The steadfastness of his guardianship indicated a stronger investment than what UP expected. *Like Rio, who's not on serum.*

Atana saw Cutter's steel eyes glint as he hoisted Tanner up beside him into the ceiling trusses. A few paces more and she saw Josie's green e-rifle igniter fade out through a vent screen in the distance, a large arm that could only belong to Panton, around her waist.

A shadow approached, with a familiar set of glowing eyes. She grabbed Kylo and slung him around a corner, pressing him against the wall. Kylo stared at her in surprise. *Linoans.* Drawing her SIs, she took a silent but deep breath to wind herself down, and make sure she was focused, then listened.

I finally understand what he's talked about all these long-cycles.

Atana looked up at the guard not much older than herself. Admiration and curiosity lifted the scowl he'd worn earlier that day. *Who?*

Kylo just smiled and tapped her SI, pointing to his sternum. *Shoot here, most likely kill shot.* He pushed her behind him, beneath the stairwell and looked up. *Clear. Wait.*

She readied her fingers over the triggers. *So you are not him?*

Huh? You don't remember?

I was in a crash.

A crash? He twisted and looked back at her.

Over his shoulder, two gangly creatures appeared, moving with an eerie slowness. She recognized their spotted flesh instantly. A hot, prickling heat pounded her body.

The pair of Linoans turned at her gasp.

"Fuck!" Realizing her mistake, Atana raised her SIs to either side of Kylo. Unprompted, he pivoted, shielding her body with his own. She took the shots and sent the Suanoan assassins toppling from the fiery onslaught.

Kylo's eyes brightened, casting blue light over her face.

Atana dropped her arms. Glaring up at Kylo, she shifted around him.

I just had to know, he defended.

She paused, curious at the unexpected tenderness in his tone.

That you were up to the task, that the rumors were true.

Her nose crinkled in disgust. Agutra had rumors. Earth had rumors. She hated the notion everyone knew her better than she knew herself. Or thought they did. With the absence of so many years from her memory, she could only wonder. Wonder amidst the infuriated chaos of digging, scraping, clawing for pieces to the torn puzzle of her past.

Atana's fingers squeezed tighter around the grips of her SIs. There was one thing she could do that always shut the rumors up, something she could remember learning. Atana set foot in the hall, muscles tensed in preparation, scanning for Linoans.

Kylo rested an urgent hand on her shoulder. *There will be at least two more. Linoans always work in groups of four.*

I am always someone else's rat. She continued on her path and felt his fingers slip away. As each shadow became distinguishable, she took them down. Flaming, aqua heat burst from the radial vent slots of her right SI, a ball of fury taking down one Linoan. Then her left vented, right, and left again. *Two more somewhere.*

A chilled awareness crept down her neck. She slid back and spun in preparation for the attack, only to be cut off by a flash of brown leather. Bennett lunged out of the shadows, plowing over the Linoan. Its body lifted in the dim light, flattening out against the wall.

Bennett stepped back, fists clenched, shoulders rolled forward. The Linoan clambered up and swiped at him. Leaning away, Bennett avoided the swinging heel and took a shot through his thigh holster, knocking the red and black assailant to the floor.

Rebel. Atana glowered at Bennett. Pairs of silent glints sprung off the floor behind Bennett. Before she thought, her SIs were holstered and Bennett was stumbling off to the side from the tug of her hand on his jacket. "I gave you an order."

Hooked blade in hand, she ducked, allowing the swinging fist to find only empty space. Atana snagged one of the Linoan's ribs and effortlessly tugged the metal into bone. Using the anchor, deep in the Linoan's body, Atana jammed a hip in its side and flung the assailant over her shoulder and to the floor. It hissed out a groan as the tightly wound bowstrings of its body fell limp.

Bennett glanced over the Linoan at her feet, shame and reverence clashing in his eyes. His voice was sharp as a new blade. "A bullshit order. Death follows no rules. I protect my team. That includes you, now."

Soft footsteps made them turn to see Kylo sprinting their direction.

"Are you harmed?" he asked.

Bennett's words dripped with acid. "Why do you care?"

A tender warmth against Atana's low back pulled her mind away from the pending argument and deep into her body.

She'd just scolded Bennett. They were fighting Linoans. Why was his hand touching her in such a way? The heat spread up into her shoulders, comforting, inundating. Atana couldn't move.

Kylo said something muffled with a few edged notes.

A finger, no, Bennett's thumb, brushed over her jacket, thrusting that cold-banishing tickle into her stomach.

Bennett's body jerked beside her as he snapped out a reply she couldn't decipher. The pulse in her ears and the rush of air in and out of her lungs made it hard to focus. She could fight all day and not blink. But this was another animal. Why was he doing this? Why after Goss's death? Why now? What if more Linoans came? *Wake up, Nakio. Get out of this—whatever this is!*

Kylo side-stepped, eyes pinned on her. Filled with worry and pinched in anger, his quick scan of her confirmed what she felt. Something that wasn't supposed to be—was. Bennett moving between them once more didn't fight back the notion.

"Bennett, why are you always touching me?" she asked, more in thought than in conscious interrogation.

He stood with feet spread, arm still around her back, glaring at Kylo. "Guards must maintain physical contact with assignments whenever possible." It sounded like a textbook quote. Bennett shifted and softened his voice. "Sniper Guards, like Panton, have the highest requirements. Tech Guards, like Cutter, have the lowest. We are taught it calms and stabilizes our Specialty Sergeants, maintains protection-capable distance, and is feedback for us to know if you are safe."

"I-I'm not used to it," she admitted.

His arm jerked away, and he turned around. "It's making you uncomfortable?"

Atana opened her mouth to disagree when she felt the floor pulse and quiver beneath her boots. She looked down. The hot rush of Bennett's touch had left her arms dangling limply at her sides. She shook them out then tightened her grip around her SIs. *Kylo, hide. More are coming.*

He left after a breath's hesitation and one final sneer at Bennett.

There was no time to wonder if relations had just been broken for good, not when 'death followed no rules.'

"How much ammo do you have left?" Avoiding Bennett's eyes, Atana pushed on his shoulder, turning him around. Backing up against him, she felt his muscle-packed shoulder blades cushion hers. It was—reassuring.

Atana scanned the hallway, focusing on the thumping pattern her feet detected.

"Plenty. Why?" he asked.

She crouched in the middle of the hallway, Bennett lowering himself with her. "Warruks."

"How do you know?"

"I can feel the vibrations of their feet through mine." She took a long breath. "My body learned to listen before my ears ever heard a sound."

Bennett's shoulders tilted, and she twisted to meet his voice with an ear. "How many?"

Closing her eyes, she absorbed the waves deeper within herself until she could isolate each pace from the others. "Full set, eight."

"Shit."

"Agreed," she muttered, returning to her visual patrol. "Ready?"

The hall brightened with blue-green light. To any other, it would've been faint at best, probably unnoticeable. She knew Bennett's SI igniters were primed, sitting at shoulder height. To her, they were suns in the sky.

"Always."

The Warruks' multicolored forms thundered around the corners, weapons raised and vibrant orange in the distance.

Grips squeezed tight in her hands, Atana narrowed in on her targets with ease, letting go of every other thought, concern, and question. It was just her and Bennett against *them*.

The hall lit up with blue-green and orange fire. The pile of Linoan bodies was an effective shield from the Warruks' assault.

Back and forth the flames danced—a circus of fireworks.

Up for the shot. Down for the hit.

Smoking flesh. Glowing metal walls, all in orange. Blues never missed.

Atana sent one last shot arcing down the corridor, a precision mass of writhing fury.

A heavy, hot body collided with her side throwing her onto her back. Panic lanced through her at the surprise of attack. Bennett's chest pressed into hers, his hands catching her wrists, preventing her from firing at his head. He didn't tense or shudder, just lay as if accepting a possible fate.

Orange bloomed overhead in a blazing rocket, punching through her recent position. It lit in his frightened eyes when it passed, an impossibility in such a position.

She spluttered, unable to still her heart. This was wrong. She was supposed to be the best, be unstoppable, invincible.

A set of feet landed at their side. The walls painted in dark indigo light to the sound of a spooling turbo. Peeking up at the whirring whine, a translucent bubble around a humanoid creature, veined in cragged light, Atana and Bennett watched it send a radiant pulse out from its back. Coursing around hundreds of thin strands, the pulses joined together before the creature's body, releasing in a string of flaring orbs. A luminous rosebud-of-a-weapon not framed in metal or initiated by any visible structure.

The last Warruk on Bennett's end fell. The hall grew silent.

Bennett's body, now having stiffened above her, lifted, his hands frantically sliding over her curves in the darkness. "Nakio? Are you—"

This level of physical contact was more than she'd had in the last thirteen years combined. It was distracting. Too much. Pushing on him, she sat up, forcing him back.

"It's my job to protect you," he said, a begrudging twinge in his tone.

"I'm fine." When she looked into his golden eyes, she grabbed his arm. A fire burned behind both irises that he seemed unaware of. The color faded after his blink and it made her wonder what she had seen.

Bennett cocked his head. But she wasn't going to add stress to an already over-complicated situation or doubt in his mind over her sanity. She had enough doubt for the both of them.

The humanoid beside Atana and Bennett offered his hands, helping them stand.

"I am Rimsan. Are you both okay?" His voice was low and smooth as they dusted themselves off. Cracks of light broke through in jagged lines on his ridged forehead and obsidian cheeks. Hundreds of long, thin, luminous strands waved behind his back—arced wings made of glowworms.

Panton broke the silence from behind, the team straggling up on his six. "What in God's name—"

The slender man twisted to his words and let out a nervous laugh. "I'm a Primvera. These are my flumes." A few of the tentacles waved like fingers. "They are a durable extension of my nervous system and send out Kilavi energy because I'm a Prime."

"Rimsan, what do you think you're doing? You want to get us all killed?" Kylo hissed through clenched teeth. "You are supposed to keep cover!"

"I am tired of hiding, like everyone else!" Rimsan's strands spiked with his frustration. "Except, apparently, you. I am glad I am not from your sector." His light vanished as his flumes rolled up like ferns against his back, and he headed into the darkness.

"Jeniah!" Tohsa wriggled free of the many hands restraining him, his eyes following Rimsan's path.

"I was following Kylo order. We all was!"

"And I was following—" Tohsa trailed off meeting Atana's gaze. "This is our chance to gain control, for everyone, including Verros."

"It was a test. They passed," Kylo said, turning to the team.

"You sent the Linoans?" Josie asked in shock from Panton's side.

"No," Kylo replied. "But you performed well. You have earned the right to walk free." He nodded. "We will discuss routes in the early-cycle."

"Why didn't you fight?" Josie snapped. "Why, if you are so good, did you hide? Like cowards?"

Kylo whipped around, his eyes a furious blue beneath narrowed brows.

Atana knew the answer but was more in shock at the sergeant's sudden accusation and implication. Josie had clearly never known anything but to plow her way through every battle. A one-track mindset like that got a lot of shepherds killed when that wasn't the needed tactic.

"Guns blazing is not how we survive up here. We obey our rulers. We warn sectors of attacks. We hide."

One of the other guards cut in. "We don't have weapons like you. Only a handful of Warruk guns we steal off the dead but cannot carry because they glow. They are stashed for when we need their parts to keep sectors operational."

A guard fingered a pair of slices through his shirt, quietly talking to someone in the back. "This is why I hate new clothes. Always ruined day one." The skin stretched over ribs beneath sent a pang through Atana's chest.

The boy from her dreams came to mind, the dew on his body a sign of the immense pain he was in. They shouldn't have been sweating in that heartless metal box. *So cold.* Atana shivered, the memory of the sting from the frosted exam table biting into her back, hips, heels, fingertips.

Another guard piped up, breaking her free of the past. "Most only have knives unless they are Elite kiatna, like Rimsan." He flipped his crudely hammered shank in the air, the handle wrapped with frayed fabric. "We fight only when necessary, to not draw too much attention."

"Tohsa, get the scrub crew." Kylo's larger shadow waved the guards away. "Eih ahna. Avi mitras."

"Eih Mitron." Tohsa grumbled but walked off with the others.

127

"You and your team remember how to get back?" Kylo asked, tossing Atana a short, defeated look.

"Yes." Bennett snorted before Atana could reply and pushed past Kylo, escorting his team through the halls.

Atana trailed behind, glancing back to where the guard stood alone in the darkness amidst the bodies. Kylo's shoulders sagged despite his attempt to straighten his posture. For a single moment, she imagined a life like his.

Fighting for scraps, for pieces, for life.

I understand.

Chapter 22

BENNETT GROWLED when they re-entered the container. "I told you we couldn't trust her!"

Every member of the team buzzed with the recent events, their hands fidgeting over their weapons.

"It was just a test," Atana replied. "Of faith and capability."

"That was no fucking test. That was a damned ambush! They're not even united. How are we supposed to fight with them?" He flung a hand toward the hallway.

"Fight? Command never said anything." Atana looked at him, a silent admiration in her eyes as they filtered into the bunk room again.

"Oh, come on. I know you're thinking about it because I am too. I just don't know how to trust these people anymore, or whatever they are. Was that Chamarel's plan? Or just Kylo and his personal agenda?

Chamarel appeared in the middle archway. "It was Kylo, wanting to make sure you could handle the shadows. I don't think he counted on the Linoans or the Warruks."

Bennett held back his urge to say what he felt: betrayed. His instincts had been right. Inside he was a twisted-up knot because he had ignored them. He'd placed a higher value on Atana's unusual skill and knowledge than his own because of Command, because he hadn't a clue what to make of this place.

He released a hot breath through his nose. "We could have died out there, lost good people, people who can help, because of your guard's reckless endangerment."

"But you did not," Chamarel replied.

Wiping a hand down his face in frustration, Bennett could feel the hot prickles of anger starting again. His serum was wearing off faster than normal. "Don't downplay the element of risk just because you took a chance and came out on top. These are my people. I am responsible for their safety. And I do not take lies and deception lightly!"

"Bennett," Atana called softly, tugging on his forearm. When he looked down at her, he caught a flicker of regret in her eyes. It crushed his fury in a cold second. "I agree, but it's in the past."

She looked to Chamarel. "What your guard has done has earned only our distrust. However, that doesn't change the needs of your workers or our people. We are two kinds of potential, but together, we can set things on a different course, if you can promise to not pull any more stunts like that. We need our people in the best condition possible to bring the least amount of pain to your crews."

Chamarel's hands had wadded up the fabric of her robes at her sides. Bennett noted her hunkered shoulders, though her eyes remained bold and serious. Kylo's intentions were not in line with hers. "Early next cycle, I will call our lead guard in to work over routes and guard posts so you may know who you can contact for assistance. I do hope your people on Earth can offer us help in return."

"I hope so too," Atana replied. "Tanner has some maps on his laptop that we were able to download from the ship's main system. I would like to discuss them with you then as well."

Chamarel bowed. "Rest well. You have earned respect among us."

She turned and disappeared out the front of the hut.

Bennett loosely gestured to the cots. "Best get some sleep. Tomorrow we check out." The crew hesitantly sat.

"Why do I get the feeling they run every infiltrate crew like this?" Cutter lifted his shotgun from his shoulder for the first guard shift. "She said earlier that many have tried."

"It's because of a prophecy." Atana shifted between her feet and looked out across the fields.

Bennett surveyed her lowered head, the mahogany waves of her ponytail draped over a shoulder, her long bangs hiding her face. "Is this what you two were talking about earlier?"

"Yeah." She said it so quietly he almost didn't hear it. "There's supposed to be someone from a blue planet destined to save the slaves from this—" She lifted a hand, directing outside the door. "The method isn't explained. But this being is described as looking like—" With an audible swallow, she lifted her red-rimmed eyes. "Me."

Chapter 23

SHE CRIED OUT.

Atana covered her face with her arms, hoping she hadn't awoken Bennett or his team.

Panton grumbled in his sleep.

She drew in a deep, silent breath through quaking lips. She didn't have the energy or the control to explain herself now—not without breaking down. Her spine was hot with the memory of Suanoan nodes: the immense pressure, the way they melted to her bone, and the seizing twinges when they wrapped around her nerves, finally taking control.

Cutter leaned inside the door from his post. "You all right, ma'am?"

Someone *had* heard. Tensing every muscle to calm her trembling, she pushed up from her bed and stepped outside. "Yes. Just wish the past would stay there sometimes, you know?" *Please don't ask.*

This place was unveiling too much for her to sort on such little sleep.

He nodded, fingering the grips on his shotgun. "Do you want guard shift, again, ma'am?"

"No. Clearing my head." Surveying the slump in the rigid posture of the man leaning against the door frame, snippets of gunfire and blood flashed like lightning in her eyes. "How are you holding up?"

"Within parameters." His gray eyes stared at her, listless. "Give me a whistle if you need anything."

He was the tight-laced, tormented tough. She could hear it right through his hardened exterior. "And you as well."

Atana aimed for a forested spot near the middle of the container, with a rock shelf thirty meters up overlooking the despondent survivors and their meager encampments below. Sitting on the edge, she scanned the imitation horizon to her right—a little over ten kilometers. She looked to the door they had entered from. *About twice the distance.* Staring, unfocused, she calculated.

That's almost 60,000 acres per container. With the irrigation system, the convincing sunlight, and stars, their method is efficient and effective. A wave of nausea hit her. *Effective but unequal.*

Straightening, Atana felt her back crackle. She let her shoulders hang forward. All the disguises she displayed to mask who she was on the inside could finally drop if only for a few seconds. She could be a plain woman, just another being, one without reputations for, or expectations of, completing impossible tasks. Perched solitude was her sole option for introspection. It was how she kept her sanity when the visions wouldn't let her rest.

There was a strange beauty in the strength of the lives hanging on to a shred of hope for their freedom. And it was a shred. They had no dignity in this place, only honor. Kylo and Chamarel had shown her that. Life had never given Atana many options. The prophecy was just added proof.

Her next decision could be their last.

"You found my favorite meditation spot." A voice boomed down on her from the mountain's crest.

She sprang up and spun around, whipping her hooked blade out of its sheath in defense, scrunching her eyes toward the sound. He was the second man to catch her off guard in the last decade. Unnerved and breathing rapidly to calm the blood rushing through her exhausted body, she began to doubt her capabilities and focus.

The man hopped off the peak, landing heavily on the shelf a few meters from her. Her boots quivered with the rock underfoot. He stood slowly, his blue eyes brilliantly illuminated between the boughs of the trees.

As the shadows slipped from the man like wind under a cloak, barely hidden beneath his faded, pocketed shirt, she couldn't deny his powerful structure. His skin was the same gray with blue markings as Kios's from the day before, though this man's were perfectly symmetrical.

Her blade remained fixed in her hand, her muscles awaiting the command. *At me, I fight; backs away, I let him go.* Scanning his ruffled haircut and sturdy dimensions, she remembered him from the yard.

"I apologize for Kylo's behavior. Sometimes he forgets his place," he said with a vocal density and smoothness of the rock they stood on. He pried his gaze from hers to pan the fields. "The closest thing you can get to peace is up here."

He's a perimeter guard. She hesitantly let her arms drop to rest at her sides. "You are larger than most I have seen. Why?"

He glanced over his shoulder at her and slid his hands into the patched-in pockets of his haggard pants. "I had a foundation on a planet. Many here did not. Here, everyone gets one item for meal. One Brocanip fruit, one Hatoga roll, or one Vesha stalk. For those like me, we make the most effective guards. We need more food and earn it pulling double shifts—

working in the fields and then patrolling. But Kylo, Tohsa, Rimsan, and I have been hunting Quinock. They eat the crops. Sometimes we catch enough to share at meal." *They breed like Japous, filthy rodents.*

A long silence stretched between them. Atana wasn't sure if he was assessing her as a threat or a potential ally. The way he'd planted himself between her and the trail left little room for escape, except maybe down the cliff. He looked away as if changing his mind over a matter previously decided. She gave the cragged edge a glance. A twelve-meter drop, few possible handholds. It would require holstering her weapon.

"Kylo and Tohsa were surprised when you saved the child that you spoke Xahu'ré." His eyes swept back to her boots. Pinpointing every crease in her leathers, they crawled up to her collar with deep focus as if to memorize every one.

His vocabulary and complete sentences, without missing words, like Teek, made her curious. This man's 'they' came out more like 'day,' his Rs rolled like a purr, and short As sounded more like short Us. Flickers of her collected memories leapt forward simultaneously, each demanding attention, claiming a connection, and then fading before she could mentally grasp them to ask why. Why were they so adamant, at hearing his voice?

"I lead the guards, so Chamarel teaches me many things." He strolled around her and confidently stopped one foot's length from the cliff. "Especially the English dialect of Ranimi. In all, I speak four languages."

The man shamelessly traced her length, again. Atana back-stepped. Attention this intense was abnormal and growing uncomfortable. "I apologize for intruding on your privacy."

"You don't have to go," he promptly offered, his stoic face suddenly creasing with insecurity. "Guards don't get much of a life up here."

Atana brushed away the long bangs that had fallen from her ponytail and tried to turn and leave. A large hand snagged her elbow.

His fingers were solid as steel. "Please."

She tugged from the panic. There was no reason to trust this male. He didn't have an assignment with her nor had he vocalized reason for his touch. He didn't have *permission*. Her reflexes kicked her arm up with force, freeing herself from his grasp.

Atana lunged backward, her hooked blade in hand as she raised her fists. Loose gravel scraped under her boots. Locked on his every move, she found herself panting, struggling through a hot rush of adrenaline.

Steadying her breath took more effort with every muscle in her body tensed for battle.

He lifted his palms in innocence, a flash of rejection crossing his gaze. "I won't hurt you, ever. I swear! Please don't hide from me. I just, I remember you." *Please don't go. I'm begging you.*

Atana's brain pounded, heavy with his thoughts, making her wince at the depth of his tone. She knew she shouldn't let her guard down, but couldn't keep her eyes from slamming shut. Thinking back to Lavrion from a few days before, and Chamarel, evoked a fresh awareness of how little she seemed to know about herself. A mission-critical conundrum. *Could they be lying? For what purpose?*

She stumbled a step away.

"My name is Azure," he said with caution. "May I ask what happened to your—"

Looking up to his eyes through the pain pressing out against her temples, she watched him motion toward her scar. Her mind rewound: tumbling through the blazing cabin, with no up or down, and chunks of metal debris pummeling her flaccid body. Thirteen years ago, she and eight others had survived the rescue, bodies broken in a crash landing, her past knocked into darkness. But tonight felt more disorienting and significant than that day. Something was about to split wide open. The tearing sensation she felt in her chest, stirred with the clouds of fractured memories, made Atana think it was her.

Azure was quiet for several moments. He blinked fast as if holding back an ocean of hurt then looked off to a place beyond the confines of the sector.

She examined his posture from the side, how oddly it reminded her of—*what was it?* The ache in her brain faded faster around him than Chamarel.

"Up here, it no longer matters where we are from." He quietly cleared his throat behind a hand, a sign of his deeply buried suffering. "Most of the planets these life forms once called home have been completely destroyed, nothing left. Vioras, my home planet, included."

There was a heavy silence, the kind that makes a person feel like exploding and imploding at the same time. It seemed pointless to say anything. No words could comfort that kind of loss.

His voice rumbled low and soft. "What do you remember from thirteen long-cycles ago?"

Atana knew it would be breaking Rule Six, again. But thirteen years was a very specific request. It couldn't be a coincidence. So she made an exception. "I lost most of my memory when I was in the rescue crash. All I have are the memories I have created since and—" She didn't really want to admit her truth to another man she'd just met.

"And what?" Azure's attention locked hopefully on her eyes.

Her heart jittered with his focus. "Well, I—I think I feel things in my dreams. I see things which seem familiar like I should remember them. The memories never come to full fruition though. I don't really sleep, can't. I'm as awake when I'm asleep."

Seeing a partial smile form on his face, she laughed nervously.

"Everything is in color. I always get the full-effect: sounds, smells, and physical sensations, not just the visualizations. They are painful, physically and mentally, usually waking me with a jolt. Memories of testing, all the procedures—" She hesitated, knowing she was breaking Rule Six again. "I'm sorry. You didn't need to know all that. I have vivid memory-like dreams."

Atana wondered what had made her open up so freely to this new individual. There was a disconnect between her and the other shepherds. They would not understand. They hadn't seen what she had. Their dreams weren't like hers. She was not one of them. Him, she was still sorting out.

Azure scanned the rock beneath, clearly working over a thought.

Her hands wrapped around her arms as if the chill from the table in testing wasn't just a memory. Maybe standing there, with him, was the dream?

He swept the dusty ground with his bare toes. "Those who survive the Suanoa testing and those of us with stronger telepathic abilities have the most vivid and reoccurring dreams. Drifting—uncontrolled thoughts and visions—is normal for us."

She slipped her blade in its sheath. "So you have such dreams too?"

"Almost every sleep cycle." He rubbed the back of his neck like he wasn't ready to say what was on his mind. "I have been praying for your return."

Atana couldn't tamp back the disappointment muddying her words. "Yes, so everyone tells me."

His brows lifted in surprise. *Right, she doesn't remember.*

A knock in the primal part of her brain made her twist to scan the trees behind her.

"What is it? If it was another perimeter breach, I would have been notified." Azure drew a tiny, metal square from his pants pocket.

Atana squinted at him. *I don't need a device to know if another life form is close, except, for some reason, you.*

I know you don't—me? A furry, rat-like Quinock skittered across the opening and down the face of the rock bluff, momentarily distracting him. He twitched as if to lunge after it then thought otherwise.

"You what?" she asked. Azure's stuttering made her face tighten. *I don't trust you, and hiding things from me isn't going to earn it. What aren't you telling me?*

Azure hesitated. *You notice things most others can't because you were born without the ability to hear. You* feel *life.*

"How do you know that?" she growled, wrapping her fingers around the handle protruding from one of her thigh holsters. When he didn't respond immediately, she barked, "Answer the question!"

"I, because we were—"

A loud cracking of tree branches, snapping like dried up bones, came from the narrow pathway leading off the mountain.

She snatched an SI from her holster and extended it, heart pounding with exhaustion, confusion, and if she were honest with herself, a little fear.

Chapter 24

SNAP.

Bennett burst out into the opening, pointing his glowing barrel at Azure. "Who the hell are you?"

Azure's tone sharpened. "Who are you?" *She is not yours.*

Ignoring Azure's declaration, Atana retracted her finger from the trigger, her igniter darkening. "Why are you following me, Bennett?"

"I don't trust these people, or beings, or whatever they are. Not after Kylo's deception." His eyes drilled into Azure. "I remember you. You passed me the first day we were here."

One of Azure's cheeks tensed.

"He's a guard, Bennett." She slipped her SI in its stiff, fabric resting place on her thigh. When the men didn't budge, she stepped in between them.

When his barrel lined up with her, she froze, her vision blacked-out.

Three pallid figures replaced Bennett, holding radiant, amber weapons, pointed at her. The room was dark and deathly cold. Rage curled her fingers tight around the wood of a bladed staff. The metallic scent of burnt blood and flesh hung in the air.

Atana stumbled.

A hand braced her back.

"Are you okay?" Azure's deep voice rippled through her memories, sending tsunamis of distortion through the images, making her dizzy.

"Don't touch her." Bennett redirected the barrel around Atana. Taking a fistful of her jacket, he yanked her back into his arms.

Atana blinked forcibly, her chest heaving. She clumsily pushed back from Bennett, her mind a muddled mess of past and present. "I was just thinking, without distractions. He hasn't done me any harm."

"I don't like it when you take off on your own like this, Nakio." His voice softened, his eyes narrowed in concern. *How do I know he won't hurt you?*

"Because I won't," Azure defended.

Bennett's face paled. "Excuse me?"

"Telepathic." Azure gave him a wickedly mischievous grin, shifting in Bennett's direction.

Azure's chest was back in his sights. "Don't. Move."

Atana stared, dumbfounded. The two men stood primed for the other to attack.

"Please, stop, both of you." Their heads swiveled toward her. "We don't need to make this situation any harder on ourselves and everyone than it already is." She placed a hand over Bennett's SI, pushing it toward the ground. "He has done nothing."

"You're missing the point, Nakio." Bennett gestured a hand at Azure. "After the recent attack, why are you defending him? And when are we going to spend time working on the routes we're going to take?"

"Tomorrow, and I'm not defending him, specifically. I defend peace, for every innocent life. It's the oath you took too." She frowned. "What's gotten into you? Have you had your recent serum dose?"

"Yes, of course. I just— I know you need to rest, not to be wasting time with this—this alien!" Bennett contended.

"Hey!" Azure's baritone voice yelled in disagreement. "Technically we're all aliens, humans included. None of us are from here."

Bennett lifted his SI, pointing it at Azure. "You need to keep your head in the game too, Nakio. You're not supposed to get involved with anyone, either."

"Ill-founded assumption, Bennett. Besides," she said, moving in close to him, "you kissed me the other night, remember?" Bennett glanced at her lips. "Twice." There was a moment of heated silence between them, cinders stirring her insides. "I can take care of myself."

Ignoring her first comment, he leaned in against her ear. "I know you can." He peered up at Azure. "It's not your actions I'm concerned about."

Azure tugged her aside and stepped in between the two of them, his glare burning bright in the darkness. His fists clenched and muscles tensed as he pushed up against Bennett's barrel. "If you're going to shoot me, do it already. It won't be the first time I've been shot, and I can guarantee it won't be the last. Get it over with!"

Staggering to the side, Atana stared in shock that Bennett would be so aggressive and that the stranger would be so defensive of her.

Bennett's grip tightened on his SI. The hot igniter charred Azure's shirt, sending tiny wisps of smoke twirling up into the stagnant air.

Atana's flashback returned.

Three flaming bursts slammed into a shield in front of her. She caved with the power of the blow. Toppling backward, she discovered it was the boy from her dreams, lying in her lap. His body smoking, burnt, and blistering, she cried out. The torches in his eyes faded. An anchor dropped, yanking her heart down to the floor, following the fluids trickling off his incapacitated form.

Vibrations of rage swallowed her whole.

"Bennett!" Atana slipped, once again, between the two men, her palms shoving him back a step. A radiant, teal color filtered over her vision. Her body tingled with anger until she saw the alarm on his face.

Bennett lowered his weapon. Holstering it weakly, he shifted away from her.

"I will see you at camp in the morning, yes? We can talk then?" He didn't wait long for a response before disappearing into the trees.

Atana wondered why he was suddenly so compliant. *Another outburst? What's happening to me? All those years of training. Come on, Nakio. You're better than this.*

"What was that all about?" Azure asked.

She fumbled through what to say, staring at the sliver of a shadowed path Bennett had retreated down. "I don't think his serum is working."

"Neither is yours." Gently drawing back a few wavy strands of her hair, he exposed the light casting out over her cheeks.

She pulled back, uncomfortable with the contact. Too many people knew who she was, what she was, and wanted to touch her. "How do you know I'm on serum?"

He hummed. "The flashing on the band around your arm saying: Serum Dose Overdue?"

"You can read English?"

"I know a lot about your kind and your planet." His faint smile fell in an instant. "Is he your mate?"

She rotated the screen of her wristband and confirmed Azure's words were true. "Mate? No."

"Good— I mean not good because you aren't matched." He cringed. "He seems overprotective. You seem like the type who can take care of yourself."

And you seem far too interested. "Members of the Universal Protectors are not allowed to mate, marry, or have any sorts of relationship connections. It leads to irrational thoughts and decisions, which create inappropriate actions." She gestured at the path. "That's why we developed the serum. Obviously, we have some dosage concerns to work out."

"You can never be matched with someone?" He frowned. "Most of us aren't either. We can if we choose though."

"Not us." Knowing nothing about his species' relationship traditions, she didn't want to step on any toes or start anything she couldn't finish. "Are you?"

"No. Been waiting."

"For what?" Disconcerted about the teal haze blurring her vision, she plucked her blade from its sheath and used its glossy, tempered, surface to discover the source.

"The right one."

Staring for a moment at the brilliant blue-green of her irises as they reflected across the metal, she debated Chamarel's words. *This man is Xahu'ré. I am part Xahu'ré. I had two visions while awake. That never happens.*

She thought about the boy from her dreams.

No, he couldn't be, could he?

A larger-than-average hand lifted and, with a single finger, directed her chin up until her glowing eyes locked on his. She could see her light reflecting in their crystal clear surfaces. She wanted to pull away. It was wrong, according to Command. It compromised shepherds. But something kept her still this time. He was a constant, a fixed point. She felt stable, though everything about him made her flounder in a storming sea of rising emotions.

She must remember something. Maybe if she could see it— Azure tilted his head, eyes devouring her every feature.

A faint, echoing alert worked its way in between them, breaking the hypnosis his presence had put her in. Atana cursed, holstering her blade, remembering her overdue serum.

The chart on her screen displayed her levels at two-fold threshold and rising. She'd never been that high and lined up to tap the flashing option to inject.

"Wait!" Azure grabbed her arms, inspecting the wristband. "Before you do, I want to show you something."

Startled, Atana looked up to the longing in his gaze.

He swiftly separated her hands from one another and moved in against her body, cradling her head in his palms. His nose delicately graced the side of hers. Something about him took the strength from her legs and the breath from her lungs.

His fingers trembled, interwoven with her hair. "Can you trust me, just for a few moments? I don't want to hurt you." *I want to help you remember.*

Atana studied the sapphire light burning in his irises. It circulated like eddies, sucking her deep, under the swirling water. Her forehead barely felt the touch of his.

A whirlwind of memories flooded her consciousness, making her dizzy. She reached out, finding only his capable arms to grab on to. Wrapping her fingers up and over his tensed forearms, she fought through the storm in her mind, toward the voice calling to her. Azure stood in the gray mist, his right hand opened. Grasping tightly onto him, the vision cleared.

A girl, jingling keys in hand, leapt over a pile of slumped Warruk guards. Her cage was open across the hall, her fingers frantically twisting key after key until one clicked. When the girl lifted her head, Atana realized it was the two of them—just teenagers.

With a gray blur, as if time were rushing forward, the rescue team from Earth, in black fatigues, appeared at the end of a hall. They grabbed everyone with amber lights pulsing in their left wrists.

"Luna!" One of the shepherds searched the cells in a panic, fear stretching his face.

Atana and Azure had met a testing subject by that name and led the way. She was in a room farther down the hall, lying on an operating slab, barely breathing. The man tried to scoop her up until blood oozed out her back. She screamed.

Another male in black appeared in the doorway. "Sensei, our ship. It's gone, in pieces. We have to take one of their pods."

When Sensei looked down, the girl had passed out. A tear stood at the edge of his eyelids. Atana and Azure watched as he kissed her forehead and carried her out the door, pulling her tightly against his chest.

"Papa's so sorry, baby," he whispered with another kiss to her smudged face, her golden baby-dreads swinging with his steps. "I love you."

Reaching the airlock, the group found three Suanoa blocking their escape. The second shepherd drew weapons and fired on them. The

Suanoa countered, launching their own attack. In a blur of lucent, red plasma, his body slammed against the wall, a smoking distraction.

Sensei yelled at Atana and Azure to run for the airlock, but they were cornered.

Azure guided her body behind his. Wisps of blood-orange flames and smoke curled up into the air. Three searing blasts hit his body, and he fell into her arms. The two of them tumbled to the floor. Her hands weakly cupped the face. Overhead, she shrieked and sobbed, a mix of fear and agony contorting her gaunt face. He reached a quaking hand toward her chin. But it fell with his eyelids before his skin could meet hers.

Atana gasped, squeezing Azure's arms, breaking free of his memory. A familiar look of powerlessness scrolled across his eyes.

Cells awakened in her, ones dormant for over a decade. The twisting, writhing energy at her core was realigning, each electron recognizing his presence, her spirit slowly pulling itself back together. Azure's connection to her was too strong for any synthesized serum to manage, even after Rio's auto-inject programming kicked in.

Her memories flooded in through open doors. Azure's features became more familiar every moment she traced and retraced them: his square jawline, the slightly crooked nose with its rounded tip, and the layers of cerulean rings in his irises set beneath a prominent brow. At the top of his forehead, the centered point of a V-shaped stripe barely peeked out from beneath his dark grey, disheveled hair. Xahu'ré stripes were like tattoos, immovable and easily identifiable characteristics, setting each individual apart from the next.

She sputtered. *The shepherds, Sensei, he tore me from you. I tried to stay!*

It's okay. He paused, looking down at nothing in particular. *Kylo found me and took me to Chamarel. Though my scars are—* His large fingers played gently in her hair. *It took many cycles to get out of bed. But I healed.* He straightened, running a tender thumb over her bottom lip.

She couldn't understand why he would sacrifice himself for her. Atana delicately touched his chest. *Can—can I see them? The scars?* She slid a finger under one of the crudely-cut twig buttons on his shirt.

You don't want to. They're not— He jerked away, running a hand over the thermo-stripe hugging the back of his neck.

Atana wasn't sure how to proceed. He had become so strong and so good, despite what he had been through, despite her having left him behind.

She had completely forgotten about UP, about her mission. All she could see was him, his eyes, his skin, and feel the guilt like liquid cement in her veins.

Chapter 25

AZURE DELICATELY traced the line on her forehead, the one that made her once loving eyes now inspect him as if everything he said was a lie. *You can change your mind.*

I want to see. I need to, to know what you went through.

Azure swallowed the consuming flare of visceral lust that sent his blood roaring through his body and prayed.

It was like meeting her all over again. Fear tore at his insides. *If she doesn't take it well, what am I supposed to do?* He knew the chances of seeing her again, that she was still alive in the universe somewhere, were slim to null. The thought had never crossed his mind that if he ever found her, she wouldn't even remember him after all they had been through.

He admired her gleaming mahogany veil, silken and smooth, her loose strands a far cry from the dirty dreads he once knew. He struggled to keep himself calm as her fingers tugged on the buttons of his shirt.

Her eyes lifted to his, and gingerly, she encouraged the fabric back and over his shoulders, letting it fall from his arms to the ground at their feet.

No one has seen these since Chamarel took me in. Are you still sure? With a nod from her, Azure took a deep breath and crossed his arms. Grasping the shredded bottom edge of his stretched-out tank top, he peeled it up and over his head, dropping it beside the other.

He couldn't look at her. He was waiting for her to scream and run or be disgusted and sick like so many of the ones who had cared for him.

The once dirty, scrawny Xahu'ré boy he'd been was long gone, replaced by a muscular weapon he'd built to protect his fellow workers. If she remembered anything, it wouldn't be this.

Atana's wristband flashed in the darkness, drawing his attention back to her.

He watched her scour the three large, silvery blotches with crooked lines, like lightning, radiating out across the surface of his skin. They marred his right shoulder, the upper left area of his abdomen, and part of his lower right abdomen, before merging with the top crest of his hip. She covered her shaking lips with a hand, tears creeping down her cheeks.

Her voice came out raspy and strained. "Do any of them hurt?"

Azure shook his head, unwilling to risk scaring her more. His skin was covered in streaks, pocks, and jagged hash-marks, not just over the muscles and joints like hers. Several of his thermo-stripes had become almost indistinguishable over the last few long-cycles, having been rearranged by so many weapons and tools.

Any other person would have backed away. But empathy reflected in her eyes, and she moved in close, her fingers gingerly reaching for him. The nerves beneath were too damaged to sense her touch over the scars that were proof of his unwavering love for her.

The fingers of her left hand found the rounded divot beneath his clavicle, from their first encounter with one another. When the flashbacks flooded her thoughts, he opened himself to observe, curious what she would remember.

She leaned over his testing slab, tears in her eyes. The blood on his chest and pooled at his back were devastating. "I don't want to be alone anymore." Her forehead drooped enough to connect to his, a child unknowing of the significance of such intimate contact.

Azure's spine tingled, as she traced the outline of the black markings crawling up and over his left collarbone. *The Marakou gave me symbolic armor for protecting sector 219,* he offered. *We were in their area to track down a group that was raiding bunkhouses and raping the females. I pulled a girl out of their grasp before she could be harmed.* He sputtered to a stop. *I'm sorry. I didn't mean to ramble.*

Atana vacantly scanned the distant fields behind him, her other hand resting on his side.

The heat of her skin against his sent a wave of relief through him. *It's okay. I know this is a lot to process.*

She whined a grunt and slid her arms around his bare back, pressing her cheek to the broad planes of his chest.

His arms lifted in reflex, coupled with a back step. She clung to him as if she never wanted to let go again. Closing his eyes, he basked in the sensation. Azure wrapped himself around her, nuzzling into the feathery waves of hair on top of her head. She was so clean, filled out, and effervescing the sweet scent of life. His lungs shook as his protective walls crumbled, finally breaking down after cycles of hopeless faith. Azure drew in a deep breath of her and held it, letting every last bit of her scent reassure his brain this was real.

She was alive. Thirteen years he'd waited, wondered, prayed, busied himself to the point of exhaustion so the thought that she was gone didn't have space to creep in. And now he felt her healed skin beneath his fingertips, her lusciously long and combed out hair sweeping over his bare arms so lightly it made his muscles quiver and his stomach dance. Atana was familiar and different, healthier, stronger, but still falling, with all her weight, against him.

Memories flickered into her thoughts once more. Azure caught them in Ether.

With the glaive in hand, her muscles burning with fury, she stared down the three Suanoa that had taken him from her. In a blur of blinding steel, she cut them down, savoring the moment each succumbed to a spattered pile across the floor. And all too quickly, she found herself limp, on the floor, being dragged away. Her throat ached and scratched, screaming for Azure, her fingers straining toward his fading silhouette.

Droplets sparkled down Atana's face, illuminated by the re-emerged light from her eyes. *Thank you for reminding me.* Her breaths choppy and violent, she bound him tighter to her. "I have been lost for so long."

I know how you feel. Azure rested his mouth to the top of her head, hot drops slipping between his closing eyes. *Thank you for remembering me.*

...

Bennett couldn't quite make out the shadowy figure heading toward the hut from the tree line. He jerked forward, away from the doorframe where he stood guard. Pointing Cutter's shotgun out across the darkened fields, his right eye trained down the faint, green sights. Two teal orbs appeared, the figure closing in. Breaking out into the starlight, he saw her and let the gun rest across his front.

"I apologize for my outburst." Atana touched his shoulder with the lightness of a butterfly. The soft timbre of her words was unexpected. "Thank you for giving me some space, Jameson. I'm sorry I was so hard on you."

He fumbled, felt his mouth hanging open, and slammed it shut, giving her only a lethargic nod.

"You are right to be concerned because this place is different, something our rules were not prefaced to handle. But we should not judge others before we get to know them. Up here, we are the aliens to them."

The fire in her irises shut down his retaliation. Questions flooded in like a burst dam. *Who was the stranger she was with? What made her eyes glow like his? They don't look alike. He's telepathic? And what caused her sudden change in attitude?* Not that he minded. It just wasn't normally like her, or the reputation she had as a shepherd. Then again, he had only known her for a few days.

She smiled from the shadows as she lay on her bunk and closed her eyes.

Ultimately, he was left with one thought replaying in his mind. *She called me 'Jameson.'*

Chapter 26

ATANA ROLLED HER HEAD in confusion the next morning as she and Chamarel sat, once again, alone in the front room. The team had remained in the bunk room, reviewing the pairing order for the mission that day, leaving her a few moments to talk alone with Chamarel. "I don't understand. You want me to do what?"

I am entrusting you with the task of saving Teek and Paramor. Please, you need to practice. Chamarel motioned to her forehead.

Atana tried to relax her body, hoping it would help her focus. It had been a long time since she had been able to concentrate enough to meditate for more than a few seconds. Memory-visions came to her easily now after the events of the previous evening, though she was having exceptional difficulty in quieting the conscious thoughts in her mind.

Only telepaths can see images when we communicate openly through Ether. This is Healer Paramor. He is the one who must lead the workers if the chains that bind us are broken.

Blocks of color sharpened in Atana's mind.

She squinted up at the bright lights obstructing her already blurry vision, pain screaming through her stomach. Platinum hair flowed down his back, matching his silvery skin. His gray and white irises seemed honest, worth the trust he requested. A tiny, white feather stuck out of a corner seam of the burlap behind him. Her mind faded into the familiar, murky dimension between.

Atana lifted her head to confront Chamarel about this vision, wondering why the perspective made it seem like a memory of her own.

You must save him. He is our only hope for a future on a new planet. Chamarel's eyes opened. *He is the reason you and Azure are what you are and why you are alive today.* Atana's heart broke into a sprint. *And yes, I know about you two. Azure tells me everything. I hope you know how important you are to him.*

Atana instinctively covered her heating face, embarrassed, though she had never felt such a way before.

Do not fight it. There are many ways in which emotions are more important than not. He would not have made it here without something to hope for. When he heard of the prophecy, that you were to return, he held onto that. It was the only reason he could piece himself together, why countless workers cling to life. Because of you.

And if I fail, what then? I didn't ask to be part of someone else's plan, Atana said.

Chamarel's eyes fell to the floor, the sheen of her skin dulling. *You are going to leave these workers to their deaths?*

No, I just don't think it's smart or fair to put so much weight and hope on one life. Atana drew a deep breath and forced the frustration out in whorls that stirred up the loose straw on the floor.

Fairness doesn't matter in our world. You are the single piece left in this universe that can make this happen. You are the one that can reverse the cycle. Chamarel snatched one of Atana's hands, turning it palm up in hers.

Atana gasped at the heat she felt beneath as the woman's touch evoked a tiny blue flame from the surface of her scarred skin.

You cannot deny your spark, child. I feel your conviction wanes. Chamarel released her and sent another vision tearing through Atana's mind.

Azure's thin, teenage frame writhed on the cot. Chamarel's helpers held him down while she cleaned his wounds. His arms reached out, grabbing handfuls of cloth from Chamarel's robes and her helper's shirt. He cried out, begging for the torture to cease, tears pouring from his eyes. "Sahara—"

His body quaked and fell limp, unconscious on the worn sheets. Chamarel applied a thick, mint-colored paste to his raw flesh, and then touched his forehead gently with hers, softly reciting a prayer for him in her native language.

Atana choked. *Sahara* echoed in her mind. Her lashes locked behind the fingers hiding the shock of her mistake. *Lavrion—*

"No one should have been capable of living through such devastating injuries." Chamarel's voice wavered. *I'm sorry, young one. You needed to see it. You have power because you bond with others strongly and readily, without judging. You bleed strength into them through your love and conviction. Have faith.*

Atana nodded stiffly and excused herself.

Stepping outside the hut, the clashing emotions built to an intolerable level. She couldn't return to the team like this. Heart pounding in her ears, Atana broke into a run. She had to get away, find a quiet place she could process. Workers scattered from the fields around her. Hot tears streaked her face with every thrust of her legs and pump of her arms.

Regret welled like a bag of rocks in her stomach. The image of Azure kicking from pain as drops of fluid drained from his frothing skin disjointed Atana's stride. She stumbled and fell to her knees in the middle of the tall grasses, her face screwing up as she tried to push the image away.

That level of agony, she knew it. A sickening ache invading deep inside the body, curling its hungry fingers around bone and muscle, clawing its way up around the stomach with nauseating effectiveness. The heart was always the next to suffer. Weak and fast its beat. Atana choked out a cough from an empathetic palpitation. Last was the mind, tingling with the hot pricks of dehydration and the notion the pain would never end. But there was always the incessant itch that couldn't be scratched without tearing open such a delicately healing wound.

She rolled to her side, joints aching from the distress. Tremors shook her body, her lips, and her lungs. It was her fault. His pain belonged to her.

Why did he step in front of me? I'm not—

Her true self-image reared forth, and she flopped back to stare, lungs heaving, at the golden heads of the Hatoga grains waving carefree across her bleary vision.

Not fast enough. The memory of his blue eyes pleading for mercy was now planted within her, permanently.

Not strong enough. She could've stopped it, stepped in. Should've. Atana's back arched, her muscles straining to push the surfacing self-hatred back down, beneath the mask.

I was a sack of bones. Just another hopeless person in testing. I wasn't—worth it!

"Sahara." She heard the name echo between her ears again, a dystopian mantra.

Bracing her head in her hands, she cried out, hiding her face from the world, hoping no one saw her finally crack.

...

Azure burst in to where Chamarel sat in the front room, out of breath. "Ma, a group of new workers broke out of their container, Sector 169. I sent Kylo's team to go help collect them before the Warruks take out too many. Is the team ready to talk?"

I hope it is a useful distraction. Put Imara in charge for now.

"Imara?" He didn't like the way her discolored eyes fell from the fields to her fingers. The motion spoke of regret. Her ignoring his question about the team meant there was a bigger problem. "Ma?"

Azure, I had to show her.

He seized. *You didn't.*

She needed to see you as I did when I found you, to understand why she must fight.

Hopeful bliss fell to his feet, replaced by a dismantling fear. "What if it scared her off? Did you think of that? She only just opened to me last cycle!"

What is necessary isn't always comfortable. Chamarel calmly laced her fingers together in her lap. *You know this, Azure. Please, still your spark.*

He realized he was panicking, his breath rapid and shallow, his body trembling—signs of a novice guard likely to make mistakes. "Which way did she go?"

Chamarel glanced at his hands.

In lifting his shaking fists, he forced them open. Azure snarled, wiping his face like there was a mask painted across it he didn't want to hide behind any longer. "Which way, Ma?" *I need to know she's okay!*

She sighed and lifted her nose in the direction with which Atana had vacated her seat. He leapt toward the front door-opening. *Give her some space. She may not be ready.*

A warning growl burst from the depth of his lungs as he left the hut. The team would fail their mission without her. She was the element that would sway the odds. He'd seen enough infiltrations end in disaster to know. Azure frantically scanned the fields, jogging along the perimeter, checking each quadrant.

A worker pointed, and he looked.

Through the golden haze, Azure saw her standing still, mindlessly inspecting the awn on the crops. He could almost feel the softness of her wavy hair, the strands from her ponytail dancing like kite tails in the subtle breeze. He didn't hesitate to cut through the grasses and run down the row to her side.

She hung her head when he approached.

Azure struggled with the uncertainty of her reaction and fought back his urge to touch her. "Suriah vi ahna trus?" *How are you feeling?*

When she turned to him, her lips parted and quivered. *I'm so sorry.* Atana leaned into him, wadding up fistfuls of his shirt. *I shouldn't have left you there. I should've tried harder.*

Azure looped an arm around her and wiped the tears from her cheeks. *I have you now. That is what matters to me.*

Her eyes fluttered closed.

You can do this. You can figure out how to kill them. You've done it before. He wanted desperately to feel her against his skin like he had the night before. Dipping his head, he pressed his lips to her ear. "Just let me guide you. I can't lose you this time. Not again, not ever."

Atana's nose swept over his cheek and into the nook between his jaw and his neck where she noticeably drew in his scent. Azure's heart leapt into second gear.

He was uneasy about taking things too fast, not wanting to overstep his bounds, uncertain of how much of him, or them, she remembered. The girl he had once known, the one whose memory he had clung to for years on end, had transformed into a fully-curved, healthy woman. His carnal urges were tugging like rabid dogs on chains, straining to be let out.

Slipping his arms around her waist, he bound her tight to him and sank his lips into hers with so much force it made their faces flush with the heat. Her presence made his insides thrum, his bones feel like they were filled with the dust of stars. *I have missed you so much.*

Atana pulled back to nuzzle his cheek. *And I you, in too many ways.*

Chapter 27

BENNETT SCRUBBED HIS FINGERS through his hair, trying to massage the headache away. He hadn't slept much after he traded off guard position with Panton.

Command granted a maximum of five days to complete any recon mission before taking action based on the assumption their people were being held against their will or deceased. The team was already on day three. Two days wasn't much time to complete recon and return. But it would have to be enough.

The team was packed and waiting as millions of tiny lights above alluded to the next cycle, their black-and-white pattern blurring into a vibrant yellow-orange.

Josie and Tanner sat on their bunks discussing the potentials of what they would encounter. Panton and Cutter stared quietly at the ceiling, on guard, the direction they knew they were headed later that morning. Atana had stayed up, talking with Chamarel in the front room and wanted to be left alone. She had disappeared at one point and returned with Azure and Teek, who carried a box full of wires.

For that brief time she was gone, Bennett had paced the bunk room until he'd dug a shallow trough in the dirt with his boots. Atana could order him to leave her alone. But like any decent guard, he covertly stood watch from a distance, listened to what he could, and never let himself get distracted from his paused purpose. It was obvious Atana was upset upon exit, yet Chamarel stopped him in the doorway.

"This place is a bigger burden on her than you understand," Chamarel had said. "Give her the space she needs if you want to succeed."

Bennett deepened the trough.

"You were out late; so was Sergeant Atana. Were you two—" Tanner trailed off when Josie lurched in between them, brows raised in shock.

"Were we what?" Bennett stopped and threw him a glare.

"We were wondering why you were both gone so long," Josie stated, sounding genuinely concerned.

"It's nothing. Just keep by your guards." Bennett jerked his nose toward the other sergeants.

"Yes, sir," they replied.

Chamarel appeared in the doorway. "Come."

The team gathered their things and filed into the front room.

Atana was bent over a detailed sketch of the vessel's schematics. Azure pointed at a location on her screen. She looked up. "Did everyone sleep all right last night?"

They acknowledged her with unconvincing agreements.

Bennett's eyes narrowed, catching sight of the tall man so close to their leader and wondering why she was suddenly concerned about such non-regulation things. The nods between them suggested a conversation. But he couldn't hear it.

Panton, sweeping Josie behind him with an arm, hopped on the question before anyone else could muster the words. "Who are you?"

Chamarel lifted a hand. "This is Lead Perimeter Guard, Azure. He is the reason so many have survived this long."

"While we appreciate the help, he's not coming with us." Bennett glared at him before darting his gaze to Atana.

"Yes, he is. He can help us navigate undetected." The emotion was gone from Atana's features today.

It wasn't what Bennett expected or wanted. "You didn't clear it with me. And after last night, I'm not allowing it. We picked the routes on Tanner's map this morning before your meeting. Why are you changing the plan?"

"Fine-tuning the plan with some new route information from Healer Paramor," Atana countered.

Inside, Bennett felt like throwing his hands in the air. They'd finally agreed on a course of action and she'd changed it already. Sure, assignments shifted often in the field, and Command had suggested he needed to adapt to her. But that didn't make the concept any easier to work with.

Atana rose from her seat and asked Bennett out into the next room where Kios lay sleeping. "What's your problem? We need all the help we can get, and you know it," she said quietly.

"No, Nakio. I don't like it. You hardly know him." Bennett paused, considering his statement might not actually be true after the events of the previous evening. "I don't trust him."

"I barely know you. I trust you, because of Command, despite your infractions." Atana glowered at him.

Don't remind me. Bennett cursed himself inside for breaking code with UP's top shepherd. "You trust Chamarel?" He glanced sideways through the archway to where she sat in the front room answering Tanner's questions.

"After our conversations, yes. We need him on the crew."

Bennett rubbed an aching temple, wishing he'd had more than an hour of broken sleep. "I don't want him that close to us, to you. I'm not putting my guys at the mercy of some—"

"Fine." Atana cut him off. "But we need to get more information from him before we go. There are a few perimeter teams on each level that are aware of our plans and are ready to support us however they can. We need to be able to make contact with them discreetly."

"Fine."

Kios stirred on his bed. His tiny fingers reached for her. Atana hesitated then slipped past Bennett to gingerly take the hand extending in her direction.

Bennett turned to watch.

Azure stepped inside, his frown softening when he noticed Atana in the corner with Kios.

The boy produced a weak smile as he threw his arms around her neck, to Bennett's surprise.

"Vi sisano," Kios whispered.

Something in the way Atana's eyes caressed the boy spoke more than words ever could.

...

Atana wrapped her arms around Kios and cautiously laid him back on the blankets. "Rest."

She was lost in little Kios—the uneven stripes on his neck peeking out of his torn collar, his dark hair, and those big starry-night eyes. His hair was a mess of mud-stiffened weeds. He needed a bath, medicine, and hope.

Taking his small hand in hers made her think back to her own abduction, how scared and angry and confused she'd been. But Kios had no anger in his eyes. Only love. And pain.

His face contorted, a sobbing whine bursting out of his lips. Kios tried to curl his knees toward his chest, but they fell limp against the tattered blankets.

The sight stung like hot poison in her ribs. Atana tenderly brushed the bangs from his forehead. They rustled like dried hay. "Kios?"

His hand squeezed tightly around her fingers like a last attempt to cling to life. "Miia zi du viia—"

He didn't ask for help, but Atana felt the nudge in her mind. Seeing a tear form in the corner of one of his eyes, the shell around her heart fell into a million pieces. She could save him, through Ether. Chamarel and Azure had reminded her of that. Chamarel also had to ration her own skills to hundreds.

Atana knew by the paleness of Kios's face and the way his eyes rolled around in his head, he wasn't going to make it through the night. Not without help. Somewhere, deep in her gut, she knew Kios wanted her, not Chamarel. Maybe it had something to do with that name he kept calling her. She couldn't explain why, for certain. Kios just needed *her*.

Stabilizing him with her hands, Atana scooted closer on the cot's edge and leaned forward, carefully connecting their foreheads.

A rush of cool air swept over her body, and she opened her eyes. Lush, blue grass cushioned her feet. A silver pond sparkled unusually bright in the distance. Above, she noted the iridescent sheen of a thick bubble surrounding Kios's small Ether. Beyond was the darkness of space filled with black planets cragged in orange light. She squinted and took another step to get a better look. She knew the team was waiting, but right now, this was her reality. And what Kios saw in his world didn't seem limited by constructs he could have known. He hadn't been alive long enough to see so much destruction. His personal Ether was small, but its reach seemed infinite.

The Suanoan plasma colors were like that of molten mantles of— *Terraforming.* Atana gasped as she frantically scanned the desolate planets. This wasn't modification; this was destruction.

A giggle behind her made her spin and look. Kios chased a glowing blue butterfly in the distance. He hopped, hands in the air, then stopped and curled forward, wincing in pain. He straightened and tried to catch it again but stumbled and fell beyond the tall grass. She didn't see him get back up.

"Kios?" Atana hustled over and knelt at his side. When she rolled him over, dirt was caked to the wet streaks on his hollow cheeks. She lifted him into her arms and gave him her best smile. "Hush. Let me share your burden."

Sobs shook him. "Everyone is dead!"

She looked up again at the planets in the sky. "We aren't. Not yet. Can you hang in there a little while for me? I need to help the others."

Kios stroked her face with a hand as if seeing something that wasn't there before. His fingertips felt too calloused for his age. Atana closed her eyes for a moment, soaking in the tenderness of the boy's touch. It made no sense why anyone would love a scarred and broken thing like her. But she felt it as she sat there holding him, his strange connection to her. She sensed him sinking into her heart.

"I must go," she said, peering down at him.

"I know." His bottom lip quivered. "Please, come back."

Atana leaned forward. "Vi tiisa, be strong." Touching her forehead to his, she broke free of Ether.

Delicately kissing his closed eyes, she stole the tears from the shallow creases and pulled the loosely woven, burlap blanket, not worth its threads, up and over his chest. *Don't cry, little one. You will be okay.*

Atana stood to find her stomach cramping. Keeping her back to the men, she lifted the edge of her jacket to see a faint bruise darkening her skin. Realizing her mistake, she took a deep, calming breath and stifled a curse. In healing Kios, she had taken his pain, literally. She had forgotten that part of Ether. A bond was a two-way street. It's how she was able to give him her health, by taking the burden of his injury.

She spun around to find the two men staring at her. Atana froze for a moment, unsure what they might think. It was then that she realized she didn't care anymore what anyone thought or what the rules were. She was going to do what was right because someone needed to.

Concern crossed Azure's face. When she tried to push between the men to get back to the mission, he caught her arm.

"Let her go," Bennett snapped, grabbing Azure's wrist.

Spreading her feet, Atana stiffened as she scanned between the tensed men.

Azure's eyes burned into her. *You shouldn't have done that. You have endangered yourself, your mission, everyone.*

I know. Atana bounced impatiently on her toes. *I forgot the consequences.* She glanced over at Kios sleeping peacefully. *I can't explain what I feel for him. When he's in pain, it feels like a part of me is dying. I had to help.*

Dying? Azure's lips parted as he studied her.

Bennett tugged Azure's grip free from her arm and corralled her into the front room.

Azure spoke in her mind, an edge to his tone. *I will follow in the shadows since I am not tolerated by your guard. Just in case you need help.*

Atana glanced over her shoulder at Azure. Her stomach ached deep, stealing her strength to object to Bennett's rough handling. *Thank you.*

...

Bennett cut off Azure as they rejoined the others, long enough to throw him a glare no one else could see.

Atana lifted a wire-thin crown from a bale. "Teek has developed technology to send and receive telepathic communications between individuals, for non-telepathic species."

Teek scurried over to Tanner, looking eager. "For you, we put two nodes here and one here." He pointed behind each ear and at the top of his forehead.

Atana lifted the largest node. "The power switch will attach at the base of your head. You must try to hide the cable under your hair. The nodes can be visible. This will make you look like a Ryson."

"Who the hell are they?" Panton asked.

"Strong workers with motion sickness," Chamarel responded. "Teek's predecessor designed that unit. All perimeter guards are Telepaths. It is a requirement for the position so we can communicate without drawing the attention of the Warruks or Linoans, who are not. If we are reduced in numbers, this unit allows non-telepaths to fill in."

Connecting the last of the nodes to the base of Tanner's skull, Teek asked, "You ready? May hurt."

Bennett didn't like the concept of his team being guinea pigs and took an urgent step toward the young shepherd. He was always quick to try new things, often without regard for his personal safety. Innocent, wanting to please. *Like Jack.* Or what Bennett could remember of his little brother. "You don't have to, Remmi. If you want, I can go first."

"It's all right, sir. I'm curious anyway." With a reluctant nod from Bennett, Tanner signaled to Teek, "Okay, hit it."

A long, gray finger pressed the button at the top of Tanner's neck. He winced. Tanner's wristband beeped, stating the influx of adrenaline in his bloodstream. But seconds later, the noise subsided.

He let out a breath. "Feels like normal."

Bennett slid open a tab on his wristband displaying five faces and their physical status with Atana at the top center, just to confirm. Tanner and Josie were where they were supposed to be, and Cutter was below, almost flat like Atana. On serum, his numbers only flared in the moment of necessity. Panton's testosterone and adrenaline were higher than normal. Bennett would have to check in on his sniper guard again soon.

He cleared his throat to regain their attention. "Tanner and Cutter, you're assigned offensive capabilities, power, and propulsion systems, whatever information you can get and stay in one piece. Josie and Panton, I want you to meet up with Healers, Saemas, guards, whoever you can on each level, in silence, and sort out sector, sway, and testing numbers. Don't lead them on, but find out who all can fight, in case this gets out of hand before we're ready. Atana and I will figure out what the commanding crew situation is."

Atana nodded her approval. "We'll regroup near sector 157. Tanner and I found a way home."

They hadn't actually discussed a plan in the typical sense, more of a set of goals. Bennett was merely improvising like Command had implied he should.

The beeping from Josie's wristband diminished, and Teek moved over to Panton. "So, how do they know we're on the same side? And why are they so eager to help us if so many others have failed?" she asked.

Chamarel folded her hands together in front of her. "Because our guards are telepathic, they will sense your presence and know you are not harmful. The Suanoa and their crew have a different aura. It is impossible to mistake one of us for one of them. If they hear you communicating, they will know purely from your language. Each perimeter team has at least one guard that knows every language used on this ship, including yours. They will understand you or at least track down the guard who does."

Everyone waited for the answer to the second part of Josie's question, but Chamarel stopped.

"I was able to get a hold of this from Paramor in a neighboring sector," Azure pointed to Atana's wristband. "It shows you most of the hidden routes we train the perimeter guards to use. We converted it this morning."

The team huddled around Atana, peering down at the map. Her shoulders drew inward, and she slid back a half-step. With a swipe of her finger, she sent a copy to each person, their bands flashing with the incoming data.

Bennett noted her recoil, something she'd done more every day. "Okay, team, gear up, check your doses, and silence your alerts," he ordered as Teek finished installing his receiver.

Chamarel touched Josie on the shoulder. *It will get easier in time.* Josie cringed.

The words banged around like pinballs in Bennett's mind.

"Ha! I heard that!" Tanner cracked a bright white smile like the team had never seen before.

"Of course you'd love it." Bennett chuckled.

Tanner fingered the node on the top of his forehead and nudged Teek. "You have to show me sometime how you came up with this."

Josie's brows furrowed. "It's definitely louder and clearer than I anticipated."

Cutter gestured at Atana. "Doesn't she need a receiver?"

Atana sighed. *No.* The entire team flinched, including Bennett, as her words punched through their skulls. *The last time I was on this ship, I killed three armed Suanoa. With a glaive. Any other questions?*

The team stood in silence.

Azure waved a hand at the back of his neck. "Make sure if you get caught, you power down your devices with the button behind your head, or the Suanoa could do some serious damage to your minds."

"Uh, yes. But, no worry," Teek said nervously. "I make better. This time keep power low and now have better unit to stop much signal." He gestured something small in his fingers.

"A fuse? Too much power and it will pop so the device doesn't blow up." Tanner gestured an explosion with his hands.

Teek nodded vigorously. "Yes, yes that! Feeuzze—"

"Comforting," Panton muttered sarcastically.

Bennett's eyes snapped to the one man of comparable size to Azure in the room. *On the edge, Sergeant.*

"I'm fine, Bennett. I hear your thoughts now, remember?" Panton adjusted the shotgun on his back.

One of Bennett's cheeks lifted in a poor attempt to smile. "Thank you for your generosity, Chamarel." He dipped his head. "Teek." Pensively canvassing the tall man, there was a moment where the urge to think about what he wanted to do to him took over before he could shut it down. "Azure." Bennett's upper lip twitched, watching the blue eyes brighten, despite the man's vacant face. He turned to his team. "We've been sitting around here with thumbs up our asses long enough. Let's move out."

The team gave him a variety of acknowledging remarks and stepped outside the hut behind him and Atana.

Chamarel, Teek, and Azure followed at a distance behind the crew. Letting out a whine, Teek ran after them, bolting past Bennett. "Atana, I come with?"

"No, Teek." She trudged ahead. "It's safer here with Chamarel."

"Please, I give anything," he begged, running around in front of her.

She stopped in her tracks with a hand up, halting the crew behind. "You are still needed here. What we are doing is not safe for you right now."

A thick, blood-red tear broke free and slid down his cheek.

Bennett watched as she wiped away the line tainting the gray fur, leaning over to whisper in his ear. *Why is she like that to everyone else?* A half-smile from Teek's wet face made her eyes crinkle in the corners.

Sir? Cutter approached his side.

Nothing just—

Trying to figure her out. Cutter nodded. *Me too.*

Atana signaled the team toward the end of the production facility, passing Teek on the side of the path. Tanner gave the teen a quick pat on the shoulder. With everyone filing through the door at the opposite end of the fields, Atana stopped and looked back. Bennett stopped with her. Chamarel and Azure were just specks in the distant fields.

Chamarel lifted a hand. *Siisa mamua layha. Good luck, friends.*

Atana braced herself in the doorway. *Please, watch over Kios.*

I will. The spot of color that was Chamarel in the haze shifted closer to Azure.

Between Bennett's ears, Chamarel's voice was calm but trimmed with worry. It put him on high alert. Palming an SI, he waved Atana out into the hall and pulled the door shut.

Chapter 28

IN SILENCE and pressed for time, the shepherds of Earth moved quickly through the stretch of main hallways. Bennett studied his wrist map, directing the team with a hand. *Head to the left. We have several kilometers of hallways to get through before we can separate.*

The team silently rounded the next junction.

Anyone want to play a game? Test the limits of this crazy shit we're wearing? Cutter's steely tone held uncharacteristic notes of amusement.

Tanner squinted at him. *Hell yeah! Rock-paper-scissors on the count of three, you and me. Ready? One, two, three—*

Bennett couldn't help a fraction of a smile when the two shouted their answers into everyone's heads. *Okay, let's focus guys. Clock's ticking.*

Even though Bennett and Atana led the pack, the pairs checked every intersection. Walking backward, Tanner monitored their six, his SIs outstretched, their igniters glowing.

Josie's teeth gritted. *Yes, couldn't you do something calm and constructive to practice?*

Cutter spun around. *Like what? This is constructive.*

I don't know, maybe— A cacophony of disheartened voices ripped through their receivers, cutting Josie off.

Bennett crumpled with the team to the black, metal floor, his head throbbing heavy from the noise.

Josie gagged and ripped the receiver off, holding her head. Panton put a hand to her back, glaring at Tanner and Cutter.

Rotating on her toes, Atana surveyed the group. The screams faded with her blink. "Sorry, I was drifting."

Bennett peered up at her through watering eyes when she hurried away from them. Picking himself up, he intended to jog after her but stumbled to a stop. Heat, like he was huddled too close to a bonfire, flooded his body. Wavering and soft at first, it grew until the sensation tore through him. A quiet gasp fought back the lightheadedness from his sprinting heart. Clenching his fists, his fingers balled up with abnormal force.

He closed his eyes to focus. *What's going on? Is this a side-effect of the receivers?* Chamarel and Teek hadn't mentioned anything.

Concerned, he listened to his crew, still picking themselves up behind him. No one had noticed he was in zombie-mode. They grunted and grumbled and resituated gear.

Bennett's heat was holding steady. But the rush of energy accompanying it was so tumultuous inside his veins, he squirmed.

The mission. Get back on it. Stop this nonsense.

Lifting his eyelids, all he saw was Atana's silhouette fading into the shadows. His feet picked him up on command, carrying him to her faster than expected. *Is that what you hear, in your mind?*

I should get a little way ahead of all of you. If I stay out about twenty meters, I won't interfere with your communication anymore. Atana scanned ahead and then inspected an intersecting hall.

How do you sleep at night? Bennett twisted his neck, his fingers digging into the tight muscles.

I don't, not really.

Right, trouble sleeping. He bobbed his head. *Atana, I'm really sorry about last night. It didn't sink in that Azure was the Lead Guard we'd need to coordinate with. I didn't mean to hassle you.*

Her brief inspection of him made Bennett pause and reconsider his word choice.

Or threaten the mission.

Atana's leathers swished softly in an even pattern, her pace unaltered. *It's fine.*

It was too mechanical, too programmed for Bennett's liking. *No, it's really not. I compromised you. Brushing me off suggests you're upset.*

I am not compromised, Bennett. We just don't have time for this right now. I need you to focus.

His steps slowed, the heat lingering with him. *How do I help her?* He glanced back at his team, finally heading their direction. *She's a shepherd, like all of us. Why is she so determined to do everything on her own if we're all right here? She is so headstrong and so damned—* He couldn't help but look back and drag his eyes up her strong legs to the curves of her hips and waist, ending on her waterfall of soft hair. His heart thumped hard against the serum.

Atana spun on the balls of her feet, squinting at him. *You are the compromised one, Bennett. None of this makes any sense.* She flung a hand in the air. *Why the hell did they send me up here with, of all the shepherds, you?*

The team stopped in the distance. He couldn't see them. They were behind him. But he *felt* them stop. It was the strange *knowing* that stilled his boots.

Her jaw visibly flexed. *I'm here because they believe what I saw and experienced would give us an advantage, not to watch over you.*

She moved closer, causing Bennett to backpedal at the last second. His shoulders pressed against the rounded steel wall. Her eyes cut into his like icicles piercing the soft earth on the first day of spring. *You know the rules—no emotions, no relationships, only rational and impartial decisions. You have serum for this. And yet, I saw you do not have enough for this trip.* She thrust a finger at his wristband. *Not that it seems to matter with you. You're still a mustang on the inside: untamed and uncontrollable. I don't think serum works for you. I don't think it ever has.*

The sweet spice of her skin warmed the air around him, teasing the receptors in Bennett's nose. *How did you know?*

Because of what I am, she gruffly replied. *It's not like you hide it well.*

"I can explain." Not giving a second thought to her words or the consequences of his actions, he reached an arm around her waist, pulling her against him. It felt right and wrong all at once, as if the serum had completely lost all effect and something else had slid into its place. It was something hot, primal, and left him feeling so full of energy that he wanted to burst. So simultaneously empowering and alarming, he shoved his awareness of it out of his mind. Bennett holstered his SI, slipping his other hand behind her shoulders.

"Bennett," she whined. *There are billions of lives relying on us.* Wedging her hands in between them, she placed them on his chest, pushing.

His grip on her loosened. "Stop and just listen a moment. We're finally away from the view of others." He paused, seriously considering his words. It wasn't the time. But she needed to know his weakness. It was a shepherd's duty to report all vulnerabilities in the way of mission success. *You're right. The serum hasn't been working.*

Bennett wiped a hand down his face, trying to rub the stress away and awaken his mind from its sweltering dreamland.

Her brows furrowed. *Why now? Our mission is at stake because of you! We don't have time for this!*

Bennett grabbed her upper arms. "There's no way I could have known this change would happen right now. Besides, you were with Mr. Perimeter Guard, Azure last night, and this morning. You've been awful close to him."

He threw a finger in the direction of the Hatoga fields. "And not uncomfortable with it, yet you were uncomfortable with the team standing around you an hour ago. What's going on with you?"

He's a friend from before I was a shepherd. I didn't want to give away I was telepathic before the time was right.

The heat kept building as did Bennett's frustration. And the chaos within. The voices through his receiver were abnormal, too clear, too easy for him to understand. His team was still rubbing their foreheads. Bennett fought back inside. Fought the growing doubts in his mind. About himself. And her. The urges were so strong. They took over every cell. His need to touch her, shield her, defend her. Yet his anger at her, at the system, at the invaders, swelled like high-sea waves in a storm. He was alone, different. He should tell them, shouldn't he? Like Atana should've told him? But they wouldn't understand. No one would. Because they couldn't feel what he did inside.

His serum had failed.

He was free.

He snapped.

Oh, so it's okay for you to break the rules but no one else? You think you're above the rest of us? He shoved Atana into the center of the hallway. *Is he the reason you never include us in the plan? Or was it Chamarel? You never told me what upset you so much after your talk. Why won't you talk to me?*

Atana's glaring eyes illuminated. She squared her shoulders. *I'm just different, not like you.*

Because you're telepathic? Is that it? Or because you're an R4? He spun a circle, palms slapping his forehead. *God, always with you Independents.*

It was thirteen years ago. You don't understand. "You can't understand!"

His hands fell open before her, heat flaring inside again. It swelled in his chest, spreading out into every fingertip and toe until it felt like he wielded twenty hot pokers. *I'm trying to! But instead of seeing it, you just rip my heart out instead and go after grumpy gray guy? How is that equal? How is that to code?*

How is you kissing me to code, Bennett? You need to focus on the mission!

Very hypocritical. Bennett replied in reckless contempt. *Typical Independent.*

She lunged at him, clawed fingers reaching for leather. He shifted out of her path. They scuffled, at nearly equal strength, each trying to knock the other down. They fought in sync too well, blocking everything the other attacked with. Atana went for a drop, but Bennett twisted, landing and pinning her to the floor, caging her within his arms and legs.

Heart pounding, Bennett felt like he could crush the world the way his muscles quivered with energy. It was a foreign feeling and, he realized, if he didn't regain control, he might crush *her*. Through the mirage of impulse and desire that had replaced his serum-regulated bearing, his hoarse voice mustered a request. "Stop fighting me."

She pushed angrily against his chest, squirming, trying to break free. His body remained solid, planted, like iron bars buried in concrete. He didn't know how. It was as if something else had control.

He closed his eyes, trying to shut out the heat and energy, ignore it, defy its power over him. This, he was quickly realizing, was stronger than a withdrawal session and any serum burnout on record. But he required special doses. Rio never told him *what* made them different.

His fists relaxed, smoothing out the leather they had wadded up, his hands forming themselves gently around her shoulders. "Please. I can't control it anymore. I don't know what's happening to me."

When her hands softened over his chest, he let out a breath, relieved she didn't truly intend to hurt him.

I want— He paused to dip his head, locking onto the eyes that avoided him, needing her to know she was more than an assignment. *To protect you. I'm trying to fight it. But it's deeper than serum, UP, all of this.* He leaned back, waiting for another, more violent shove.

The scrunch in her brows lifted. "Want?"

Her surprise was unexpected.

"Not *that* kind of want." He stammered and shook his head. That was a lie. "I mean, maybe it's because you're so important to everyone on earth, and now here. I don't know. But I need you to work with me. I need you to know something's different and serum isn't fixing it. I need you to try to understand. I know it sounds crazy."

The radiant, blue rings in her eyes thinned, filling with the darkness from the center. Her scent morphed into something he couldn't identify, but it drew him in like the song of a siren. "I—understand."

He couldn't believe the calmness in her voice. "You do?"

"Bennett, I'm not human. I understand."

His palms moistened, breath locking inside his lungs on strike.

Not human? It wasn't that the thought hadn't crossed his mind, with all the anomalous characteristics she possessed. He just hadn't stared it in the face before.

Cutter broke the silence. "We got company!"

Atana and Bennett squinted down the hallway at the team.

This is getting too complicated. "Hold it together, Jameson. I need you." Placing her feet up against the wall, she thrust herself out from underneath him. Rolling backward, boots over her head, she planted her hands, pushing herself into the air and back onto her feet.

Ashamed he had let himself fall, *I need you* echoed in his mind, easing the violent spasms inside his ribs. He picked himself up.

Atana yelled at the crew, waving them their direction. *We're almost to the central hub. You've got your assignments. Bennett and I will take care of this. Go!*

Chapter 29

BRIGHT ORANGE streaks illuminated the halls. The Warruks' steps pulsed through the floor like an earthquake. Atana and Bennett both whipped an SI back and took the Warruks down.

Turning a corner, stark flashes of light made them screech to a stop. Atana hadn't felt the Linoans under her feet, their steps too light.

Bennett aptly ducked and lunged at one, his shoulder burying in its gut, throwing it back. One shot and it was down.

Atana blocked the swing with a forearm, but the blade grazed her left cheek, the metal so sharp she didn't feel its effect until her face tensed and the skin peeled open. Ramming her SI into the Linoan's chest, she squeezed the trigger. It hopped and fell, charred and smoking. *Teams of four. Two more Bennett.*

Copy. He backed up against her in the middle of an open area with several adjoining hallways. *This is a sway junction, isn't it? That place where they sort new slaves? I think I saw it on the map.*

Yes. A blip of grey and blue darted from one hall to another. Atana smiled. She thought momentarily about the collectors and Lavrion. Sway processing would likely be where he was, but which junction on what level? Her eyes unfocused for a moment. *Sahara.* He had said it, and Azure too. It was her name, then. And if that was the case then Lavrion wasn't lying. He'd made her hesitate. The cheekbones she'd stared at every morning in the bathroom mirror reflected in the doorway of her apartment that unfortunate day. *Oh, stars! I have to find him!*

Sahara? Bennett glanced back at her. *Find who?*

My— She looked up as the shadows shifted, but not in time to stop the vicious heel flying at her side. She blocked, but her stomach cramped up from her recent healing of Kios. The steel, razor sharp, sliced through her leather layers, splitting her skin below her ribs. She cried out as the force threw her against the wall, her head slamming into metal.

Bennett had a second's more time and swung around, catching the slender black-dotted ankle in his callused palms. With a thrust of a foot, he broke the standing leg of the Linoan. It tried to retaliate and drop a fist onto Bennett's thigh.

Atana heard a crack. The Linoan slumped to the floor.

168

Bennett spun and shot down the Linoan hunting Atana.

With a grunt, she collapsed sideways onto the floor. *Get up,* "Katana," she muttered, the stabbing pain leaching up her side. It squeezed the breath from her lungs and coherent thought from her mind. "Must fulfill—" *sword of Command.*

Her body trembled in a poor attempt to get herself upright. Bennett made a move toward her side. But a grunting Warruk quickly stole his footing, his body caving with the snarling force. All she heard after was the brush of fabric being dragged across the floor.

Atana whined, her consciousness slipping, fighting to stay awake. The sinking in her belly told her she wasn't going to get to scope the commanding crew from the shadows because the shadows had found her.

Sensei. She thought back to her first day with him. Her only hope now was the one thing Chamarel had advised against. But she was not so out-of-training. She had practiced Sensei's lessons every night before succumbing to the memory-visions. It was the only way she'd kept her desire for vengeance under control, her job, and her sanity.

With the amount of warm blood she could feel seeping through her fingers, she knew she had to find that sliver-thin rope of existence and calm her heartbeat if she hoped to survive. *Sensei, it hurts. Please, help me.*

I know, a voice whispered. *It is only a signal in your brain. Control your breaths, slow your thoughts. Be deliberate. Focus on the thing you want most. Shut everything else down, and you will live.*

...

In an adjacent hallway, more Linoans appeared, bounding at Bennett and Atana from a neighboring sector. Without thinking, Azure, who had been cautiously following, leapt across the hall to attack the flood of fighters. This wasn't his first encounter. His scars were proof. And the fury he felt toward Bennett for what he'd just done to Atana needed to be released. Azure had almost broken his cover just to slit the man's throat. But he was well aware of the value of silence, of his role as backup for the team.

They had to be successful.

Having been caught in the center several times, Azure knew exactly how the Linoans started their combative formations. One well-placed punch from them was a brutal way to die—split open and bleeding out like a gutted animal.

Azure launched himself at the impending fight. Approaching the first pair, he drew the heavy throwing knives from his belt and dropped to his knees. He slid on his back across the dirty floor, directly between, jamming one steel blade into a thigh of each Linoan. He came to an abrupt stop just behind the two.

Whipping forward, he planted his palms on the ground. Kicking his feet up into their chests when they turned to face him, he knocked them over. He put his feet down, somersaulting backward. Yanking his blades from their legs, he slit their throats in symmetrical movements with surgical precision.

Close enough now to be accurate, Azure threw his knives at the necks of the second pair. The Linoans froze, metal burying in flesh. Azure jumped up, ramming his palms against the pommel of the blades and shoving them through the Linoans' spines. He ripped the knives back out the front. In a matter of seconds, he had cut all four down. Surveying his work, he clenched his teeth in disgust.

The distant sound of her strained voice hollowed out his heart. Warily peeking into the hallway, he found four Linoans down and a male and female silhouette, both limp and fading into a thundering darkness.

Oh, Diete. No!

He sprinted out after them with everything he had, following two trails of smeared blood on the floor, laying out dismal but perfect paths. They ran through an engine room, two more gravitational maintenance rooms, and up several flights of stairs. The amount of blood the shepherds had lost was building.

Come on, Azure, he growled. *You're losing her!*

Nearing an intersection, his footsteps slowed, his heart beating faster. Frantically inspecting the intermittent splatter patterns for their direction, he feared they couldn't live much longer. Tracking the droplets off to his right, he felt a sudden breeze behind his head and realized his mistake, a moment too late.

Chapter 30

PELTING his laptop keyboard, Tanner whipped through the propulsion system control panel that was trying to lock him out. Cutter had positioned himself to Tanner's six, monitoring the whirring room. Cylindrical generators radiating white light surrounded them, connected together by thick, luminous bundles of cables strung out around a central column like spokes in a wheel.

Tanner stood between two of the three wall screens facing their corresponding power grids, scanning the systems. He typed in a command and hit Enter.

"Son of a—"

What? Cutter stole a quick glance over his shoulder to see red streams of data pouring schematics and directions onto Tanner's screen.

Sergeant Atana wrote one line of code for me. It's downloading everything and giving me access to control half of what's in here, including the maintenance rooms below. How the hell? Tanner's fingers froze midair as he tracked the flood of information.

Cutter caught a hulking shadow enter the main doorway. Its head lowered and swayed as if catching an odd scent. *Time to go!*

Okay, five more seconds! His fingers pummeled the keys, rushing the process.

Tanner!

Okay, okay. He typed in one last command, clearing the log of his presence before pulling the cords and shoving them in the pouch below the laptop strapped to his front.

The two of them crouched, sneaking around the central hub and out the opposite door. They crept down several hallways, reaching a stairwell. Their last stop was plasma engineering. Cutter steadied his shotgun and led the way.

So what do you think of Atana? 'Cause I can't wrap my head around it. Tanner said behind him.

The receiver picked up the direction of Tanner's thoughts as if they were made of audible sound waves. However fascinating a concept, it unnerved Cutter with the personal vulnerability it created. His mind was a private space.

171

She saves that boy, Kios. Then she's fighting in the hall with Bennett. Isn't that what manics do, the ones that the serum doesn't work on?

Cutter paused for a moment on the landing of their fifth flight, hearing mucus-filled voices pass in the hall. He leaned out of sight, his shotgun igniter primed. When the sounds faded, he shifted cautiously to the edge of the doorway and peered in while Tanner joined him on the opposite side.

Several stories below them, bundles of white cables illuminated the walls and a large pipe which circled off into the distance. Above them, the ceiling glowed red-hot.

What is this, some sort of nuclear fission? Tanner eyed the pipe. *Looks to be circling around the core of the ship.*

Cutter glanced at their backsides. *Maybe it's how they generate power?*

I have to study the download later. Tanner shook his head. *Solar is their main source. This could be what they use when they're between stars.*

A fizzing snap and a scream sliced through the air. An emaciated young man in ragged clothing crumpled in the room below, a set of parallel lines burnt into his calf. The others in his crew hurried to compensate for his absence, pushing a large, translucent obsidian column into a set of metal braces against the far wall.

The room began to hum, like the weapon the Linoan held. The Linoan's vertical mouth barked another command, and the man with the injured leg was dragged off by a pair of Warruks in loincloths. The creature spun the bow-shaped device in its hand, sending the dual arcs snapping and popping. The blood-orange light glinted off the Linoan's fist blades and the individual scales of its black chrome bodysuit.

There were many groups of workers, and a Linoan assigned to each. Some innocents were rewiring, others cleaning up an orange fluid spill with rubber push mops, and a few replacing exterior panels on the pipe.

Cutter retracted from the doorway and continued their climb.

You see the guy get smacked by that Linoan for no reason? Tanner shuddered, following close.

Cutter chewed the inside of a cheek. *As far as Atana and the serum goes, the manic stage occurs first, when shepherds initially begin treatment. If they don't transition within the first month to the passive phase, they aren't accepted for duty. Ones like Bennett, who took the longest to tame, are accepted but are reassessed more often and more carefully than the others. Then there's the special category that isn't instructed in class. They are called the "unbalanced." Command created it for the survivors of the rescue mission. She's the last one.*

He continued with a shake of his head. *You know she came out while I was on guard last night. I had this eerie feeling she knew something. I guess it makes sense now if she's telepathic.*

Tanner shifted beneath his tech harness. *I couldn't imagine being an antenna for so many other people's thoughts. I don't know how she holds it together. No wonder she has so many headaches and nightmares.*

Yeah, let alone keeping Bennett's obsession with her at bay.

Tanner stopped on a step. *Wait, you aren't going to say anything, are you?*

I'm not saying anything to anyone about him.

Good. Tanner started moving again. *I was concerned the reason you were sent to our team was because UP might've thought him compromised after—*

The fight between him and your former guard? Cutter squeezed the textured grips of the weapon he refused to set down. *Remmi, your last guard, Cara, wasn't on serum. Bennett could tell. She hacked the CENA protocols so she could stay off. Cara wasn't focused on her job. She was interested in you.*

Weird. Tanner's face scrunched. *So why are you still here, with us?*

Got tired of moving. Command wanted to keep Bennett a Team Leader, so there was a position open for your guard. Besides, to break up a team as cohesive as ours would not be conducive to the effectiveness of UP.

Tanner scanned behind them, the volume of his thoughts dropping. *I wonder if he's ever studied the rest of the team.*

Of course, I have. It's what I do. Cutter's words froze Tanner in his boots. *I'm here because I want to be here, not to study you guys. Besides, you are one of the most levelheaded people I know.*

Really? Tanner asked.

Yes, so stop worrying, before I'm forced to change my mind and report you.

You wouldn't! Tanner scoffed.

I won't if you don't make me.

You— Tanner called him a name Cutter didn't think was in his vocabulary. But before Tanner's fist could plant in his partner's shoulder, a Warruk came around into the stairwell from a doorway, a few steps ahead of them.

Cutter reacted with deadly precision, knocking the beast to the ground in a shower of flaming pellets.

Where's the partner? He ran up the last few steps to the landing, jumping over the body he had just taken down, and checked the hall. *Nothing.*

Spinning around, he saw a large shadow approaching Tanner from behind. "Three o'clock, move!"

Tanner sidestepped to his right. Cutter lifted his shotgun and pulled the trigger. The Warruk stood for a moment, dazed. Leaping off the platform, Cutter rammed a foot in its stomach, knocking it over and sending it toppling down to the next level.

He turned to his partner, frantically scanning Tanner for injuries. *You okay?*

Yeah, you?

Relieved, Cutter blinked slowly as he tried to block out his apprehension over the situation he'd permitted his assignment to be in. *That was too close, Tanner. I can't—*

Can't what?

Never mind. Cutter shook his head and scanned the landing and the stairs above and below, wondering if anyone would respond to hearing his shots or the tumbling body. *Keep quiet.*

I call Bravo Sierra. Tanner blurted. *You're holding something inside. I heard it. What are you hiding?*

Ignoring the matter, Cutter continued silently up the steps.

Hey, I'm invoking the rule.

Cutter stopped, irritation tensing his back. This was why he didn't like the receivers. *I trust you won't talk, even about me? I'm your team psych.*

Tanner cocked his head, confusion knitting his brows. *Never do. Part of the rule. You know that.*

Cutter's throat ached, and he was suddenly thankful he didn't have to use it. He was trained to be a machine by Command but in a deeper sense of the word—always watching and solving others' problems, never his own. He spent his time in a colder, more heartless place than anyone ever knew.

I let myself slip once and— Someone good died. Glancing back at Tanner, he briefly studied the rings of color in the man's eyes. They looked like solar eclipses in unnaturally blue skies with a thin ring of green in between. A corner of Cutter's mouth lifted in a poor attempt to smile. *It's like I'm still protecting her when I'm protecting you.*

Her? Tanner's brows lifted. He, thankfully, didn't ask what happened. It was Rule Six and also a respectful way to handle mission situations no one else would understand unless they had been there. *I—I'm sorry man. Well, if you need anything—*

Not to talk about her. Cutter gave him a cold look. He knew it made the younger shepherd uncomfortable. But it was effective.

A deep sigh released from Tanner's lungs. He stepped over the Warruk on the landing and, together, they continued their ascent.

Cutter knew it was his duty to be the strongest impartial influence on every team. But Bravo Sierra was their team rule for good reason, and he didn't want Tanner to think he had other priorities. *I'm finally content with my position, with good people, people I can trust, people I'd like to think of as—*

You don't have to say it. Tanner clapped him on the shoulder. *We know.*

—Azure—

Chapter 31

THE DIM LIGHT, the putrid smell of Yakna firewater, and steam from cooking Fimus noodles brought back memories that always made Azure regret one, specific, past decision.

"Drékor!" he bellowed, clambering out of the bed they had dumped him on. The damp air of the makeshift fort, built in the open web of structural steel of Agutra's core structure was thick with Samacca incense, used to lighten the mood. His head spun when his legs stood his body upright.

Ramura, a Xahu'ré girl he had taken a personal interest in guiding, ducked beneath a truss, holding a small plate of food scraps and a gourd filled with water. Pulling down the strip of fabric from her nose, she smiled with all the hope of youth, her scars proof of anything but naivety.

"I brought you some things to help with your headache." She offered the woven plate to him.

The sight of her dark charcoal waves and charismatic smile were comforting, but Azure had a much more pressing matter to attend to. He scrubbed his fingers through his hair to awaken his drowsy mind. "Where is Drékor?"

She sighed. *In the den with the girls, like always.*

Charging around her and out into the main room, his veins searing with anger, Azure confronted the male relaxing on a pillow bed, three Xahu'ré females under his arms.

"What the hell, Drékor? Why?" He glared at the straight nose and pristine skin on his face. The Xahu'ré warrior was a sweet-talking freeloader, a liar, and one of Azure's first mistakes. Azure hated the man, and himself for ever believing there was an easier way to survive Agutra that held any moral weight. "I was closing in on them!"

Drékor scowled and stood. His thinner form was muscular, like every Xahu'ré, but his mass did not compare to the warrior towering over him. "What on Vioras are you talking about, brother? I prevented more harm from coming to you."

Azure's fists balled up so tight, his short fingernails dug into his palms. "You have no idea what you ruined or how many might die now because of your actions!"

"That is no way to talk to your own flesh and blood." Drékor leaned forward, a devilish grin spreading his cheeks.

"You are no Xahu'ré brother of mine," Azure muttered under his breath.

Drékor clicked his tongue, shaking his head. "Let me guess." He paused to pick up a gourd of red Yakna from a table on the side. "You've been hallucinating about that female again, haven't you?" He downed it and returned the hollowed out fruit to its tray. "Why don't you take one of my miia? They are capable matches, would bear you strong warriors."

"I am faithful." Azure's eyes burned into him. "Unlike you."

Drékor shrugged, downing a second shot. "Your decision."

"There are real problems threatening survivors." Azure checked the throwing knives on his belt, reseating them in their sheaths. "We have a real chance at freedom for everyone, yet you stand here, drinking and drifting the ether."

"Don't ruin this for me," Drékor hissed. "Every time you get the idea in your head someone is here to rescue us, all it does is destroy the peace! Warruks flood the halls. Linoans are released from their protocols to hunt us until the traitors are shredded, or enough of the workers are that we make the rebellion stop of our own accord. Then we get stuck in here, because we can't leave to get supplies without being caught!"

Azure's bare toes grabbed the metal floor. "It is not about you! All of this is at the expense of the other lives working hard every cycle, living in constant fear of death if they don't produce enough. Your actions make you no different than the Suanoa!"

One of Drékor's minions spoke up from his slouched position in a hay-stuffed chair on the side of the room. The female in his lap purred as she nuzzled into his neck—a post-mating ritual. It made Azure's stomach turn in jealousy and disgust over their misplaced priorities. "This will only bring more pain to them, Azure, giving them false hope, just to suffer again when we fail."

Azure gave him a blazing glare. "You don't know the first thing about pain, you little Japous."

"Oh, here we go again." Drékor rolled his eyes. "You think you're so special because you're different from the rest of us."

"Asii!" Ramura slammed the plate she was holding for Azure on a shelf. "Drék, you were born on this ship. You didn't go through testing or even the sway. You and I— We can't understand; we will never understand!"

"Shut it, Ramura. You're more worthless than him," he sneered.

Fury heated in Azure's chest. "Don't you dare talk to her like that! She has proven herself on more occasions than any of you. You don't even know what we are doing! We want to find a real home, a place where our kind can be safe and established, somewhere we can begin to heal and rebuild, before we disappear, like so many others from this universe. A place where we don't live in constant fear!"

"That chance at normalcy for us died a long time ago, brother." Drékor dismissed his words with a wave of his hand. "You must relax before your heart explodes from working too much or your brain from the foolish thought your miia is even alive."

"She is alive—here, now! That's who I was chasing in the hall!" Azure growled. "So what if *we* don't see such freedom? But our future generations could. We have to fight together, for each other!"

It was the motto perimeter guards lived by, and he believed in it completely.

"I'm not risking my life for someone who's not smart enough to do what I'm doing." Drékor smirked.

Azure was growing weary, wasting time on such an unproductive conversation. "You mean hiding like a coward?"

"Me, a coward? I kicked your ass out there! You had no idea I was following you!" Drékor barked, throwing a hand toward the door. "Perimeter guard my—" he muttered a few choice words in Xahu're that Azure ignored.

"You blindsided me in the head. And if I remember right, you said originally you were 'preventing more harm from coming to me.' You are contradicting yourself. Now, who is the stupid one?"

The room chuckled at Azure's remark, but his nerves were growing thin.

"Shut up, Ehru!" Drékor balled up his fists. His irises brightened and movements slowed. The firewater was kicking in.

Ramura shook her head. "Azure has done a lot to keep us from getting caught, and this is how you repay him?"

"When are you going to grow up and realize the full gravity of our situation?" Azure asked. "True Xahu're warriors stand up and fight!"

"Never! Look at this place!" Drékor scanned the room smugly, a palm open and up as he swaggered a circle. "This is the life. We built this. This is our home!"

Azure looked away, ashamed of ever having been associated with the wanton lifestyle of the male in front of him. "No, the Suanoa built it.

Everything in this place has been stolen from honest, hardworking life forms on this ship. If either find out about this place, you will wish you were dead." Azure snorted. *Some days I regret saving your worthless ass.* "All you have done is disappointed me and let those who cared about you down."

With a shake of his head, he turned for the exit. Talking was wasting time.

"Screw you!" Drékor spun around, reaching out to push Azure.

Grabbing him by his shirt, Azure lifted him and tossed his flailing form at the bed, causing the girls to screech and scatter.

"Don't get in my way again!" he shouted over his shoulder, charging the guards blocking the exit. He was too fast and reached them before they could move. Azure rammed a double uppercut into their stomachs, his veins bulging from the fury tensing his forearms and fists. The two doubled over and sank to the floor as Azure stormed out of the den.

Drékor's arrogant shout was a whisper behind him. "Or what?"

Azure barreled through the crosscuts, leaping from one truss to another, desperation his driving force, the image of Atana's broken body—dragging limp behind the Warruk—burning in his thoughts. *I'll crack your ribs open and darken your spark with my bare hands.*

At the faint sound of skin landing on metal, Azure looked back to find Ramura catching up. Her silhouette sat perched in the light from the doorway on an angled beam for only a breath before jumping another beam closer to him.

I will not let my guard down again, Drekor, Azure warned. *Nor will I ever forgive you for this.* He heard the warrior's scoff in Ether fade as the distance between them grew.

Can I help? Ramura asked. *Drék keeps me locked up and in the dark most of the time.*

He hasn't been letting you out? Azure glanced through a set of louvers to ensure the hall was clear. Climbing down through the vent, he dropped silently to the floor.

No, and I didn't realize it until I was inside. You know he likes his control. She lowered herself into his open arms and closed the screen. Azure set her down, and she followed him around a corner with soft-footed grace.

Of course. Suddenly worried, he stopped in the shadows to examine her, his fingers caressing her cheeks. *He didn't hurt you in any way, did he? If he did, I'll kill him.* He paused. *After I find the team from Earth.*

Ramura shook her head. *I'm not tall and pretty like the other girls, so he made me his servant. A few slaps is all.*

As if we need to add to the misery of this place. Azure's face twisted in disgust. *You are so beautiful. He doesn't know.* He cautiously moved out into the hall. *Drékor's the one who's an Ehru, so power hungry. He's not intelligent enough to be a leader. He makes careless mistakes, endangering good warriors like you. You need to go to your sector. It is safer there than it is with him.*

Can't I come with you? she asked.

No. Sahara's been taken to the hollow, deep in the sway, for interrogation. I'd bet my bones on it. The Warruks only injured them, and I followed them through the sway shortcuts. I just hope I'm not too late, now.

You really found her? Her indigo irises lit above a hopeful smile.

Yes. Azure motioned to the ground and then the direction of her sector. *Lisano Ramura, niema. Beautiful Ramura, please.*

Disappointment darkened her eyes. *Yes, Martiis.*

Hey. He left a tender kiss on her forehead. *It was good to see you. Vi sisano.*

—Grit—

Chapter 32

A HAZE, like hot cotton stuffed in her brain, blurred Atana's focus. Her body felt like a sack of potatoes being dragged along. The garbled grunts of a Warruk echoed overhead.

Lavrion—must find— She groaned. Atana had sworn after escaping testing no one would ever take control of her body again—a broken promise.

Blanched colors filtered into her thoughts, disrupted by sharp tugs on her gathered hair. Shifting and blurry, unrecognizable faces. Shadows dancing between. Comforting warmth. Sunlight. Golden hot. Hand in hers. Fog pushing them apart. Suffocating darkness stealing her again.

"No." Some primal part of her resisted and reached for the fading fingers.

Her body jerked, rolling across the moving floor. Stings preceded a repetitive, dull ache. The hardness of each hit was not absolute. It flexed, bent to her body. Wood. Through her arm, back, legs, the pain burst inside. She choked down a sob. They would not win.

She would not give them the pleasure.

Breathing was hard, the beat in her chest too slow.

"Don't sink." But she couldn't stop the descent. Only fight against its depth.

Her head snapped sideways with the strike. Atana felt tears gush from her cheek across her lips and nose. Hot. Tasting of iron.

The black blanket of nothingness curled around her.

Clouds of gray puffed up in the darkness. Sparkles and flashes, yellow-white in hue, made her squint. Through them stood a small log cabin. Laundry flapped in a gentle breeze. Her skin warmed in the light.

Atana searched for the cool sensation at her feet. Water from the shallow creek babbled underneath her, reaching her ankles. She could barely make out a reflection of her small, round body on the surface, her tiny toes sensing the unevenness of the pebbles at the bottom.

Her little fingers combed over the hem of a thin, plainly-woven dress. The pale, faded-yellow cotton and its ink-printed red roses rippled lightly in front of her.

Few scars. She rotated her arms admiring them. It had been so long.

Would you like a spin? A pair of women's hands spoke into hers in the glittering light. Atana forgot her worries, reveling in the glorious sunshine and warm fingers around her wrists, as she swung round and round, her feet drifting upwards.

The kaleidoscope of butterflies dancing in her tummy escaped in giggles.

She looked up at the woman when she was set down. Why did the circles have to end?

Pale hazel eyes smiled back, framed with ivory skin and tawny-blond waves of hair. A golden angel. Young Atana begged for more, forming O shapes with her hands and tapping her fingers together. She reached up.

More— It rang so familiarly. *More, uh-more. Uh-more-uh.* Where had she heard that before? It meant 'garden of life,' 'the one who would bear the children of the future.'

Atana reeled as she listened to it in her mind again, thoughts spinning when the connection finally clicked into place.

A gentle kiss planted on her cheek.

Amora was her mother.

Sahara. Her voice was sweet syrup to a starved soul. *I do not have the strength your father did.*

Did? Atana wanted to step back from the memory, turn and run. Her body didn't flinch. Struggling against the vision rendered nothing. She was bound in a mental strait-jacket, skin and muscle and bone, completely numb and asleep. She wanted out.

It's what she needed to live.

Blond curls and a pair of blue eyes peeked out over her mother's shoulder.

Lavrion. Guilt churned in Atana's heart.

A ball of light collided with the cabin, sending pieces of the logs flying into the air and a ripple through the ground beneath Atana's toes. Her mother clutched her tight, eyes darting back and forth over the sky. Chunks of flaming wood rained around them, some of it floating down the creek. Her mother sheltered her, beautiful face contorted with denial.

Her mother started screaming. Atana knew she was. She couldn't hear it, but she could feel the vibrations against her body.

Miima? Atana had never seen her mother so afraid.

As a child, she hadn't understood what war was, only that their world was on fire. And her miima was crying. Now grabbing her by the wrist. Now pulling, painfully hard.

Atana's bare feet stumbled to keep up.

Skirting a chicken coop, they scurried into the weather-beaten barn. Her mother grabbed the reins and yanked their horse out of the stall. Atana watched from the ground, hands twisting, eager to hold on to her mother again.

Her mother climbed up, swinging baby Lavrion around to her front.

Another rumble beneath Atana's feet startled her. She cowered in the corner as flaming boards crashed to the ground from the ceiling of the barn.

Give me your hand! Her mother steadied the horse shaking its head and reached for her. Atana didn't hesitate to leap for the comfort of her mother's fingers. Her young body flung through the stifling hot air to land on the back of the saddle. Amora took her little hands and put one on each of her sides, tapping hard. Atana wadded up fistfuls of her mother's yellow dress. Singed holes appearing in the cloth sent Atana's small heart racing.

Her mother couldn't get hurt, could she?

But embers burned through to Amora's skin from the fiery skies. Yet she didn't stop, didn't hesitate or try to wipe them away.

Their horse, Buster, was fidgeting, not following Amora's commands. A swift kick to the sides and he listened better. They launched out of the barn and sprinted down the narrow road. More pieces of burning wood fell around them, ash darkening the day to dusk. They were heading into the mountains. Away from home, from Mamoo, their cow, from the soft grasses and blossoming crops. Everything Atana knew.

All of it was burning.

Little Atana wept as small hills rose around them. The saddle swayed with Buster's steps as they climbed the twisting trails. Rocks broke free in the loose dirt and fell. Her mother wouldn't change course no matter how many times Atana tried to get her attention. Why wouldn't she listen? She could hear.

A pair of aircraft passed overhead sending heavy vibrations through Atana's lungs. An explosion from a ship crashing into the mountains made Buster rear back. Tightening her fingers, Atana strained to hang on as her mother fought to regain control of Buster. He jumped and shook his head, not meeting her demands. Fabric slipped.

Atana felt herself falling and the wind tugging at her dress. The ground was jagged and unforgiving upon contact, knocking the breath out of her lungs. Dirt caught in her eyes and mouth, each tumble landing another blow.

Sahara!

Atana slid to a stop at the bottom of a slope, body aching, head pounding, cuts throbbing. She had never been in so much agony. Rolling onto her stomach, she squinted up the hill to her mother, a blurred mess of spinning colors. Atana blinked and cried and pushed herself up.

This time, when she looked, her mother was clear, as was the approaching shadow in the sky behind her.

Her mother turned the horse around, panic in her voice. *No.* She said it over and over.

A ship. Coming up fast. Fear tightened Atana's throat. *Miima!*

A cold, green light blinded Atana, filling her with regret for not behaving better, not saying she loved her more, not holding on tight enough. As the coils snugged in around her, frosted ropes of stinging nettles, her stomach lurched.

The ship didn't take her mother.

Green columns of light. An invisible hand yanked her into the sky. Into the belly of a mechanical beast. Then icy fog on her skin. Then silence. She couldn't move. Only pain and blackness. Nothing else, but the tomb.

She waited.

Someone would come. Let her out. She could feel the vibrations of footsteps nearby. With shaking hands, Atana squeezed the knife her mother always strapped to her waist. Its familiar weight calmed her fear. Its purpose eased the confusion.

Whoever they were, they had destroyed everything. Killed Mamoo. Burned her home. They hadn't played fair, or nice. Her miima would scold them.

Anger strengthened her fingers and spread heat into her veins.

She waited in the dark. In the cold. Alone.

Atana knew her brother was now a victim of the green light. It had to be him. Finding Lavrion wasn't an option right now. Maybe he was still too far away. But she had to try.

Through the emptiness, Atana called out his name, hoping he could hear her. Wishing she could calm his fear, a fear she knew too well. *Lavrion—*

...

The gravity swayed back and forth like a boat on calm ocean waters, making it difficult for Bennett to clear his head. His eyelids were heavy with exhaustion and defeat. Blood from his knuckles had dripped between his fingers, making them sticky. His SIs were gone.

Behind him, the cold wall numbed some of the burn from the hit.

"Damn Warruks," he grumbled.

Out of habit, Bennett lifted his left arm to check on his team. Black-chrome ropes snapped taut around his wrists, restraining him stronger with each passing moment.

A surge of adrenaline sharpened his senses. Bennett felt the threads squeeze and the blood pool in his hands. Looking past his smashed wristband, the last vial of serum cracked and empty, he saw the dark fibers curl like tentacles around the metal grid of the grate in the floor. He wasn't tied to the room; he was tied to something living beneath it.

As reality came back into focus, he noticed a faint light blinking before him to the rhythm of clinking chains. He squinted up at the source.

Suspended from the ceiling of the cell, Atana faced Bennett, her eyes shut. Wisps of hair floated as she swung, blocking the light from a tiny window in the door, her hands tied behind her. Black and blue splotches covered her face.

Bennett clumsily scrambled to his knees in the sludgy grit on the floor unable to take his eyes off the discoloration. *Atana, are you awake?* His heart pounded harder when she didn't respond. "Nakio."

The cables holding his wrists clung tight, preventing him from leaving the wall. Whatever resided below him burbled its disagreement.

Bennett strained with all his available energy, desperately trying to reach her, his breath faltering. "Nakio?" His eyes moistened, racing across her closed eyelids, wishing they would open just a little, anything to let him know she was holding on. A four-centimeter gash on one cheek had left a trail, drawn by gravity, toward the top of her forehead.

His face was close though too far to sense if she was radiating any warmth. Bennett tore angrily at the cords that held him. "Please!" The veins in his neck and forehead rose. He jerked once more out of frustration, but the creature was unforgiving. A growl burst from his exhausted lungs, his shoulders screaming in their sockets.

From inside her collar, a plum-red drop slipped free, decimating his rage when it splattered in the puddle before him.

Bennett stared wide-eyed at her motionless face. He had failed. This was his fault.

An overwhelming sensation of fear, guilt, and isolation struck him. He slumped back against the wall, his muscles too weak to hold him upright any longer.

She was right. I shouldn't have come on this mission.

His mind, not accustomed to the influx of negative emotions, shut down into darkness.

Chapter 33

BLOOD DRAINED from Bennett's lip. Two Warruks had stormed in, trading off punches, their fists heavy as sandbags against his body. The final hit sprawled him out on the floor.

Something clicked on the Warruk standing over his head and the creature below bubbled out a whine. With one eye, Bennett peered through the grate to see a crackling, red collar light up a set of eyes narrowed in pain. The ropes retracted.

His muscles burned and throbbed in such totality it left him numb as a Warruk lugged him out of the door.

Bennett's boots squeaked and screeched as their rubber tread slid along the sludgy, wet hall. His bloodied drool wasn't helping. He didn't have the strength to fight, not now.

Nakio— Surveying Atana's flaccid body, her hair tangled in the grasp of the Warruk beside his, he feared the worst. *Nakio?*

After several failed attempts to communicate, he inventoried the jingling belts the Warruks wore to keep his mind off the possibility she was dead. Their thunderous steps and the end of a wooden pole pounded like the pulse in his skull. The edges of a doorframe passed by and they entered a white-walled room so bright it made him squint. *Adapted to the darkness*—

He checked on Atana again. She was still hanging by her hair, her limbs unconsciously following her Warruk, who stopped next to his. The colors of her injured face in the light made him queasy and furious. He calculated the distance between their bodies. *Three meters.*

His guard picked him up with a hand to the back of his jacket, sitting him on his knees. The heavy, sickening chill permeating such a vibrant space could only originate from one thing: *Suanoa.*

Three pairs of blood-orange irises, encircled by smoky fingers that clawed the light from the room, glared down upon the two captives and their keepers. Dull-red fabric draped off a jutting shoulder of each, accented by small, sage green, cuspidate-like bones. Their stygian robes glinted beneath—a grid of pointed, overlapping, placoid scales.

They sat atop raised pedestals. Beyond dual panes of radial glass. Walls that caged him.

Bennett could hear their chatter over his receiver. *We have to decide what to do with the intruders. Punishment for disobedience is death.*

Brooding, in the middle, the screeching overlay to his rumbling voice made the words torturous to decipher. "Why were they not properly punished?"

The Warruk's shifted, mumbling incoherently in response. Bennett stole a glance at them. Their large, quatrefoil irises were constricted with fear. Even the most reckless beasts feared Suanoa.

"The deaths of your brethren were fair punishment for your incompetence!" the Suanoa to the right remarked. The guards' disagreeing grunts evoked only more agony. *Silence!*

Their minds rang with the sharpness and volume of the word, causing the two guards by the open door to cover their ears, though no physical sound waves were created. The Warruks guarding him and Atana winced.

Bennett doubled over, squeezing his eyes shut, the noise echoing between his ears. Chamarel had warned them about the potential harm of the Suanoa's telepathic abilities. He cleared his mind the best he could, trying to focus on the sensation of his forehead against the dirty floor that smelled sickeningly of raw meat.

Why their breath smells like iron, she'd said. His stomach clenched. *Don't think about it. Just don't.*

Voices scraped through his brain like ice picks, screeching and digging like vengeful thieves ransacking a vault. Bennett fought back, forcing his watering eyes open. Lifting his head, he took a meditative breath.

"For every action," he rasped, "there is an equal and opposite reaction."

Bennett's jaw clamped tight as he struggled for control. *Aren't getting shit out of me.*

"On Earth, it's called Newton's third law." The voices backed off. His conscious distraction was working. "Some call it equilibrium, some Karma." He sucked in deep, filling his hungry lungs to capacity. A defiant grin curled a corner of his mouth. "Either way, she's a bitch when she comes for you."

The third made a sound, which Bennett interpreted as a haughty laugh. "Who is going to stop us? You?"

Bennett cleared his throat and spit the blood from his lip onto the floor. "Do you truly want nothing from the places you visit but to use them and throw them away?" He peered up at each of them.

"How dare your insolent being look at us!" the Suanoa on the right barked indignantly. "You are not worthy!" Its nail-less, knotted fingers opened like reanimated spider's legs, signaling to the Warruk holding Bennett.

He caught a glimpse of the gleaming detonator embedded in the Suanoa's palm before the bundle of knuckles against his cheek sent his face and shoulder smacking the floor. A hoarse curse softened the stinging waves rippling through his body. A hand picked him up and plopped him roughly back on his knees.

The leader stared at him with a predatory fixation. Its three-fold mouth scrunched and squirmed, its long, gar-like teeth clinking together. "We are a self-preserving species and seek no need for humility. It is weakness."

Bennett was exhausted and couldn't help but let his head droop toward the floor, despite its toxic scent.

"You are making so many enemies." Sucking the fresh blood into the center of his mouth, he spit it to the side. "They will, in combination, bring the downfall of your kind. How do you not see that?"

It was a game, theirs and his. Their goal was to break him down. His was to break them open: arrogance, their tyrannical reign, and the transparent panes protecting them—all describing weaknesses.

"We do not fear your petty threats. Your kind are unintelligent, naïve, and slow to adapt, all of the worst characteristics any could have." The Suanoa to the left rubbed the knobby ridge in the center of his face as if it ached. "The reason your type have been allowed on this Agutra is that you can perform the same tasks as Dagganak, Xahu'ré, and Marakou, with less resource consumption. Otherwise, we would've rid your planet of your disgracing presence." It leaned sideways, remarking to the others, "Pitiful, really, their kind. No special skills or characteristics."

"Selfish barbarians think they're the center of the universe," the one on the right added. "They know nothing and think they know everything." Chewing casually on a soft, splinter-thin bone he twisted between his fingers, his lambent eyes gleamed with wicked intent. "I want to see how hard he fights."

The leader nodded, still scrutinizing the sergeant below.

Screams blasted through Bennett's brain like bullets released from their cages, ripping through his past. Everyone he had ever watched die, every injury and aching loss, replayed vividly behind his eyelids, pummeling his newly serum-free heart. Their familiar faces flashed before him like strobe lights. His nervous system flooded with pain from dull to sharply inundating: lost fist-fights, bullet holes, flying metal fragments, knife cuts, burns from flaming beams, and the deplorable notion he was the forsaken one.

He cried out, his body shuddering and lungs heaving. Bennett strained for the few pieces of himself he could collect inside, the things that gave him hope, things he didn't want to lose: his team, UP, and— *Atana.*

The Suanoa shouted silently in his ears. *Worthless, hopeless bastard. You will always be alone. No one will come for you. You are a disgrace to your kind! Your partner is already dead. You will join her soon, you pathetic brute! You have failed.*

His guard squeezed the glaive tight in his hand, sticky skin squeaking over wood.

Bennett could feel its gaze burrowing into the back of his neck. Twisting, through quivering and blurry eyes, he inspected Atana's incapacitated body. The bloodied strands of loose bangs framing her dirty, inanimate face only put gasoline on a building fire.

His life dwindled, a candle flame in a sudden draft. The matchbox lay at his side. His eyes drooped shut. Her soft hair and bright teal eyes made him want to blow up the universe and anything in his path, just to get five minutes to stare at her undisturbed. The ginger-sweet spice of her lips had knocked the serum dead the first day in the fields. But the spark between their hands upon meeting was what implored his protection of her. Command's mission didn't matter after that moment. This purpose ran far deeper. Consumed him with need. An unalterable fate.

Bennett's lips thinned, peeling back from his gritted teeth. It couldn't end this way.

All I need is one match, one sign there's still fire in that merciless heart of yours. He forced his eyes open and focused on her. *Come on, Atana. Give me something to work with.*

Chapter 34

THE FIRST HIT had knocked loose a cascade of memories. The Warruks were too simple-minded to be aware of her manipulation as Atana repeatedly stood, dodged their attacks, and tried to run. It was a mistake for them to release her. She remembered that now.

After they caught a leg, they dragged her through more halls, into a sway cell, and hung her up by her ankles. She couldn't run. Couldn't move, not with her hands tied behind her back.

Blood pooled in Atana's head. Her focus sharpened.

Unbeknownst to them, they had helped her meditate, helped her stay alive.

Even in her declining state, it was flawless manipulation.

Cool, gray clouds billowed around her as she sat, Quarter Lotus, in her mind-space. She opened herself to the sensations of the world around her, waiting for their black storm to invade, waiting for the Suanoa. Dreams and memories drifted in and out, but she held her ground, letting them pass around her like wind in a storm.

It was difficult at first to block out the agonizing signals of damage to her body. And when Bennett had called to her, she'd felt the urge to wake, to reassure him she had a plan. But she couldn't, not if she wanted the Grey to work, and not if she wanted to survive.

Her limbs tingled with blood loss. But it was the prickle running down her spine that told her it was time.

Atana blinked and looked down at the white floor, splattered with blood. The room rippled like a watery curtain around her. Awake in Ether, in the dimension between dreams and the physical realm, she pushed her soul up from her broken body. It was like ripping off a bandage—a quick sting followed by a dull throb, then relief. Beside her, Bennett swayed in obvious pain, seated on his knees. Her being, now of pure, willed energy, drifted upwards. She didn't want to leave him there. To suffer. There were just things bigger than him she needed to face first.

Atana knew she had to stay calm for the Grey to work if the Suanoa's capabilities were as powerful as Chamarel had warned. Any disturbance could draw their attention. Willing the gray clouds back in around her, a cloak of shadow and mist, her body melded with the air like a chameleon skin.

It had always been a suicide mission, in the eyes of Command, in hers. She'd felt death's grip on her from the moment she'd seen Lavrion disappear. It was karma. Goss's death, Ekiipa's plea to not be forgotten, Chamarel, and the failed prophecy—all taunted her.

A twinge of doubt within said she wouldn't make it long enough to relay any information she might gain. If she could even figure out how to do it. It wasn't her original plan. Bennett had screwed it up. Of all the hours, he had to crack on their departure, expose his vulnerability, and then cage her beneath him so she couldn't run, couldn't lead the Warruks and Linoans away from the team. She'd forced out the voices, tried to knock the crew down when she had felt the distant thunder through her boots.

She hadn't detected the Linoans, their bounding footsteps too light. They came too soon.

Improvising was normal. But this telepathic land, this Ether, was something she was only beginning to remember. *A last resort.* Her only option.

The mission was officially a mess, like her. At least they had something in common.

Floating through the air was weightless, like space, with the pressure of swimming through the deep ocean. She thought about the radial glass wall and, to her surprise, drifted toward it. Her fingers reached out, frustrated by a barrier she hadn't expected. She should've known Suanoa wouldn't leave themselves vulnerable.

Her fingertips dipped into its surface as if it were made of water. Atana's eyes slammed shut. She took a steadying breath and hurtled herself to the other side. It felt like diving into a deep pool, the air beyond much thicker, a transparent molasses. The panes rippled back into place behind her.

She spun to face the three tarnished souls in their arc, staring down at the shepherds' limp forms and the Warruks holding them. This is where her plan ended. It was difficult to lay out checkpoints when she had no idea how to search within the Grey. She needed guidance. Needed Chamarel— or Sensei.

Atana knew Sensei the best. She didn't see his eyes straight on very often. He was always meditating. In the few glimpses, she'd never sorted out the color. One day a hint of blue, the next brown, then green.

He would say, *silence yourself, and listen to the energy within.*

Thinking in words was too easy for bystanders to comprehend. She'd learned that the hard way with Chamarel. She had to do it by essence, by aura, by feeling. It was the only way she could navigate and not get caught. Lucky for her, the serum stopped working.

Atana did not want the Suanoa to know she was watching. There was no telling what the punishment would be if she was found. A slow, agonizing death was the only certainty.

A whisper, in urges, said, *Touch what you wish to see: the one in the middle.* It had the thickest stripes over his eyes, the most animal teeth accenting his uniform. It would likely be the highest ranking.

Him? The one that had ordered such brutality.

Cruising around behind him, she looked at the churning vat of tar that was the essence of his being and shuddered. What would his spark look like in Ether? Was it even a spark? Or something else altogether?

Her fingers inched out, anticipating a lashing cobra's venom at any moment. Ever so lightly, she touched the glinting armor on his shoulder.

Ripped from her own mind, she was thrown into another dimension. A pit of glossy and matte black creatures crawled and oozed over her body. Fear ravaged her control, stripping her down to the barest instincts.

Get out, get out!

Only, there was no up or down, left or right, no sense of gravity, no direction she could see to safety. Frantically, she pawed at the sea.

This is his mind? His heart? There was no air, no space between, only fractions of light to indicate her fate. She felt a tongue thistle in her ear. A thick rope curled around a leg, creeping up and over her chest, pressing the breath from her lungs. Short-haired legs trotted across an arm. The grating slither of scaly skin over itself made her seize.

Brushing a thousand tiny legs from her face, with a humming scream, she protected it with her hands. She tried to suck air in, but it felt like little beetles pouring inside. Closing her tearing eyes, she tucked herself in the farthest corner of her mind.

Sensei!

One of the first lessons he'd taught her, came to mind. *What you feel inside will form the world around you. In consciousness our instincts protect us. But in the twilight, our subconscious must be controlled with reason. What are you, Nakio?*

In her panicked state, she could only recall a piece of the Shepherd's Oath, a promise drilled into her since she was a teen. *Even on the darkest night, we are their shepherds, their guiding light. I am a shepherd. I am a—*

The creatures fell like hail to her feet. Pure air poured into her lungs. She stood in infinite space, her body a single beacon of light, the rays penetrating the depths of their black hole Ether. Their mental network, the dimension where things existed as plain energy, was a far cry from the gray and blue Ether she had connected to with Azure and Kios or the multicolored, sparkling world Chamarel was linked to. She had never felt such emptiness in anyone, other than herself.

She stepped across the crunching, squishing ground, wobbling but listening—their squirms and cries beneath her, dismissed; her breath, accounted for. Looking up to the skies above, she saw the Suanoa, their minds playing like fifty-three translucent screens around her.

Somewhere in the locked away memories, she knew it was not the first time she had seen the system. She had infiltrated once before, a blurry, incomplete picture. She worried they might recognize her but hushed herself before the words could manifest. Circling the clouds, she studied the moving images.

One burst white with the sight of an exploding star. It spread, flashing on every screen, a chain of dominos around her, different perspectives, but all the same content: fear of the light. Theirs.

Staring wide-eyed at the opalescent net of expanding energy flying at the window of a rumbling ship, the shattering planets of a galaxy visible through the glass, she gasped, reaching out for something to brace herself against. Two Suanoa huddled together in another memory, releasing squeaks and bubbling noises, what she could've only figured was their version of crying. Backing away, she denied the signs of humble humanity that had long since vanished.

You know this. The wretched sounds of its voice filled the expanse. Her light faded on instinct. She slipped away from the others as the memory windows rolled and spun into bodies of no identifiable detail. *Remember your ancestral lines. When your conviction softens, your loyalty weakens. Remember their sacrifice for us. Take everything. Leave nothing. Survive.*

The multitude joined. *Take everything! Leave nothing! Survive!* Their voices were like the peak note of a child's scream overlaid with the lowest rattle in a mother's chest as the frozen void stole her spark.

Atana's panic dislodged her senses, throwing her soul out of the darkness and against the floor at the feet of the jury.

Already dead, she heard one say. Lifting herself, she saw Bennett's pleading face turned toward her body in the other room and the glaive as it rose, her panic rising with it.

No! "Bennett!" Atana clambered up and thrust herself at the glass, only to find it had solidified. She banged frantically on its cruel, clear surface. "Bennett!"

But she was still a mere apparition. Her voice made no sound. Not in the physical realm.

Atana's head was jerked backward by a fistful of hair. She screeched, her hands tugging, clawing at the spider-leg fingers. Shock flayed her nerves, leaving her quivering beneath three sets of red eyes.

Her throat tightened, the heat of a plasma implant hot against her neck. If she died in Ether, she died in the waking realm. The Grey would be no different.

This was all wrong. It wasn't supposed to happen this way. She was supposed to be invincible. The prodigal child.

"I'll show you what you want to see, worthless sack of dregs." His eyes boiled with wrath above her, his grasp unyielding. "I'll show you before you die."

Why did its insult hurt so much?

She fought with every ounce, worked herself nearly into the grave from lack of sleep and food. What more could she give? Fighting for life was all she'd ever done. Humans and non-humans alike depended on her, whether they knew it or not.

A sack of worthless dirt.

It was the feeling she feared, she carried inside, she believed to be true.

Smoky clouds poured down around her face. She choked on its breath, stinging embers in her lungs. Her body was unwilling to her command. Disappointment, self-hatred, and fear locked her arms and legs in place. Stilled her thoughts. She couldn't look away. It would be so easy to give in, to let go, to die.

But they didn't play fair.

Plan or no plan, she would show them she wasn't afraid. She wouldn't surrender. She wouldn't give them the gratification.

We have a fighter who wants an honorable death. The sneer twisting the leader's face bled of arrogance and success.

The two at his sides remarked at her puerility as she was knocked back into their black Ether.

A white-hot explosion amidst the depths of space blotted out her vision. And then she saw them, thrown along their warpath through the stars searching for salvation. Planets and peoples, gone, obliterated without question. The galaxies blurred past, faster with each moment.

Every Suanoan voice joined in the mantra, rumbling through her with earthquake force. *Take everything. Leave nothing. Survive. You will not deter us. A fleck of ash in wind, you will be forgotten. An empty sacrifice.*

The chill of space, of the hopeless battle, crept up on her, weaving trails of ice into her hair. Her wristband and fingertips frosted over. Her lashes encrusted with tears. The sting was too much. Her scream hung in the air, high and shrill like the slice of the glaive.

Somewhere in the other room, between her sobs, she heard a growl.

Atana replayed the sound as the universe slipped away, the familiar darkness invading.

Please, let that be Bennett.

Chapter 35

ONE MATCH.

Atana's Warruk yanked her head upward and adjusted its grasp in her hair.

An eyelid flicked.

The hammer in Bennett's ribs swelled, dumping fuel into his body. There was no serum to halt the advancement of adrenaline. When his Warruk's swing reached peak height, he planted a foot.

With a bellowing growl, Bennett rammed himself into the body behind him, switching off his receiver. The monster stumbled, its bladed staff clattering to the floor. Jumping his rope-tied wrists, Bennett kicked a foot back, throwing the Warruk against the wall with inhuman force.

He crossed the three meters between him and Atana in a single stride, grabbing her guard behind its shoulder before it could react. Bennett threw a knee with all his might into its lower abdomen. It caved, releasing its grip on her.

In one graceful arc, Bennett shoved his bound wrists at the blade tied to the kneeling Warruk's side, fraying every thread, and then drew it from the sheath. The glistening point found the soft spot between the jaw bones of the snarling face, punching through with ease.

His Warruk had regained its ground and charged. Yanking the knife out, Bennett spun, striking his guard in the chest with so much force the metal tip burst through its bulbous body, spurting dark, plum-colored blood against the wall.

The two guards from the door came running at him with heavy feet. The soreness from their beatings had faded from consciousness, leaving only fury thrusting out from his core, coursing hungrily through his muscles.

Bennett took the closest down with an arm across the throat, its windpipe flattening on contact. The blade slipped his grasp, plinking off the far wall. Bennett somersaulted over and took the last Warruk's knees out from underneath with one swooping kick.

Ripping the elliptical gun from the guard lying at his feet, he shot it, center mass. With a weighted sigh, he pointed the weapon at the jury.

"She is the only thing that matters to me."

The Suanoa on the right chewed apathetically on a bone, watching Bennett. But the others leapt to their feet, the notable leader in the center barking commands at the third. A radial screen illuminated like magma around the third's hand. It frantically typed across the symbols at the leader's direction.

Keeping his mind silent, Bennett hustled over to where Atana lay and peeled her up from the floor. Slinging her limp body over his opposite shoulder, he backed out of the room, heart pounding. This mission had turned to utter shit. He had no plan and no idea what the repercussions were of his actions. Bennett was operating on instinct—and anger.

Warruks barreled out from every intersection. Bennett effectively fired upon them without thinking. Passing a stairwell, he peered down, hoping for an escape. Four Linoans were headed up and only a few steps away. Tightening his free arm around Atana's knees, he sent rapid fire down the shaft. They were the last thing he wanted to deal with on his six.

Two more Warruks approached his nine-o'clock position. He swung the weapon, smacking the first in the face. It stumbled away, far enough he could take it—a smoking hole through its gut.

The second approached, shooting now from his blind side, the shoulder Atana was folded over. A heat wave barreled past his middle, singeing his leather jacket. He slung the weapon across his stomach and took a careless, but lucky, shot. *Thud.*

Jetting down an adjacent hallway, he studied the map on Atana's functioning wristband, searching for a hiding spot. A potential location appeared inside a small hydro-facility maintenance closet between the Hatoga fields and the proposed backup transport Tanner and Atana had found. He tapped it, illuminating a path.

Hearing pounding footsteps off to his right, he ducked into an unlit alcove, placing the radiant weapon behind his back. Atana's wristband lit up the shadows. Sliding a finger over Silence, the screen blinked out.

Four Warruks stopped in the opening. One leaned into the nook concealing the two Earthlings, its heavy, rasping breaths covering up the sound of Bennett's adrenaline-infused heartbeat.

Bennett edged back until his body pressed into the darkest corner. Grumbles came from a Warruk in the hallway junction, summoning the other three to follow. The one searching the shadows sniffed the air before releasing a snort of disapproval. Reluctantly, it turned and left with the others.

When the heavy tromping faded, Bennett let out the breath he'd been holding and crept toward the main hall. With the coast clear, he set course for the maintenance closet, listening for the faintest sounds. He hustled along the suggested hidden paths as best he could with Atana over his shoulder.

After what seemed like hours, Bennett's legs were exhausted, his back aching. He slipped into the secret passage above the sprinkler systems and forced his weary muscles to obey, cautiously bending forward to shift Atana off of his shoulders. Bennett braced a palm behind her head and rested her battered body on the floor like a sleeping baby.

Utilizing the communicator on her wristband, he reported the trouble to his team. The pairs responded.

ETA: 1 Hour

When Bennett had acknowledged, the screen cleared. Her pulse blinked in the lower, left-hand corner, slow but present, to his relief. He slumped down next to her listless figure, stretching his stiff spine as he slid his jacket off. Lifting her head from the ground, he cushioned it with the leather.

With her unconscious, he knew he had to be the one to find and care for her injuries. Bennett brushed the bangs from her face and inspected the gash on her cheek. Several more clean cuts from the Linoan knife blades had ravaged her body. Her jacket was soaked in blood, though it had mostly dried on the surface.

"Jesus," he whispered. *What did they do to you?* His fingers trembled, palpating each injury. Thick blood seeped out with the lightest of pressures.

Unzipping her shredded jacket, he unbuckled her corset. In lifting her shirt up, he found two deep, parallel slices below her right lung. Blood had covered her stomach.

Fuck.

A field guard's worst nightmare: their specialty sergeant was clinging to life, and the bleeding wouldn't stop.

Drawing a large coagulant-infused bandage from his cargo pants pocket, he frantically tore the package open, nearly dropping the contents. Bennett fought the smarting sensations in his eyes with several blinks. Placing the gauze over the cuts, he taped it around her core with pressure. He gently pulled her torn shirt down and closed up her corset and jacket, to help stabilize her abdomen.

Bennett snatched a strip of sticky, butterfly closures and a cleaning wipe from his kit. Gently scrubbing the dried blood from her face so the adhesive would stick, he peeled two closures from their backing. Delicately pressing the edges of the cut on Atana's face together, he tacked the gash shut.

Staring at her face, he hoped for eye movement, to reassure him she was at least dreaming. There was nothing. Anguished by the bleak outlook for her recovery, his unregulated system overrun by emotions, he tenderly ran a fingertip up the center of her forehead the way his mother used to when he was sick. It was a comforting gesture in his memory. "I haven't given up on you. Just promise you do the same for me."

Her wristband alerted to a changing condition. Picking up her left arm, he addressed the flashing health summary. Atana's heart rate had spiked momentarily and then crashed, her vitals now cutting close to their lowest survivable thresholds. Seeing her Serum tab light up red, he tapped it open.

Serum Dose Overdue
No More Vials Available
Last Three Doses: Ineffective
See Serum Specialist Immediately

She's—like me? He slid a hand into hers. The static zap between their skin evoked a strange but elating tingle of heat in his chest.

Many minutes passed that he couldn't break his gaze from her face. He'd finally found another shepherd like him. Most accepted the serum and their solitary life of service without objection.

Bennett couldn't.

"Please, forgive me. This is the last thing I wanted to happen to you." *I was trying to protect you.*

He squeezed his eyes shut. *As if she can hear me now. Should've talked to her earlier. No secrets, remember? Bennett's Sanction. It's your own damn rule! Bravo Sierra, you idiot.*

He tried to rationalize his feelings while caressing the top of her head. The sensation of her wavy hair through his fingers was uncharted territory and so wonderful that he wanted to claim it, protect it for all eternity. It was a startling sensation, but so strong he couldn't fight it and didn't want to.

Timidly, Bennett rubbed the back of her hand with his thumb in an attempt to feel more of her scar-flecked skin against his. With an incredulous shake of his head, he prayed to whatever god was out there. If there was no god, then he prayed the universe would hear, and drifted off, her chilled fingers bound tightly in the heat of his.

Chapter 36

AN HOUR PASSED.

Something squeezed Bennett's hand, rousing him from his exhausted slumber. His eyes flew open.

"Nakio?"

A sinking feeling in his gut told him someone was coming. With Atana still unconscious, he lifted the Warruk's weapon, rose to a crouched position, and peered around the corner of the doorframe. *Nothing.*

When he spun to check the opposite end of the hall, he met a blue glower so intense it could only belong to one individual. Bennett sighed heavily, letting the weapon rest at his side.

"You don't look so good," Azure chided, eyeing the dried blood on Bennett's t-shirt from several slits in his chest and arms.

Bennett stood, his distrust of the warrior growing. "How the hell did you find us?"

Azure braced himself on the wall when his gaze fell upon Atana, lying behind Bennett's feet. "Is she alive?"

"Barely. I need to get her to Home Station. We have better medical care there."

"Let me carry her to our sector. We can use the maintenance ship." Azure leaned around him.

Bennett stepped in his way. The hell he was letting a man as secretive and surly as Azure so much as look at her wrong, let alone touch her. "I'm carrying her. I know where her injuries are."

Carefully sliding his jacket out from beneath her head and down around her shoulders, Bennett lifted Atana, cradling her in his arms.

Azure picked up the Warruk's weapon, readying it in his hands. "You should have let me come with you."

"How did you say you found us again?" Bennett thread of trust with this man grew thinner with every encounter. He only put up with the guard because of Atana.

"I didn't." He led them through an intersection and descended a set of narrow steps.

No shit. Bennett stifled a grunt of annoyance. "Okay. How *did* you find us?"

Azure studied Atana's pale face long enough to make Bennett uncomfortable. "I followed her scent. It is much easier without Warruk's stench masking it."

Scent? Bennett squinted at the man. *What are you—a fucking animal?*

Humans tend to think so about most of us up here. Azure tossed him a look that suggested they move on.

The team reconnected in the hallway, ripping their receivers off.

Josie's eyes peeled open. "Sir, what happened?"

Bennett adjusted Atana in his arms, drawing her face closer to his neck until he felt a faint breath. "Linoans. Didn't get much on the Suanoa, but she is more important at the moment."

"Our M45 is in the bay." Azure directed to a large door in the corner of the facility. All of the workers in the fields rested their tools, tracking the unnerving haste of the shepherds.

Tanner jogged over. "Who's going to operate it?"

"I can." Azure handed off the Warruk's gun to a worker, providing instructions in another language.

"You?" Doubt crept into Bennett's voice.

"Many things can happen in thirteen long cycles." Azure stuttered. "I mean, years. It's our maintenance vessel, what we use to fix essentials on sectors that we can't reach from the inside. Suanoa expect a good harvest. Low production or sickly yields mean death, or worse. We must fix everything ourselves."

"What's worse?" Tanner's question faded as if he'd changed his mind last minute.

Azure scanned the group, a blank mask on his face, his words cold and flat. "They lock the doors on the food storage containers. Watch us work ourselves into stumbling sacks of bones. Many won't make it. More work after, for those that do. Suanoa think we are not worth our brocanip."

Because they weren't starved and thin already? Bennett tamped down his building hatred. Atana's situation was time-critical.

Though bare, Azure's feet carried him across the rocky soil toward the corner of the fields without a flinch. "I've been modifying ours. I should be able to fly under the radar long enough to get us out of here."

Azure looked over at Panton. "We never used the ship to get people home because we wouldn't get away with it twice. Something this small isn't good for much except an emergency." His attention fell sharply to Atana's lifeless face against Bennett's shoulder. "I never mention it to infiltrate crews. But yours is special."

"This is hard to get used to, the whole mind-reading thing." Panton rubbed a nervous hand over his neck. "But that definitely makes sense."

Bennett paused and rehashed his impression of Azure. The warrior considered Atana's fading health a qualifying reason to put his own people at risk. "I hope you know what you're doing."

Outstretching a hand to one of his guards, Azure called him over. "Tell Chamarel we are taking the M45. It is time to spread out the crew."

The guard ran off toward the hut.

An ugly expression crossed Azure's face as he inspected Bennett in the light. With a snort, brows drawn in determination, he spun and marched for the maintenance door, Bennett and the team following humbly behind.

...

Sliding the door open, Azure prayed his modifications were ready.

Imitating a teardrop, the M45 sported a large viewing window for the pilot and a flared tail for the maintenance crews to stand and work from.

Punching his code into the control panel on the side of the ship, a ramp dropped at the rear of the vessel. With everyone on board, Azure depressed a red button on the wall. An airtight door rolled down from the ceiling, closing off the crew from the fields. The only exceptions to the resulting darkness were his eyes and the ramp lights.

He hopped up, passing Bennett, who strapped Atana to the workbench with Tanner's help before buckling in next to her.

Azure sank into the pilot's seat, fingers flying over the controls faster than he'd ever managed before. Pulse pounding in his ears, he tapped in the startup sequence. The dash surrounding him illuminated a vibrant blue. Several processes he could do in his sleep. He'd flown hundreds of maintenance flights, but never a mission so personal. The worry was distracting.

Tanner took the co-pilot's seat. "Boss wants me up here. I hope that's okay."

"No time to change now. Strap in." Azure commanded the door shut. It sealed with a whistle. Muffled clanks of metal confirmed the magnetic locks had released. He slid his fingers up on one of the screens and the M45's thrusters boomed louder, slowly lifting the ship.

As the airlock doors opened to the stars, Azure rested his shaking left hand on the primary thruster control lever beside him, watching the flashing red warning on his screen.

When the door brackets blinked blue, he slammed the throttle forward. With a compounding vibration from the rear, the ship erupted out into the cold void of space. "Where am I taking us?"

"Good question." Tanner signaled back at Panton, catching a device tight in his palms just before gravity dissipated completely. He called in, "Hotel Sierra Nalli, Alternate Transport One. Echo India Sierra Three Seven, requesting a location for landing."

Azure took the quickest course away from Agutra.

While waiting for a response, Tanner studied the dash, its warped surfaces and curved controls snaking around the nose. "This is amazing. I would kill to learn about all of this if we get the chance."

Azure's fingers stilled over the controls. He looked over at Tanner. "Kill?"

The shepherd paled. "Just an expression—to—indicate level of interest. Some people say 'love.'"

"Those are very different things." Azure nervously checked the perimeter. No vessels were following that he or his scanners could see. It was almost too quiet. The Suanoa couldn't possibly be letting them escape. Something was wrong.

"Wouldn't know." Tanner tilted to peer out the window, back at the ship. "So if none of the Suanoan ships are ground-worthy—"

"This is. Modified it myself. I thought it might be helpful at some point if there was any truth to the prophecy." Azure inhaled deep, summoning the courage to admit his one true doubt. "Though I've landed in artificial gravity more times than I can count, a planet I have only done in theory."

"Ah, well let me see if I can assist." Tanner flipped open his laptop. "I need whatever information you can give me about her."

"Her?"

"Yeah, the ship."

A blazing ray of red light shot past them, followed by another. Azure strained to hold his position, his fingers flying across the controls, banking the vessel hard to the left. This was more like them.

"They're shooting at us!" Panton's booming voice echoed from the back.

Josie cursed as three more shots went by, a little closer. "What'd you think would happen?"

Another band of plasma bullets lit up the sky to their right. Azure swayed the ship, never repeating the same response. He knew the Suanoa would expect that. But patterns were predictable. Azure pulled a hard right, spiraling around the next barrage, Earth growing larger before them.

"Atana doesn't have time for games!" Bennett growled.

"You want to get shot out of the void?" Azure slid two power-draw settings to their highest position, stealing all available energy for the main propulsion. "Making it to the surface is sort of important for her to survive, don't you think?" The lights in the cabin went out, dash lights included. He didn't like operating in the dark because of the increased risk of error. But the vessel tripled its pace. With a quick dive, Azure circled them around the dark side of Earth, hiding from the mothership.

Redirecting a small portion of the power, he brought the dash lights back on. Azure inspected the scanners, watching the shots fade out far behind them now. Stealing a quick peek over his shoulder at Atana, he noted Bennett's hands were on her shoulders, the man's forearms stabilizing her head. Bennett's glare shimmered like golden fire in the dark. Azure did a double take just to make sure he'd seen what he thought he had.

"Shouldn't you be facing forward?" Bennett's directed at the sky with his eyes.

Azure turned back around with a snort, righting the vessel so its belly was to the Earth's surface. His heart was drumming so fast that it made his entire body tremble. He sighed heavily, calming his nerves so he could focus on the nearing atmosphere.

The communicator popped and crackled in Tanner's hand. "Echo India Sierra Three Seven, Hotel Sierra Nalli. Landing coordinates sent. Request status report."

"An M45, I think I've got it on record somewhere in here from our initial scans," Tanner mumbled. Depressing the microphone button, he studied the images on his screen. "Sergeant Atana in need of immediate medical assistance. Sergeant Goss down, 501 down, Xahu'ré—an alien— pilot fill in. Name: Azure. Returning in, confirmed, M45 maintenance vessel, sending schematics."

Azure's mind wandered. It had been many long-cycles since he had been on the surface of a real planet. He was curious about the types of plants that grew, rooted in depthless dirt under a real sun, instead of grow lights. Would the sun be warm, the nights cold, like on Vioras?

"So—modifications?" Tanner's voice pulled Azure from his daydream.

"Oh, right. Added an extra fuel tank, fifteen litrons, four more control wings to help manage the effective air pressure, and two secondary direction-adjustable ion thrusters so we can hover in higher gravity. The extra fuel tank is for the chemical thrusters, two under each main wing. I did a lot of this based on estimations and the small bits of data I was able to steal from the Suanoan database."

It was mostly the truth. He glanced at the shepherd beside him, drawing in the changes to his schematics at his direction. Tanner wouldn't understand. Only Atana was capable of that if she remembered.

Tanner surveyed the dash display, pointing at the readout on the side of the central illuminated screen. "Are these the updated mass and power outputs of her?"

"Yes." Azure kept them on target, internalizing his concerns about Atana's health, the M45's capabilities of landing on a planet, and what the beings of Earth would think of him. He hoped Chamarel and the workers would be safe without him there to protect them. After decades of prayers, the prophecy was coming together. Their future was now on an unpredictable path, and he was a part of it.

"It seems you have overcompensated. Nice work. We're a little nose heavy. Go light on the rear thrusters so we don't pitch, and we should be fine."

Relieved, Azure slid open a program on the dash and made an adjustment. "Can you give me the acceleration of gravity value for your planet, for the landing program algorithms?"

"Standard is 9.8 meters per second, squared, or Newtons per kilogram for force."

Breaking the crest of the Earth's atmosphere, the dash controls beeped and flashed, alarms stating contact with the ground was imminent. Azure entered the value into the system's computer, ignoring the alerts.

Behind him, the team shifted and seatbelt straps zipped tighter.

"Relax. It will stop when we get within 300 meters of the ground." Azure reached up, pulling four levers down from the roof. "It's still calibrated for spacewalks. It was next on my list of things, just didn't get it finished before you got here. It's a notification sensor. It doesn't affect anything."

"Anything else you didn't finish we should know about?" Such an acerbic tone could only belong to Bennett.

Azure offered no verbal response to accompany the twitch of his cheeks. He prepped the additional control wings, opening their slots on the hull.

Tanner selected a 3-D map of the globe on his laptop, showing Azure the best path for travel to the drop site. "They are going to have a transport waiting for us at this location. It's in the Sahara Desert, Zone Three. We're landing in the sand."

"Understood." Pushing the button between the four levers, they hummed and disappeared up into the ceiling. Long-bladed wings spread into their descent positions. Azure glanced back to either side of the pilot's window to see the wingtips had successfully moved. His tickle of excitement was fleeting.

The Sahara Desert? He wanted so badly to look at her again but controlled his desires, remembering his duty to the Agutra innocents and the team of Earth's guards, their lives in his hands.

Hesitant but curious, he swallowed the leery edge threatening to creep into his voice. "Are we going to have to destroy the M45 when we get to the ground? And what about me? I'm not like any of you."

"I'm sorry, Azure. I don't have answers. It's up to Command." Tanner double-checked the device in his hands. "We are called Universal Protectors for a reason. I'd hope they'd be accepting of you after all your help."

Plummeting through the thermosphere, a real horizon appeared in front of them. The dark sands and deep blues of the sky made Azure's heart jitter. Breaking through the burn phase below the mesosphere, the M45's vibrations smoothed out.

"Can we get there any faster?" Bennett asked, his tone sharp and clipped. "Her heart rate is dropping! Readout projects minutes to failure!"

Dread thrust Azure's fingers into a frenzy over the screens. "Yes, everybody hold on!" He kicked the wings back into the hull. His stomach greeted his throat, the seat harness catching hard over his shoulders. Several shepherds let out groans behind him.

At five kilometers from the surface, Azure reinitiated the landing program. The wings sprung back out, guiding their descent along the continent's crust. Everyone sank heavily in their seats. He redirected all available power to the main propulsion and raced them through Sand Zone Three with Tanner's instructions.

Dropping within 300 meters of the blurred dunes, the alerts on the dash subsided, a new one taking its place.

"Redline warning. Thirty-seconds to overheat."

"There!" Tanner pointed urgently. "Looks like a mirage, a sort of extra hazy area. They have the chameleon skins up."

Azure squinted across the shadowed desert sands. A matte gray ship unskinned ahead of them, white lights blinking along its perimeter.

Waiting until the last possible second, Azure rotated the wings down, creating drag. The M45 shuddered with the reverse in force, their bodies slinging forward into the harnesses.

Setting the secondary propulsion units to Hover, Azure's heart thumped heavy, sending heat flaring through his body in a mix of nervous anticipation and heartsick worry. Coming to a standstill, Azure slowly dropped the ship to the surface with a heavy clunk.

Chapter 37

THE WIND-RIPPLED DUNES glittered like the night sky above, the moon casting light across the crests around the M45. A rush of air from the dropping ramp wove a long-forgotten warmth through Azure's shabby clothes, so unexpected that it sent a hot shiver of awareness through him.

I'm on Earth. I'm on a planet! We made it!

Unbuckling and reading the flashing updates on their wristbands, the team greeted and directed the medical crew from, what Azure overheard was, a Med-Evac transport. They rushed on board and were out seconds later, carrying Atana on a litter. Bennett and Cutter hustled with them, their hands firmly wrapped around the frame at her head.

Tanner returned to his seat beside Azure. "I'm staying with you. Don't worry."

Down here, on the surface, there were too many unknowns for Azure to calm his nervous jitters—things he had no experience with or so little so far back in his past they might as well not exist. The young shepherd had no idea how comforting those few words were.

One of UP's pilots bounded up the M45 ramp, a tall man with blue eyes. "You understand English?"

Azure nodded.

"Great, we are going to hide your ship." The pilot motioned with a hand toward a dead, dried-up ball of twigs rooted into the ground not fifty meters from their current location. "Take her over there and hover above."

Azure closed the gate, reignited the thrusters, and lifted the M45 guiding it over the vegetation. The sand gave way underneath the ship.

"Ease her down."

Azure lowered the thrusters' force, and they found themselves dropping below the dunes, into an underground passageway. His ears boomed with echoing pulses. Azure rested the ship on the floor without so much as a bump.

"Nice job, man!" Tanner gave Azure's shoulder a congratulatory slap.

Opening the ramp, Azure gave a half-hearted smile in return. His concern had moved on to Atana.

The pilot waved them out to the tunnel floor. Sand poured around them in whispering sheets from the gaping opening overhead.

The ends of three knotted ropes dropped down as engines rumbled in above. White navigation lights blinked to either side of a glowing door. The three grabbed a hold and were hauled up and out of the tunnel.

The night breeze pushed against their shadowed forms, swinging them as Azure, Tanner, and the pilot continued their ascent. Passing through a vibrant ring, a port in the belly of the hovering Med-Evac, Azure found himself in the grasp of two men, who promptly directed his feet onto a platform, before waving him to back up toward the wall.

He joined Tanner to the side of the transport's deck. The pilot, whose eyes were as bright blue as his own, nodded at him before heading to the cockpit without another word.

Hearing metal scrape and pound in the way it groans under pressure, Azure frantically spun around.

At a separate floor dock, a large chunk of a wrecked vessel, similar in size to his M45, swung from chains above another open portal. The commanding yell of a woman sent the wreckage falling and the chains swinging free.

Curious, Azure crept around the closing door beside his feet toward the commotion. Tanner stuck with him and didn't object.

Despite the mirage from hot engines, Azure saw the metal fracture upon impact with the dunes. The transport lifted, exposing a murky image of the destruction through the solid floor. Azure slid back from the panel he stood on in a panic he would fall through, arms flying out to the sides, wanting to catch a handhold.

"One-way chameleon glass." Tanner proudly tapped the toe of a boot on the surface. "I helped with it. Cool, huh."

Azure swallowed his heart back down and out of his throat. "Yeah." It was unusual.

Across the large portal in the floor, an arm's length too small for the M45, Panton had clipped his harness in a crisscross pattern to D-rings in the ceiling and the floor of the Med-Evac. Running his short shock-absorber line to the hook between Josie's shoulders, he held her steady by the handle on the back of her vest and an arm around her waist. The transport continued its slow ascent. With one shot from Josie's e-rifle, the wreckage burst into flames.

"Med-Evacs don't have weapons, only defensive measures." Tanner rubbed a finger up the side of his head where Atana's scar was. "Covering our tracks this time."

Azure braced himself on the wall, the reminder of her injuries draining the strength from his body.

Panton pulled Josie up to him, his arms cinched tightly around her, the floor iris whistling shut. Two crew members picked up and threw long latches, locking the doors by their feet. The engines thundered louder.

Tanner tapped Azure and motioned toward the handles above. "Hang on."

Grabbing on with both hands, Azure scanned around them for Atana and the rest of the crew.

"Up front. We'll just be in the way up there." Arm stretched to the strap overhead, Tanner wearily rested his mouth on his shoulder, his elbow a cradle for his head. The man looked beat and discouraged the way he hung from the handle. He twisted to stare out the crystal-clear window beside them, muttering something familiar to Azure's own heart.

"Wanting to help doesn't mean we're the most qualified."

For someone not telepathic, Azure considered Tanner a surprisingly thoughtful young man, one he felt would be safe to stick alongside.

The ship dipped and launched, tugging hard on their bodies. Azure clung to the straps, his bare feet stumbling across the warm metal floor.

Tanner swayed gently not far from him, feet planted firmly. "You okay?"

"Your gravity is stronger on the surface than in the cage." Azure released a shallow breath. "I'm thirty-some long-cycles and feel like I'm three."

A faint twitch of a smile crossed Tanner's face.

Smiles were a rare sight to Azure, almost as foreign as the endless, sparkling pinpricks in the inky veil over the land. No walls surrounded him, no ceiling, no Warruks or Linoans—just freedom. But his elation upon arrival and concern for the hours ahead clashed like fire and water in his stomach. All he felt within was a smoldering, soggy pit of insecurity—his Ether spark unable to alight with hope.

Yet he refused to let it drown in fear. Not any more.

...

Through the hangar and into the elevator next to Atana and her medical staff, the team was silent, gazing solemnly over to where Bennett stood, escorting their leader. The bustle of nurses and EMTs around her made them uneasy.

Cutter hustled up to them, glancing at Azure's worried face.

"Stable for the moment. Let's hope she stays that way." He stepped inside the closing doors with the team, muttering to Tanner. "Bennett's another story."

The computer system beeped a warning. "One passenger not cleared for descent."

Tanner leaned forward, looking into a blue light. The screen flashed green. Azure watched the shepherd type in a code. A prompt for the guest scan appeared. Tanner waved Azure over.

"Just look at the blue dot. It scans your iris into the database. We're all programmed into Home Station three different ways. One is enough for you to be coded a guest."

Azure dipped down and did as Tanner requested.

An automated voice responded, "Cannot distinguish pattern. Please rescan."

Squinting at the screen, Tanner tapped in some adjustments. "Try it now. I think the light in your irises is making it hard for the computer to register your pattern."

Azure tilted in again, the bar of blue light drawing a circle momentarily over his vision. "Sorry. They do this when we're emotional." *Or drunk.* He straightened. "I have no control over it."

"New passenger accepted." The elevator finally began their descent, thrusting Azure's stomach into his lungs. Down a thick, transparent shaft, they submerged below the ocean. Azure steadied himself on the handrail.

"You hide the typical symptoms of emotion well, so don't worry about it." Tanner pointed outside. "I'm guessing you haven't seen this before."

The glowing, underwater station in the distance had Azure transfixed in an instant. Several schools of silver and green creatures swam by the elevator, their iridescent scales reflecting the pale lights. Earth was a spacious, radiant place of surprises. It felt like a dream.

He paced the glass walls until he could see Atana's car, which had left mere seconds before theirs.

Or a nightmare.

...

An attending nurse held up the crew at the entrance to the Infirmary. "I'm sorry we can't let any of you go in. She needs surgery. Some of her cuts are pretty deep, and she's bleeding internally."

"How long is it going to take?" Bennett's hand tensed around his wadded up, bloodied jacket. She'd shoved him out of the surgery room upon arrival and gone to fetch it.

He didn't give a damn about the jacket. He'd wanted to stay with Atana.

"Maybe two or three hours," she replied. Turning the corner to the infirmary, she darted her narrowed eyes at Bennett one last time.

Azure shifted uneasily beside Panton and Josie. Shepherds rushed back and forth in the hallway, many of which were staring at them. "I will stay. You should go talk to your people."

Even with medical staff on hand, Bennett didn't like the idea of Azure remaining unguarded near Atana. "I'm not leaving."

"Your leaders need to talk to you. I am going to be out of the way, here," Azure defended.

Bennett eyed the guest wristband on the warrior's left arm. It would track Azure as long as he stayed on station, only permitting him into public spaces. But it was still a rather retroactive solution for guests in his mind. The shepherds wouldn't *care* because of the serum. But Azure was definitely in their sights, judging by the sets of eyes pinning on him as teams passed.

"Tanner put me in your system so I could stay." Azure grabbed the screen, adjusting it as if it were uncomfortable.

Clenching his teeth, Bennett sneered, "You're lucky this is a time-critical mission and we're willing to deal with the consequences of your presence later."

Cutter stepped between them. "We will go and report what we have, and you can both remain here. We have plenty to talk about for a few hours until you're ready to join."

Giving him a single nod, Bennett walked over to the observation window. His throat ached to yell out in rage and helplessness seeing Atana unconscious on the gurney. He raked a hand through his hair, letting out a sigh instead.

Azure trailed behind but kept his distance, to Bennett's relief.

"Hey, B." Tanner hustled over to him as the rest of the team headed for Command's conference room. "I called Rio so he could get you set up with a new wristband and serum. He should be down in a bit."

For several breaths, the two stared at the rush of nurses around Atana. Tanner hooked his hands on his vest and turned to face Bennett. "It's not your fault."

Bennett crossed his arms, standing frozen except for his eyes, and tracked the movement of the room before him. "She was my main responsibility, given by Command and Rio."

"Oh," Tanner hummed, straightening his back. "That explains why Rio was so quiet."

"Mad?" Bennett half-listened for the answer.

"I don't know, didn't get a lot of words out of him."

Hiding his bruised knuckles beneath his elbows, Bennett visually traced the dark orchid and orange splatters peppering Tanner's armor. "*You okay?*"

"Cutter's ten times what Cara ever was." Adjusting the case on his front, Tanner glanced down the hall after his team. "Don't blame yourself. There's a reason you're an R3."

With a consoling pat to Bennett's shoulder, he left him alone with Azure.

They glared at one another in brittle, judging silence. Azure obviously had his convictions. It was the question of his motivations that ate at Bennett.

The warrior's face softened when he looked back into the surgery room. Bennett saw a flicker in the man's eyes, a raw emotion Azure was holding inside. It left Bennett feeling relieved yet torn.

Chapter 38

THE FRANTIC WORDS of a nurse through the open doors of the surgery room stole the breath from Azure's lungs.

"No, Doctor. We aren't ready. She's lost too much blood. We're low on type—" Metal tools clanking in trays muffled the rest.

Desperate to help, Azure impulsively rounded the corner, caught a closing door, and stepped inside. "Take mine."

Bennett pounded on the large picture window between them. His voice was barely audible, suppressed by the thick panes. "You are not authorized to be in there!" His brows knitted with fury. "Get out!"

Azure ignored him. He cared about one thing only. Atana had lost too much.

"You can't be in here," a nurse yelled. "This is a sterile environment!"

"I'm the right type." Heart pounding, Azure outstretched an arm and rolled up his tattered sleeve. *I know I am.*

The surgeon put a hand to his arm, stopping him. Their eyes met. He was being inspected.

Anger flared heat through Azure's veins. "We're wasting time. Let me help."

With a hesitant nod, the surgeon waved for the nurses to continue the preparations then urged Azure through the double doors and into an office down the hall.

"Please, sit." He lifted a hand at the open seat beside his desk. "I have to do a test."

Azure thought it strange how easily the man found his vein, given how deeply embedded Xahu're circulatory systems were. The elastic strap around his arm encouraged his vessels to surface.

The surgeon drew one vial of translucent, indigo fluid with swirling silver-metallic flecks. "Lisano—amazing."

Azure studied the man before him. *That had to be a slip of the tongue.*

Releasing the tube into a slot in the machine on the counter, the man slammed the top shut and tapped a button with a green triangle on it. The device hummed to life.

He tried to wait patiently, but Atana's fading health had Azure drumming his fingers.

Numbers and colorful bar graphs jumped up on the glass lining the walls of the corner office. The surgeon's fingers flew over the smooth surfaces, opening Atana's serological spectrum analysis and cross-match breakdown.

"I don't believe it." He swiftly scrolled through the output data. "That's impossible."

Azure's nerves heated in panic, concerned his leap of faith with this new environment, for the one true motivation in his life, had been a mistake. He had spent so much of his life caged, poked, and prodded; he feared it was his destined life occupation.

"It's our lucky day." Grinning, the surgeon sprang out the door to the surgery room and shouted for a draw bag. A few muffled words came from the closed doors. "No mix. He's it."

He popped back in, requesting Azure lie on the table against the wall while he quickly hooked him up to the pliable container.

Azure didn't feel the needle slide in. The bag filled at a rate that appeared to surprise the man.

They would save her body with this. But that was only one of the triad that was all beings. Azure worried more about her mind and what the Suanoa might have done to it.

Some called the third component a soul. But to all Xahu'ré, and most other life forms, it was called a spark. Hers had looked dark when he'd seen her lying on the gurney. He couldn't literally see it, only the paleness of her skin under the harsh light and feel the fading energy of her aura.

In all his memories, she'd burned brightest, spread hope to the hopeless, defended those weaker than her. Endless in her fight, her resistance. Her love.

All three had to function for the triangle that was existence to remain stable, strong.

"Why do you want to help this Sergeant?" The surgeon delicately inspected the transfusion adapter attached to Azure's arm.

It wasn't just a want, but a need. A compulsion. He'd do anything for her. "She is important to many, in ways I don't know how to explain." Azure's mind rewound to the blood trails he'd followed through the hallways. "I know she's lost more. I can give more." He'd give her every drop without hesitation.

How does he know how much she's lost? Did he know he would be a compatible match? Does he know the truth? No, he couldn't possibly— The man's thoughts trailed off when he met Azure's eyes.

219

Azure shamelessly listened to everyone.

"You're right. Are you sure you want to give more?" The surgeon promptly unhooked the bag.

"Yes."

The man clipped in one more bag and left the room immediately after, carrying the full one to the nurses in surgery.

The second bag filled with encouragement from Azure's clenched fists. Disconnecting it, the surgeon pressed a cotton ball against Azure's vein, slipping the needle out and tossing it in a bin in the corner. Wiping the surface of Azure's arm, the tiny puncture plated over. "That's enough. How are you feeling?"

Azure sat up. "Not even lightheaded."

"You've lost a lot of blood." He held out a disc with spots to Azure. "You want a cookie? You're a big guy. You might need a few."

"It's not the first time I've lost that amount in one day. What's a cookie?"

"A sweet food to get your blood glucose back up."

"Does it have nuts? My kind can't have nuts."

"Nope." The man released the treat into Azure's large hand. "Make sure you stop by the lunchroom and get some good food in the next hour or so, please. I don't want to see you here for another reason. For now, please return to the viewing area. I have to go into surgery and get to work."

Azure padded out of the office behind the surgeon, splitting off to join Bennett in observation. Seeing the man wave the nurses forward with surgery, Azure lifted the 'cookie' in his fingers to study it.

Bennett scowled. "You're supposed to eat it, not stare at it."

Growing weary of the man's relentless criticism, Azure looked over at him. "I am sorry for whatever I did to make you not trust or like me. I am only trying to help."

Letting out an irritated sigh, Bennett dropped onto the edge of the bench, facing the view pane. Two nurses came to tend to his cuts.

"I'm fine. Go check on my crew. CR-1," he grumbled, waving them off.

Sniffing the cookie, Azure figured it did not have nuts and consumed it in three large bites, all the while watching Bennett. The shepherd's fixation on Atana brought an old worry back to the surface. But Azure would show them all, soon. She was different. What they had, no one else would understand.

Wiping his fingers on his frayed pants, he sat on the opposite end of the bench.

"Yeah, you stay over there." Bennett cracked his knuckles.

If she doesn't make it— Azure licked his lips, throwing Bennett a crooked smile. Her 'guard' would meet her fate—but *much* faster. Refocusing on the woman sprawled in a bed of bloodied sheets, he closed his eyes and dove inside Ether.

We are all here, all with you. Do not give up. Azure didn't expect a response, but the silence threatened his composure, nonetheless. Lacing his fingers together, he squeezed until the physical pain in his fingers distracted him from the fear swelling within. *Niema, Sahara. Fight back.*

Chapter 39

HER BLOOD STAINED his hands and clothes. Bennett wanted to punch something. It felt like the last thing left within his control. The plum color taunted him, its pungent, iron smell nauseating. Yet his clasped hands rested on his lips, bouncing periodically as he retraced his steps and decisions.

The two men sprung from the bench when the surgeon came out, despite the stiffness from not having moved for hours. His face was stretched with exhaustion.

"Thank you again for your donation." The man nodded to Azure. "It's definitely given her a fighting chance. We've stopped the bleeding, for now. Some of her surface injuries are still oozing a bit. She's being moved to a recovery room down the hall. Her pulse and blood pressure have been fluctuating, so we'll have to keep tabs on it."

"Why do you suppose the readings are inconsistent?" Bennett asked while Azure remained quietly by the far end of the bench.

The surgeon sighed. "It's difficult to say. It doesn't seem to have anything to do with her physical status. I think she's locked in some sort of unconscious state. You know the brain will shut down with too much trauma or stress."

Bennett cleared his throat to steady his gravelly voice. "How long could she be in this condition?"

"Minutes, hours, or even weeks, I can't say. It's up to her."

"When can we see her?" Bennett wrung his leather jacket nervously in his hands. "I'm her guard."

"Of course you are, Sergeant Bennett." The surgeon eyed him, a hint of disappointment in his tone. "She will be in recovery in about fifteen minutes, R22."

The two men thanked the surgeon and left for her designated room. In ear-splitting silence, Azure and Bennett walked next to one another, yet divided—by galaxies, ethnological experiences, and a chronological order beyond their control.

...

The medical team rolled Atana into her private room. Counting off, they lifted her limp form from the gurney onto the bed. The staff

222

connected her heart rate and blood pressure monitors to the small table and switched her nasal cannula feeder to the one on the wall.

Another nurse came in, setting her folded leathers beside the machines. She informed Bennett someone would be in every hour or so to check on her. "If you need anything, press the red button on the side of her bed frame."

Bennett couldn't take his eyes off Atana's bruises or the paleness of her mocha skin between. "Thank you."

With the room empty except the three of them, Bennett slumped to her side, his hands rising and falling, unsure where they could touch without causing more damage than they had already allowed.

Azure stuttered behind him as he moved to stand at her other side. "Aye Diete." The warrior drew in a sharp breath and promptly stalked out of the room, the back of a hand over his mouth.

Bennett turned to watch him leave. If Azure tried anything, security would catch him, easily.

Machines peeped all around her. Their colorful, dancing analyses seemed almost disrespectful compared to her blanched and broken body.

He stared at Atana for several long moments, collecting his thoughts. *What happened, Nakio? One second you were fine; the next, you were down. I dropped my guard when I saw you. What were you and Chamarel talking about the other morning? What was so dangerous she didn't want you to do it?*

Bennett slipped a finger under one of her icy hands, wanting desperately to hold it again.

Why are you trying to do this on your own? Hiding his searing eyes behind his free hand, his teeth clenched. His split lip tore open, his swollen cheek throbbing. *I'm going to fucking destroy them for doing this to you.* His veins, strung like Detonating Cord through his body, wouldn't need but a single spark to explode. *Tipping, Jameson, teetering on the edge.*

His control was crashing, adrenal fatigue setting in. The serum might counteract the effects of the adrenaline, a regulation tactic, a buffer. Rio couldn't stop the glands from functioning themselves because some level of hormones and neurotransmitters were essential to live and to fight.

Bennett had burned through it in the recent hours. His lungs drew in hard, like the first breath above water after swimming the length of a pool beneath its surface. He couldn't get enough. He was slipping into the manic stage of serum withdrawal.

A cool softness, her skin slid over his. Bennett's eyes snapped to her hand: perfectly still.

Relaxing or reaching, unconscious or waking? He couldn't tell. A whine slipped from his throat. Leaning forward, he took her wrapped hand, his forehead resting on the bleach-white sheets beside it.

I'm so sorry. I was wrong. With a blink, a tear hit the floor like a lead weight. *Don't leave. You have to fight. We need you.*

Azure's booming voice rasped from the door. "She used the Grey."

Bennett jolted, retracting his hand from Atana's to wipe the moisture from his face. "Christ, what's your deal? Always sneaking up on people."

"Why can't you be happy there is someone else who cares for her and wants to protect her as much as you do?" Azure fired back.

"Because I don't trust you." Bennett's fists clamped tight when he spun and rose to his feet.

Azure's brows furrowed. "Even after everything I've done for you and your team? I brought you here, in one piece, in a ship I've been working on for over a decade!"

"Skill and earned trust are two different things. When are you going to get it in your head? She'll never be with you—or anyone!"

"That means you too, Bennett." Azure's tone darkened and cooled when he pointed at him. "Strong leaders lead by example. Your serum isn't working."

His accusation stung more than Bennett anticipated. "Shut it, Azure. You don't know shit about us."

"You think you know anything about my people, our life up there?" Azure snorted in disapproval.

The pilot stopped in the doorway.

"It's an honor to have you here, sir." The comment was directed at Azure. "Sergeant." He paused, giving Bennett a once-over. "Command wants to speak with you soon, after you—collect yourself. Get that band fixed. And the armory for new standards, after."

He disappeared down the hall.

"Yes, sir." Bennett sighed, forcing his fists open and his heart to slow. *Why can't we both care about her, and never tell her, just pretend everything is normal?*

"Because she already knows we both care and because she's like me, Bennett." Azure rubbed a hand over his chest as if to push an ache away. "She's better than me, but she's like me. She knows a lot of unspoken things."

Bennett's hand slapped the cargo pocket with the receiver in it.

"Telepathic, remember?" Azure arched a brow.

"Right. So what do you mean, really, that she's like you?"

"She's half Xahu'ré."

"She's what?"

Azure touched the point of the stripe on his forehead. "Xahu'ré: my species. We could be separated by many levels and sectors, but I will always find her. When others are unconscious, I search by scent." He inhaled deep through his nose and hummed. "Spicy Jesiar petals and sweet Zusha nectar—"

Bennett rolled his eyes. "Yeah, okay, Rule Six."

"Rule Six?"

"TMI, too much info, man." Bennett frowned. "So why don't you take her and leave? Obviously, you two have some sort of connection the rest of us don't understand."

Azure looked down, wiggling his bare toes. "I would never make her do something she didn't want to do."

Bennett studied the woman on the bed wondering what she wanted and what she was dreaming about. *Damn prophecy.*

Straightening to his full height, Bennett felt every bruise protest. Staring at her in such a state had him drowning just enough to lose clarity on the mission. He needed serum.

Bennett reluctantly turned to the door and paused, glaring back at Azure's illuminating eyes. "I have to leave for a while. That band will monitor your every move. If you hurt her, I'll burn you to the ground."

...

Azure sat beside her, studying the curves of her face like they were undiscovered. But the creases in the corners of her eyes and her bulging jaw muscles were familiar. She was deeply focused—to the point of clenching her teeth. He knew she was adrift in Ether, straining to hold on to life. He'd seen it thousands of times. Thirteen years apart couldn't dull those memories.

He had traded the metal cage of Agutra for the one of Home Station, fended off an endless darkness, to be a beacon amongst it, searching through the void for her, only to find her light already guarded by another's. Sergeant Bennett.

A lone warrior atop a mountain of skulls. For nothing.

Azure knew what she had done. Chamarel had talked to him about it, long ago. He was built of fire then, with only vengeance on his mind. And he had learned his lesson the hard way, like most perimeter guards—self-willed, bullheaded, reckless. Their last breath was their promise. It's why they were damn good. And few.

Taking gauze from the counter next to her bunk, he gently dabbed at the draining stitches on her cheek.

The machine monitoring her pulse and blood pressure screeched. Azure's heart leapt into his throat. Picking up one of her wrists, he positioned his fingers over her veins to check her pulse. It was a faint, two beats per minute.

He knew what she desperately needed. Standing up, he shut the door, locked it, and switched off the lights. Covering her with a blanket from the shelf over her bed, Azure sat next to her on the edge.

Bracing her face delicately between his massive palms, he opened the window between their souls. *Hang on, Sahara. I'm coming.*

The Grey rushed in. Her pain, his pain. Her injuries, his. The pangs seized his insides until his every muscle trembled. He grunted.

Yet, through the clouds, he called to her, a man in a fog, his hands reaching out, barely able to see. The darkness was suffocating and deathly cold. He felt a fingertip and folded his hand around hers, pulling her sobbing shadow into him.

"They are infinite, Azure. Infinitely cruel, infinitely ruling, infinitely terrifying, infinite—"

He held her head against his chest and buried a kiss in her hair. "It's okay. You are safe now. I won't let anyone hurt you again."

...

The ruckus of nurses trying to get into Atana's room caught Bennett's attention from down the hall. Through the tinted glass walls of her room, a resplendent blue filtered through. He ran back and pounded on the door. "Open up! Azure, open this damned door, now!"

Security hustled down the hall as Bennett reared back, ready to kick the door in. They placed a handheld recalibration device to the doorframe above the latch, unlocking it with a *ca-chunk*. Bennett flung it open, fuming. Flipping the light on, he peeled Azure off of Atana, shoving his body to the floor. Nurses swarmed inside.

"Five minutes! I can't leave you alone for five fucking minutes with her!" Bennett rolled him over, fingers clawing into his threadbare shirt. "What did you do?"

Azure reeled like he was drunk. He tried to grab the arms that held him. "You don't understand. I was helping—"

"Helping her? You call this *helping*?" Bennett growled, thrusting a finger at the flashing screens making the racket.

"You don't—"

Bennett's fist split Azure's lip open. Blood sprayed across the floor. "Go fuck yourself."

He slung the warrior at the guards, who stared in confused hesitation. "Got something to say?" They shook their heads. "Detainment."

"No, you can't! I need to check her pulse!" Azure kicked and fought, blood draining from his mouth in an indigo trail across the floor.

"Yes, sir," they stammered, clumsily dragging the large man out into the hallway.

The machines were still analyzing. A nurse lifted Atana's wrist and counted. "About sixty beats per minute."

Bennett's eyes slammed shut. *Oh, I'm going to catch hell for this.*

"We'll have to wait and see if she stays that way," another muttered. She watched the screens carefully, making notes on her tablet.

Minutes passed that Bennett stood in a blur of rushing nurses, waiting for the official status report. He slumped back against the wall, sudden exhaustion creeping in. Resting his hands on his gear belt, he forced his breathing to slow, hoping it would calm his heart. No luck. But at least none of the nurses seemed to notice his major infractions.

Or, at least, they weren't saying anything.

The sheets rustled. "Jameson?"

He looked to find Atana had rolled onto her side, eyelids cracked—revealing their bone-chilling aqua beneath.

"Nakio?" He crouched down in front of her, taking her warm hand in his. "How are you feeling?"

A nurse interjected, touching the top of his shoulder. "Sir, we need to take care of our pa—"

"I'll move when I'm ready," he growled at her hand. The nurse snatched it back.

"How did we get here?" Atana scanned the room. She cupped Bennett's fingers with a gentle squeeze.

"An M45 from the Hatoga fields." He tenderly brushed a strand of hair from her face.

With a subtle nod, she mumbled, "Command's probably waiting for their mission debrief."

"Yes, but—"

"I'll be up to the meeting in a few minutes. Twilight afterglow."

"Of course." Bennett rubbed his thumb across her knuckles, not wanting to let go. "I'm glad you're all right."

Still unsure he trusted Azure's actions, he accepted whatever he had done. It had awoken Atana and stabilized what the surgeon and nurses couldn't. He stood and released her.

Walking toward the door, Bennett glanced at her once more, just in case he never saw her again, having failed at his most important job. Relieved to see her still smiling beneath open, blue eyes, he returned her gesture for a moment, then pushed himself toward Rio's office.

Chapter 40

BLACK AND BLUE, a security sergeant's eye was swelling shut. In his grasp, a gray male, whose scowl turned to a grin when Atana entered the office.

"This one's a fighter, ma'am." The guard struggled to hold Azure back when he stepped toward her. "You sure you want to let him out?"

Rounding the desk, the detainment clerk rested a coder to Azure's wristlock. "He was cleared by Command, nothing we can do." The spreader bar clicked and blinked green, the cuffs snapping open.

Atana sensed their apprehension when she outstretched her arm, exposing the bandages on her wrist. "Don't worry. He won't misbehave around me. Will you, Azure?"

"No." *Not the way they anticipate.* Azure licked his lips, his lungs visibly swelling with a breath. He devoured her with his eyes.

Heat rushed to the surface of her skin, and she wasn't sure if it was embarrassment or lust. *Mission first.* She wrapped her hand around his bicep, chewing her cheeks to restrain the urge to smile, and escorted him out into the hallway.

When they were out of earshot, she tightened her grip to get his attention while they walked toward the main Home Station doors. "You didn't have to do that for me."

"Your pulse was too low. You could have died." Azure's brows knitted with concern.

They rounded a corner, and she peeked in, stealing him off into the dark, vacant corridor. "You took more pain than you needed to, and you know it."

"I hate seeing you suffer," Azure said, brushing his thumb over her chin.

Atana scoured the discoloration on his face, his split lip. "What happened to you?"

He rolled his head away, clearly not wanting to talk about it. "It's nothing."

Tracing his fresh injury, she listened to his thoughts. "Bennett did this?"

"He doesn't understand."

Atana frowned. "I don't care. That's not how a shepherd is supposed to act."

Taking her hand, Azure met her gaze with sincerity. "Nakio, I'm fine. All new workers are the same until they learn our ways." He sighed, checked the hall, and returned to her, concern in his eyes. "Are you sure there isn't something—"

She cut him off, not wanting to get into it with the fate of the world at their mercy. "I don't know. Serum apparently doesn't work on him."

"He was trying to protect you. He doesn't know me."

Her mouth parted in disbelief. "You're defending him after the way he's treated you?"

Azure shrugged. "I've endured worse for less, lisano miia."

She held a finger up to his mouth and looked longingly up into his sapphire eyes. *Thank you.*

Drawing a wavy wisp of hair out of his way, he dipped his nose to tenderly nuzzle her cheek. Her lashes hung low with the tingling sensation of his hot breath against her lips. "We should get going."

Azure swallowed audibly. Looking away at the floor, he nodded once. With a supportive arm around her back, he helped her up the steps to Command's conference room. "You need to rest."

She placed a hand to his chest. "You and I both know I can't. The Suanoa won't hesitate now."

Azure pulled the door open for her but wouldn't look her in the eyes. She gave his arm a reassuring squeeze and stepped inside. Atana felt like a key forged of thin glass in a heartless world made of steel. One wrong move and she would shatter. They had a chance if she found the lock in time. But she didn't have much left.

Tanner sent digital blueprints to the main screen on the wall behind the Coordinator. "The plasma drives are definitely designed for destructive purposes, considering their logged properties and extremely well-shielded containment units, terraforming or otherwise."

Atana interjected, lifting a feeble hand to point at the image. "They can use them in combat but, primarily, for restarting ecosystems."

Bennett squinted at Azure.

"Welcome back, Sergeant Atana," the Command member closest to her commented with a shallow bow.

She made a weak attempt to return the gesture. Her stomach cramped up, the pain curling around her lungs. A nauseating wave of prickling pressure throbbed through her. She shivered. Bennett jolted to his feet, but Azure shifted forward, supporting her. She let out a short puff of air.

"Azure, what happened to your face?" the pilot asked.

Bennett's eyes widened just enough for Atana to notice.

"I apologize. I resisted detainment because of a misunderstanding." Azure stood completely still, a hint of bitterness clipping his words. Atana could tell he was working hard to keep his control. "You have strong guards."

"Sergeant Cutter." Atana switched subjects, wanting to avoid confrontation in front of Command. "You take Goss's band for processing?"

"Yes, ma'am, dropped it off for the download before the meeting."

"Thank you." She gestured again to the schematics as Bennett sank back in his seat. "The pulses originate from the mother ship and are then distributed around the planet via Linoan collector clusters."

Atana connected wirelessly to Tanner's laptop via her wristband, pulling up the vessel diagrams. "Fifteen, when docked together create a deflector surface, which they use to direct the pulses toward the weaker spots in a planet's crust."

She zoomed in on one of the vessels. "Their underbellies are made of a uniquely thermal-resistant element: rhizoras, something we don't have in this galaxy. The redirected plasma pulses boil the core of the planet so hot it folds in on itself, destroying any life on its surface."

"How long does this process take?" a member of Command asked.

"For the size of our Earth, once the pulses start, they have estimated four hours and thirty-three minutes. They won't begin until after they have assembled the collectors and recalled the agricultural containers from the surface. Unfortunately, people won't live even close to that length of time. They will do this soon to Earth. It is imperative we return and stop the Suanoa."

"How do you know all of this?" another member questioned her.

Atana shook her head. She was already working on a plan and didn't have the time or the thought space to answer. "Tanner, what have you covered?"

"Everything, now."

Bennett leaned forward in his seat, watching her. "Command has already agreed to our return and has sent out a team request to assist with whatever maneuvers we—"

"Fine," Atana interjected softly, picking at her bandaged hand. "Then I need a word with Command, alone, please. Can you all wait outside?" Her eyes flashed at Bennett, whose mouth was forming an objection. "Rule Six."

He pursed his lips and stood with the others.

The team picked up their gear and headed out into the hallway. Bennett took the longest, stopping beside her, scouring the features of her face for the reason.

She looked up at him, wishing she could tell him the truth. He wasn't ready. None of them were, including her.

The pinch between his brows melted until his hazel eyes looked at her with remorse. He huffed a breath, shot Azure a glare over her shoulder, and stormed out.

"Azure—" She had hoped he would leave too.

"I'm not going anywhere," he protested, the door closing behind him.

"What's so important you're keeping secrets from your team?" a member of Command asked.

Atana had been confronted with the question since she and Chamarel started communicating telepathically. "Do you know *what* I am?"

The council deliberated for a few moments, talking low.

Growing impatient, her fingers curled up, nails biting into her palms. "We don't have time for this. Do you know or not?" she barked, scanning the members through narrowed eyes.

A male member glanced at her long enough that she caught the violet and green rings around his pupils. His chair screeched when he pushed back and stood. He waved a hand over a ceiling panel. The glass walls and overhead tiles solidified to an opaque, heather gray. The lights along the metal framework of the room brightened. Command stood and stepped away from their seats.

She slid closer to the door and found herself bumping into Azure's body. His protective arms were around her in a split-second, a faint rumble of warning in his throat.

…

Out in the hallway, Cutter stood beside Bennett. "We'll meet you below in a few."

Josie, Panton, and Tanner acknowledged, disappearing down the stairs.

"What's up?" Bennett asked.

"Sir, the whole team can see Atana's effect on you, especially after the last day's events." Cutter looked him straight in the eyes. "And luckily, I'm the only one who saw you kiss her."

"What?" Bennett put a hand over his flushing face. He scanned the floor, wondering what Command would do to him when they found out. *Why, Jameson? Why couldn't you control yourself?* "Shit."

"Sir, I want to help you," he whispered. "Bravo Sierra style."

Bennett's fingers slipped from his eyes. "Help me? Why?"

"About four years ago, I worked with another shepherd to gain access to some records from that terrorist group that wants to take over UP, the Kronos Clan. I was required to go off my doses. She was assigned to be my wife, so we were convincing as normal civilians. We went as financial contributors to a benefactor's function at the leader's house. She was shot because I slipped up."

Cutter shifted the shotgun strap digging into his shoulder. "She didn't make it."

"Married?"

Lifting his hat, Cutter ran a hand through his black hair. His tone fell with his eyes. "I wanted to quit UP. Wanted to take her away from here, start a new life."

"Whoa, you're serious?" Bennett stared at him, tongue-tied. *How has he hidden this from us for so long?*

Cutter checked down the hall. He pinched the top of his nose bridge hard. "I fell for her honestly, and her for me. She died from her gut shot when we were discovered, or so Command told me."

"What the hell, man? Why didn't you ever tell me?" Bennett slapped a hand to his head. "Team rule was created so you don't have to endure this shit alone."

"I'm a psych. I can't have mental weaknesses. Besides, try telling someone you swear you saw her still breathing even after they shut down the equipment and called it. They think you're delusional from the hormones." Cutter shook his head, muscles dancing in his jaw. "I don't know. Maybe I was. First time off." A shoulder twitched like he wanted to shrug. "She was so beautiful, so kind, and fought strong, like—" Cutter gestured toward the door. "And someone took her from me when I wasn't paying perfect attention to my surroundings."

"I'm so sorry, Steven."

"Don't be. My point, sir, is you have to control yourself. The serum can't block out memories. You must learn when to listen to the hormones and thoughts and when to tell them to get the hell out and stop haunting you. Our people need you to be strong and focused. The next part of this mission, you have to keep your head clear, whatever it takes. Keep control until you're alone. If you need to talk, holler at me, okay?"

"Thanks." Bennett patted his teammate on the back. "Same goes for you."

Chapter 41

VIOLET AND GREEN. His eyes were like Chamarel's.

The Command member who had closed the blinds walked to each individual at the conference table. When he touched them, they morphed into something entirely unexpected.

Atana and Azure stood stunned before eleven different species. Her lips fell open. Azure slumped around her in a relieved hug then straightened and squeezed her arms.

The pilot who had greeted Azure and Bennett an hour before was Xahu'ré, standing two seats from the far end.

Asiivé Martiis. His blue eyes lit with a nod at Azure.

Eih ahna. Azure grinned. *Martiis.*

The Coordinator spoke from the far end of the table. "The people of Earth don't know there are many refugee species here. In truth, we now outnumber humans in combination."

The woman to his left hung her head. "We sought refuge from the Suanoa, who destroyed our planets."

Another chimed in, "We began hiding beneath the cover of the human face when the first few refugees were attacked and killed thousands of years ago. The humans were not ready to unite with the galaxies. Not even in recent centuries." He glanced at the unchanged individuals. "No offense intended."

"None taken," one replied. "We weren't ready. For many of you, the timing was impeccable, arriving at our most humbled hours, concerned only with our planet's survival. And we are grateful for your help in building this foundation that has protected so many."

The members muttered and exchanged meager smiles.

"So to answer your question, Sergeant Atana, we know what you are." Directing outside of the room, the member who had changed them continued, "They still care if you are human or not. We have shielded all of Earth from one another to protect all of you. To protect the peace."

Returning each to their masked form, he lifted the shades.

Atana recognized four of the species: Human, Mirramor, Xahu'ré, and two Primvera like Rimsan. Three of them were telepathic. "Then you understand the Grey?" From their confused mumblings with one another,

Atana guessed they did not. "It is how I know what I do and is one of two ways the Suanoa can be physically destroyed. The Grey is a deeply subconscious connection to Ether. An individual has to be in this mental state to avoid the Suanoa reading into our minds' preconceived actions."

"So how does one do this?" a member asked.

"The Grey can be reached through a near death experience, or—" Her eyes shifted to Azure.

"Sergeant Atana?" The council awaited her answer.

"Or the individual has to be void of all hope or desire to live, with no fear of death. If there is nothing to connect them to the realm they are in, the Suanoa have nothing to base their actions off of. They can't anticipate anything from something that doesn't have the element of predictability."

Azure hooked her elbow, turning her to look at him. *The rescue, when you killed the Suanoa after I was hit?*

She licked her lips and gave him a single nod. *Yes, Azure.*

He blinked, a sparkling blue glow brightening in his eyes.

Returning her attention to Command, she saw the pilot lift a corner of his mouth and look away.

"Why can't we use our Taz, the unmanned fighter, and take out their control center?" a member across the room asked.

Azure waved a dismissive hand. "There are Suanoa spread throughout the ship and many ways to manually discharge the plasma. Earth will be restarted like all the others. They have calculated for twenty-seven pulses, only half of what it took for my planet, Vioras."

Atana looked up at him, realizing how deep he'd dived when he'd healed her.

"What about destroying the mothership?" one of the human members asked.

"No!" Azure and Atana said in unison. They stared him down. Command shifted in their seats.

Fury ignited a blue filter over Atana's vision. "There are good beings up there who deserve to live and be free just as much, if not more, than the rest of us down here. They have been suffering for longer than you have, scraped from their homes, your homes! Many of your kind are up there too." *Human—* The effort of her argument left her body quivering and her lungs struggling to expand.

"Nakio." Azure grasped her upper arm. "You aren't strong enough to fight. A smart warrior knows when to rest so he can fight in the next battle. I don't want to lose you again."

"We don't have time for me to heal," she countered impatiently. "And I have a plan, another solution, thanks to Teek."

Atana pulled up a schematic she'd copied from Tanner's laptop of Agutra and addressed the expectant members. "There are fifty-three Suanoa in total up there: thirty delegates in the distal core of the ship and twenty-three imperials, which command from the apex of the vessel. I think we have almost the perfect device for our people, to keep their movements unpredictable—to put them, artificially, in the Grey. I'll need to re-engineer some parts on it to make it work for others and likely need Teek to help me finish the calibrations."

She motioned to Cutter, who was in the hall outside. He handed her his receiver. Noticing the other team members had disappeared, Atana lifted her wristband. "Sergeant Tanner, how much time until the collectors are done and begin assembling, you think?"

"Some sector containers have lifted off of Earth and are heading for Agutra. So probably—" The sounds of keys clicking on his laptop popped over the speaker. "Seven and a half hours, ma'am."

"Teek?" a member of Command asked.

Atana bobbed her head only once, the slosh of blood inside making her dizzy. "Someone I worked with when we were up there. We need to make more of these." She lifted the receiver. "It's for non-telepathic species, so they can communicate silently across distances without drawing too much attention. I'll need to make full use of the replication lab downstairs ASAP, to redesign some parts."

Command agreed. "You can take anything you need. But before you go, you said there was another way to physically destroy the Suanoa. What was it?"

"A supernova."

—Axiom—

Chapter 42

BEWILDERED, Bennett held Atana back, letting the door to the lab shut in front of them. "What happened? Why are you—" He bit his tongue, seeing her face contort. A breath rushed from her lungs.

"I—I'm sorry," he stammered.

She pressed a hand to her ribs, grimacing. "We are a different species. We can share the pain of others, sometimes heal them, though usually not completely."

He braced her arms. "Did I hurt you?"

"It's fine. You and I can talk later if we survive this, all right?"

Bennett released her and hesitantly pulled the door to the lab open, waving her in first. They passed Azure, whose arms were crossed in irritation, his glower pinned on Bennett.

The team was gathered around a digital design table, Command on speaker. "We have assigned you seven more teams, per your request. They're in staging, ready to deploy when you are. We are also sending several technicians down to assist you in the lab. What else can we do to help?"

Bennett stepped forward, meeting the faces on the screen. "Let us get up there and try to shut things down before you take out any collectors. We still have people on them." Turning to his crew, he asked, "Any ideas for how we'll get up to the ship without being noticed? They will know it's us if we try to return with the M45, and they've already destroyed one of our ships."

Azure stroked a thoughtful hand over his mouth. "Do you think you could fly me close to one of the Linoan collectors? They usually have space on the top level for fifty or so, above the life-slots. Their flight controls are similar to the maintenance ship. I know I can fly them."

Bennett's eyes narrowed. He didn't like Azure, but he wasn't being given a choice in the matter. They were wavering at the edge: a chance at keeping freedom, freeing others, or being incinerated. And getting to the mothership weighed on one man—or whatever Azure was.

"Yes." The Coordinator nodded to the woman on his left. "We are designating an F201. Tanner and Cutter, you'll operate. Josie and Panton assist. Pick up a collector from the closest Pacific Zone reporting infiltration."

"Understood." Azure and the team set out for the staging area.

Command had surpassed Bennett and given his team orders to work under yet another independent person. Starting to feel out of control of his situation, Bennett hustled behind them into the hall, several lab technicians sprinting past as they donned their lab coats. "Azure."

"Sergeant Bennett," the Coordinator boomed out over Bennett's wristband. "You stay."

Bennett froze.

"Your job is to protect our most valuable asset. You failed once. Last chance." The call clicked off.

Last— Bennett growled with force. "Azure!"

The large man slowed and spun, running backward. "I'm just trying to help!"

"That's my team! I'll—"

"Burn me to the ground with your fists." His glare sliced through Bennett like two fiery blue knives. "Got it." With a snort, he left.

When Bennett, dumbfounded and frustrated, opened the door to the replication lab, he heard Atana giving instructions to the technicians. She demonstrated how a receiver should fit before sliding it off and setting it on the table in front of her.

Walking back to her station, he watched the computer below the surface scan and separate diagrams and specifications for each layer inside the device. Compiled schematics filled the screen. She rearranged traces, microprocessors, chipsets, pin grid arrays, and power integrations without pause.

"Why didn't you go with the others?" she asked.

"Because it's my duty to protect you." Bennett drew the bottle of water and electrolyte pouch from his cargo pocket, setting them in the corner of the console in front of her. "I expect both of these to be empty before you leave this room."

She stalled to inspect the items. Her eyes darted up to his, a flicker of gratitude in her gaze.

His updated serum dose and new wristband were helping him focus. The hum of the high from the drugs in his brain clouded some of the effects she had on him, though it was never quite enough. His desire for her was insatiable, no matter her condition. "I'm sorry, I hurt you at the door."

"I know you didn't do it on purpose." Her dispirited tone was subtle but enough to catch Bennett's attention. Swiping the diagrams of the device to the screens at each lab station, she yelled at the technicians. "One hour!"

The replicator machines kicked on, whirring to the max, the shepherds a blur of white and gray coats and components. Rubbing her palms into her eyes, she sighed heavily.

He put a hand gently on her shoulder. "We're going to make it."

Atana braced herself on the table and peered up at him. "How can you know?"

Sliding his fingers down her arm, he took her hand behind the shield of the workstation, brushing his thumb across her knuckles. Her eyes displayed the cold, hardness of glacial ice. The longer he dwelled the clearer he saw the helpless creature frozen inside. "I have faith."

She scoffed. "In what, a god that doesn't exist?"

Bennett shook his head, understanding her doubts. "In the hearts of those I trust." He gave her fingers a tender squeeze. "And those who have suffered enough."

Chapter 43

INTO THE DARKENED SKY, Tanner piloted the cloaked F201, Azure riding shotgun, the team prepped in the back.

"What position do you want us in?" Tanner asked.

Azure squinted out the front window and pointed. "Stay topside. Their collection ports operate below the spread. There's a hatch in the middle of the roof I can climb down."

Jerking the fighter up, Tanner let a Linoan vessel pass underneath them, shooting out to their nine o'clock. Banking it hard to the left, he kicked the power up, launching them forward, in pursuit. "Go."

Cutter stood by the narrow, dropping gate while Azure hurried to the back. He held a rope hooked to the inside of the fuselage. "In case you change your mind."

The fighter pulled ahead. Azure looked to their pilot, confused.

"Wind drag!" Tanner yelled over the air whipping around the deck.

Azure hesitated for a moment but thought of Atana and took a breath. The fall was endless, the whirling, cold, night air biting his skin like the scortiiga beetles that infested sector twenty-seven and left the workers' skin bubbled and frothing.

He landed heavily on the collector roof. With an explosive shiver, the memory of their cragged pincers dissolved.

Two arced turrets popped up in the front, their mounted, black-chrome units humming as they circumvolved to point at him. Josie provided cover fire, disintegrating the glowing red hubs. Flaming green and red sparks flew around his body. He braced himself against the hull, shielding his face from the chunks and cinders.

Azure planted his bare hands and feet against the metal as the collector dove off to the right. The F201 disappeared down a side street of the small city, a mere shadow blinking between the distant buildings. The apprehension of fighting alone made his palms moisten.

He checked the length of the collector over his shoulder. *It's okay, just alone like always.*

On the roof, downwind, the hatch flew open. Four spring-loaded assassins crawled their way toward him. Azure knew the winds threatened the traction of their lighter forms. He pushed himself carefully to his feet and reduced their numbers with two precise punches. The air lifted the Linoans' stumbling bodies, carrying them over the edge. Leaping at the last pair, Azure rammed a foot into each, catching the hatch just in time, the hinges bending and groaning with his weight. They slipped on the smooth hull, falling with soft thuds before tumbling to the earth below.

Azure peeked over the opening in the roof and found two more prepping to climb up. Drawing a pair of his throwing knives, he tightened one in each hand and hopped down into the cabin, thrusting his arms out, driving a blade into each of their skulls.

Above, the end of a rope appeared, to Azure's relief. The cloaked F-201 was back overhead. Josie and Panton slid down, Panton lowering her to Azure through the hatch. "Sorry, we lost ya for a second," he said.

The Linoan vessel jerked left then right. Azure grabbed her waist, his toes latching onto the ladder steps like fingers. Josie and Panton's wrists snagged on the edge of the opening.

She shrieked in desperation as the ship threw them around. Panton grunted, trying to grab the hatch frame with his free hand. Azure reached out and firmly gripped a wrist, hauling him through. The three tumbled to the floor.

"Thanks." Panton gasped.

Azure bolted upright, thrusting himself into the front of the ship. Swift and precise, he took the co-pilot's head in his hands, the resounding crack of its neck gratifying. The pilot snarled as it banked the collector. The floor beneath yawed.

At the sound of bodies slamming into metal, Azure looked back. Panton had caught Josie in his arms, taking the brunt of the fall.

Four more Linoans bounded up from the stairwell at the tail of the collector.

"Rear gate!" Azure pointed.

Josie sat up, swinging her e-rifle around in front. Panton's hands steadied her hips over his. Her rifle clacked, unleashing rapid fire. The four fell into a pile, no shot wasted.

The pilot left the controls unmanned to take a swing at Azure. They struggled until Azure had the Linoan positioned in front of the cockpit door. Bracing himself against the seats, Azure rammed his heel into its middle, knocking it through the doorway. He drew one of his throwing knives and hit his mark with bullet force—straight through one of the Linoan's eyes.

In their fight, the rear ramp had opened. With the hatch on the roof exposing the sky above, the air inside became turbulent. All eight Linoan bodies were sucked out.

Panton and Josie started to slide. He caught one of the bench straps along the hull, clutching her against him. The fierce gusts tugged at their tactical clothing. She let out a screech, and he tightened his grasp on her. Several containers and cords flew out the open back, plummeting to the ground below.

"Can you shut that?" Panton yelled, his eyes squinted tight.

Azure spun around and took the controls. Flipping a switch, the gates closed, dropping the wind pressure down until it only whistled through the hatch. "Looks like we're clear. I'm turning us around."

Josie stood with a relieved sigh, outstretching her good hand to Panton. "I'm going to radio in to let everyone know we have control and need a space-worthy patch ASAP."

Azure grumbled, banking the collector back toward Home Station. "I did not anticipate breaking that."

Josie shrugged in his periphery. "We have spaceframe guys for a reason."

"Let me get your wrist wrapped before you call," Panton offered, standing up in front of her.

She inspected her soaked sleeve. "Oh, shit."

Azure listened to the grating sounds of tape unraveling and paper rustling behind him as he increased their speed. A shadow appeared overhead. Through the cockpit window, he saw Cutter wave from the deck of the F201. Azure hesitantly lifted a hand in return.

"Let me see yours." Josie's soprano voice echoed through the empty fuselage.

"I'm fine, scratches is all," Panton said, nearing the cockpit.

"Josh, you're bleeding."

He back-stepped into the pilot's guard box just behind Azure, his palms in the air. "I'm three times your size, Yalina. It's nothing. Go call Home."

After a huff, her boots paced away on the deck as she called Dispatch.

Panton settled into the co-pilot's chair, focusing inattentively out the window at the ocean whizzing by beneath them.

One of the screens in front of Azure displayed the full and empty capsules in the cargo bay below. "Forty-five of fifty life-slots filled." *Acceptable for sway dump.* He pointed to the display. "We have to keep them on board to make our ascent convincing."

Panton turned to him. "Life-slots?"

Azure drummed an armrest, monitoring the collector's speed and course. He knew their fear and disorientation. "New slaves. They're just sleeping right now. Will only feel like a second or two when they wake."

Panton acknowledged, sending Josie a written message via his wristband. When she joined them in the archway between the pilot's guard box and the cockpit, Panton jerked his head away, toward the island.

In an awkward moment of silence, Azure picked up on something neither Panton nor Josie seemed aware of. Shepherds had rules to follow, acceptable codes for action. But as Panton's arm hooked around her waist and hers around his neck, their eyes attentive to the land ahead, Azure knew it was the truth.

Deep down, they were more than co-shepherds.

"We all clear?" Panton asked her.

"A-firm. They want the collector in the field atop Home Station." She pointed to the flat, grassy area they approached.

In an attempt to be a little more human, Azure used a term he'd heard in the staging area. "Roger. Best hang on. My last set down was not so good."

"Oh, that is so bullshit, Azure." Tanner's voice crackled over Josie's speaker. "His last one in the tunnel was perfect! Better pilot than he lets on."

Azure felt his face heat.

"A humble protector is wise and effective," Cutter's steady voice added.

"We can handle anything," Josie said.

Setting down on the Home Station field, Azure brushed off their compliments and refocused on the mission. "We should get moving. We don't have a lot of time."

"Yes, sir." Josie and Panton were promptly on their feet, descending the opening gate.

Sir? Azure looked over his shoulder at them as they exited. *They respect me?*

Shepherds with Spaceframe patches on their navy coveralls hiked up the ramp to fix the twisted hatch. Catching several of the crew staring at him, he snorted. "What?"

They looked away, picked up their tools, and got to work.

Azure grunted in disappointment. *The same with every new kind.*

Spinning around in the seat, he brought the collector's main computer back online. He wanted to assess the ship's systems to ensure everything was in order before their ascent into the void. They couldn't afford any mistakes.

Chapter 44

ATANA GRIMACED. "I am—sorry, Bennett. I should have explained things to you."

The last of the receivers were being snapped together and set in a pile with the others. She had been attempting to calibrate the nodes but needed Teek's help to finish. Her focus was intermittent, broken up by pain. This much agony wasn't normal. She fought through it like usual, only to have it overpower her seconds later.

Stabbing throbs matched every inhalation. "I was trying to figure everything out—the survivors, the Suanoa, feelings, myself—before I put any of you at risk. With so many unknowns—"

"I know. Logistical nightmare." He sighed through his nose, monitoring her every movement.

She tried to take a breath to utter an agreement, but her lungs wouldn't expand. Pressure was building in her chest, her skull, her stomach. Her hands froze mid-air, dropping the calibrator to the desktop. Denying the symptoms seemed to make them worse.

Agitation at her weakness thrust heat into her face. To her dismay, jabs shot around her injured lung, seizing both instantly. It felt like she was tearing in two.

Bennett reached for her arms, worry widening his soft, hazel eyes.

Her growing dizziness caused her to stagger back from the table. A despairing uproar of voices re-emerging in her brain made her cringe. Where had they come from? There were never this many individual vocals on earth. Her hands shielded her temples on instinct, her shaking knees defying the order to keep her upright.

Something in her had changed after the encounter with the Suanoa. They'd broken through a barrier. Or maybe it was the Grey. There was no way of knowing the how or why. What *was* mattered. That's what she had to deal with. Nothing more.

"Nakio!"

Arms collected her. She didn't feel the hit of smooth concrete like she anticipated. A warm body cushioned hers.

"Nakio, talk to me."

When her lungs finally relaxed and she could draw in a breath, hot fluid coated the inside. *Oh no.* This was deadly bad. Atana grabbed her side and covered her mouth with a trembling hand, coughing violently. Blood spattered across Bennett's armored vest.

He looked down. "Oh God, I have to get you to the Infirmary, right now!" Bennett adjusted his grip, reaching for his wristband.

It wasn't Earth languages she heard. They held within them a prickle of a warning. Atana grabbed his shoulder to steady herself. "We need to go. Stop worrying about me. They're running out of time."

"*You're* running out of time, Nakio." Bennett's mouth set in a hard line.

She took a fistful of his jacket, pulling his face close to hers. Why was he so defiant? Command had her information. The receivers were complete. They didn't *need* her for anything else. Staring into his eyes, she envied him. His life. His strength. A hot breath from his parting lips curled between them. His—desire.

What she wanted didn't matter. "You have to promise me something." The words were a struggle with the blood swirling through her teeth.

The tension in his eyes faded, his face sagging like he already knew what she was going to say. "Anything."

Atana soaked in how he studied her, never shying away at the sight of her skin. His breath was warm, like the hands that braced her and the thighs beneath her. He smelled of leather and metal slag. He had encountered the Suanoa with her and survived. He could do it again. "If I don't make it, you tell Teek to reverse the receivers, *push* the telepathic signals away. He's smart. He'll figure it out."

"Nakio—"

Panton's deep voice popped through their wristbands. The collector was up top and ready.

Bennett's head swayed.

"Load." Atana directed weakly to the assembly bench. "Receivers." She held out her free hand.

Reluctantly, he helped her stand. "I'm not leaving you."

She tilted her head in warning, leaning heavily against the design table. "And I need a moment alone," Atana said from behind her hand.

Bennett grumbled an indecipherable objection, started for the bench, then spun around. "If you go—" His lips hung open when he paused. "I don't think you're going to survive. You definitely can't fight like this."

An accurate assessment she wouldn't confirm for fear of putting more doubt in his heart. And doubt was motivation's archenemy. She tamped down the urge to gag at the metallic taste, every exhale begging her to cough. Any verbal response was a bad idea. Releasing her ribs, she shooed him away with a reddened hand.

With a disapproving glance, he gathered the piles of receivers and gently packed them into a duffel bag.

Picking up the calibrator she had at her desk, he gave her a once-over. "If you aren't five minutes behind, I'm coming to look for you." At her nod, he hustled through the doors slinging the bag over his shoulder.

When Bennett was gone and the lab technicians were cleaning up the equipment, leaving half of the room to herself, she pulled the garbage can out from underneath the workbench and spit the blood from her mouth.

Chapter 45

"YOU ARE IN NO CONDITION to go with us." Bennett placed a hand lightly on Atana's shoulder when she hiked up onto the main deck of the collector. The teams had finished loading, the rear gates closing up with a whistle.

Her eyes spoke her unease, behind her stubborn mask. "Jameson, you know I have to." She walked around the crates of e-rifles and receivers toward the cockpit. Atana had wiped the blood off her leathers and retied her hair.

He followed at her side while she glanced over the cargo. It was all they could fit. It had to be enough.

"There are things I can do that no one else can." Her grimace was a twitch too many.

Bennett wanted to stop the launch, escort her off, in cuffs if it meant saving her life. But the concept was tarnished with a sense of abandonment. He couldn't do that to her. Didn't *want* to. "That only works if you're alive to do them."

Turning in the archway, she faced the teams buckling in against the perimeter of the collector, giving him one last look that said she knew.

Tanner nudged Bennett as their team took seats closest to the pilot's guard box. "That guy's insane."

"Azure?" He glanced at one of the gray arms reaching out to touch a screen in front of the co-pilot's seat.

"Yeah, B. Jumped 201 to the roof." Tanner looked up. "No harness, no rope. Unbelievable. We have to get him on the crew." He hesitated when Bennett lifted his brows. "I mean, if that's okay, sir."

"We'll discuss that later." Bennett tilted his head toward the co-pilot's seat. "Monitor, please."

"Yes, sir." Tanner slipped past him to sit beside Azure in the front.

It was a slap in the face. Bennett begrudgingly admitted Azure had been successful, making them one step closer to doing what needed to be done. Looking at the Linoan blood spatters on the floor, Bennett realized he needed to follow his team's example this time and work with Azure, instead of doubting him.

Atana addressed the UP crews new to the mission. "This is a standard facility sweep. Our job is to scrub the ship of every combatant. No talking unless absolutely necessary. The on/off switch is here." She directed to the base of her skull with two fingers. "Focus on clearing your mind. This way, we can surround the Suanoa and take them out if they cannot determine our maneuvers. Believe it or not, this *is* our advantage."

She leaned out of view of the crews to spit blood from her mouth.

Behind her, Azure's fingers danced across the switches and screens, illuminated crimson. The vertical thrusters kicked on, and the Linoan collector lifted, its nose lagging until their speed picked up.

Bennett watched Atana sputter and wipe her mouth on her sleeve. He decided to continue for her. "It's like fighting regular people. Your e-rifles are your primary weapon. Set your SIs to their maximum intensity. The Suanoa's skin contains a plasma layer, so you have to either attack with high heat or cut them by hand with a blade to take them out. Blunt contact will only cause their skin to harden, like punching rock. Got it?"

The crews nodded.

"You will be matched up with teams from different sectors on the ship. Azure has many perimeter guards who are eager to assist." He motioned toward their pilot. "They have been protecting the enslaved workers like we do the people of Earth. They will help you determine when you see a Warruk, Linoan, or a Suanoa. Each of you will take an extra receiver and e-rifle from the bins upon arrival. Those items are for the perimeter guards you will be fighting alongside."

One of the new crew members looked dazed as he surveyed the pilot. "Do they all look like—him?"

Atana squinted at the sergeant. "Some do. Most do not." She harshly cleared her throat. "There are no human perimeter guards, so be prepared. They are, however, all good at heart. Something we have yet to experience and understand." Her eyes cut into Bennett.

Their situation, the rules, Azure—they would never change how Bennett felt for her inside. Tonight, she needed support greater than UP could offer.

Bennett thought about the young shepherd's question, and who they would be working with. He knew he needed to set them straight, quick. They had to trust one another if this mission were to succeed. "At our initiation, each one of us swore to protect every innocent life, no matter the cost to our own. We would have nothing, and be nothing, if it were not for those who rescued us and brought us to safety, in some cases giving up the ghost themselves, for our sakes. It is now our job to pay this forward.

"We are equals in this battle," Bennett scanned the teams packed into the fuselage. "Equally vulnerable, equally capable, with common goals. The Suanoa must be neutralized, or we will all perish. Together is the only way we can make this happen successfully.

"These life forms you will encounter have been caged, tortured, and enslaved, living in endless fear for their lives, at the hands of the Suanoa and their crew of Warruks and Linoans. Some slaves were born into this nightmare and do not know the true colors of a sunset, what it feels like to have clean rain on their faces or breathe fresh air. They may appear different to us on the outside, speak different languages, but the necessities for their lives to exist are the same as ours. This is our chance to lift their burden and free them from the chains of their forced captivity."

The engines rumbled louder. His feet pressed harder into the floor. Atana's hand tightened around the metal arch at her side, her knuckles paling. Bennett braced her, urging her into the seat behind Azure.

Atana slumped down, lethargically pulling the straps around her shoulders. He helped hook them in front of her and startled at the chill of her fingers. Clipping into the pelvic harness, she yanked on the straps to tighten each buckle, removing the slack from the loose ends and gave him a nod.

Azure reached a hand behind him, taking hers with a worried glance at Bennett. "We're almost ready to jump."

Belting in across from her, Bennett looked out at the crews, the image of Atana's hand in Azure's sparking one last thought.

"Our purpose has always been to prevent our people from falling victim to such feudalistic ways, no matter the perpetrator. The universe has given us this chance to transcend to a new level, to rise above the expectations of ourselves, and protect more than our world." He lifted a hand, gesturing at Azure. "Countless planets have been destroyed by the Suanoa, the native survivors then displaced to these Agutra vessels to exist only as slaves. We were trained to never waste an opportunity. Let us make full use of this one. This may be our only chance."

The engines whirred faster, the pitch of their sound elevating. The crews sank heavily into the tall seats.

Bennett could sense the tension in the air. Even on serum, he knew the shepherds were nervous, traveling in some unfamiliar vessel to a location they knew basically nothing about.

His voice carried through the ship. "My strength comes from those before me. I honor them now and forever, as I continue their tradition."

Bennett's team was the first to respond to his words, continuing the Shepherd's Oath in zeal. "I solemnly swear: to be honest and fair. With integrity and a balanced mind, for this vocation I was designed. Not akin to any zone, we call Earth our only home. We're the last true armor for the vital spark. We disarm evil and preserve peace for every heart."

The transport jerked, lifting vertically, shooting up above the stratosphere.

Atana grabbed a strap hanging down from overhead, gasping sharply.

The remaining teams joined in the recitation. "The greed of others will not sway our actions, but fuel the purpose for our reaction. Our decisions remain unbiased and objective. In this state, we shall be effective."

Atana yanked open the top of her harness and bent forward, slamming the door shut between their seats and the fuselage. Blood splattered on the floor at their feet and up the door from the change in direction of gravity.

Bennett freed his chest clip, his hands supporting her shoulders. Strings of blood and saliva dripped from her lips, sending his heartbeat into a thunderous frenzy.

Tanner stopped reciting the oath when he spun in his seat, his laptop open to the flight plan. "Oh, shit."

Their voices were muffled by the door as the oath concluded. "We will continue to safeguard the innocent until every last drop of our blood is spent. Though our bodies may weary, as long as they're warm, we'll stay calm and controlled, amidst the storm. We are a symbol, for those who see, no matter our pain, we will set them free. Even on the darkest night, we are their shepherds, their guiding light. We fight for each other 'till the wicked succumb. We are all equal, united as one. We are the Universal Protectors!"

Bennett knew the repair to her hemorrhage had failed, and she was bleeding internally again. Atana's sunken, peeled-open eyes flicked up at him. He looked through the pilot's window to the nearing stars.

Please don't take her last drop, Universe. We still need her.

Chapter 46

A BARRAGE OF ROCKETS broke the stagnant air in their primed ears. The bloodshot light above the dock door flashed, the cabin pressurizing to the mothership. Azure hadn't docked a collector in months, but it was seamless as ever.

Harnesses yanked free, every shepherd standing promptly with e-rifles in hand.

"Sergeant Cutter, two Warruks," Azure shouted the reminder over his shoulder.

"Ready when you are!" Cutter replied.

As soon as Azure triggered the airlock, Cutter burst through the doors, releasing two cracks from his shotgun.

A pair of Warruks piled up in the sway entrance at the opposite end.

Cutter explained what they were to the unloading crews. Sounds of several e-rifles switching to Multi-round Burst filled the silence.

Azure followed Atana as she leaned on Bennett's shoulder.

She switched on Bennett's receiver, looking up to both of them beneath heavy eyelids. *We should hide the crews until we find Teek and get these recalibrated.*

Part of Azure wanted to rip the two of them apart and then Bennett a new one. But seeing the blood on her bottom lip, his heart stalled.

He picked out two spots least likely to be active from the schematics on Bennett's wristband. *Stage at hydro-facilities: P3KJ and P5KJ.*

Bennett signaled at his team, sending Tanner and Cutter with half the crew to P3KJ and Josie and Panton with the rest to P5KJ. Then, he sent them a message:

We're going to look for Teek.

Azure led the way back to the Hatoga sector with Atana and Bennett at his heels. *Kylo! Tohsa! Jeniah!* Azure called for his guards. *Where are they? At least one should be here.*

Atana touched his arm when they neared the fields. The skin on his neck prickled.

Something's not right. Bennett glanced over his shoulder. *It's too quiet, feels too empty.*

A non-telepath sensing a dip in the energy of Ether was not a good sign. Azure studied him a moment. His guards would never leave their posts unless—

"Oh, Diete." His rising fear matched the widening eyes of both shepherds.

The three bolted simultaneously, knowing in the pit of their stomachs why the guards weren't at their posts. Azure grabbed the latch on the bay door and flung it open.

Strewn about the fields were lifeless bodies, the grasses matted and stained in areas where the innocents had been slaughtered at work. Azure's perimeter team had been cut down with the rest.

Atana gasped and covered her mouth, her fingers gently touching Azure's back. He stood in stunned grief and guilt.

Bennett slung his e-rifle strap across his chest and messaged the teams.

Blackout Status

Safe Zone Compromised

"We need to find Teek," Bennett reminded them with a glance before running off into the fields.

"Azure, I'm so—" Atana started.

He swayed his head, cutting her off. "It's too late now. There are others to save." His guilt made him pull away from her.

Running through the grasses, he called out for anyone alive while searching for Chamarel and Teek, praying they were hidden somewhere safe. He passed countless workers, some he recognized, a few he didn't.

A familiar silhouette appeared beyond a cluster of trees in the waving grasses, the soil beneath a muddied indigo. The terror the sight spiked in Azure's heart blurred his vision and made him stumble into a sprint.

Azure dropped beside the guard, lips quaking. He slid a hand in Kylo's, inspecting the charred, smoking hole in the warrior's thigh and slices in his gut and neck. "What happened?"

"They came right after you left," Kylo sputtered. "There was no time. You were right, brother. All they are is death. Forgive me, niema Martiis. Promise me you kill them. All of them."

I promise. Azure knew Kylo was beyond hope by the size of the puddle beneath. He guided their foreheads together, forcing the few moments of love and friendship he could through the fog in hopes of making the warrior's pain easier to bear.

The guard grabbed his arm, looking him square in the eyes. "I see it, brother. Why you dreamt of her. She is special. Don't let her go. She is—"

"I know," Azure said softly.

"End this pain for all, for Lerona—" Kylo let out his last breath, the vibrant light fading from his irises.

The angry ache burning inside crushed him. Another good soul was taken before its time. Kylo was the best guard Azure had ever worked with: reliable, compassionate, and faithful. He was the one true male Xahu'ré Azure had become friends with, the one who had found him after the earth Rescue had left. Verros or not, Kylo had given him a second chance at life, at finding *Sahara*.

Rearing back, Azure released a howling grunt in agony, before pressing his face to the one wrapped up in his arms, his body nearing convulsions from the sobs. His fingers dug into Kylo's shirt, wishing he could hang on forever. He screamed through his teeth at the bitter clay that taunted him, his sounds coming out in whispers from the overload of rage that left him weak.

"Sim verso, marrat, sur sim veriia," he choked out, tears breaking free. "I promise, brother, on my life. Sim verso," he whispered. "Sim verso—"

Chapter 47

SMALL SWIRLS OF DUST formed near the blood draining from the lower corner of Atana's mouth. She hadn't made it far before her legs grew too heavy and her body had fallen to a pile in the fields.

A barely audible sniffling—a young voice, a child—gave her something to focus on in the light-headed haze.

Atana's heart knocked like a rock on an unforgiving iron cage when the notes registered as familiar.

That's Kios! Get up, Nakio. Get up! Each limb felt like it was filled with hot metal when she pushed herself onto all fours. She crawled toward the sounds, parting the grasses with aching arms. Atana passed several bodies, all burnt and sliced open. A couple had blood staining their nostrils as if something had erupted in their brains.

She reached the source of the sound to discover Chamarel, motionless. An iridescent sheen freckled the grasses around her body.

Oh, stars. "Azu—" Atana coughed and gagged, painting the golden grains red. Letting out a screeching whistle, she rested in front of Chamarel. "Kios."

A tear-soaked eye peeked out from underneath the bloodied robes.

"Vi ahna rass'ii?" *Are you okay?* Atana struggled to sit up.

He leapt out and hugged her tight, burying his wet face in her jacket. "They—" His shoulders shook. "Hurt Ma!"

Chamarel's fingers dug into the soil. *You must save them from this prison.*

Tremulous and teetering, the internal pressure building, Atana squeezed her eyes shut. *I don't know if I can.* The weight of her world's fate and those on the ship in her hands wasn't helping her breathe.

Kios's eyes widened in fear when he withdrew a hand from Atana's side, his fingers covered in blood. "Miia zi du viia, ahna—" Fresh tears sprung from his navy eyes. "Niema, nigh!"

Atana guided Kios away and doubled over, coughing out dark, plum-red blood. Unable to bear the load any longer, her body sank into the dirt.

...

Azure staggered through the bodies, scanning the tops of the grasses, trying to pinpoint where the whistle had originated.

256

"Miia, nuxia!" The voice was faint, high pitched, and frantic. Azure moved toward it. Someone was alive.

I called, and you came. You can't leave me now! Azure heard a child's sob and broke through the grasses in a mad dash, bursting through another cluster of trees.

Niema, miia zi du viia, nuxia!

He saw Kios, just meters ahead, shake a flaccid shoulder in his tiny hands, then sit back between two silhouettes and cry out at the sky.

"Kios!"

The boy blinked, his head swiveling as he searched for the source of the voice.

Azure bounded into the clearing, slamming to a stop when he saw Chamarel's drenched robes to one side of the boy and the stained soil by Atana's lips to the other. "Ma? Nakio?" Azure sank to the ground in front of Kios. "Are they both gone?"

Kios bounced in frightened impatience. "Almost."

Chamarel lifted a finger. *Let me touch her.*

"Ma, you're in no condition—"

I can give her a chance.

Azure hushed Kios and, with a gentle touch to his back, directed the boy to Atana's head. Carefully scooping up Atana's body, Azure placed her next to Chamarel. "Can you even save her? She's lost so much blood."

That's not what she needs, my son. Curled on her side, Chamarel reached out a shaking arm, tapping her fingers on top of Atana's leather jacket. *I need you to expose her skin to me.*

Azure knelt over Atana's lifeless body, unzipping her jacket and freeing the bottom buckles on her corset. Pushing the fabric of her shirt up and out of the way, he saw her bandages, drenched.

Oh, Diete. He covered his face with a hand.

Chamarel palpated around Atana's abdomen.

She needs you Azure, more than she lets on. Settling her fingers over the stitches in Atana's right lung and a hand underneath her, frosted orange light danced over Atana's body, mending the lacerations. *Her mind is lost in the dark. You must guide her back.*

How?

Chamarel smiled. *The same way you did before.* After a few moments, her hands weakly retracted from Atana's side. *It is your turn, my son.*

Azure studied Atana's lifeless face, attempting to put himself in the same mindset he had been in the last time. Framing her head with his arms, as gentle as he was able, he touched their foreheads together.

Reality faded until only the colors of night surrounded him. A single, angled light laid a silvery path through a sector door. He could feel the smoothness of the warm metal doorframe beneath his fingertips and the roughness of the concrete tiles under his toes when he passed through its opening.

A warm breeze filtered through his loosely woven clothing, gently wrapping around his skin. He had never experienced Ether when it wasn't a memory, and nothing as quiescent or complete as this world.

Outside, he discovered a woman standing on a rooftop under the cover of night. Horns and sirens echoed faintly amidst dreary lights below. He stepped out into the starlight. *Nakio?*

She spun around. Every bit of her was darkened. Her straightened hair, her outfit, her skin, and even the whites of her eyes had turned a dusky, light-absorbing nothingness. A tiny blue orb was all that remained at the center of each iris, dim at best.

Azure moved cautiously toward her, steadying his voice, despite the doubt creeping up his throat. "What are you doing here?"

"I don't know." Her voice was hollow, her eyes vacant.

"And this place?" He scanned around them.

Sensei's home, my—

Why are you here? He guessed the answer: this place was safe to her like the mountaintop was for him. They could see everything from up here.

I don't have a home. I've failed my people. She stared at the streets thirty stories below, whispering, "Those people."

Her image morphed as if to become more of a shadow than a physical person.

No! Azure grasped her arms with urgent force, sending tiny plumes of sparkling onyx dust whirling away from her skin. Her body locked up with a gasp.

"Nakio, you have not failed anyone. It is a manifestation of your mind." He loosened his grip and rubbed her shoulders. "And you do have a home, with me. Yes, there are lots of lives counting on you. But, you are not alone. I am here for you, with you. I have always been with you."

Her lips trembled, the light in her eyes nearly fading out. *I don't want to lose you again. I'm not ready to die.*

You're not going to die. And you will never lose me. Azure slid a hand up and around her cheek, caressing the arch with his thumb. Reaching his other hand around the small of her back, he carefully gathered her in his arms. Her eyes brightened as he traced each side of her nose with his.

His heart jumped when their humid breath mixed under the stars.

"Sim verons ahna. I love you." Brushing her plush, moist lips with his, he admired how they shimmered under the night sky. *I always have, always will.*

Her eyes consumed with fire. Grabbing two fistfuls of his shirt, she pulled his mouth against hers.

His fingers dug in, feeling the spark in her reignite, warmth radiating from her lips, her tongue, her body. Her waves of hair reddened. Onyx dust slipped from her clothes and skin, carried away by the wind, exposing the gleam of her leathers.

The ground shook beneath their feet. Breaking the kiss, they looked down.

Time to go. Atana touched her forehead to his, snapping them back to the physical realm.

Atana sat up in Azure's arms, her fingers running over her healed lung in shock.

Chamarel's voice quaked like the surrounding fields. "The container will purge soon."

"Come on, Ma." Azure reached over, taking her hands in his.

It is all right, son. It is my time.

"What? No," Azure contended.

"You and Atana will save us. Take good care of Kios. He is important to the future." Chamarel took Atana's hand and his shaking one, placing them together. "*Vi tiisa amah verons.* Be strong in love."

The vibrations grew heavier underfoot.

Azure felt himself hyperventilating. *Ma, don't do this.*

Go— The metallic sheen on Chamarel's face dulled with her last breath, a trickle of blood draining from her lips.

Azure couldn't stifle his whine completely. Chamarel was the embodiment of love and strength. Staring at her lifeless face was unbelievable and undeniable. Feeling the soil quake again, he reluctantly leaned over and left a trembling kiss on her forehead. It was too late to save her now. "Pelaeso sur ahna."

Teek rushed up beside them. "I saw teams. They say you need me for—Ma?" He tried to lean down next to her.

"We really need to go," Atana interjected, picking Kios up. Grabbing Teek's wrist, they sprinted toward the closest container door, the rumble growing stronger and more violent with every passing second.

Azure glared at Teek. "Where were you?"

"Running Ramura back to sector. I sorry, Azure!"

"Did you clear out everyone else?" Atana raised her voice over the compounding noise.

"Yes. Imara help when I return. She back on post." Teek tried to look back at Chamarel as they ran, his eyes turning pink around the edges.

"Bennett!" Atana shouted, scanning for him. "They are purging the container! We need to get out!"

The shepherd appeared, a limp teenager in his arms, the boy's red quills swaying with Bennett's long strides. The thunderous roar of the motors for the massive doors made their strained words seem like whispers. "Are we safe out there?"

"Yes, they just drop the Ag floor. We have to get the hall doors shut," Azure said.

"Ekiipa, where you find him?" Teek stammered. "I look everywhere!"

Azure lugged the door open pushing Atana, Kios, and Teek through.

"Human blood is red. Camouflaged himself and crawled out from beneath a pile of bodies when he saw me." Bennett carried Ekiipa into the hall, the young Kriit's body soaked and shivering in his arms.

Azure stepped out and grabbed the handle to pull the bay door shut. The sudden changing pressure in the room fought back, winds ripping, tugging, sucking him back inside. He grunted, squeezing the handle tight in his hand as his feet slipped from the ground.

Atana shrieked, calling out his name. Then a firm hand grabbed a fistful of his shirt, yanking him into the hallway again. They wrestled the door shut, latching it just in time to hear the container depressurize and several boulders knock against the metal sides as the fields were evacuated into space.

Azure sighed heavily and turned to Panton. "Thanks."

"You saved my ass," Panton reminded him with a friendly slap on the back.

Azure felt a tender finger graze his face. Atana's gaze was stretched in fear.

He smiled. *I'm fine.*

I know. Just scared me after all that.

Kios clung to the leather over Atana's shoulders, tears streaming down his face. She drew him close. *Ahna vi mitrasso. You're safe.*

Bennett warily eyed her injury. "Teek." He lifted the calibrator. "We need you to adjust the receivers, in reverse. There's a lot of them."

"What you mean?" Teek rubbed his face.

Atana tenderly wiped away a red smudge from his cheek. "We can use them to block Suanoa's telepathic signals. Just help me switch them. Then I want you to hide, anywhere safe, no containers. Understood?"

Josie gave one of the receivers to him from the duffel strapped over Panton's chest.

Bennett, having released the device into Teek's fingers, moved on to address the Ekiipa's swelling ankle. He used a series of generic gestures to speak silently with the teen about it. Ekiipa couldn't speak. He could hear. But it was the difficulty in communicating, so many overlooked, that appeared to earn Bennett reverence in Ekiipa's eyes. Bennett's smile slowly infected the teen, despite the pain he had to be in.

Azure grumbled to himself but made note of the shepherd's compassion.

From his satchel, Teek retrieved his calibrator. He drew a thin, flat tool out of the pocket of his shorts and popped the cap off the frontal node. "How you make so many so fast?"

"We have a replication lab at Home Station. I hope we get to see it again. I think you would enjoy it." Atana leaned over his shoulder as he showed her his process. "I based the redesign off the buffer system I had to install in my transport's cranial communicator so dreams wouldn't equate to unnecessary commands."

Teek bobbed his head. "I been working on telepathic drift dampener. No luck. But this—I think—yes."

Pausing a moment, Atana shifted Kios against her side. "Azure, can you take him? It will be faster if I can help."

Azure outstretched his hands, eager to care for the child Atana had attached to and take the burden of holding him off of her recently healed body.

But Kios didn't want to let go. She stopped and leaned the boy out on her hip. "I need you to be strong. Can you do that for me?"

Sticking his bottom lip out, Kios pressed his face into her shoulder. "Azure is kind. He will protect you until Teek is able, okay?"

"Rass'ii," Kios mumbled, wiping his running nose on a tattered sleeve of his shirt.

Azure gently took the boy, small for his age, and lifted him up to his side. Kios's eyes opened wide when he looked down, his hands wadding up Azure's shirt tight in their grasp.

"I won't let you fall," Azure boomed, dipping his head to catch the boy's gaze. He tried out a smile.

Kios peered up at him, looking doubtful.

"Yanir sim niveriia vehr." *Until my dying breath,* Azure reassured with a nod.

The boy's face contorted, his scrawny arms flying up around Azure's neck. The gesture made his eyes sting. He soaked in the precious embrace.

Atana beamed up at them with a short laugh. Giving Azure's bicep a squeeze, she reached down to tear off the unnecessary bandages around her midsection while they followed Teek and the others back to the teams.

...

"Nakio?" Panic made Bennett stumble and reach out to stop her.

She looked up at him, the last bandage slipping off her ribs, showing her healed skin.

He stilled in confusion, staring at the faint marks where moments ago she was bleeding profusely. His stomach heated. He'd never seen so much bare skin on a woman when it wasn't covered in blood. Rotating to the side, he averted his gaze to keep his control.

"Is Ekiipa okay?" she asked.

He gestured to the pair of medic sergeants attending to him. "Yeah, just the injured foot, I think. What happened?"

"Chamarel healed me." Atana wadded up the bandages and chucked them in a corner. "She's with the stars now."

Bennett caught her arm, lifting her chin to inspect her eyes. They were attentive, steady, and backed with fury.

"I'm fine this time, really." Her gaze darted in the direction of Azure. Slipping Bennett's grip, she made a beeline for Teek's position. He stood, recalibrating receivers, inside a ring of shepherds guarding his back.

Dropping his hand, Bennett followed her suggestion. "I'm sorry about Chamarel and your fellow workers," he said to Azure.

"Thank you." Azure licked his lips, his face sagging with indescribable loss. He clutched Kios tighter. "They were family."

Family— Bennett spun and headed for the crews gathering in the hallway intersection, finally able to focus once again. Except his attention was back to the closest thing he had to such a concept. Undoubtedly many, maybe all of his would die too. There was no telling, because no one had gone into battle like this with Suanoa before and survived. "Can you direct them on where to find the perimeter teams on their wrist maps?"

"This time, in the cycle—" Azure closed his eyes, tilting his head. Bennett held up a hand, and the crews stopped moving. The subtle hum pattern of the hydro-facility's pumps became more distinguishable.

Azure tapped on Bennett's screen, highlighting the guards with white dots, illuminating the locations on every shepherd's wristband. "Those are the same positions for the teams in every sector, on every level."

Several shots went off behind them. Bennett and Azure whipped around to see a female sergeant rest her e-rifle at her side, her eyes honed in on the two Warruks piled up not far from her boots. Checking the hall they had come from, she returned to her team.

Kios trembled in bursts. His skin was pale, lips split and peeling. No one closed their eyes on Agutra without someone else standing guard. Bennett had observed that much. Kios had to be hungry and his energy low from all the healing his body was doing. Jolts of fear and panic would only compound the problem. It was best for him to rest. Convincing him he could, safely, would likely be a tough battle.

Releasing the hand from the blades on his belt, Azure patted the boy's back and sighed. "You can crash Kios. One of us will watch over you."

Kios whined softly, trying to pry his eyelids open. "Miia zi du viia."

"Don't worry about her. Just rest." Azure cradled the boy's stick-thin frame tighter.

Bennett silently reformed Kios's words with his own lips, looking to Azure.

Azure pointed to Atana. "I will contact my lead guards personally so they understand the plan and help spread the word. Just in case, the code is ongkrat, if any of you have trouble communicating. They know what that means. If they look at you for a moment, it is because they have never heard it when it meant something before."

"And it means what?" one of the sergeants asked.

"Mutiny." Azure glanced at the blue-eyed man nearly matching him in height.

Teek outstretched recalibrated receivers to Bennett and Azure. "We done."

Checking on Atana as he donned his headgear, Bennett watched her inspect her SI intensities and sling an e-rifle over her shoulder. But it wasn't until she wrapped her hand around the handle of the hooked knife strapped to her low back that she paused for a breath and closed her eyes. When they opened, they darted to him, blazing aquamarine. Atana's fire was back. And it pleased him to no end.

Azure cautiously traded Teek the receiver for a sleeping Kios and picked up a pair of e-rifles. "Stay behind so we can clear the pathways. I want you by Paramor. Find him and don't leave."

Teek nodded and braced Kios, slipping out of the way as the teams formed up.

Bennett called out to the crews. "Make sure each one of you has an extra receiver and e-rifle for the guard teams you will be working with."

Atana waved a cluster of shepherds over to her. "Igniter Five Five, with me. Our job is to take out the imperials, top deck. Azure's leading Eagle crews, lower eight levels. Viper crews with Bennett, one through seven, plus engineering."

"I still think you should take more than one crew, Nakio." Bennett mindlessly racked the e-rifle between his hands, a soft green glow warming above the forward grip. "The plan was to clear sectors then move up."

"What I saw when I drifted— I can't explain in words. I'm the one who should take the risk with the imperials. I'm only taking a team so you two will *let* me go." Atana slung a second e-rifle over her shoulder and drew her SIs.

Bennett hated the feeling she was right. He picked up another e-rifle. "And if you don't make it?"

Her gaze was icy again, hard, her voice equally cold. "Then you rain hell down on their heads with everyone left, Sergeant."

His jaw jutted to the side, wanting to argue. "Yes, ma'am."

Atana circled a hand in the air and moved toward the stairs, her team following.

Bennett cracked his neck, steadying the hot e-rifle in his hands. "You heard Atana; Vipers with me."

With Ekiipa under Azure's protective arm, Teek and Kios bringing up the rear, the remaining crews crept into the stairwells—igniters hot and ready.

—Dust—

Chapter 48

AZURE SCREECHED TO A STOP, halting his crew behind him. Imara, his second in command, bolted down the hallway shouting his name. The strongest female perimeter guard on the ship, she knew the hidden roads as well as he did.

"Another sector just got purged!" Her face darkened with fury. "I've got reports in of seventeen other containers that either have been or are in the process. We need to figure out how to shut it down!"

Someone yelled behind her. She spun and, in another language, directed the frantic mass of life forms to a possible shelter slapping a hand to her forehead. "Why are they purging their containers now? It's too soon. The other sectors haven't docked from the planet. We are losing so many workers!"

"Why, in Diete, didn't anyone come get me earlier?" Azure demanded.

Her brown rag shirt and pants were splattered with different colors. "It's chaos on every level. I couldn't break away. A couple of the Verros locked a team in a container when it dumped. Ours and theirs." Imara's striped cheeks were stained with angry tears. "I don't know why they would do that! This is their home. It isn't Kylo's way!" She threw her arms to the sides. "Taking over Agutra would be the best of both to them." She covered her face. "We had to kill those Verros, Azure! We had to!"

"Kylo's dead."

"Nigh—" Air rasped through her parting lips, fresh streams of water escaping her eyes. "Niveriia?"

Azure reached out and gave her a squeeze, partly to calm her, mostly to reassure himself she was still real, still fighting at his side. With Chamarel and Kylo gone, the two that had been his anchors, Azure was feeling the full weight of leadership. And the stress. "Vi tiisa, Imara." Burying a kiss deep in her hair, with a silent prayer to keep her safe, Azure stepped away and frantically called out over his wristband. "Tanner, where are you?"

"Three levels above your position, sir." In the transmission-crackled background, Tanner fired off several shots, Cutter's voice shouting behind him.

"Any idea how to shut down their purge process? Imara told me they've dumped about twenty containers." Azure tracked Imara while she

266

paced a circle, fingers digging into her baby dreads the way they always did when guilt and panic butted heads within her. She was a tender creature on the inside and often beat herself up over a perceived failure that was no fault of her own. But the anger, it would undoubtedly evoke, made her fight stronger.

She stilled and looked up. "They wouldn't purge all of us, would they?"

Azure didn't like much about his position as Lead Guard. His least favorite part: telling others the truth about the place they hated calling home. "You know better, Imara. Do not count on that."

Bobbing her head, she scrubbed the water from her face with bloodied hands, smearing dark streaks across her cheeks. "I just needed to hear you say it."

"Do you think we would find them up in the imperial ring around the abaddon deck?" Azure asked Tanner. The concept of willingly ascending to meet the Suanoa face-to-face in their territory made Azure cringe inside. It might've been easy for Atana. She hadn't lived under their rule for decades, like him. But he'd push through anything to stop this.

An explosion rattled the speaker. Tanner whooped. "Nice one, Cutter." He paused. "Yes. Our teams just finished cleaning this level. We will be there as fast as we can."

Azure addressed the five members on his team. "Go with Imara. Help move and secure workers. Keep your eyes open for Suanoa."

The readout on his wristband listed:

Program: Delegate - 26 of 30
Cleared: Levels 1-8, 10-14

He shouted after Imara in their native tongue. *Four Delegates remain! Levels nine and fifteen left!*

Eih. Vi sisano Martiis. Her blue eyes flashed once more at him, fury in their colors again, before disappearing around a corner.

Azure's grip on the e-rifle tightened. He flew through the hallways, grinding his teeth.

"Veriisaht Ehrun!" Hustling to an ascending ventilation shaft, his muscles flexed, begging for the release. *We're at least several weeks from Zephyr station. Why do we come here to get more resources, just to dump everything?*

He crouched and slipped in behind the vent screen, closing it firmly behind him. Slinging the e-rifle across his back, Azure stepped to the edge of the shaft. Bow to stern, it was the longest fall to one's death on the entire ship. Heart pounding with rage against his ribs, he eyed the duct across from him. It was a familiar, three-meter jump.

There was always the possibility the Suanoa knew what they were planning.

Gripping the frame with his toes, Azure thrust himself to full extension through the air. Arms outstretched, he felt the other ledge beneath his fingertips just before his body thudded against the metal, e-rifle pressing between his shoulders. He tugged the reversed receiver down, tighter over his head.

The noise of the jumps never concerned him. Warruks were too heavy for the ducts. They fell through. Linoan heel-blades caused too much damage. Azure knew he was safe until his exit.

His first few jumps were always a bit clunky, until he got his momentum and the rhythm synced. A glance at the next duct above and Azure pulled his body up, taking a hold with his feet. He launched again. A twist mid-air and, his fingers caught on the edge. It was faster and safer than climbing stairs.

Maybe they figured out who Atana really is. Azure's focus tunneled with belligerent anger. *Doesn't matter. I'm fulfilling promises tonight.*

...

Cutter peeked warily through the half-open door. Slipping inside, shotgun at the ready, he and Tanner found the team from Earth and the two perimeter guards assigned to Atana sprawled throughout the circular command center. "Shit."

The two of them scanned between the curvilinear operations desks molded up into the outer wall, searching for survivors.

"Where's Sergeant Atana?" Tanner asked.

"Bennett probably knows where she is. Let's find the purge switches." Cutter scoured the room but couldn't see the figure stealing the heat from his spine.

The ship rumbled again, shaking the ground underfoot. Tanner growled and took off running.

Cutter spotted an orb of fire peeking out around the ring-shaped room. "Cover!"

Tanner dropped to the floor, sliding under a desk, his body toppling a chair.

Lifting his e-rifle, Cutter sent three bundles of flaming, green pellets arcing across the room and into the Suanoa's blood-soaked body.

The wall behind Tanner's recent upright position dripped globs of red-hot plasma and molten metal onto the floor.

At several soft sounds behind him, Cutter whipped around, pointing the glowing end of his e-rifle at Azure. The warrior jumped back, throwing his hands up.

Cutter immediately lowered the barrel.

"Where's Tanner?"

Tanner's tousled blond head poked out from under his table. He sprinted over to the station the Suanoa had been working at. Lifting his wristband, he checked the symbols of the sectors that had been reported purged. "Found it!"

Bennett stumbled in the doorway. "I heard you guys over the radio. Did you find them?"

Tanner finished pressurizing the sectors. "I just need to pull down the last lever to lock in the settings." He tugged on the handle. It didn't budge.

Cutter hustled over and urged Tanner's lighter form out of the way. Using most of his bodyweight, he forced the lever over, snapping it into position.

"I know that's what it's for," Tanner insisted. "I studied it in the logs last night. I don't know why it's almost nature-welded unless they don't use it. But they could've bumped a switch."

"This is how they purge us?" Azure took a step closer, scanning the grid of switches. "What do you mean, bumped a—"

Seeing the mortification stretching Azure's face, Cutter corralled the large man away. "It's done. Let's focus on finishing these bastards off, yes?"

Azure nodded numbly, still trying to look back.

"Level nine is almost clear, only two sectors left." Bennett twisted, scanning the space. "Where's Atana?"

Tanner pointed past the group to the far arc of the ring. "That's her entire team."

They collectively jogged to the downed shepherds and perimeter guards.

Cutter began unclipping wristbands and shutting down the computers. "All dead, sir. I don't see Atana."

Bennett's shoulders rolled forward, a hand running over the scruff on his face.

Azure squinted at Bennett. "Neither one of us should have left her."

Cutter scanned between the two as he freed the last wristband, resting the female sergeant's hand over her burned stomach. Azure was telepathic and wore a reversed receiver. Yet he seemed to have heard something Cutter had missed. "If we have over twenty unaccounted for imperials and we've cleared almost every level, where else could they be?"

The ship jolted, knocking everyone from their feet.

"What on God's green Earth was that?" Cutter asked.

"It's the plasma drive!" Azure scrambled up, slamming himself to the radial windows of the internal wall to peer down. "Your planet is running out of time!"

His contours were cast in red light. Cutter, Bennett, and Tanner exchanged glances before jumping over the bodies to Azure's position. The stacked, cylindrical towers at the center of the ship bloomed red.

"Tanner, can you shut it down?" Bennett asked.

When the red light mixed with Bennett's hazel eyes, Cutter could've sworn they looked like they were on fire.

"I—I think so." For someone always so focused, Tanner's stutter made Cutter look.

Tanner wasn't paying attention to the lucent rings. His eyes were locked on a circular room of glass far out in the raised center of the ship. Standing in a bubble of orange light were the remaining Suanoa. Amidst the red flickers, a pair of blue eyes couldn't be mistaken.

Sergeant Atana. Cutter had studied Tanner's map of the ship enough to know that chamber, suspended between the spires far above the rest of the ship, was labeled as the abaddon deck. *Abaddon, a place of destruction, condemnation. Hell.*

Sickened fear swirled in Cutter's belly.

"Do it!" Bennett commanded. "We're going to find Atana."

"Yes, sir!" Tanner swung his e-rifle in front of him, leaping for the door.

Cutter thrust a finger her direction as he lifted the large shotgun slung across his back. "Found her." He tossed his shotgun to Bennett, who eagerly caught it. "You might need it. Never know."

With one last glance between the two men, Cutter lifted his e-rifle, bursting out into the hall after Tanner. *Please let those two make peace even if just for a moment.*

Lifting his wristband, Cutter selected All Teams. "There's at least one Suanoa in plasma engineering! I repeat, Suanoa, plasma engineering! Anyone available, take it out!"

Chapter 49

"PLASMA DRIVE INITIATED! I repeat. Plasma drive initiated!" Panton and Josie heard Cutter's call come in. Their team had been finishing up level nine, with two containers in the core structure left to clear.

Another team crackled through the comm. "We're coming up on nine. You four go!"

"Copy, we're—" Josie's response was cut short when the food storage container they were in filled with sounds of gunfire near a side door. She and Panton spun to discover the commotion had ended. Several Warruks lay dead, along with the Marakou perimeter guard assigned to their team, his tattooed body painted with pale olive blood.

The guard remaining let his e-rifle rest by his side, the tip glowing from the intense heat. He shook his head, his long, red, segmented quills swaying with his movement.

There was no time to mourn the loss of a comrade. Several more Warruks and Linoans closed in on them from all sides. Josie and Panton backed farther out into the center of the tall, cylindrical room, searching for an exit. In scanning overhead, Panton realized the vacant catwalk above was within his reach. He grabbed her and pointed up.

Catching sight of his silent suggestion, she nodded. He lifted her until her arms reached the bars above. Pushing her feet up, she climbed over the railing. Panton followed, setting his boots silently against the metal.

Her eyes told him she was watching the level above and he was to monitor below.

A blazing projectile whizzed out of a Warruk's gun, hitting the side of the catwalk just behind Panton, fusing its orange glow with the railing. That small fireball had been enough to kill Goss, along with many other UP members and perimeter guards. It was no matter to be trifled with.

Panton let loose, spraying rapid fire down over the enemies swarming in from the doors. Josie released multiple shots overhead. Three bodies fell from above, two landing on the floor below. One folded in half over the metal handrail of the walkway they stood shooting from. The Warruk's body slipped off the bent metal and fell, crumpling a Linoan below with its weight.

271

A blast skimmed the Kriit guard's upper thigh, taking him to the ground. Panton yelled, waving him toward the door of the neighboring sector. When Josie and Panton spun to provide cover fire, a young male, bandaged but holding a Warruk's gun, popped in the doorway, firing with repetitive accuracy.

"Ekiipa?" The man's voice faded, the younger arms dragging him off, into the shadows.

During their moment of distraction, two Linoans appeared on each side, running at Josie and Panton from the ends of the narrow platform. She whipped around, shooting the one closest to Panton, just in time for him to grab her vest and sling her behind him, the Linoan on her side closing in.

He tried to dodge the punch, but the Linoan's bladed fist struck his upper chest, cutting deep into his skin. The force knocked Panton backward into Josie. Bracing himself on the handrails, he kicked a foot out hard into its gut. She promptly swung around and shot it in the head, raining currant-colored blood onto the floor as it fell.

An arc of amber-red light came from above, exploding against the catwalk. The frame jerked, splitting at the end and buckling in the middle, sending the two of them tumbling as it twisted and caved.

They rolled off and into the exterior wall of the facility, several more arcs raining down from above. Panton frantically crawled over Josie, shielding her in the corner. A bruise was forming beneath the dirt on the side of her face. Shelving toppled. Bits of clay jars and bundles of grains filled the air. Dust filtered the light. The scent of burning hay and hot metal slag filled Panton's lungs.

Another blast from above made her gasp and flinch. He knew what her reaction meant and did his best to reset himself for the impact.

A metal panel fell, slamming down across Panton's back. It sent sharp pains radiating out from his spine into his shoulders and arms. Pieces thundered down on top of it, rattling his body. He braced himself against the wall, above Josie's head, taking the beating. A vein bulged in his forehead so strong he could feel it.

He coughed and sucked in.

"Let it go!" Her voice came out scratchy from the thick, smoky air. Blood dripped from the cuts in his chest, falling to her vest with several pops. "Let it go!"

He grunted and shook his head. "Guards protect, at any cost."

Blinking forcibly, he attempted to clear his mind and renew the fortitude of his fight. But the weight was too much, pushing his exhausted body down, forcing him onto his hands and knees.

"Even if it means dying?"

Her voice was the softest, most frightened he'd ever heard it. Tears formed in the bottom of his eyelids. He couldn't look at her. "It's my job, to my last drop."

Afraid she would be crushed if he let the structure win, he jerked his nose toward the best possible escape. "You have to climb out."

"No, I'm not leaving you!"

Another blast smacked the floor of the middle storage level. Her body quaked, gobs of molten steel dripping like rain from the misshapen edge. "I—I don't want to."

The structure jostled with another clang. Panton's arms trembled under the weight. "Please, Josie."

"Why are you doing this?"

He couldn't understand why she would ask such a question. The answer was obvious, a given. "If it doesn't kill me when it collapses, I'll climb out and find you."

"Josh." His name on her lips was a retort and a plea.

A cool finger grazed his jaw, summoning his attention. Staring down into her emerald eyes, so clear amidst the haze of destruction surrounding them, broke down the last barrier he had inside. Her warm vanilla scent hummed through his system, a justification for the pain. His wristband sent out flashing alerts in rapid succession.

Serum Dose Overdue
No More Vials Available
Last Five Doses: Ineffective
See Serum Specialist Immediately

"For you, Yalina Cera Josandizer—" His voice was rough from the sting of the cuts that sent feverish pulses up his neck. "I would do anything."

...

Josie tried to find words to rationalize their situation. His chocolate eyes stared longingly at her, unwavering, despite the agony she could tell he was in. Caged amidst the mayhem, no one left to rescue them, she felt the depth of their bond. It was something that, until now, she had believed impossible. Her flashing wristband proved the truth.

Auto-Inject Sequence Initiated
No More Vials Available
Dose: Ineffective

See Serum Specialist Immediately

A blast hit a few meters from their location, startling her emotionally young heart. More pieces of clay burst into the air, pelting down around them. She cursed, realizing her distraction.

"You have to go," he said, body trembling above her.

"No! Not after all those years! No shepherd left behind!" Josie's focus leapt through their surroundings, assessing combatants, calculating a target plan. She picked up her e-rifle, attempting to line up through a small opening for a shot. Her arms quivered, the muscles refusing to obey her commands. She was a mess of emotions with no serum to knock them down.

"Brace it on my shoulder. You've got this." Panton's words were comforting, calming the unfamiliar sensations. Another explosion from the Suanoa's hands came from above, a meter closer than before.

Realizing the danger for the first time, the risk to Panton's life as she began to place a new value on their relationship, she felt something she never had before—anger.

Her arms stopped shaking. A rush of heat swept over her body. Time slowed. She watched the falling clay hang in the air.

Panton turned away when she confidently reset the e-rifle over his shoulder. Every one of her cells honed in on a single point. Through the narrow peeled-back opening in the mass of twisted metal, she took Warruks and Linoans down like trees in a hurricane.

Nine shots and nine of their enemies met a blazing, green demise. A cool chill passed through her calming heart, syncing her chronologically, once again, with Panton.

The Suanoa above kept shifting, its shadow blinking between pillars and shelves.

"Come on. Move into the clearing, between the shelves," Josie muttered her sadistic encouragement. It peered down at their position from behind a large clay pot. *Just a little more. That's it.*

Another bullet ignited from her chamber, sending a jolt through her shoulder. It ripped through the air, climbing two levels, boring straight through the Suanoa's head. "Got you," she whispered with quiet satisfaction. Its body hit the floor with a thud. The resulting cloud of dust painted a moving object. Slouching down and pointing her e-rifle between Panton's spread legs, she searched.

"Josie?"

"One more. He's trying to hide. Might be a little warm."

He stifled a whine through his nose. Her eyes grinned, tracking the movement out on the floor. She took her first clear shot. The bullet punched hard, rolling the Linoan over, exposing a burnt e-bullet hole through its chest.

Panton coughed. "I don't think I can hold it."

"Then, let it go."

"No, Josie—" His rugged face contorted with a string of nos. Panton's body sagged and quaked when he resisted.

Watching him fight so hard sent a stab through her chest. She gingerly braced his cheek. There was no one else she'd rather die with. "I'm ready."

His shaking arms gave out, and he collapsed onto her like a lead blanket.

Metal screeched, crushing clay as it shifted, toppling down on them. Air burst from Josie's lungs at the increasing weight slamming down on her.

Panton's forearms braced her head, his cheek pressing to hers as he whispered a quiet prayer. A shelving unit pitched toward them, dragging several beams and clay containers with it.

Lacing her arms around his neck, she pulled him close and tensed for impact.

One after another, the items sent jarring blows through their bodies, each one heavier than the next.

She shrieked, and a sob slipped out, knowing he was taking the brunt.

A gust of hot air hit her ear. Panton groaned and everything came to a standstill.

"Josh?" She blinked the tears from her eyes, trying to get a peek at his face. He didn't move. The dust settled around their bodies until the air had almost completely cleared. Her lungs jumped into a sprint, and she patted his face. "Josh!"

His legs shifted to either side of hers. "Yalina—"

Beneath her fingers, she felt his cheeks lift in a grimace, another breath warming her skin. Nuzzling the sweaty side of his head, she sent a silent "thank you" to the stars.

He struggled to push up, powder and pieces of clay rolling off his shoulders. "Are you okay?"

"I'm more worried about you." Brushing his face clean, she traced the edges with new admiration.

Panton's muscles quaked with the effort, but he propped himself on his elbows above her. "Be honest."

She bit the corner of her lip. "Just not sure which one of our guns is digging into my hip."

Panton's cheeks pinked. They shared a light chuckle until blood from his chest dripped onto her vest again. She frantically tossed her e-rifle to the side and reached into his cargo pocket. Drawing out a bandage, she ripped it open and shoved it under his shirt and over the slices.

Panton's head drooped. His eyes rolled shut. The tip of his nose drew a line along her neck so delicate it sent an unexpected rush of desire through her. "I don't mean to make you uncomfortable. After the last eight years I—" His jaw clenched. He jerked away.

She lifted his face with her free hand until his eyes met hers again. This was dangerous, especially on such an important mission. Something about that was deliciously appealing. "Your secret's safe with me."

His dark eyes scoured her features. "Why?"

"The last thing I want is a newbie protecting me." Reaching into his pocket, she drew out the medical tape. Josie tore off several strips with her teeth and tacked down the bandage.

"Oh." He nodded and zoned out at the floor beneath her. "We might be able to get free if we both try."

Sitting up, Josie placed her palms on the metal overhead and pushed.

The pile lifted just enough for him to crouch beneath it. Together, with every ounce of combined strength left, they shoved the debris out of their way.

"After eight years, Josh Panton," she paused as he helped her stumble through the mound to the bare floor. He peered down at her, pain and rejection in his gaze. She offered her most genuine smile. "There's no one else I'd rather work with."

He reset the e-rifle in his hands then stilled. "Really?"

Panton's stocky frame was coated in dust and sticky with blood, his dark hair a ruffled mess. She knew she had to be similarly disheveled. Yet he stopped to stare at her a moment, like the surrounding destruction didn't exist.

An abashed tickle crept into her voice. "That and, I don't think anyone else could handle me."

Chapter 50

AN EXECUTION.

They checked the Suanoa spires, the stairwells, the halls—nothing.

No one. Anywhere.

The moment Atana and her squad entered the imperial ring was like a drop of water in a vat of pure acid. The ring boiled with fire. Blue-green, blood-orange, blue, blood. And a slurry of red was thrown against the walls. Only seven imperials down—and her entire team.

Her leathers smoking and charred, Atana stumbled to her feet, drawing her hooked blade in preparation of their attack. Her SIs were empty. The Suanoa formed up around her—an impervious ring of fate.

Thousands of voices raced through her mind, crying out to the universe, to her. She dropped to a knee. Her knife clinked to the floor. Lifting her heavy eyelids, she caught a glimpse through the window of the containers' contents in space, one after another: crops, land, and innocent, lifeless bodies. Her heart quivered, trying to flow the wrong direction, pining to turn back time.

A bright, carmine fire burst from the circle of raised hands, each coalescing with the next. Flaming fingers crept their way around her throat—a noose. Clawing at the calescent rope, she met nothing she could grasp. The soles of her boots lifted from the floor.

They slung her out of the imperial ring and onto the abaddon deck. At the center, her back slammed into a hollowed-out metal cast. Locks clamped her wrists above her head, despite her resistance, so even when her knees gave out, she would be forced to watch. Through the window wall lining the circular room, between the towering spires along the ships perimeter, she saw Earth, her view speckled with the tragedies of war.

The stories were coming back to her. This was part of their ritual. They took a prisoner with each new planetary consumption, who was forced to witness their home planet fold in on itself. She never thought she'd be the one to helplessly watch Earth's undoing.

A tremor shook Atana's cage. A pulse deflected, burrowing into crust. White clouds of steam puffed out of nearby mountain ranges.

Panic lanced through her. She jerked on her cuffs, her heart crying out for mercy.

The Suanoa weren't waiting for the collectors and containers to clear Earth's surface. It made no sense. *All will perish. There will be nothing left, nothing to return to. You have failed.* Their words grated through her brain.

Another pulse bounced off a Linoan deflector. When it drilled into the planet, she felt the burst in her chest, like a dormant volcano awakening. Hot with fury that had been stifled too long. The pressure within growing intolerable. Begging to erupt.

Her head swayed and hung in defeat. The noose was immovable as the cuffs, stealing her breath, her strength. Every ounce of hope.

You are a disgrace to your kind. You lie to them, make them think they can overthrow us.

Atana closed her eyes and listened, absorbing the truth she felt inside.

You deserve this pain for ensnaring them in your selfish scheme.

She repeatedly thumped her head back against the cage in frustrated agreement. *Yes.*

You will join them soon, in the cold darkness, the hollow veins of the universe.

She *wasn't* here to watch then tell. She was here to die.

Their rumbling voices rattled her bones. "Sahara—"

Her eyes flew open. They knew. Atana tore desperately at her restraints. The lack of oxygen going to her brain blurred the lines between morals and justice. Plumes of volcanic ash blotted out the sparkling oceans. Horrified and aware the temperature would soon hit its threshold, fragmenting her planet into a churning, molten mass, she choked. "Please, stop! They have done nothing to you! Niema!"

Her cries were met by deaf ears. "Take everything. Leave nothing. Survive. This is our way. You have impeded our way, wasted our time, time we cannot afford to lose."

"You have already taken my planet!" Atana's throat ached with the force. "You have taken Vioras! I am Xahu'ré!"

Their blood-orange eyes focused on her as if they moved as one being. "You lie!" Their booming screeches rang in her ears. She shuddered and pressed her body to the back of the searing cast.

Another wave of specks drifted by the window, silent victims to the heartless hands of space. Her eyes froze, tears burning in their rims, tormented by the never-ending suffering and death. She tugged, weaker now, at the unforgiving shackles above. Her lungs pined for air, wanting to scream, to fuel her fight.

A fleck of charring paper floated before her. The heat of the room suddenly became more apparent. She looked down to see holes burning in her clothes. *Ekiipa's note.* She jerked, trying to reach for it, but it incinerated and fell to dust, ripping her heart wide open.

—And then we are nothing, sent to the stars and—forgotten.

Like the workers tumbling by the glass, like earth, like— She studied her thighs, the leather crinkling and curling back. Her skin remained untouched. Atana gaped, dwelling in the sight. Denying its reality. Fighting its implication. Then slowly accepting her fate, too much evidence pointing to this.

A rare Xahu'ré characteristic, Chamarel had said.

And the prophesy—Embodied in flames.

The first invasion of Vioras was stopped by an explosion on the ship. Atana remembered the story she had heard back in testing.

The Suanoa were hunting him—Martiis zi du viia. He never came back.

Around Atana, the red-hot flares strengthened, the Suanoa tightening their boundary. Fifteen voices spoke as one. "The only thing that follows you, Sahara, is death."

I know. She growled, twisting and writhing with the erratic fire building inside. "I know!"

Beneath the hatred was a whisper, strengthening a purpose inside her. A familiar voice, not Sensei's, sang of something deeper than what she held on her own—a raw, primal power.

It's what we are.

The Suanoa were hunting *him.*

Tears evaporated from Atana's stinging eyes. The heat-tolerance wasn't from her mother. Atana swayed from the heaviness of the strength humming in her bones and the notion she'd finally found her link home.

She was her father's daughter.

Iridescent, white dust illuminated, effervescing from her skin as Atana bathed in a new energy. She felt as if a hundred thousand hands suddenly braced her back, each person holding a weapon, ready to fire over her shoulder at her command.

Death did follow her. But not the type the Suanoa implied, not *their* kind. Atana pinpointed the set of lurid eyes across from her as she drew in a ragged breath. "The difference between us is—" Her tone darkened to a blood-thirsty growl. "I kill for others, not myself."

Atana's fury swelled from her core, her heart the synergist. It fed into her veins, burnishing them a spark-blue. The pounding of blood in her body heightened to a smooth thrum, balanced, tuned to a frequency that resonated with every cell in her body. *Even on this darkest night, I am a shepherd—a guiding light.*

Infuriated chatter erupted from the Suanoa as they staggered back. At a shout from behind her, the Suanoas pressure swelled like an invisible weight crushing her body, the noose squeezing tighter around her windpipe.

She was slowly suffocating but didn't have time for fear. The escalating firestorm within her would end this. She just had to hang on long enough to complete this one, final mission.

Disarm evil— Another plasma pulse deflected around Earth, submerging into the depths of the Arctic Ocean. The heat within her grew.

Her head and shoulders slumped forward, debilitated by the lack of oxygen, her lungs collapsing. But the fire swirled fiercely inside. It felt separate from her body—an entirely different animal, a new level of existence.

With every last drop—

The murkiness in the earth's atmosphere expanded.

Amidst the storm. She struggled through a breath.

Bit by bit, the Suanoa tore apart the one place she could remember clearly, with the people she had worked alongside and those she had sworn to protect on its surface. The sight threatened to choke her out before the noose could.

She shivered and jerked in the cage, fighting through their suffocating grip. *I must set them free.*

Her previous reservations, the emotional control she had worked so hard to acquire, had lost its appeal in this moment. *The wicked will succumb.*

Atana's brows narrowed from the fizzing tingle in her limbs. The energy within her was on the edge of combustion. *I fight; I die; I live. Repeat. For once, let this be enough.*

Drawing with all the might in her ribs, slipping air through the noose, her lungs slowly filled to capacity. Atana pulled every deplorable memory she could out of hiding—her continuous source of drive when she was starved, exhausted, and teetering on death. She clung to the trauma, welcomed every moment she relived, absorbing the reawakening rancor and channeling it outward.

Atana belted out a battle cry, releasing decades of contained wrath. The pitch of her scream elevated until her body sent out a blizzard-white pulse.

Time lurched to a creep.

Air poured into her heaving lungs, the red collar feathering away. The Suanoa were one of the oldest species and powerful. But they stood still around her, like everything else. The sparkling clouds vibrated, waiting for a command.

Atana bared her teeth, relishing in the savagery of her final domination. *Cut—them—down.* Blood boiling with rage, she wrenched on the cuffs, twisting her body with a jerk. Time sped forward, and the explosive light coursed into a cyclone at her direction, tearing through the abaddon deck with catastrophic force.

...

Bennett and Azure raced around the imperial ring to the door leading out onto the platform. Through the glass, they saw her locked in and surrounded. The loop of billowing, lucent red energy around the prisoner was more pressure than any average life form should have been able to tolerate.

A murderous scream led waves of white flashes into the hall. The two shielded their faces, leaning away.

"Is that her?" Bennett squinted into the room.

"The prophecy didn't say anything about this." Azure's shaky voice gave away his surprise. "She's a Nova Xahu'ré?"

No! Azure's hands pressed to the door. *I can't endure this anymore! Stop taking her away from me!*

"Jesus." Bennett held his head and staggering sideways into the wall, muffled noise banging around in his thoughts. "Why's that such a bad thing?"

Azure's eyes lit with a fire like burning copper. He lifted his contorted brows to look at Bennett. "The last died! He died protecting our home, Vioras, from the first wave of Suanoa infiltration! But they just came back. They always come back!" He desperately pounded on the panel. "Nakio, stop! You have to stop this!"

Bennett wasn't sure of what he was witnessing or hearing. His mind clouded with words and voices different from his own. But he knew he didn't want to lose her either. Pushing himself upright through the ache, he swung Cutter's shotgun off his shoulder. "Step aside."

281

"Like hell!" Azure rammed a fist into the door, the metal surface caving from the force.

Bennett flinched. "Christ, Azure!" He knew it was going to take more than a punch or two to get through a door with no visible keypad or lock. There was one way in. Lifting Cutter's shotgun and pointing it in front of the warrior, clicking the safety switch off, he barked, "Move!"

Glaring back at Bennett, Azure's expression lifted, and he stepped out of the way. Bennett directed several shots at the frame which split. Cutter's gun ran out of ammo. Bennett gave Azure's size a quick calculation and tilted his head toward the door.

Together?

Azure dissected him in length.

"I don't know shit about Xahu'ré or whatever magic is going on in there." Bennett impatiently spread his feet. "But I'll help you get through if you think you can help."

Stepping back beside him, Azure gave him a sharp nod.

Throwing care to the wind and their shoulders into it, they tore the panel from the frame, slamming it to the floor and sliding inside, onto the deck.

The heat in the room made the air thick and hard to breathe. Torrid winds combed through their hair and clothing. When they screeched to a stop, Bennett reached up and grabbed Azure's forearm in a handshake.

"Go get her," he yelled over the deafening roar of fire.

Azure returned Bennett's grasp and hauled him to his feet. "Best get back."

When the heat from the abaddon deck swelled, Bennett stumbled away until he was in an all-out sprint through the hallways. His skin moistened, an ache of regret burrowing from his chest and into his bones. He was leaving Atana behind. But if he sacrificed himself too, there was a chance no one would be left to continue the fight if this wasn't the end.

In a Suanoan spire, far from the soupy grit and stench of rot and blood and bile, the hot gusts of air still followed him, tasting of iron. Looking down from this vantage point made the sectors below, and Earth beyond, seem much smaller in comparison, fitting perfectly with how the Suanoa viewed all things not akin to themselves. He was above the abaddon deck now and could see the other massive metal arcs, like his. They protruded from the guts of the ship, an open claw, as if to scrape the stars from the sky.

The Suanoa were all over the universe. This wasn't the end. Deep within, Bennett knew they'd started something bigger than the survivors and shepherds understood.

Hot as an iron chain over his shoulders.

He *felt* it.

...

Azure sprinted between two Suanoa, breaking into the fiery circle. He immediately crumpled in agony, his skin scalding from the swirling flames pelting his left side. The roar of the Suanoa's storm in his brain wasn't helping. It screeched and pounded like grinding metal, never pausing, never fading. There was no relief. He grabbed his head and cried out.

It was the song of death.

Azure crawled away and stumbled to his feet, his body smoking. The Suanoa paid him no mind. Their eyes were on her.

Taking a few steps around the perimeter of the luminous twister, Azure searched for a better way in. Every second grew hotter than the next. His time dwindled like the breath in his lungs.

The outline of a woman appeared amidst the waves of white as he circled to his right. Repositioning himself directly in front of her, he prepared for the worst. He knew the fire could strip him clean down to his elements and maybe even take him away from her before he got any words out. A gust of flames licked at his body. He tensed, enduring the onslaught that shoved him sideways. He stumbled a step. It was a risk he had to take and a sacrifice he'd make—for her.

I'd rather die than live without her again.

Turning on his own mental noise to block some of the Suanoa's telepathic control, he leapt forward, bursting through the outer edge and into the depths of unforgiving heat. Halfway to her, his steps slowed. He cried out as he reached her feet, his brainstem demanding he retreat. Shivering from the excruciating sensations, he fought to lift his failing body up to her face.

"Nakio." Flecks of his skin peeled away into the storm. He let out a pained howl and looked at his bloodied hands. *For her, this is for her.*

The two became wrapped in a blanket of sparkling blue and white flames. The fabric of his clothing was scorching. Hers had completely vanished, though he couldn't see much through the blinding light.

"You know this won't be the end. Don't do this! Your people still need you!" His throat dried and scratched itself raw with the effort.

The world pulsed. Scanning her face, he searched for any sign she was listening. Her curled lashes were locked shut. Motionless.

"Please."

Azure's lips trembled. His faith faltered. The nerves in his skin assaulted his consciousness with signals of irreversible damage. The thought of losing her and dying there, hopeless and helpless once again, was too much.

He choked on the scorching air, tears evaporating from his eyes. "Niema, Sahara— Sim tus ahna." *I need you.*

...

His voice rippled through her, the missing fragment to join her past and present. He stitched Sahara's furious determination and Atana's unrelenting control together. Because he'd never left. Not even when the crash had taken most of her away. He was still there, in her broken dreams.

Atana's eyes flew open to see Azure clinging to the blistering hot edges of her metal cage, his skin braised and disintegrating. He had found her and chosen to spend his last wheezing seconds at her side, sacrificing everything to beg her to fight fate.

Her heart caught in her throat at the misery on his face. "Why?"

Azure's forehead touched hers. "Because," his lungs heaved through cracked lips. "I love you."

The guilt she felt for not having saved him during the rescue tore at her. He was the one person she knew she could fall into that would catch her in his capable arms, even after thirteen years.

Tears steamed from her eyes. A mixture of reverence and regret made an aching desire to fight fate spring to life in her veins. She let go of the hatred she held for the Suanoa surrounding them and reached her nose toward his.

Azure stiffly lifted a hand inside her ripping, blue cocoon, the skin on his fingers whisking away. "Don't cry." His palm cupped her cheek.

She couldn't let this happen to him. Not after so much sacrifice. Not again.

Nuzzling into his hand, she found time easing its pace around them. His forehead rested to hers in apparent exhaustion. He hadn't connected to Ether, but it gave her an idea.

Closing her eyes, she honed in on the cool prickling sensation she felt inside, like delicately sleeping limbs. Gathering herself inside, coupled with the feeling, she thrust it through Ether and into him—a conscious healing. Blue chains of static danced over his skin, crawling down his hand from her cheek and up his arm to his body and toes.

He gasped, straining to pull away from the sparks. Their foreheads were frozen together.

"Not yet." Atana felt them nearing the balance: his energy rising, hers falling. He healed. She calmed.

Azure wiggled his repairing fingers, sapphire sparks trailing off their tips. He laughed in disbelief.

The moment of equilibrium came, a unity of forces between them. Atana took a deep breath, looking up at her creation. One of two things was possible when she let him go: they'd survive the heat together, or they would vanish with the winds.

His thumb trailed blue static over her chin. "We'll survive, lisano miia. I can feel it."

Atana's heart kicked hard against her chest. Their bodies hummed and pulsed, hot with energy. She pulled back.

A triumphant smile lifted with his brightening eyes. "Faith in you."

Slipping her hands through the deforming cuffs, she caressed the broad planes of his face in admiration. "Don't let go."

"I won't, ever again." Azure brushed his fingers over the healing cut on her cheek. They tickled her skin as they trailed down her neck to her bare shoulder.

In the distance, the blare of alarms followed by heavy thuds told her the bulkhead doors to the deck were closing. Atana couldn't help the grin spreading on her face. Surviving had never been a part of the plan. And the Suanoa were stuck on the deck with them.

Azure's caress sparked a new fire within. She rose up on her toes, slid her arms around his neck, and summoned him down to her lips.

Skin to skin, he gathered her in his arms, hungrily returning her kiss, an ardent glimmer in his eyes.

The room pulsed with teal and sapphire winds—the melding energy of their individual sparks. Metal panels peeled up from the floor, taking flight in the firestorm like silver kites. The windows warped and stretched out toward the stars as a rumbling groan shook the room. The structure tilted.

Breaking their telekinetic bonds, the Suanoa stumbled back in the white-out, their plasma layers broiling with the heat. The robes and scales of their armor tore free and shredded. One at a time, their skin burst, and bodies singed. Their embers were swept off until only a gray ash swirled through the space their feet once occupied.

Atana's bare toes felt the hot steel beneath slip away. Shredded pieces of trusses clanked against one another, joining the massive tornado. As one unit, she and Azure found themselves drifting upward inside the eye. The sounds around them diminished until all that was left was the rush of the storm and the occasional *tink* of hot metal.

"I don't know how this will end," she admitted, gazing deep into his vibrant eyes, afraid it was the last time.

Azure nuzzled her cheek sending static tingles over her skin. "Doesn't matter. The Suanoa are gone. And there's no place I'd rather be than right here with you."

Chapter 51

THE PLATFORM BURST, a bluish-white ring of light ripping out across the ship. Then everything fell dark.

Bennett uncurled himself, and peered through a window, out to the abaddon deck. Every red light on the ship flickered out. Hollow echoes of clunks brought a tier of lights back, then another.

Agutra was restarting.

The glass walls around the platform had melted into rounded droplets and were floating away into the vacuum of space. The metal frame of the ship was scrunched down, and the plasma drive wasn't visible.

Not a single soul remained. No Suanoa. No Xahu'ré. No shepherd.

The abaddon deck was broken and *empty*.

Bennett buckled, slumping against the wall. He covered his mouth, thinking of Atana and their fight the day before, saltwater blurring his vision. He regretted letting her leave his sight and not making peace with Azure. Aching loneliness consumed his heart, the cold of the metal floor a far cry from the chill in his bones. At least, it was something familiar.

The ground beneath Bennett pulsed. He lifted his heavy eyelids.

Wiping the moisture from his eyes with his palms, he pushed himself to his feet.

At this distance, the bodies and dirt looked like sand through a sifter made of trusses and pylons.

Another purge? I swear we shut those things down. Their joy of freedom had been so short lived. His hands pressed to the window, fingertips digging in as fresh abhorrence stirred inside.

He scanned to the imperial ring just below him and saw it.

Somehow, they had missed a Suanoa.

It stood, curled over the purge controls.

Bennett's fists squeezed tight. "Fucking bastard."

He was the last one remaining on the upper level who could stop the Suanoa's actions. Bennett sprinted down the halls toward the imperial ring. His heart pounded behind its walls, fueling every dynamic launch from his legs. The thoughts in his mind subsided, his endgame: death.

Leaping off the ground, Bennett rammed through the door to the ring, despite its latch. He somersaulted to a stance a few meters from where the

Suanoa stood. Drawing his Sls, he emptied the cartridges with successive blasts.

The Suanoa put up a radiant, orange shield in defense. Bennett's fiery blue bullets pinged and ricocheted off like the barrier was made of metal. Sparks shot out of several surrounding machines.

Bennett tossed the useless weapons to the side. Kneeling down, his fingers grasped the two blades he kept hidden in his boots. His hands squeezed tight around the leather-corded handles.

The Suanoa's teeth clicked. "You—"

Bennett cocked his head with a menacing grin. It was from the jury, the leader, seated in the middle. "Pitiful humans. No useful skills. Sound familiar?"

Growling, Bennett didn't give it time to answer. He charged, prepping to take a swing. He didn't care if he died. But he wasn't going to go out alone.

A fireball barreled his direction. Bennett ducked, adeptly dropping back on the floor.

Opportunity presented itself when his momentum carried him past the imperial. He reached out, with a warmed blade in hand, scoring the Suanoa's leg, down to its dense core. Dark blue blood seeped out of the gash, giving the sergeant a flicker of hope.

He came to a stop several meters beyond, his knives held at his sides, and snap-kicked himself to his feet. The imperial sent another flaming orb at Bennett.

He dodged, the hot threat passing his left side. Propelling himself at the Suanoa, Bennett lunged off a desk, swinging a knee to the central ridge of its face before the imperial could lift its shield. He thrust his knives into the base of its long neck, his weight taking the two of them to the ground. Tearing the knives out, he rolled to the side and stood.

Wavering like a drunk, the Suanoa picked itself up off the floor, the orange barrier flickering out. It tried to retaliate, throwing a punch. Bennett blocked with ease and threw one of his own, blade in hand, striking the Suanoa in its lower abdomen. He ripped the hot metal out and, in picking up a foot, shoved it backward. It slipped and smacked the blood-painted floor.

With a heavy sigh, Bennett's jaw relaxed, and he leaned over to his left, assessing the purge systems for the dumped container. Finding the sector, he pressurized it and locked in the settings, ending the purge, once again.

Searing pain radiated up his right shoulder, wisps of acrid smoke crawling through the air. Bennett grunted and grabbed his arm.

The imperial approached with a plasma insert red-hot in a palm, a wicked gleam in his eyes. "You?" He swung his hand toward the console. "Or them?"

Bennett stepped in front of the Suanoa's raised hand. It wasn't even a question.

What the imperial didn't know was Bennett had calculated the lag between the swelling glow and the plasma's discharge. There was just enough time.

A swift kick took out the imperial's knee. With his good arm, Bennett drove a blade deep into its neck, through the rubbery outer layer, past the plasma membrane. He shoved the Suanoa to the ground, directing its arm away from the console. A loose blast skipped off through the desks.

"For taking the most beautiful thing in this universe from us." Bennett gritted his teeth and thrust the knife deeper. There was nothing more satisfying than the resulting crunch. So many lives were wasted because of the festering mind now under his control.

It choked and coughed. Blood-orange irises squinted up at him. The imperial did not beg for mercy, nor cry out in pain.

Bennett would've liked that.

"You've taken what is not yours to take." Bennett glared at the pitchy stripes to either side of the Suanoa's corrugated ridge, glossy like war-paint.

Fluid drained out of the Suanoa's three-fold mouth, staining its knobby jaw an oily blue-black. "It is how we survive."

Bennett scoffed and gave the blade a slow twist. The Suanoa squirmed. Lips curled back in disgust, Bennett lowered himself to meet its eyes straight on. "You have forgotten the definition."

The imperial tensed then grinned maliciously. "More will come for you." It spluttered, navy droplets freckling their armor. *More death awaits.*

Bennett tightened his grip on the handle, forcing the gnawing fear back inside. This *wasn't* over. "Beginning of the end, then."

It screeched out a cackle. "You speak before you think. The gold of fools."

Muscles trembling with building rage, Bennett sneered, "Maybe, but I'm starting with you." With one swift crank of his hand, Bennett severed its head.

Chapter 52

SLICK WITH BLOOD, Bennett's fingers slipped when they contacted the smooth surface of the screen, selecting the flashing Respond button. "What is it?"

"Get down here. We're all in plasma engineering," Tanner said.

"What the hell are you doing down there? Is everyone all right?" Bennett stared for one last moment at the tattoo his knife had punctured on the Suanoa's neck. It was in a dark, oily ink, a creature of some sort with curled limbs. He couldn't sort the importance of it and tucked the image away in his mind for later.

"You told me to take the plasma drive offline—which, I did." There was obvious confusion in Tanner's voice. "Josie and Panton took out the last delegate in here."

"Okay, so what's the problem?"

"No problem. I found Sergeant Atana." He paused, clearing his throat nervously. "And Azure."

Bennett scrambled to his feet and sprinted out into the hall. "Are they—alive?"

"Yeah, I'm pretty sure they're okay, B."

"What's that supposed to mean?" Thundering down the steps, Bennett became impatient and took to hopping railings. He burst out of the stairwell toward Tanner's logged position on his wristband.

"I don't know exactly. I've never seen anything like it."

Bennett flew through the door to engineering. The rest of the team stood inside, every one of their faces tilted up. He screeched to a halt when he caught what they were staring at.

The middle of the upper platform was an orb of swirling, blue light. Inside, Azure held Atana close, one hand bracing her head against his bare chest, the other wrapped firmly around her waist, supporting her naked body.

Seeing the two of them alive made Bennett thank the stars though their unclothed state made his insides sick. "You both all right?"

"Think so." Azure's haggard voice conveyed his exhaustion. "Anyone seen Teek? Or have any ideas on how to fix this hole above us? I don't know how much longer she can hold this."

Teek appeared through the door. Scurrying over, he lifted a shotgun of sorts to his shoulder, nearly the same size as him. He wobbled then widened his stance. Panton chuckled. With Cutter's help, Panton stabilized the device, and Teek, who blushed.

Surveying the hole, he programmed the controls on the side of the stock. Discs slammed into position, jolting the device in their hands. Bracing himself, Teek launched several shots at the void's perimeter.

The individual guidance systems shot out electrical arcs, like sheet lightning, the discs adjusting their positions to their calculated destinations. Depressing a button on the side of the gun, the attached units fanned out. Locking together, they created a web of metal, narrowing the opening. Ejecting one more set, the hole disappeared. A second button on his device ignited yellow-white sparks, welding the metal in place.

"Okay. You can come here. Fixed," Teek said with a big smile on his face, looking proud to use another one of his inventions.

"For how long, exactly?" Panton eyed the patch overhead.

"Long enough; better fix in few hours." Teek nodded sharply, pulling the radio from the strap across his body and setting the patching device on the floor.

"You're all right kid," Panton said with a slap to Teek's back. The teen staggered and blushed brighter.

Tanner put a fist over his mouth, repressing a laugh.

Picking Atana up, Azure cradled her in his arms. Jumping down from the walkway, they landed heavily on the level below, the light reducing to swirls around their bodies. Gently, he set her feet on the floor.

Bennett stared, bewildered by the wavering bands. "What happened?"

"Yeah, what is that crazy blue stuff?" Panton asked.

"The floor melted when the abaddon deck exploded. She saw Tanner and the rest of the team in here and used her—" Azure paused. "She blocked the opening."

Atana leaned against him. "Teek, what are you doing here? Where's Kios?"

"I listen to guard that watch! Everyone listen!" Teek hesitated. "Um, Kios with Ramura." He stuttered. "She my friend. She coming."

Bennett caught a quick glance from Atana before she hid her face in the crease between Azure's pecks. "Sorry about your clothes," she whispered.

Azure visibly squeezed her in against him, sending a pang of jealousy through Bennett's heart. "I have breath and you. I don't care about much else."

Ramura ran in with Kios on her hip. Dotted with tears, her purpled eyes widened. "Hu'te sur Vioras?"

"We need clothes." Azure adjusted his grasp around Atana's body. "And a place to rest. We didn't exactly plan on whatever this is."

Setting Kios down, Ramura pulled the frayed blanket off her shoulder, handing it to Azure over the top of the light bands. "You can use it to, you know, wrap around you."

She picked the boy up and spun around with a giggle.

Panton slid his black leather jacket off, handing it to his partner. He slipped the shirt over his head and tossed it to Bennett. "For Sergeant Atana. Sorry about the blood."

"I'm sure she won't mind." Bennett saw the pair of slices and spun to inspect Panton. "Linoan?"

"Yeah, I got fixed up." Panton pointed at his bandage. He reached out to take his jacket from his partner. "Josie?"

Her glinting jade eyes were wandering over his exposed muscles.

"Josandizer." Bennett arched a brow handing the shirt off to Azure.

She let go, clearing her throat. "I apologize for staring."

"Don't be." Panton grinned and thrust his arms back in the sleeves.

Azure scanned the crowd. "A little privacy?"

Bennett reluctantly turned with the rest. He looked up at the patched ceiling, listening to the rustle of fabric, silently scolding himself for ever letting himself fall for her. The worst part was that she knew how he felt. Bracing his hands on his hips took some of the burden off his back.

Cutter gave him a sidelong glance.

All Bennett could do was shake his head. He didn't want to talk about it.

The blue light petered out.

"Covered," Atana said, meek and low.

The team turned around. Bennett held back, not wanting to seem too eager. Cutter was still studying him.

You okay? Azure surveyed Bennett's stained hands.

He forced a smile. *Never better.*

Well, I'm glad you are here with us. Eih ahna, thank you, he replied, catching Bennett off guard. *She wouldn't be here without what you did.*

"Come to my sector." Ramura sniffled. "We're still intact and not far."

She headed out and into the hallway, wiping the re-emerging tears from her eyes, Kios in tow, his arms slung around her neck. Azure followed close behind, carrying Atana delicately in his arms.

Bennett rubbed his hands on his pants and caught an extra pellet magazine from Cutter. Pulling the shotgun from his shoulders, he released the empty one and replaced it, racking the first shot into the chamber. "Josie and Panton, I want you with me to help set up patrol rotations. We have a lot of collectors with our people on them, along with more Warruks and Linoans. Tanner, I want you to radio Home Station, find out what the status is of the planet, and let them know we have control so they don't start taking out the collectors now that we have the plasma drive down. We also need to get someone to monitor the purge controls and the position of the ship so we don't send our people down the road of the dinosaurs by accident."

"The ship's on a sort of auto-orbit, right now." Tanner adjusted his harness, opening his laptop to scroll through the feed. "I saw it when I was studying the propulsion systems log."

Teek directed a long-fingered hand at Ramura. "Paramor is Healer for Jesiar fields. He from maintenance sector 105. He knows who are Doku, slaves that help fly Suanoa ships."

A flare of heat spread through Bennett's upper back. He rolled his shoulders, shrugging off the post-battle adrenaline withdrawal. "I imagine our people saw the blast from Earth. Can you help Sergeant Tanner with that, please? Cutter, stay with them."

"Always, sir." They left the room, heading for the imperial ring, discussing Teek's repair mechanism, with Cutter leading the way.

"We're going to check in with the remaining teams." Bennett hustled out the other side of the room with Josie and Panton at his heels. "So what happened to you two? You look like shit."

"Livin' the dream," Panton drawled.

Chapter 53

JESIAR BLOSSOMS SWEETENED every breath of freedom. Atana awoke to freckles of warm light on her face that peeked in between the fluttering rag curtains of a hut. Sensing the woven blanket against her skin, she stirred, enjoying its simple comfort. Releasing a sigh of contented relief, she gazed around the room.

Something floated close to her, drifting toward the ground in the gentle breeze—a white feather. It settled to the dirt by Azure's bare toes in the doorway, the fractures of light playing with the waving downy tufts.

A silvery face appeared over her body, scanning her with a handheld device. She grabbed his wrist, lifting her head to ascertain the stranger's identity.

He stopped and calmly looked over at her. "Hello, Sahara." His voice was mellifluous and reassuring.

"Paramor?" Seeing him smile, she let out the breath she was holding and laid back on the pillow.

He finished his evaluation and rose.

"It is good to see you alive and well." Paramor's movements were smooth as molten metal when he shifted up to Atana's head. "You will be fine in a few cycles. Until then, you must rest."

"Thank you."

He gave her shoulder a light squeeze and walked out.

...

Paramor pulled Azure off to the side of the structure and lowered his voice. "No species has ever witnessed anything like this." He studied the screen in his hands. "It isn't logical for anyone to survive such heat, let alone two individuals. But you did. A Nova." Paramor shook his head in disbelief. "The universe accepts things in equilibrium. Two equal parts balance each other, leaving nothing for it to interfere with. However—"

Azure hadn't let himself sleep when she had, even when Rimsan had offered to stand guard. He couldn't bring himself to close his eyes for fear of waking to find her gone, and this was just another dream. "Is something wrong with her?"

Paramor gestured an open palm under Azure's forearm. "You think she did something to your skin, and it stopped burning?"

E. L. Strife

Exhausted, Azure could only muster one word with internal panic shredding his last ounce of resilience. "Yes."

Paramor held the scanner over his skin. It hummed and peeped. "As I suspected. She changed yours, making you able to tolerate the higher temperatures. But you also changed hers. In a few days, she will be like you, Xahu'ré gray with thermo-stripes and all."

"But she's okay?"

"Better than okay." Paramor's eyes crinkled in the corners with his tired grin.

Azure rubbed the ache from his mouth with a hand. He used to wonder what she would look like in her Xahu'ré form, where her stripes would be, and if her hair would straighten or crimp more. Guilt now welled in his gut, having wished for a change she might not even want.

"She saved your life. In that moment, you two were one being. You are like each other now. You're the first nova survivors, ever, bonded down to the cellular level."

Azure leaned through the doorway to gaze at the woman lying on the cot. The flowing waves of her hair lay draped around her like a dark halo. His angel had finally returned. "I don't understand how this is possible."

"It was probably the Mirramor in her. Novas are uncharted territory for us." *It's hard to know for sure what's written in the stars, prophesied or not.*

Entering, Azure knelt beside her and lifted a hand, drawing the mahogany bangs from her face.

She rolled toward him, her eyes radiant. Her fingertips were soft and warm as they gently coaxed his lips to hers.

He held back, concerned about her team in the fields outside.

She smiled. *It's okay. My job isn't my priority right now.*

Wisps of blue light enveloped the two, his lips meeting hers with strength, desperately trying to make up for lost time. The taste of her skin was sweetly exhilarating. Their noses brushed, her intoxicating scent blurring his vision into something reminiscent of a fantasy.

He finally had her in his grasp, the oppressed were free, and their future had hope.

She drew his hand to her chin, their eyes connecting in mutual adoration. His fingers swept over her skin, the way he had wanted when the pain was too much to bear.

"Sahara!" Kios burst into the hut, giving Atana a desperate hug. His cheeks were wet with tears.

"Why did you call me that?" she asked.

"It's your name." The boy climbed up onto the bed to sit next to her. His hands took the sides of her face, and he leaned over, touching his forehead to hers.

Azure admired the boy's quick imitation.

After a short moment, Atana pushed him away. She frantically pressed her fingers into the skin on one of her forearms.

Azure watched the last of her injuries vanish and her skin dull with gray.

The boy crumpled, holding his head, whimpering.

Bracing Kios, Azure stared at him in awe. Most children didn't acquire the skill of healing until closer to ten years old.

Sitting up, Atana wrapped the boy tightly in her arms. "Kios, promise you will never do that again."

Azure rubbed the boy's back. "I have never seen a Xahu'ré so young capable of connecting to our Ether. Already a little warrior."

Kios's dewy eyelids cracked open. "Ma told me I am special."

...

Bennett posted himself on a bench of twisted Jesiar wood. He grasped the receiver node on his forehead and removed the unit, placing it behind him on a blue lapis boulder, streaked with gold. Glancing into the hut, he traced Atana's curves, grateful he could still look at her.

To his surprise, he heard her dulcet voice resound softly between his ears. *We need to talk, tonight.*

He thought it odd.

She did say that after I took this off, didn't she? His fingers toyed with the pliable cables connecting the nodes. *But they were reversed.* He shook the concern away. *Too much weird shit going on to know what's normal anymore.*

Imara sat down beside him. The fields around them were in full bloom. Deep-red Jesiar flowers sent sparkling, yellow pollen floating up into the breeze.

"So what now?" he asked her.

She shrugged. "Hard to say. Just enjoying freedom for the moment. No Agutra has ever experienced this." Lifting a hand, Imara gestured to the chatting workers as they mingled and strolled carefree through the rows. "I have never heard this sound before." Her eyes purpled when she hung her head. "The Saemas and Healers will likely discuss finding the survivors a planet if we can figure out how to operate this floating pit from hell."

Bennett leaned back into the warm rock. His heart throbbed strong, competing with the sickening burn in his arm for attention. "Makes sense not to rush into anything. Maybe we can help find you all a place, if Command permits it, which I hope they will after all this."

"You saved us from infinite death."

He hummed a grunt and looked away, checking on the three in the hut. "Many had to die. And you helped save our planet. We are in debt to one another."

A quiet moment exposed the faint sounds of laughing children and swishing grasses. *He* hadn't heard such things in decades. But it brought back a distant sense of home.

"I know how you feel," she muttered.

He switched to stare at the ground in front of them. "What do you mean?"

"The person you love is with someone else." She vacantly scanned the fields, a small, black bud twirling between her fingers.

Bennett lifted his head to inspect her. Imara's complexion was of a typical Xahu'ré female, though she had stripes on her face, whereas the vast majority did not. He caught her gaze, darting inside the hut, next to Atana. "You want to be with Azure?"

Her cheeks flushed violet. "You don't know him like I do. He's a strong warrior, a great guard, and the leader our people need."

"I think he's a big softie on the inside, fronts he's a hard man."

Imara grumbled a few choice words under her breath. "He's been so obsessed with this prophecy, with her—"

"Well, there must be some truth to it, don't you think? I mean they did just survive a nova. That is what they are calling it, yes?"

She tossed the bud in her mouth and chewed once. "It still, like your kind say, sucks."

Bennett rested his elbows on his knees. He had finally sorted out how to handle his own situation.

"I thought today, after seeing the explosion, I had lost her forever. So, Imara, think about this." His eyes graced Atana's outline with Kios tight in her arms and directed toward the hut with a weak wave of his hand. "True happiness is seeing the ones we love healthy and happy themselves, whether that is with us or not."

After a long breath, she smiled grimly and stood, leaving Bennett to sit alone once again.

...

297

The shepherds recently assigned to the mission continued their patrol with the perimeter guards and volunteers, searching for hidden Warruks and Linoans. Many of the workers had stepped forward during the crisis and taken to the hunt with crudely hammered knives, a handful of collected Warruks' weapons, wooden staffs, and the occasional handmade gun. Every color imaginable had been painted down the halls—indigo, plum, burgundy, orange, ochre, taupe—a three-dimensional form of abstract expressionism via merciless revenge.

One of UP's assigned Team Leaders had suggested Bennett's crew take a reprieve and stay with Sergeant Atana. Bennett accepted, reluctantly, after every other crew had backed up the offer.

Hushed winds sang softly through the unattended crops. The team watched Teek and Ramura talk in the grasses behind the hut. Kios sat between them, playing a game with small stones. Teek's tail sneaked around behind the boy, tickling one of his ears with its puffy end. Kios shied away from its touch, falling forward into a laughing Ramura's arms.

A group of children ran by in the distance, giggling as they chased one another.

Panton couldn't help a smile. Josie's body pressed into him, and he subconsciously wrapped an arm around her. None of the shepherds ever had much of a childhood worth talking about and his mind was on the youngsters chasing each other through the rows of blossoms.

"Josh," she whispered tenderly, up at him.

When he looked to meet her request, two tugs on his jacket pulled him into a pair of warm lips. His heart pounded. "Yalina?" he asked into her mouth.

"Shut up and kiss me you big hunk." Josie's green eyes twinkled in the fading artificial light.

He slid his arms around her and picked her up. Panton's disbelief was crushed with a second, intensely persuasive bonding of her mouth to his. He hummed in vanilla-flavored bliss.

Behind them, Tanner groaned. Panton chuckled and released one hand long enough to give Tanner the bird but didn't let go of the girl in his arms.

...

Tanner felt a tad squeamish at the sight of his team breaking Rule Number One. "What on Earth is going on?"

"We aren't on Earth?" With a jerk of his nose, Cutter suggested they leave. "Haven't you ever wanted a family? Most shepherds do."

Tanner didn't hesitate to oblige, and the two of them ambled away through the rows. "Well, I guess. It's just wrong. And I really don't want to go back to the junkyard they salvaged me from."

"Nothing is going to be the same after this. Can't you feel it?"

A girl Tanner had eyed briefly during the battle appeared, walking along a row. He shrugged, mumbling, "I don't know."

Cutter's voice was steady but held an edge of amusement. "Go talk to her. I know you want to."

"What? No, I don't." Tanner studied the willowy female inspecting the crop blossoms. The strength left his lungs, his feet glued to the ground. He couldn't look away from her magenta face.

Cutter cocked his head. "You really suck at lying."

Kicking a rock, Tanner licked his lips but didn't retaliate.

"Love doesn't need words, Remmi." Cutter picked a small, pink, non-crop flower from the ground and handed it to his partner. "Give her this. Trust me."

"I don't know." Tanner took the fragile blossom between his fingers. "What if she doesn't—like me?"

"With that adorable lopsided smile, you could get any girl you want."

"Dick." Tanner planted a light punch in his shoulder, tamping down his urge to grin for fear of proving his partner right. "Seriously."

"Then you won't be breaking any rules." With a swift and hard pat to Tanner's back, he whispered, "Go on. I won't say anything. Lot of B.S. going on tonight." Cutter winked and twitched his eyes back the direction they'd come.

"Under Bennett's Sanction?" Tanner nervously shifted his e-rifle strap farther up his shoulder. When Cutter nodded, he took a steadying breath. With heavy feet, Tanner trudged down her row, counting his steps to keep himself calm.

He stopped a meter away, letting out a short, embarrassed laugh. In looking up at her, he caught her studying him. "Y-you are beautiful."

"Hi." She lowered her head, hiding a bashful smile. Hundreds of thin strands, nearly two meters long, uncurled from her cloak like ferns. A bright pulse zinged through them, matching the blush on her face, to the dual beats of a heart. "Still think so?"

Tanner's lips parted in shock. "You look like a—glowing butterfly."

Her shoulders fell in playful exasperation. "I'm not a butterfly, silly. I'm a Primvera." She beamed at him. "Sergeant Remmi Tanner."

"T-telepathic—" He stammered. "Perimeter guard, right."

"I am Amianna." She hummed a giggle. "I remember you," she sang out, tracing his crooked smile in length. "The stunner with the gunner." She gestured toward Cutter, who waved, his hands not leaving the reloaded shotgun across his front. "Gunner."

...

Cutter stood close enough he could monitor his rigid-backed partner and his new interest. A memory of a familiar, heart-shaped face flashed before his eyes. His sternum cramped as if it were collapsing against his spine. The spiced breeze wrapped its arms around him—a protective blanket on a winter's night.

I'm so sorry I failed you, Essie. He closed his eyes, only for a moment, imagining the warmth against his cheek was hers.

The delicate winds whispered in his ears.

I forgive you.

Chapter 54

A BLISSFUL STILLNESS permeated the containers that night, the workers resting peacefully for a change. The amber light faded to a star-lit ink, the shepherds and guards patrolling through the sleep cycle. Kios was snuggled with Ramura in her bunkhouse, the team resting in the room opposite Atana and Azure's in Paramor's new-recruit hut.

Despite the surrounding quiescence, Bennett couldn't sleep.

He stood from his seat on the bench to stretch his legs and stare up at their version of stars. Alone, Bennett closed his eyes and soaked in the silence. *More are coming;* the words of the imperial haunted him.

"More what?" Atana's gentle voice made him jump. Her mouth twisted with the faintest hint of a smile.

"Sneaky." He rubbed a nervous hand through his hair. "And, I don't know. Something a Suanoa said before I took its head off."

"Beheading?" She arched a brow above a smirk. "Wouldn't have thought you were that type."

"I am what I need to be for whoever needs it." He couldn't admit the real reason to her face, not now.

Atana's skin had darkened, her stripes already beginning to show. Ramura had given her a short, brown fiber dress to wear, her arms and legs barely covered by the burlap. Atana's hair was turning the typical Xahu'ré dark charcoal, her lashes following suit.

Bennett shoved his hands in his pockets, struggling to contain the lovesick thoughts that flooded in. He looked away, visualizing the leathers on her instead.

In uncomfortable silence, they stared out across the fields. Clusters of green bugs flashed in the distance, glazing the twisted petals with their light.

Jameson.

He winced, enduring the unusual clarity to her voice. This had to be sleep deprivation, adrenal fatigue, something else. He figured a few odd thoughts might've slipped through the reversed receivers. But this had no rationale.

I'm not a hallucination. She lightly touched his jaw. *See?*

301

The heat of her fingertips against his skin made him want to bathe in that moment forever. *Nakio, why are we talking like this?*

She shrugged. *Maybe the receiver opened your mind. Or maybe you had the ability the entire time and needed an emotionally-charged experience to force it into action. That's what happened to me.* A corner of her mouth lifted.

Bennett thought back to the moment his innocence left and the desire for personal vengeance tarnished his soul—standing outside the abaddon deck, seeing Atana and Azure gone, witnessing another purge, and the workers floating out into space. He remembered the fight in the imperial ring, the shredded, burnt leather of his sleeve, and stepping between the Suanoa and the console.

Oh, no, Jameson! She swiftly unzipped his jacket, grabbing his collar.

His hands up, he tried to step back, only to find the bench and lapis boulder in his way. "Whoa, what are you doing?" Atana pushed the fabric away gently, sliding it off his shoulders. Blood surged through his veins.

"Nakio," he breathed, "stop." Bennett closed his eyes, trying to forget what she was doing and block out the aching signals from his arm.

"You're injured. Why didn't you tell me?" she demanded.

He caught his jacket and laid it across the rock. *I didn't want to concern anyone. Single injured shepherd versus a massacre is sort of a no-brainer.*

His heart rate, having elevated with her actions, crashed once again, crushed by the weight of inadvertent rejection. Atana gasped when she saw the damage to his upper arm. The charred crinkles of exposed muscle and flesh had dripped fluids clear down to his wrist. Her fingers felt like hot pokers. He jerked back.

"Shit, Jameson." She took off into the fields.

It's just a burn, not that bad.

Blue eyes flashed back at him. *You don't understand.*

Don't understand. He scoffed but tracked her figure hustling along the rows, reaching down and picking a few leaves and flowers. The urgency in her movement spiked a mild panic through him. Feeling dizzy, he sank to the wooden seat, releasing a breath. *It's just adrenal fatigue.*

Oh, what was the purpose in lying to himself? It was clear this was worthy of concern, or Atana wouldn't be running in her exhausted state.

Atana returned within minutes, setting a few bundles of greenery on the boulder. Disappearing into the hut, Bennett's pride worried Azure would come out, scold him for something, then cart his doctor away to bed. She stepped out carrying a mortar and pestle, a bowl of water, and a small, clay jar.

Azure didn't show.

Sitting next to him, she placed a hand over his chest. "Don't fade on me."

Only then, did he realize how ragged his breathing had grown from the throbbing leaching up into his neck. *Sorry. No serum in my veins.*

Grasping her hand, he pressed it in against his chest. His eyes rolled shut, and he slumped back against the warm rock. That tiny touch carried a comfort he'd missed. *Natural endorphins are wearing off.*

I know. Hang on, Jameson. Gently taking her hands back, she rinsed the greens, grinding them into a pulp, then mixed white paste from the jar into the mortar, forming a gelatinous substance. *I need you to take this off.* She directed to his T-shirt. *I will have to use it to wrap your arm for now. I couldn't find any bandages. I'd get Paramor, but he's working in another sector.*

Bennett slipped his shirt off slowly, straining against the growing weakness in his arm. *Well, if I survive, I guess I will at least have an awesome scar.*

You'll survive, she said without hesitation. *Awesome is hardly the right word for it.*

He'd meant it to be sarcastic but didn't have the energy to laugh through the pain. However dark the humor, it's how he coped with the inevitability of death. *Why do you say it like that?*

Her hands ground the pestle harder. "Because Azure has three of them." *He got them protecting me the night of the rescue.*

You two were together then?

Our holding cells were across from one another, in testing. Atana finished folding the paste in the mortar and shifted closer to him.

No wonder he doesn't like me.

She stilled then studied him. *Why would he not like you? Azure is like us.*

He doesn't. Trust me. He laid his shirt across his knees and tore it into several strips.

Is that why you punched him in the face? Because you're fighting?

Bennett grimaced. *Maybe.*

Over what?

One of his cheeks tensed. *You.*

Jameson. Resting the pestle, her shoulders dropped. *Fighting over me, that's—it's—futile. Ridiculous. Against Rule One. I'm probably not a shepherd after tonight anyway, so I'll never see you again.*

"We both fight *for* you," Bennett clarified. "Not *over* you. And Command won't retire or dismiss you. You're their most valued asset. My only mission was—"

To protect me? Not to save the people?

She'd read his mind despite his attempt to hide the truth. "Yeah, well, you first, then the people."

"Those priorities are no issue now." Her lips pursed. *Everything is different. Command's going to need to rework our mission, codes, lots of things.*

A wave of relief swept over him. She was so perfect: strong but gentle, hardheaded but compassionate. He couldn't understand how she kept it all straight.

Scooping with two fingers, she gingerly packed the paste into the severely blistered surface of his wound. Atana whispered a prayer while she finished applying the last of the medicine.

Bennett strained his neck, holding in a cry that begged at him, the stinging and burning sensations shooting up his shoulder. His arms tensed, controlling the urge to pull away.

Shh, just breathe. "It must disinfect first before you can begin to heal." Her voice was comforting amidst the thunderstorm in his mind.

Nakio, why are you doing this for me?

She took the strips of his shirt and wrapped up his arm, tying a few small knots at the ends. *Because you're hurt and because I—* Her eyes fell to the pair of dog tags hanging between the packed muscles of his chest.

Bennett grabbed them out of sudden insecurity. Family was illegal as a shepherd. It was also the only real thing he had that made everything worth the agony. He tracked her darkening waves as they danced in the breeze.

She turned away. *You've always watched my six, despite how hard I've been on you.*

With the pain gradually subsiding, breath filled his lungs again. "Why'd you hesitate? That's not like you."

Atana refocused on the jar she had set on the flat rock. "You know only a handful of Command are human?"

He chuckled in disbelief. "Sure."

"Yeah, six are Xahu'ré. A couple are Mirramor, like Chamarel, and Primvera, like Rimsan. A few others I don't know about yet."

"Oh, you're serious." *No shit. Our planet is run by aliens.* Bennett leaned forward onto his knees, scratching his short beard in contemplation. "I thought they seemed too calm about us working together." *It's an honor,* the pilot had said to Azure. *Bet he's Xahu'ré.*

"He is."

Bennett jumped. *Damn, can't think without you getting in my head, can I?*

Nope.

They laughed for the first time together, and the sounds intertwined so pleasantly, they both grew awkwardly still.

A deep-rooted envy swept over him, for the breeze playing in her waves, the starlight caressing her bare skin, and the frayed edge of the dress resting over the long, strong legs she had to keep crossed. Just the sight of her made his insides tingle.

Wiping a hand down his face, he forced himself to look away. "So, uh, why are you telling me this?"

"I guess, we all have our secrets."

"Speaking of, I uh, heard you mumbling in your sleep about Lavrion again. You think he's up here somewhere?

Lifting the jar, she spun it mindlessly in her palm. "I don't know. He was picked up on Earth, in my district."

Bennett bobbed his head. "Most of the collectors have yet to return, or so the perimeter guards are reporting. Maybe we can look for—"

My brother.

His chest warmed. She had an interest in family, like him. "I will be certain to help look for Lavrion as the ships dock."

"Thank you, Jameson." Placing the lid on the jar, she wiped her hands on her dress and sighed. *In one week, I've seen in you what it takes years to see in others. You're resilient. You break rules, for the right reasons. And—*

Her eyes drifted out across the fields.

A blur of rough and disjointed images filtered into Bennett's thoughts. *Fists pounding on glass. Seeing himself crumpled on the interrogation floor.* He winced, hearing her yell his name. *"Bennett!"*

In the darkness of the twilight that followed, the dimension between life and death, he saw a golden tether, a thread tied around a faintly pulsing blue hand, shaped and scarred like hers.

Bennett blinked, confused at the moving images flashing in his mind. It wasn't the right angle for him to have seen it himself.

You're an honorable shepherd who sees beyond Command's mission, to our true purpose. Everything about you—I just—I love— "Thank you for saving me from myself," she blurted and hopped up from the bench to leave.

His good hand snatched her wrist.

Wait, I don't understand. Bennett's heart fluttered clumsily in his chest. *Love?*

She cringed.

He instantly released her. "I'm sorry. Did I hurt you?"

"No." A sigh puffed out her cheeks. Atana slumped back on the bench, looking defeated. "Azure and I have just been together since we were kids." She gently inspected the knots on his bandages. "You think you're interested. I see it in your eyes."

"Think?" Bennett shook his head. He caught a glimmer of water between her lashes. It squeezed his heart, with tiny, hopeful fingers.

Nakio, it's okay. You two are something together no human could ever become with you. Taking her fingers, his thumb rubbed across her marred knuckles. *Long as you know I care, in ways I can't quite explain. I need to protect you, and not because Command told me to.*

Her attention fell to the metal pieces around his neck. She reached for them, a curious anger narrowing her eyes.

Warm fingers brushed his bare skin. He didn't try to stop her this time when she collected them.

Spreading the two apart, she studied the numbers. *Oh, stars, no.*

Bennett sat forward, bracing her shoulders. "Nakio?"

All she mustered was a shake of her head.

—Fire Within—

Chapter 55

"MY FATHER'S. Please, don't tell anyone." Bennett dipped down to inspect Atana's face. "Why do they upset you?"

Her eyes were squeezed shut. *He was on the rescue mission that saved us and took us back to Earth, brought me back. Gave his life defending Azure and me.*

Bennett leaned away. Atana was saying a lot of unbelievable things lately. It left him feeling shunned by the organization he'd fought so hard to protect. *That's not what they told me.*

She wiped the moisture from her cheeks. *Who?*

Command, when I joined UP. They said he was killed by Kronos during a raid.

No. Her eyes narrowed. *He fought beside Sensei. I saw him, Jameson.* Atana lifted the tags between them. *I'm the one that grabbed these. I remember this number.* She pointed to the code stamped at the top.

"What's going on?" Azure's snide tone made them swivel to look. He surveyed Bennett's shirtless form as he stalked up to the bench. His gaze slid over to Atana, relief washing the scrutiny from his eyes. He traced up her long legs to her soft, wavy hair. "You okay?"

"Yes, I was caring for Bennett's burn." Atana gestured toward the bandages. "He's like us, doesn't tell others when he's injured."

Bennett stood, grabbing his jacket and receiver from the rock behind him. He could sense Azure's eyes locked on his every move. It was a quick turnaround from his gratefulness, hours earlier. "I'll leave. Sorry to bother you, Nakio."

Atana hopped up from the bench, grasping his forearms. The urgency in her action made his heart jump. Sympathy and shame overshadowed her brightening eyes.

Behind her, Azure's shoulders rolled forward, his ears tensing backward. He looked like he'd been sacked in the gut.

Azure had noticed her concern too.

Licking his lips, Bennett thrust his focus to the ground between her bare toes and his scuffed boots. The last thing he wanted was to cause more problems for her. His presence was clearly disruptive.

I am so sorry. She gave his forearms a squeeze, momentarily calming the sting. *I will check on your shoulder in the morning, okay?*

Bennett couldn't return the warmth in her gaze. *It's good to see you healthy and to have you still here, with us. Please try to get some rest.* Pulling back, he caught her hands, soaking in the sensation of her fingertips brushing over his as he slipped himself free. "Call on me if you need anything."

He dared take one more look at her. Atana's plump lips hung open under the starlight. He already missed seeing them smile.

Clenching his jaw, he threw Azure a warning glare and slunk around the other side of the hut, to the bunk room assigned to the team for the night. One more glance at her curves, now shadowed by Azure's massive body, and Bennett shuffled through the doorway.

Bennett did a double take at one of the beds, finding Josie snuggled up to a shirtless Panton. His arm, with a bicep bigger than her neck, was hooked around her waist. Bennett's stomach turned.

He slumped down on an empty cot.

Tanner stirred, his bed head-to-head with Bennett's. "They've been like that all night."

Bennett buried his face in his hands. "Yeah, don't worry about it. Everything's crazy up here. We've all been a little impulsive."

"Boss, can I—" Tanner paused. "I think Nakio, I—I mean Sergeant Atana, cares about you more than she lets on. I mean, I know we're shepherds and ru-rules are rules, but all of this changes everything."

"Remmi, why are you stuttering? You never do that. You get hit in the head?"

"What? No, sir. Just a—a couple of slices, some singed hair. Cutter dislocated his shoulder. Snapped it back in himself."

"Okay, so come on, team rule, buddy. What are you—"

"I met a butterfly." Tanner slapped a hand over his face. "A girl."

Bennett sighed and fell back on his cot. *A butterfly? Must be Primvera.*

"I didn't want to say anything, B."

"It's okay. I'm happy for you, Remmi."

"She's got me all tongue-tied." Tanner fidgeted. "She literally sh-shocked me when I handed her a flower." He flushed dark enough Bennett could see it in the dim light. "I know you care about Nakio. So why—"

"What am I supposed to do?" The bandages shifted when Bennett stretched his arms over his head. His bare skin itched from the rough texture of the fibrous blanket beneath. He was too tired and distraught to care. "I'm a shepherd. And she and Azure are close, have been for ages." He took a deep breath and let it out through his nose, trying to control his frustration. "I'm not right for her anyway."

"What? Of course, you are, B. Don't talk like that."

Bennett mumbled, rolling over to face the wall. The dry straw padding crinkled beneath his body. "She isn't human. No matter what I want, she will always be better off with someone who can relate."

"You deserve to be happy too," Tanner said, sounding distant as if reliving something from the past. "The only reason I'm here to say that is because of you."

...

Azure watched Atana track Bennett's silhouette through the hut. They had an unspoken bond. He could see it in the way they looked at one another. It left him breathlessly desperate to pull her back to him.

Turning around, she peered up at him with a different smile, happier but abated, like she didn't quite know why she felt that way. *Bennett's father was on the rescue mission. He was the one killed by the three Suanoa at the end. Do you remember him?*

Vaguely, why?

She picked up her supplies and started for the hut. *Do you think he was human?*

Azure trudged along beside her. *Why are you asking this? Ma said Bennett was human.*

Then why has he been talking to us, like us? Atana set the items on the stool in the corner.

The waver in her hands was the open door Azure had been waiting for.

He rushed to her side. *You need to rest.*

Yes. Her entire body sagged into his.

Wrapping an arm around her waist, Azure caught her just in time. She hadn't changed in thirteen years, still pushing until the last second. He smiled to himself and slipped an arm under her legs. Picking her up, he carried her to the bed. *You must let everyone else take care of themselves for a change.*

Laying her gently on the blankets, he climbed over her. The pale light streaming in from the doorway accentuated the curves before him.

Cradling her from behind, Azure drew away the darkened waves of her hair and nuzzled her neck, basking in the sweet scent of her. His heart jittered when she softened into him. She drew his hand to her mouth, her fingers resting over a vein in his wrist.

A hot breeze fell over his skin. Two small, moist pillows pressed to the backs of his fingers. Her warm breath swept over his hand again. Whether conscious or not, she had remembered how they used to sleep so they would always know the other was still alive—his pulse, her breath.

Azure's eyes burned with endless admiration and satisfaction.

Two flickers of gold in the blue shadows snapped his attention to the bunk room. Through the woven wall, a pair of fireflies winked out.

When Azure looked down again at the woman in his arms, he found she had fallen asleep.

"Susse lianar im mora viiar. Sweet dreams and moonbeams," he whispered, leaving a kiss on her bare shoulder.

Chapter 56

A GRAY HAZE invaded Atana's dreamland, a gentle breeze sending her waves dancing across her eyes. In the mist, a burnt-orange-and-black feather floated before her. Not used to this type of peaceful vision, she followed it.

The feather drifted out and onto the wooden railing of a balcony. Picking it up, she spun it in circles, admiring its lightweight strength.

"This is not a dream, Nakio." The deep, sonorous voice from her right held familiar notes.

Startled, she slid back a step. The silhouette of a man leaned against the railing not far from her. "Jameson?"

"It was my name." He nodded. The fog billowed away from his features, exposing fiery eyes and silver strands in his short, umber hair. "The man you speak of is my son."

Astonishment and humility crashed through her, each fighting to take a hold of her heart. Atana grabbed the railing for support. "Oh, sir, I—I never had a chance to thank you."

A rattling explosion from the rocks below made her cast her gaze over the side. Splintered pieces of a structure similar to the deck sank into the cold, white-crested waves pounding the cliffs. Her lips moved to ask what she was looking at, but no words came out.

"This is one view of what could be if you don't do as the universe requests." He shifted his weight onto one foot, an orange glow lighting the clouds to his back. "It is my duty to guide the universe in its quest for balance. I am its prospector. To the universe, the powerful life forms—those with the most energy inside their hearts—are its gold. I am here with a message for you."

Atana whipped around to stare at the blazing red-orange sky. Shock tied her tongue.

"Do not fear. I am not Suanoa." At a rush of heated wind, the murkiness on the deck vanished. A pair of flaming wings stretched from the prospector's back at a span of seven men.

She jolted but swallowed her apprehension. Every element of his being, his clothing, his wings, infused her with the warmth of a sun, a beacon of hope so many prayed to in the night. "Why me?"

He straightened and looked her square in the eyes. "You understand the struggles of sorting scattered thoughts and memories. It is imperative you take care of my son. He does not yet know he is no longer human, not after today. You must be his guide."

Atana took a curious step closer. "What is he?"

"He is a prospector-in-training. My father was a prospector and his father before him. My son will replace me, eventually. He is not ready yet. He must be ready when the time comes."

Her hands hung limply at her sides. Bennett, her co-shepherd, the one who hung onto her through her darkest hours of the Grey, was becoming like the flaming man before her? He definitely fit the bill: his abnormally warm touch, the golden flecks in his eyes that seemed to glow, and the way he watched over everyone.

The prospector smiled. "You must have faith in yourself and in him. He needs you. Azure too."

"Both of us?" She raked her long bangs back and rubbed her eyes with a groan. "But they fight."

"I know." The man swayed his head as if fighting off an urge to say something more. "My son doesn't think so, but you two are his true family. His team members will not understand his strength of heart the way you will." He paused, cushioning the next words with a long breath. "Your attention, however, he will need the most."

Heat coursed out across her skin. His tone implied something she was unwilling to give. "I can't do that. I won't."

His head cocked to one side. "Why not? It is what the universe requires."

She sputtered. "Sure, you're his father. No one wants to see their family unhappy."

The vibrant mandarin and red-black wings on his back twitched, like a human's shoulders when flustered and guilty. With feet firmly planted, he scoured her face. "You do not want to see my son unhappy either."

"I—" *He's figured you out.*

"I am aware of your relationship with Azure. You are not expected to love my son the way you do Azure. But the universe knows there is a spark in you for him."

She huffed. "Love is a bond. Lust is a—a human weakness, a symptom."

"Nakio." The prospector shook his head. "You have them backward."

A light scoff slipped her throat.

Amusement flashed across his face, quickly replaced by a stern mask. "Jameson doesn't deserve to be alone. Inside, I think you know this. The universe has given you a mission, of which he is a crucial part. You have won this single battle but are now part of a war that was only a dream for the survivors. The Suanoa must be brought to justice. Without my son, you will fail."

"Why not someone like Imara? She is strong, telepathic, and a beautiful Xahu'ré miia."

The prospector interlaced his arms, a disdainful edge to his sigh.

Atana hugged herself and leaned a hip against the railing, peering over the edge at the wreckage. "I made a promise. There must be another better suited for such a task."

His tone hardened like his expression. "This is beyond your promise, your life. This is the fate of the universe."

Chewing a lip, Atana dragged her gaze back to him. Sergeant Bennett was the spitting image of his father: the angle of his dark brows when he frowned, the full lips that could light up the world with just a twitch of a smile, and the tuft of bangs in the center that seemed to defy gravity no matter their length.

Rubbing the chill from her arms, she cursed herself for ever thinking her efforts would be enough. Someone always wanted more. "Why does it have to be me?"

"You were chosen because of your heart and what you are. In time you will understand."

"What about Azure? What am I supposed to tell him?"

The prospector was cut off by the screech of a sliding door. Atana spun, feeling for her knife, expecting something and someone else.

...

Bennett stood motionless in the doorway. His father, who'd sprouted fiery wings and golden armor, was standing on his deck.

Glittering tangerine flames ignited on each feather. His father took a frantic step back.

A moment ago, Bennett had been watching Azure and Atana sleeping on the other side of the woven wall; the next, he was standing in his living room, staring at what he thought was a fire on his porch. "Wow, this," he surveyed the sharpness in detail of the wooden slats, Atana's wavy hair, and his father's alarmed face, "is one crazy ass dream."

"Jameson." Atana's voice was silken, her eyes filled with doubt. "You're in Ether. This isn't just a dream."

314

E. L. Strife

The radiant version of his father nodded. "This is very real, Big J."

Big J. He hadn't heard that in decades. "You—you mean you're alive?"

"Yes. How did you find us?" his father asked.

"I don't know. I was thinking about her when I fell asleep. Dad, I—" He trailed off. His father looked like a merging of a demon and an angel, a human phoenix.

The tattooed flames on Bennett's shoulders suddenly itched as if wanting to take flight. He shivered and stepped away from the sensation.

"I must go. You were not supposed to see me, not yet." His father leapt weightlessly onto the railing.

"Wait, Dad. Can't we talk?" Bennett rushed toward him.

"I'm sorry, son." His wings snapped taut. With a single downward thrust, they lifted him into the darkening sky.

Bennett's fingers combed through swirling embers left in his father's wake. They danced and circled his hands like amber fireflies in greeting before fading to dust.

This had to be a dream. His father would never be so cold as to turn a shoulder and run.

Why did he keep leaving?

Bennett let out a frustrated growl, his hands on his head, and paced the deck. Why wouldn't anyone tell him what the hell was going on? Did his serum resistance and the flares of heat in his body have something to do with this—with the fact his father was on fire?

"Big J." The name rushed through his clenched teeth. His father had said it too clear and perfect.

Dream. Not a dream. Bennett swayed with the coiling frustration waiting to spring forth. Slapping his hands over his face he growled into his palms. *Get a grip, man!*

Forcing out a deep sigh, he pivoted, honing in on Atana. "How long have you known about my father?"

Her body tensed. "A few minutes."

Bennett realized she felt just as lost as he did and lifted his hands. "Sorry."

"It's okay. Where are we?" She leaned over the railing, studying the crests pounding the cliffs many stories below. "I love the view."

"My house, over O.B. Thirty-three." He gazed apathetically across the water. "There's a storm coming." He waved a hand at the angry sky, dropping it to loosely suggest she follow him. "There always is when I'm here at night. You best come inside."

315

"Why?" Her hand snatched his elbow, the rain sprinkling across the deck. "We have control here."

"Nakio, I'm not in the mood." Reality was tumbling into more chaos every moment. He didn't have the reserves to comprehend what was going on in this freakishly lifelike dream.

She grasped his shoulders tight, positioning herself in front of him. A protective orb opened overhead, falling around them to the deck boards. Water droplets pattered against their aqua umbrella.

He looked up to the flashes of lightning shooting at them, absorbing into the shield she had put up with hollow thumps. The barrier blocked out almost all external noise. He could hear his rapid breathing and the calm heartbeat in her chest.

A humid breath fell against his neck, sending his heart racing. Her fingertips graced his with a static zap. The two of them twitched, exchanging bashful smiles. Feeling her hand slide into his siphoned away the recent images of battle and bloodied bodies until he was left with pure silence within himself.

Closing his eyes, he lingered in the peace. Bennett tugged on her hand, begging to feel her against him.

"Jameson?" His name left her lips as only air. He opened his eyes.

She was staring at his chest, a golden light crisping her curves. Seeing the reflection of two aureate orbs in her glossy, peeled open eyes, he bristled. *Those are mine?*

Bennett jerked his head down to sort the phenomenon. He didn't feel like he was on fire, but the blooming yellow-orange light spreading through his bloodstream like fiber optic trees was hard to deny. *It's just a dream.* "Nakio, what is this? What's happening to me?"

She ran her fingers down his chest, tracing a loop in his veins through his shirt. Her jaw bobbed, but no words came out. A shoulder barely lifted.

He drew in harshly and backed away. "You don't know what this is?" Bennett moved to claw at his brilliant, beating heart, but the glow of his hands made him seize. *What the fuck?*

"Calm down." Her fingers flattened against his chest. "Obviously, it's normal. It happened to your father."

"This isn't normal!" His breathing came rapid and shallow as he tried to shake the embers from his hands. But they didn't budge. They were stuck to him. *Within* him.

"This can't be real," he muttered to himself. "Not real."

"I'm sorry, Jameson." Atana braced his trembling arms with her hands. "This is."

Thanks for reading!

Your feedback is crucial to the success of indie authors.
Please help us out by leaving a review.

The Prophesy (Part 2)
Beyond the horizon a new light appears,
to end their tyranny and dictated fear.
A given lamb will bring only faith.
A blossom will fight more than fate.
Divided unity chains the sun,
rendering a vital creation undone.

Connect With Elysia

For book-inspired images, find **Elysia Lumen** on Pinterest
Follow **Elysia Lumen Strife** on Goodreads
Catch **ElysiaLStrife** on Twitter
Follow **AuthorELStrife** on Facebook
Find **Elysia Lumen Strife** on LibraryThing

E. L. Strife

Book 1: Stellar Fusion
Book 2: Requiem
Book 3: Shadows of the Son
Look for Book 4: Redshift in 2020

Visit elstrife.com for more information.

UP Code of Appropriate Actions

Any violation, as presented with adequate proof to Command, will subject that shepherd to a complete evaluation to determine if the shepherd in question is capable of continuing with the Universal Protectors. If a violation is confirmed, the shepherd will be sentenced to early retirement and begin out-processing immediately. Technical details are listed under Home Station's C:\Shepherds' Standards\Mandated Codes.

Rule 1: Never Get Involved.
Your duty is to respect your job, your responsibilities, and others.
Any personal relationships (ie: friendship, family, intimate) are strictly forbidden.

Rule 2: Serum for Stability.
Without it, our cause is lost.

Rule 3: Plan, Prepare, Perform Perfectly.
Error is not tolerated.

Rule 4: Treat All Earthlings Equally.
Do not place the value of one individual, no matter their affiliation or worth, over that of the masses.

Rule 5: Be Proactive.
Maintain physical health, skills, and knowledge and adapt to the evolving needs of your position.

Rule 6: Do Not Disclose Identifying Information,
Allowing Others to Know You as Different From the Masses.
Information concerning the UP program shall not be shared with any civilian, under any circumstances.
Release of information about your personal self/life is to be kept to a minimum,
Disclosed only as essential to successful performance of missions.

Rule 7: Honesty Prevents Failure.
Be upfront and forthright so tasks may be completed with minimal interference.

Rule 8: Lead by Example.
Guide less-experienced shepherds with idealized performance and explanation of expectations.

Rule 9: No Shepherd Left Behind.
A fallen shepherd will not be left in the field to fall into combatant possession without due cause.

Rule 10: Respect Command.
They protect us as we protect the people.

We Are **Kindred IN Death**.
It is only in life, that we can be different from others.
Let us use this time to make a positive impact.
We are all equal, united as one.

E. L. Strife

Shepherd's Oath

My strength comes from those before me. I honor them now and forever,
as I continue their tradition.
I solemnly swear: to be honest and fair.
With integrity and a balanced mind, for this vocation, I was designed.
Not akin to any zone, we call Earth our only home.
We're the last true armor for the vital spark.
We disarm evil and preserve peace for every heart.
The greed of others will not sway our actions but fuel the purpose for our
reaction.
Our decisions remain unbiased and objective. In this state, we shall be
effective.
We will continue to safeguard the innocent until every last drop of our
blood is spent.
Though our bodies may weary, as long as they're warm,
We'll stay calm and controlled, amidst the storm.
We are a symbol, for those who see, no matter our pain, we will set them
free.
Even on the darkest night, we are their shepherds, their guiding light.
We fight for each other, 'till the wicked succumb. We are all equal, united
as one.
We are the Universal Protectors!

Pronunciation Key

Names:
Amianna – Ah-mee-ahn-uh
Azure – Uh-zoor
Chamarel – Sha-muh-rel
Drékor – Dray-core
Ekiipa – Eh-key-puh
Imara – Ih-mahr-uh
Jeniah – Jehn-eye-uh
Josandizer – Yohs-ahn-di-zur
Kylo – Kye-low
Nakio Atana – Nuh-key-oh Uh- tahn-uh
Paramor – Pair-uh-more
Ramura – Ruh-mur-uh
Remmi – Rem-ee
Rimsan – Rihm-sahn
Saema – Say-muh
Tohsa – Toe-suh
Species:
Dagganak – Da-gahn-ahk
Gunre Tokta – Gun-reh Toe-kta
Kriit – Kreet
Linoan – Lih-noh-uhn

Marakou – Mahr-uh-koo
Mirramor – Meer-uh-more
Noriamé – Nohr-ee-ah-may
Primvera – Pryhm-vair-uh
Suanoa – Soo-ahn-oh-uh
Warruk – Wahr-uhk
Xahu'ré – Zuh-who-ray
Places:
Agutra – Uh-goo-truh
Lizra – Lye-zur-uh
Vioras – Vee-or-us
Other:
Brocanip – Bro-can-ip
Doku – Doe-koo
Hatoga – Huh-toh-guh
Japous – Juh-poos
Jesiar – Jess-ee-ahr
Kiatna – Key-aht-nuh
Marusa – Mar-ooh-suh
Quinock – Quih-nohk
Rhizoras – Rise-ohr-uhs
Verros – Vair-ohs
Vesha – Vay-shuh

Translations - Xahu'ré to English

Agutra – Suanoa Ag ship
Ahna – You
Aht – No
Ahtz – Not
Amah – In
Asii – Hey/attention
Asiivé – Welcome/hello
Avi – Go/be over there
Dak – Give
Diete – God/spirit
Du – The
é – All
Ehru – Ass/Derogatory
Ehrun – Bastard
Eih – Thank(s)
Evus – Up
Evus' ii – Sky
Giyam – Hello (in Simsa)
Grat – Hot
Grekrat – Control
Hu'te – What
'ii – Surround/encompass
Iitues – Have/hold
IL – Is
Im – And
It'yan – Item/something
Itu – With
Ituviia – Mate
Iveron – Eternity/forever
Izanot – White mush meal
Ja'aht – Different
Japous – Rat/Rodent
Kiatna – Lifeforms/ beings
Krat – Kill/murder
Layha – Friends
Li – A
Lian – Sleep
Lianar – Dreams
Lisano – Beautiful
Mamua – Luck
Marra – Male
Marrat – Brother
Martiis – Warrior/Sir/Sgt
Miia – Female
Mitras – Protect
Mitrasso – Safe

Mitron – Protector
Mocohas – Purpose
Mora – Moon
Naaht – Wrong
Niema – Please
Nigh – Stop
Niveriia – Death
Noa – Leader/ruler
Nux – Fight
Nuxia – Wake/Resist Sleep
Ongkrat – Mutiny
Ongx – Resist (fight back)
Pelaeso – Blessings
Ras – It
Rass'ii – Alright/okay
Ruut – Out
Saema – Sacred Mother
Shirrahs – Here
Siisa – Good
Sim – Me/myself
Sisano – Careful
Su – Sad
Sua – Cruel
Sua'o – Cold
Suanoa – Superior (cruel leader)
Sur – On
Susse – Sweet
Sussia – Warm
Tiisa – Strong
Tsu – Yes
Tuess – Get
Tus – Desire/need
Tusan – Use
Veriat – Family
Veriia – Life
Veriisa – Soul
Veriisaht – Soulless
Verons – Love
Verso – Promise/swear
Vi – Are/Be
Viia – Light
Viiar – Beams
Virrahs – Stay/be here
Yan – This/that
Yui – Can
Zi – Of

Acknowledgments

To the supernova in my sky, William, who encouraged me to chase my dreams, I took it literally. *Stellar Fusion* erupted from my night visions, inspired by the infinite light in your eyes. Thank you for being my support in every way. To my wonderful and extremely patient editor, Jeni Chappelle, thank you for turning chaos into order. I have learned so much from our short time together. Ruth, I owe you more than I will ever be able to repay. Your generous heart astounds me. Anthony M., you have always been fundamental to my confidence and especially so with this first book. I am grateful for your training and guidance. Joseph, thank you for teaching me about flight, radio communications, and tolerating my creative mess. You were the perfect roommate. Jacy, Kristen, Lenn, Nicholas, and Skip, your feedback and support have drawn out the best in me and helped me tune this into the dynamic piece it is today. To my grandparents, spending the summers as a child on the farm and ranch was by far the best way a person could grow up, even down to the few chores I'm sure I complained about. But what I learned about respect, love, faith, family, and hard work became the foundation on which I built the individual I am today. Mom and Dad, you are the reason I am so lucky. Thank you for taking me in and not letting me know anything but unconditional love. Without you, the void would have surely taken my spirit.

About the Author

 Elysia Strife was born in the U.S. in 1986. Since she was a child, she's been making up characters and stories in her free time. Discovering her passion for science fiction, futuristic dystopias, and conquering impossible odds, the mix swirled together into the vibrant world of fantasy she creates today.

Adopted by two educators, she developed a love of learning. She holds two Bachelor's of Science Degrees: Exercise Sport Science and Interior Design. Her past wears fatigues, suits, and fitness gear, sprinkled with mascara and lace. She likes the kick of a 30-06, the rumble of a hot, 350-ci V8, and snow and sand beneath her tracks.

Strife loves connecting with readers and welcomes all feedback and questions.

53286215R00181

Made in the USA
Lexington, KY
29 September 2019